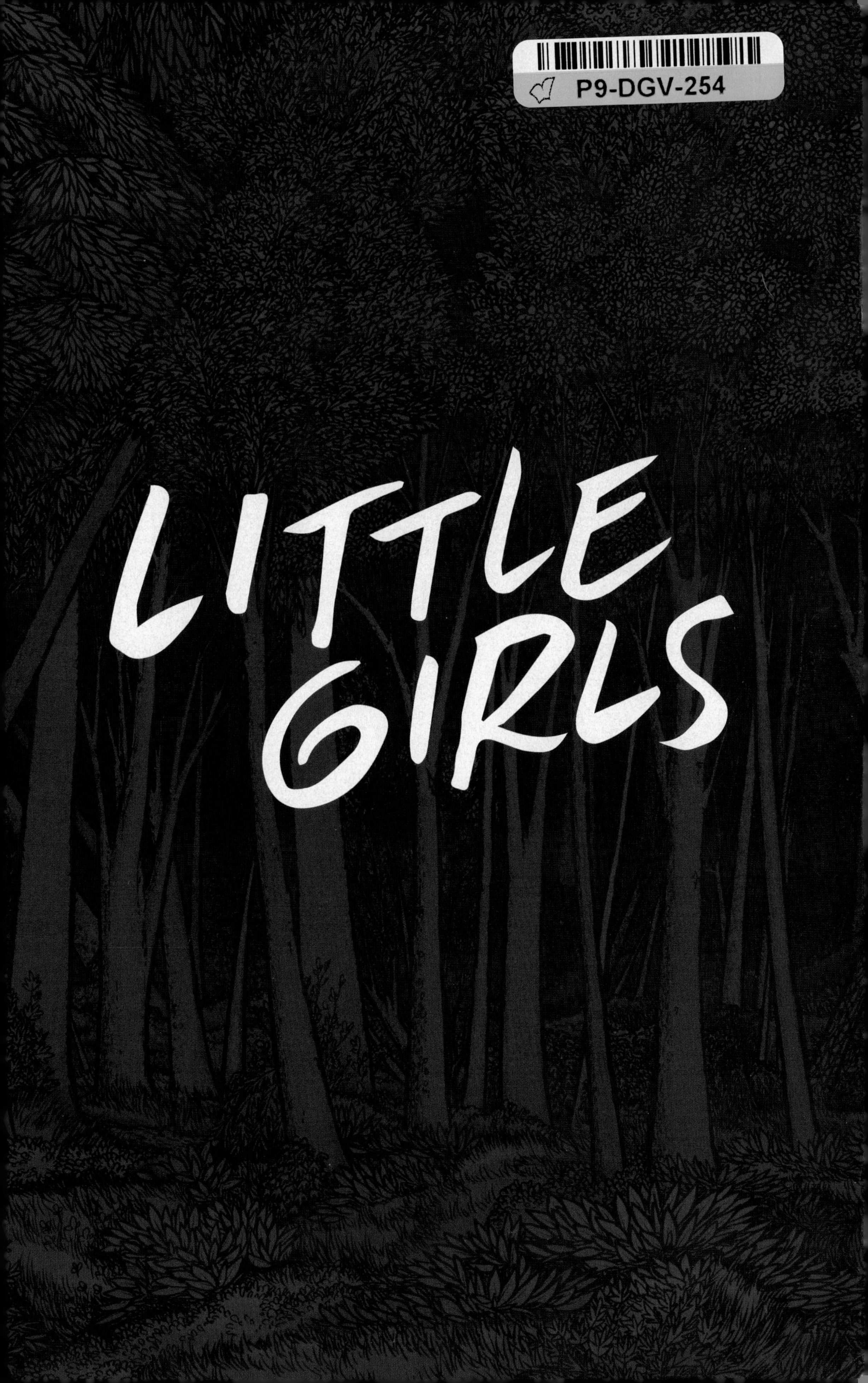
LITTLE
GIRLS

Writer—Nicholas Aflleje

Artist—Sarah DeLaine

Colorist—Ashley Lanni

Letterer—Adam Wollet

Color Flatters—Leonardo Muglia
& Gregory Ottaviani

Editor—Riley Bragg

Logo Design—Comicraft

Production Design—Drew Gill

IMAGE COMICS, INC.
• Robert Kirkman: Chief Operating Officer • Erik Larsen: Chief Financial Officer • Todd McFarlane: President • Marc Silvestri: Chief Executive Officer • Jim Valentino: Vice President • Eric Stephenson: Publisher / Chief Creative Officer • Corey Hart: Director of Sales • Jeff Boison: Director of Publishing Planning & Book Trade Sales • Chris Ross: Director of Digital Sales • Jeff Stang: Director of Specialty Sales • Kat Salazar: Director of PR & Marketing • Drew Gill: Art Director • Heather Doornink: Production Director • Nicole Lapalme: Controller •
IMAGECOMICS.COM

LITTLE GIRLS. First printing. April 2019. Published by Image Comics, Inc. Office of publication: 2701 NW Vaughn St., Suite 780, Portland, OR 97210. ISBN: 978-1-5343-1059-9

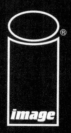

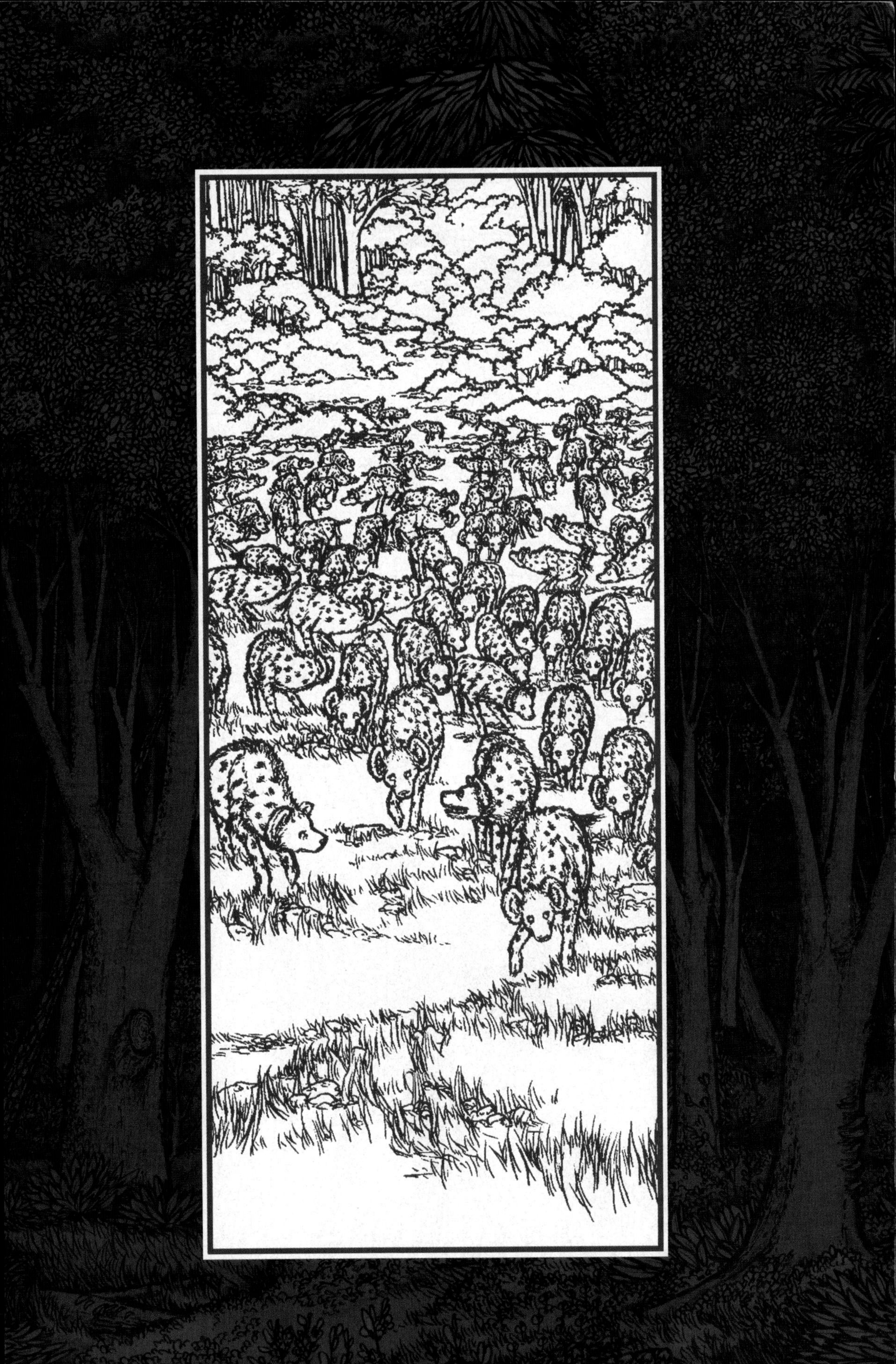

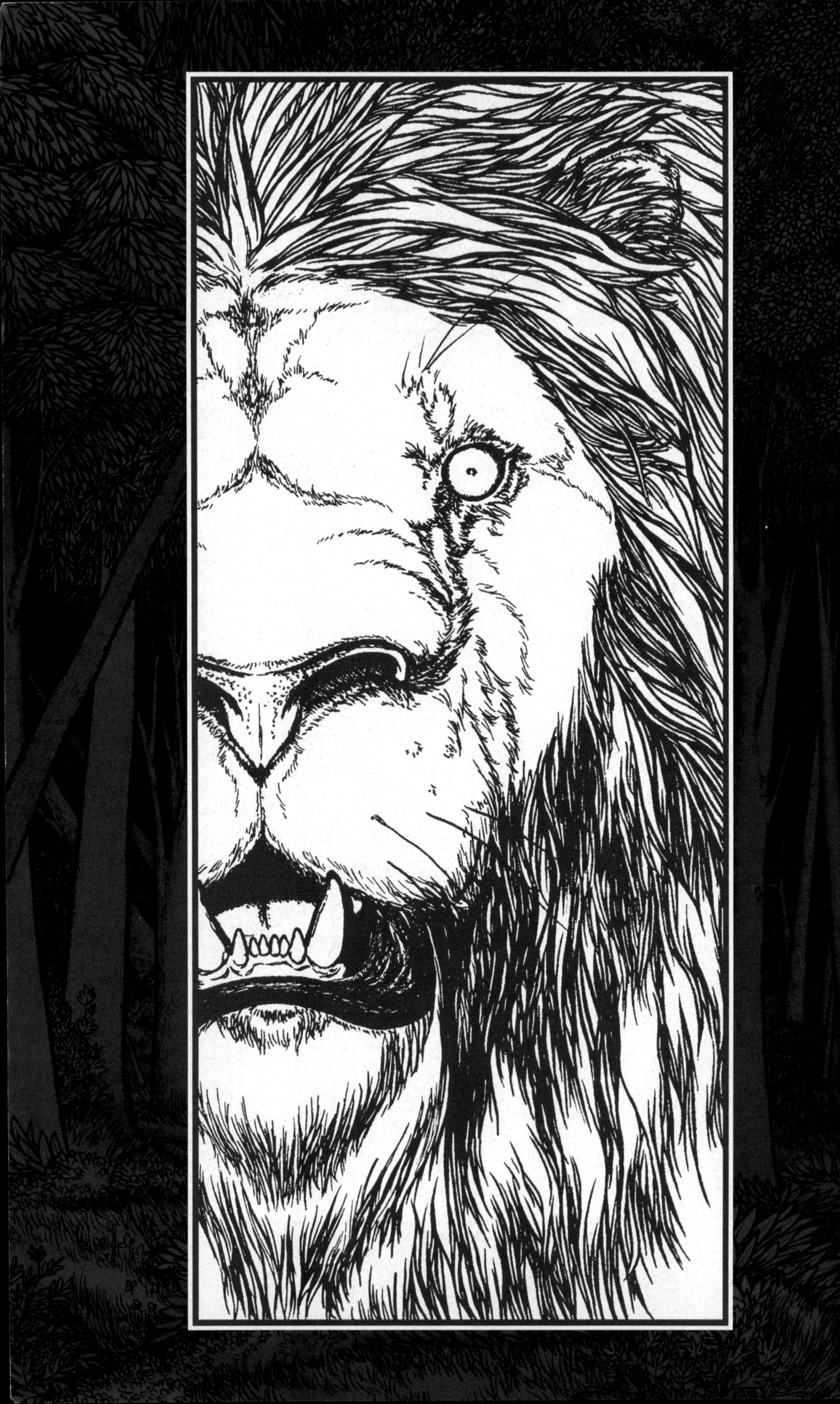

Little Girls is the perfect graphic novel.

I don't mean that in the sense of being a perfectly executed story with expertly drawn panels—although there is much to be said about both, and I'll get there shortly. What you have in your hands is not some refurbished Hollywood script, or a yarn that could be digested in 20-page chunks. It would not work as a prose novel. Maybe there'd be some value to a serialized podcast—nah. *Little Girls* is a feast that knows exactly what it is: A perfect graphic novel.

Writer Nicholas Aflleje and artist Sarah DeLaine take their sweet time introducing you to the inhabitants of Harar, Ethiopia. As creators, they revel in teaching you the rules of their world, so when they triple down on the fantastical elements, the reader is all the more gripped to see how everything unfolds for our remarkable heroes Sam and Lielet. There are parallels to real-world issues contained within the story of two friends pursuing mysterious slayings that may or may not be tied to a local legend, but never once is the narrative burdened by trying to beat a message over our heads. *Little Girls* takes place in another country, but I don't feel like any pandering is done, and similarly whenever a grisly scene occurs, never once does the art become grotesque or vulgar.

Speaking of...the artwork! In describing the majesty of Sarah DeLaine's crisp and confident line art, I told a friend: "It's like if Geof Darrow drew girl stuff." I don't say that with any tone of denigration. There is ferocity, dynamism, and suspense in the pages ahead, but you'll also find a level of care and refinement applied to each character, to each set, to each blade of glass done in a way I've really only seen depicted when a page is translated through the wrist of a woman. All this is to say, Sarah DeLaine uses her femininity as another tool to amaze us, right down to Sam's bushy, questioning eyebrows. I still can't believe this is her first full-length work of graphic storytelling. No spoilers, but wait until you see her lions.

At this point, it's prudent to admit that I know the creators personally, and have been eagerly awaiting the day Sarah would finish laboring over the beautiful inks and share this treasure with comics readers. That said, I am friends with a lot of people in the industry, and I don't stop everything to read their work, nor do I typically devour the material in a single sitting. The hard work of the creators transcends their individual contributions to deliver a singular and fully immersive world that is full of threats and danger, but I want to live there nonetheless.

That's what a perfect graphic novel should accomplish.

—Sina Grace

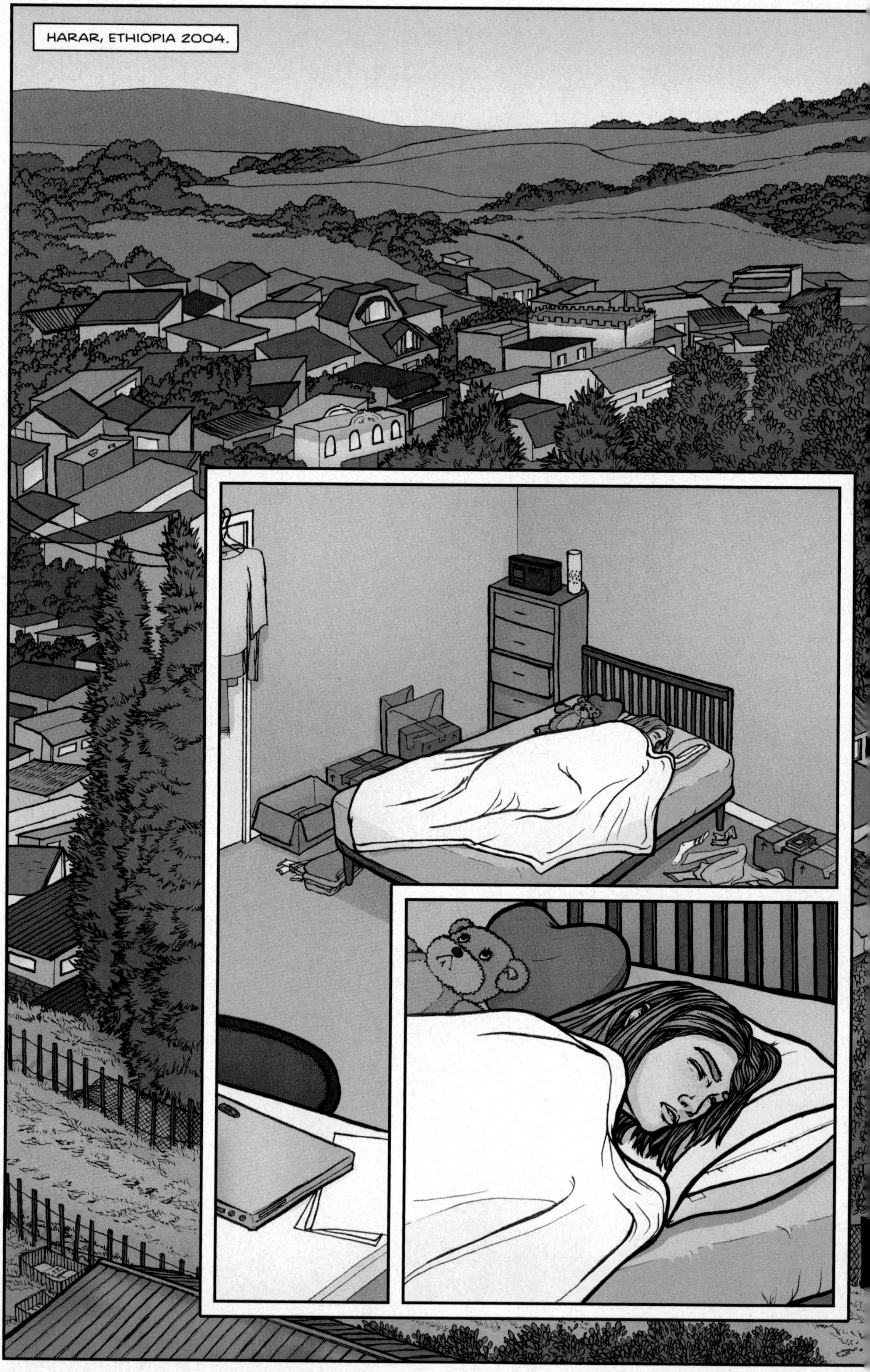
HARAR, ETHIOPIA 2004.

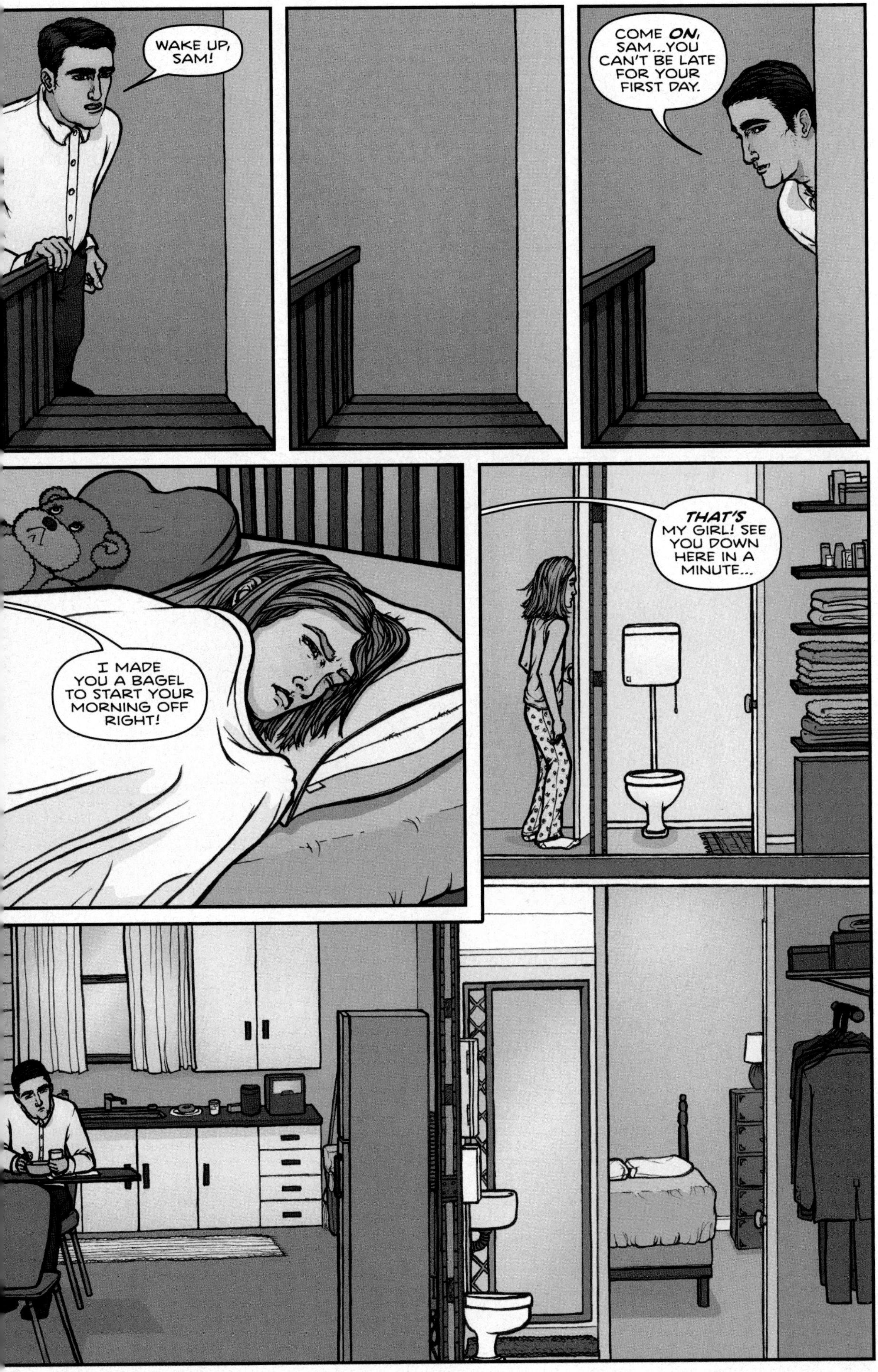
WAKE UP, SAM!
COME ON, SAM...YOU CAN'T BE LATE FOR YOUR FIRST DAY.
I MADE YOU A BAGEL TO START YOUR MORNING OFF RIGHT!
THAT'S MY GIRL! SEE YOU DOWN HERE IN A MINUTE...

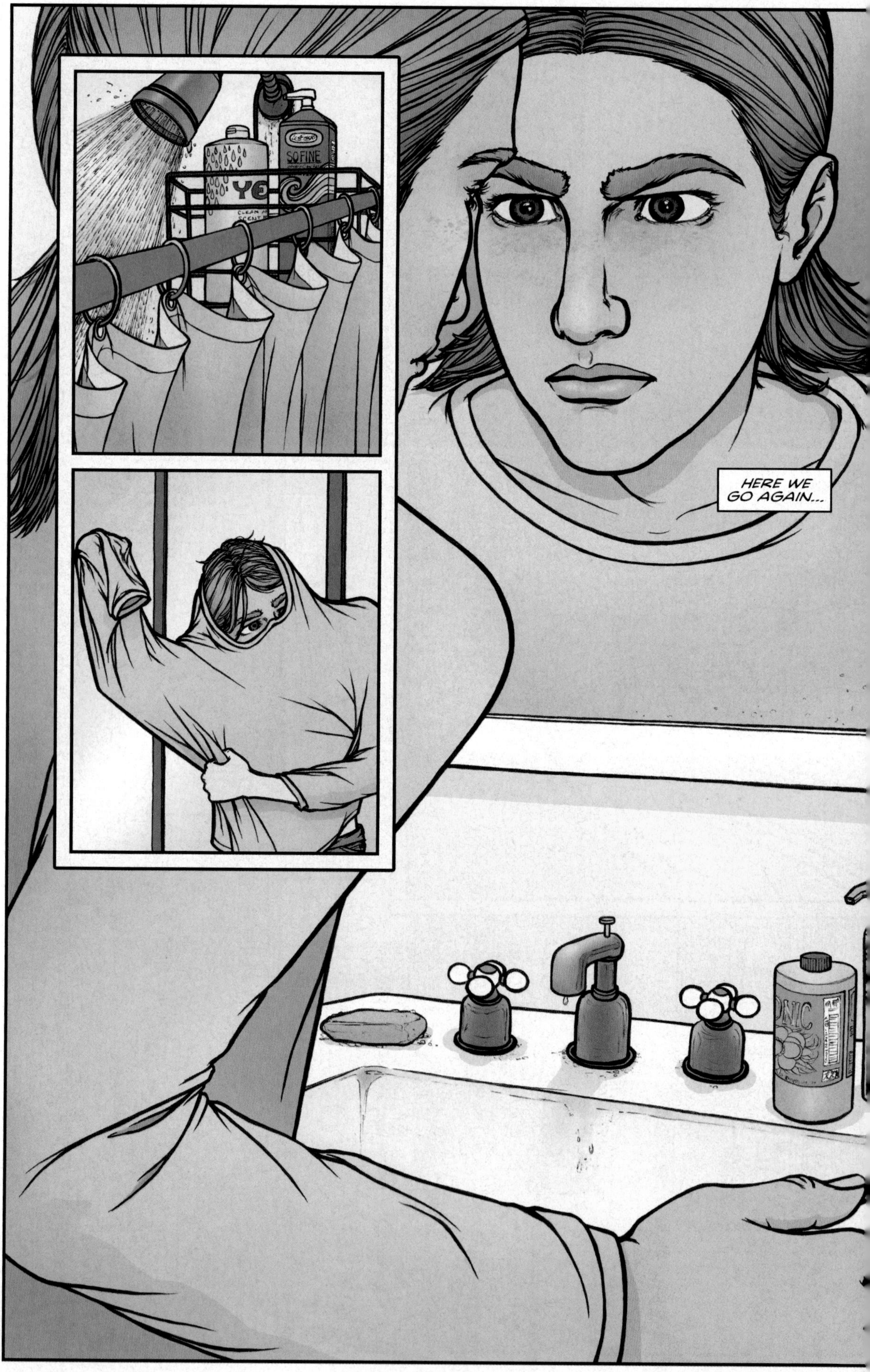
HERE WE GO AGAIN...

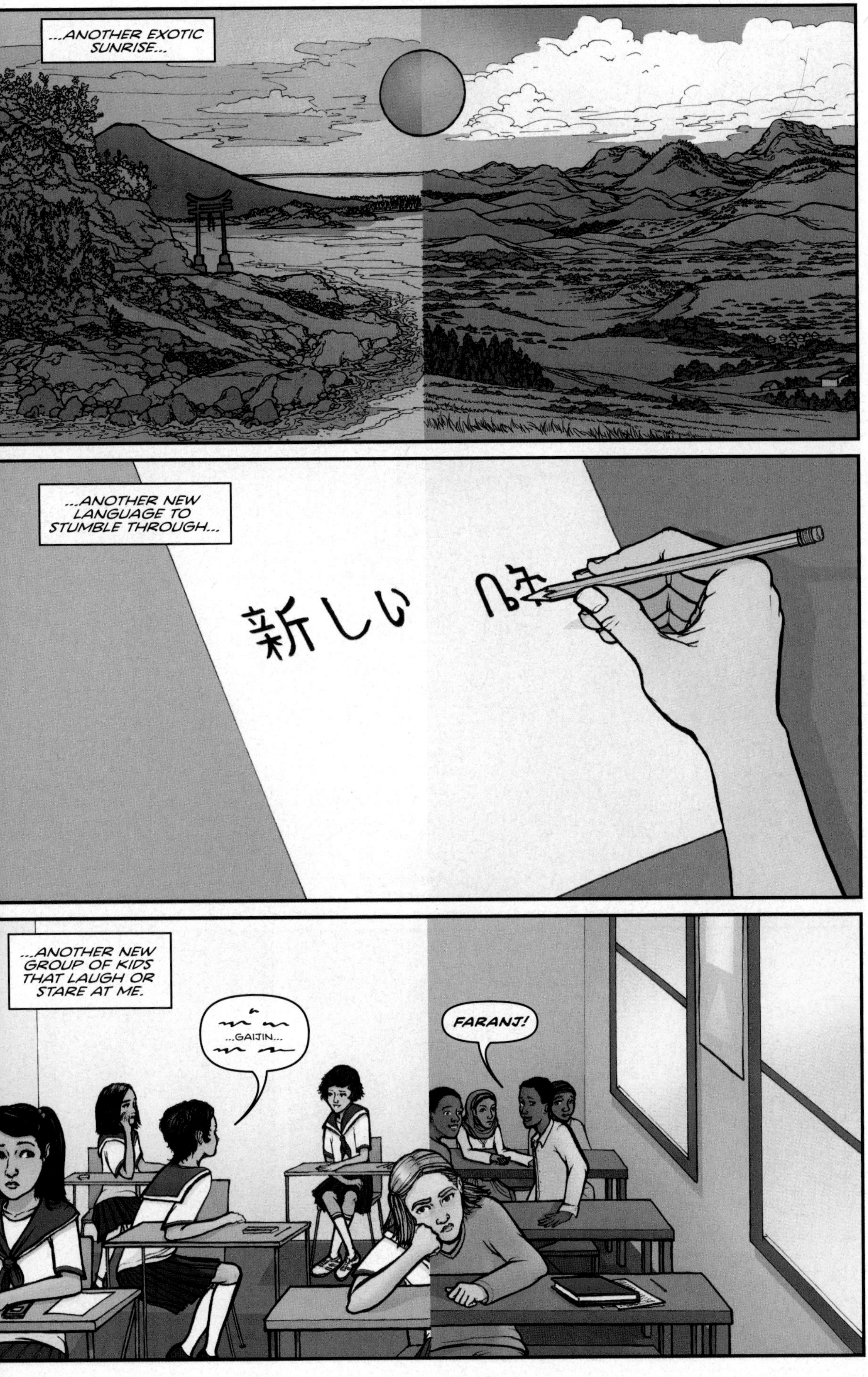
...ANOTHER EXOTIC SUNRISE...
...ANOTHER NEW LANGUAGE TO STUMBLE THROUGH...
新しい
...ANOTHER NEW GROUP OF KIDS THAT LAUGH OR STARE AT ME.
...GAIJIN...
FARANJ!

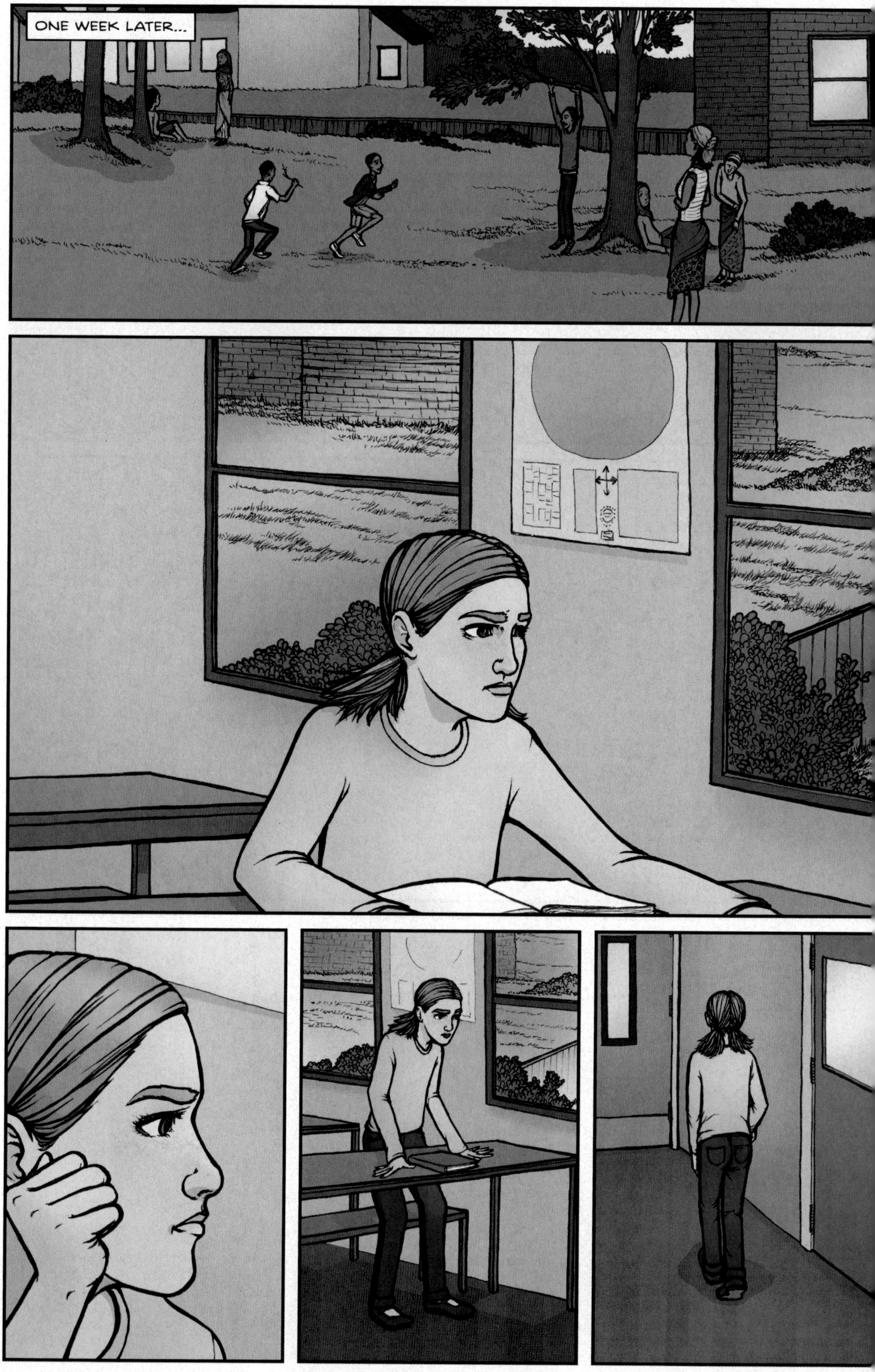
ONE WEEK LATER...

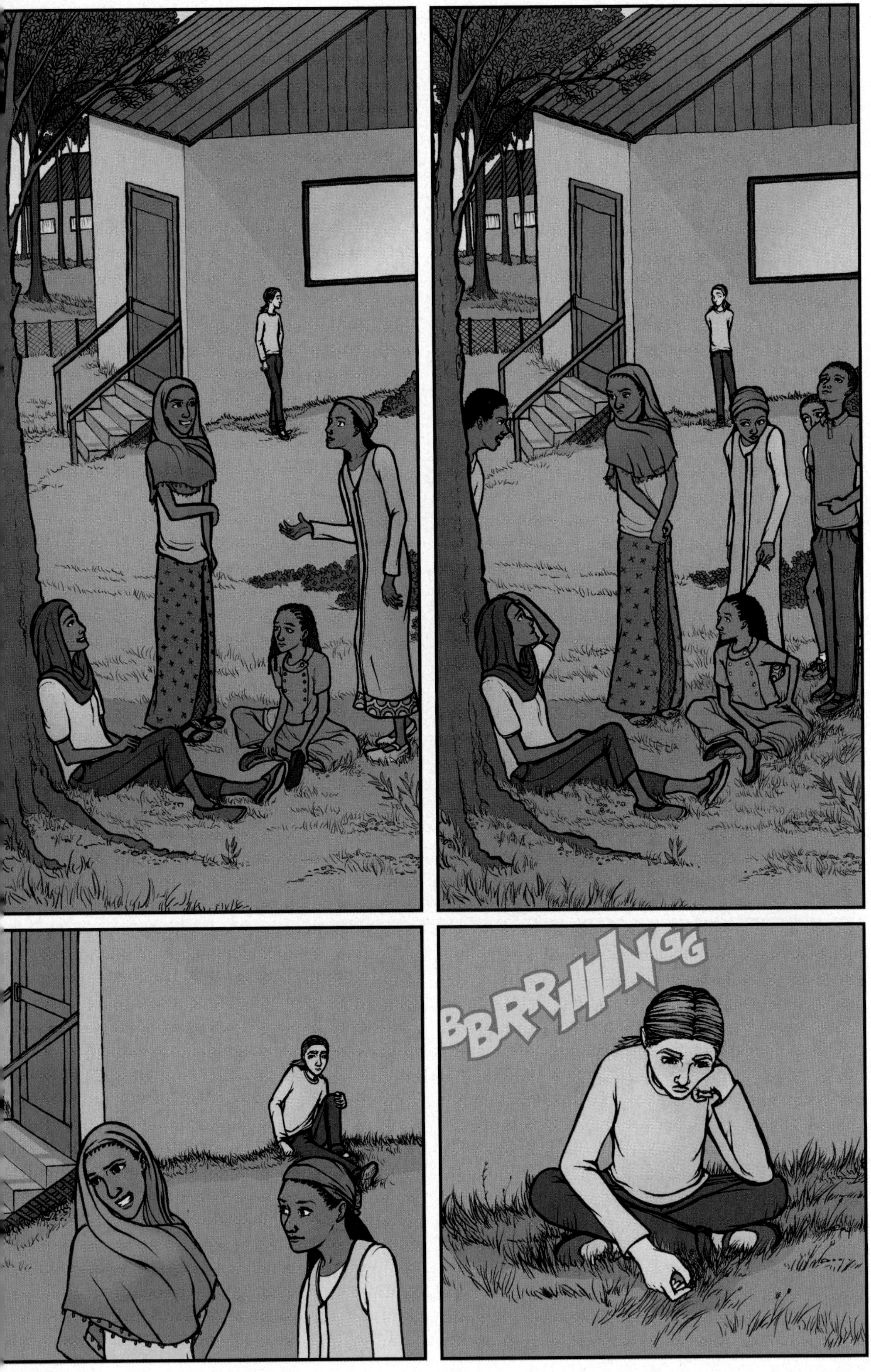
BBRRIIIINGG

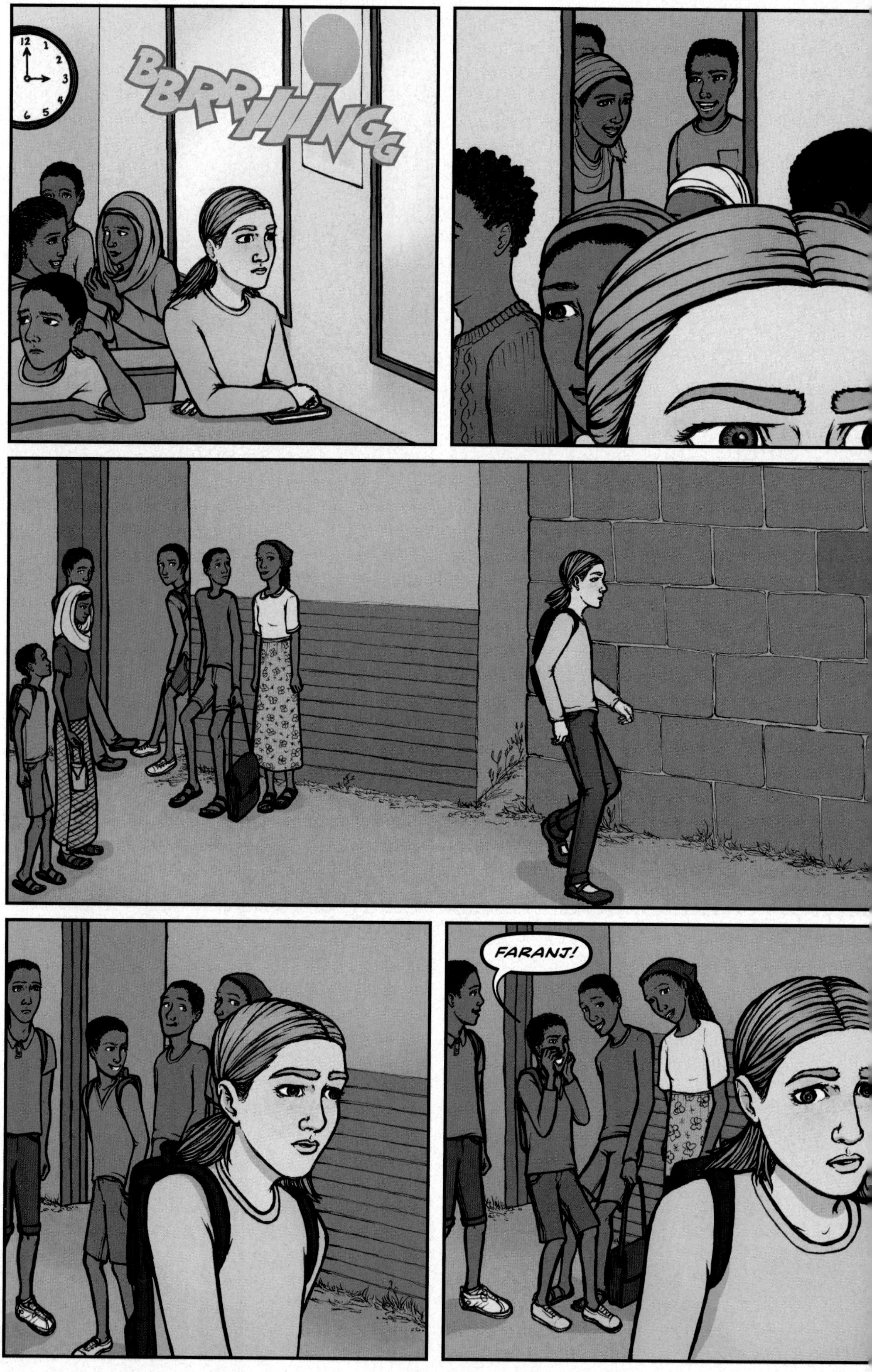
BBRRIIIINGG
FARANJ!

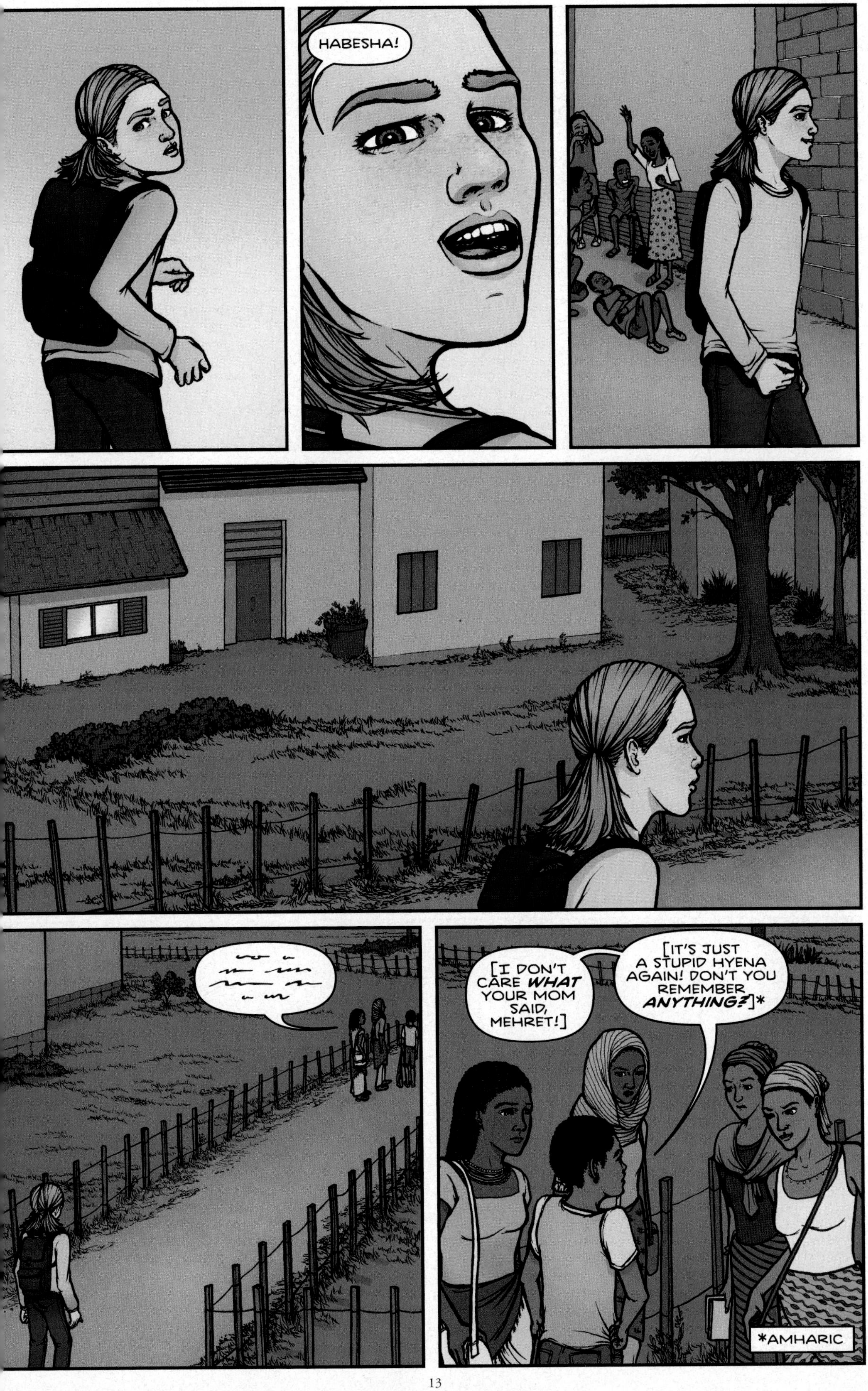
HABESHA!
[I DON'T CARE *WHAT* YOUR MOM SAID, MEHRET!]
[IT'S JUST A STUPID HYENA AGAIN! DON'T YOU REMEMBER *ANYTHING?*]*
*AMHARIC

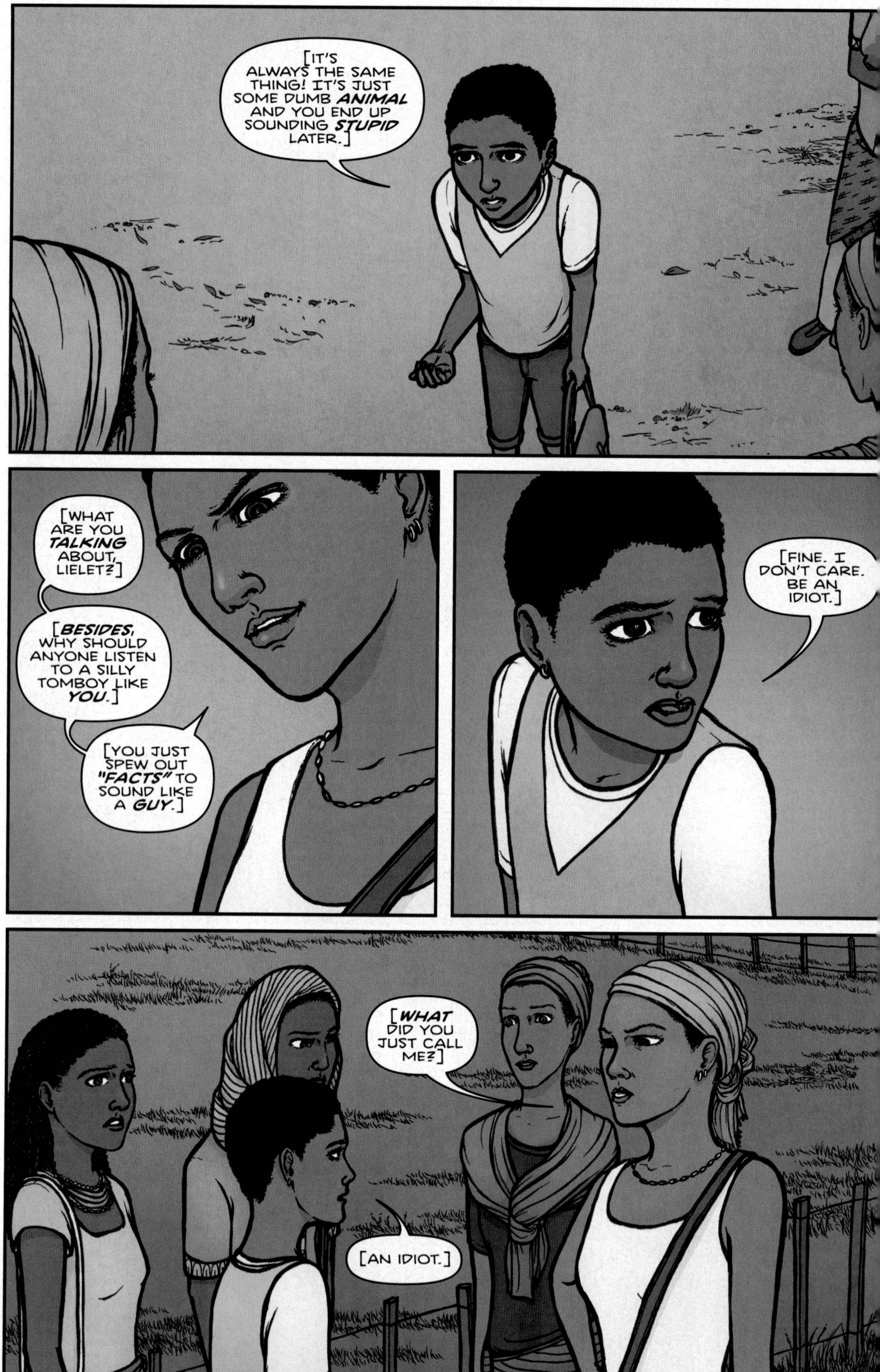
[IT'S ALWAYS THE SAME THING! IT'S JUST SOME DUMB ANIMAL AND YOU END UP SOUNDING STUPID LATER.]
[WHAT ARE YOU TALKING ABOUT, LIELET?]
[BESIDES, WHY SHOULD ANYONE LISTEN TO A SILLY TOMBOY LIKE YOU.]
[YOU JUST SPEW OUT "FACTS" TO SOUND LIKE A GUY.]
[FINE. I DON'T CARE. BE AN IDIOT.]
[WHAT DID YOU JUST CALL ME?]
[AN IDIOT.]

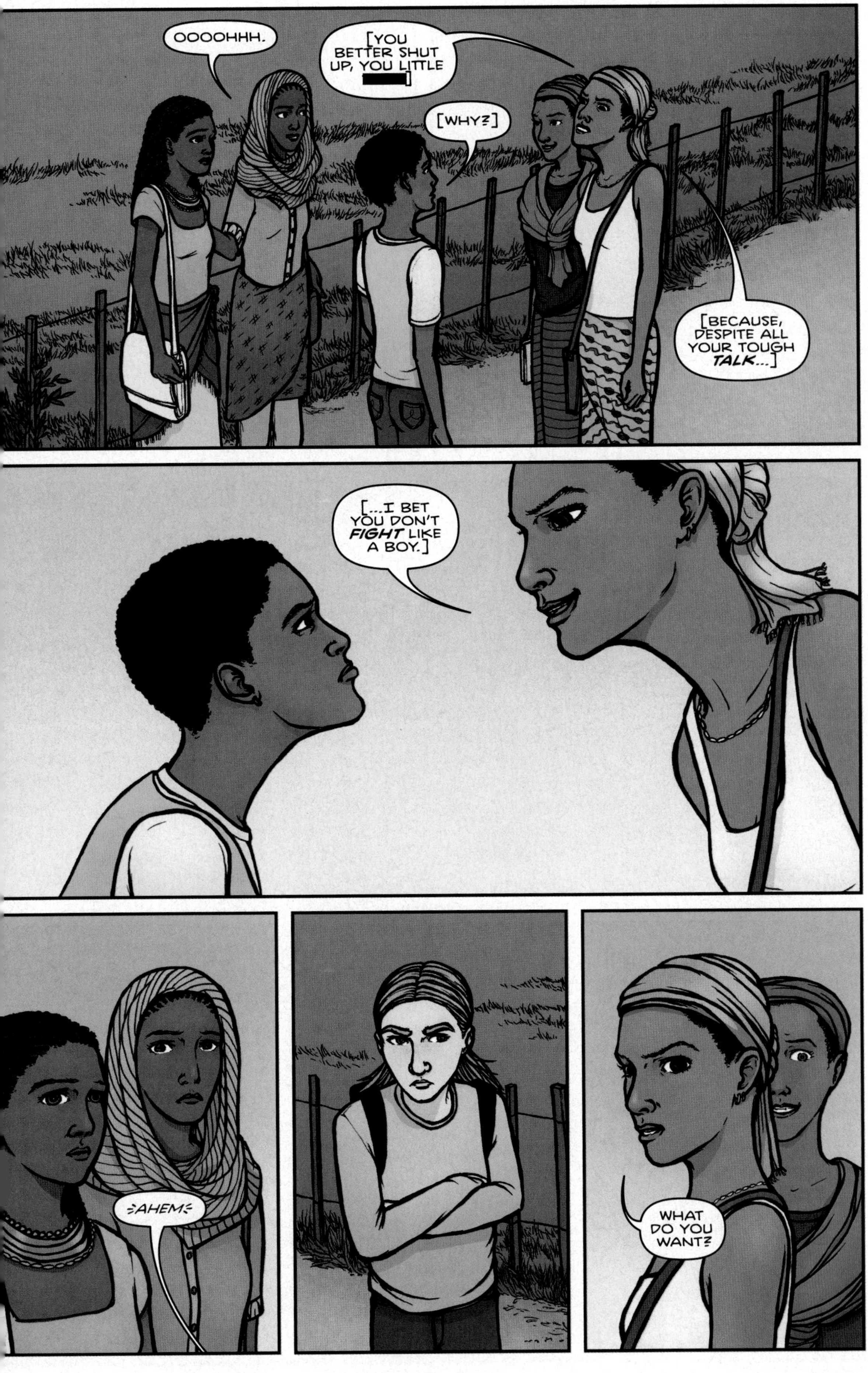
OOOOHHH.
[YOU BETTER SHUT UP, YOU LITTLE [redacted]]
[WHY?]
[BECAUSE, DESPITE ALL YOUR TOUGH *TALK*...]
[...I BET YOU DON'T *FIGHT* LIKE A BOY.]
AHEM
WHAT DO YOU WANT?

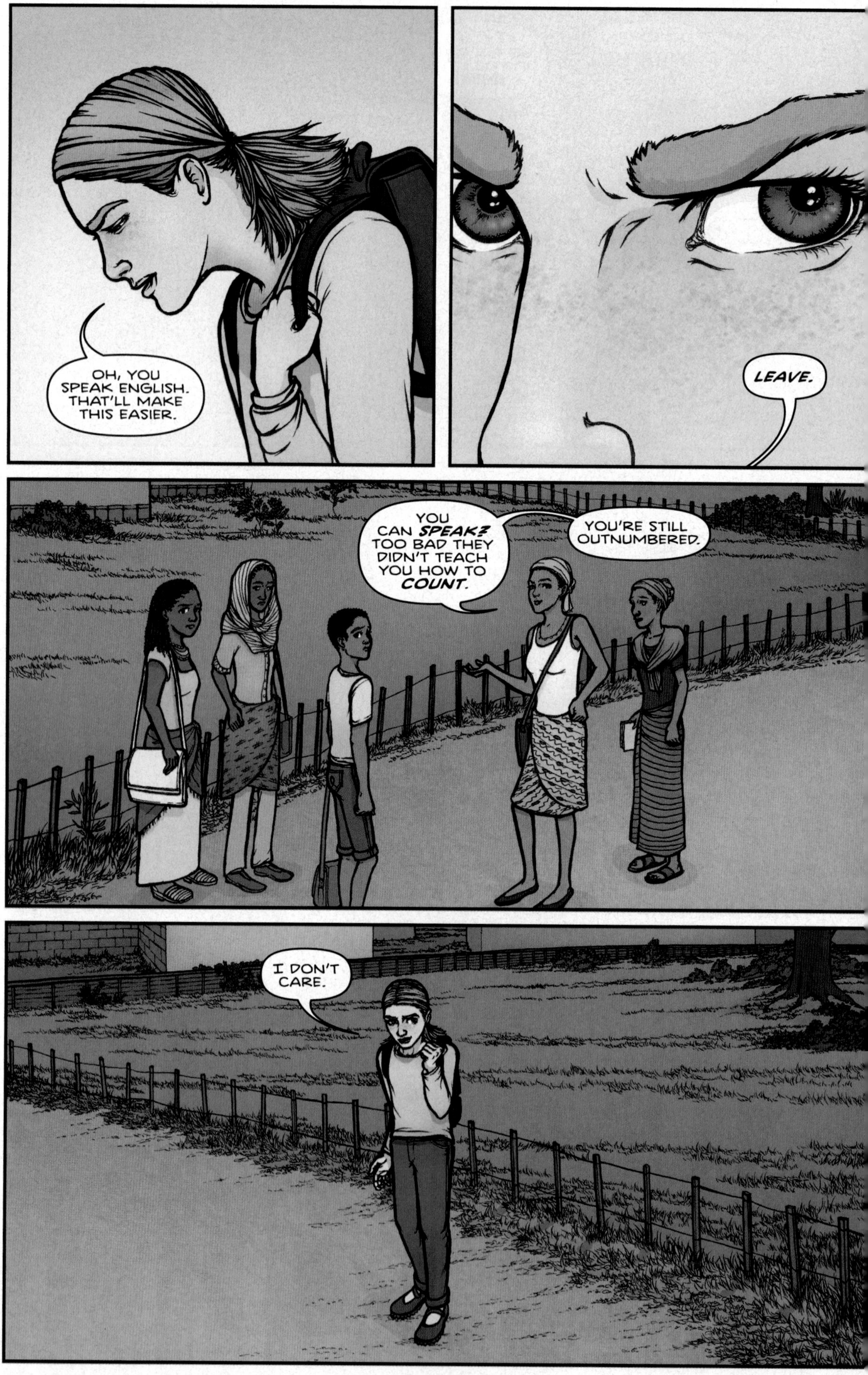
OH, YOU SPEAK ENGLISH. THAT'LL MAKE THIS EASIER.
LEAVE.
YOU CAN SPEAK? TOO BAD THEY DIDN'T TEACH YOU HOW TO COUNT.
YOU'RE STILL OUTNUMBERED.
I DON'T CARE.

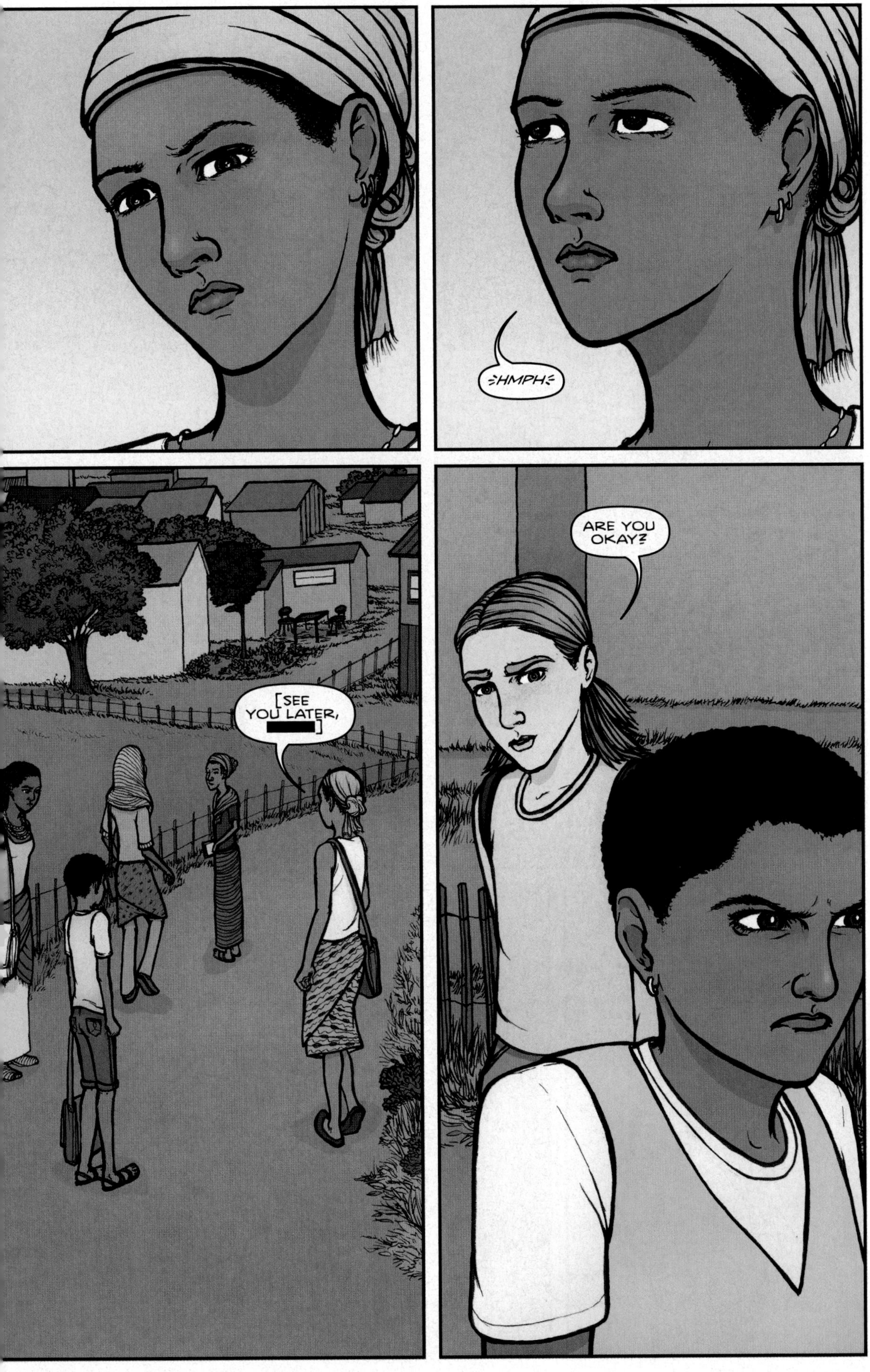
HMPH
[SEE YOU LATER, [redacted]]
ARE YOU OKAY?

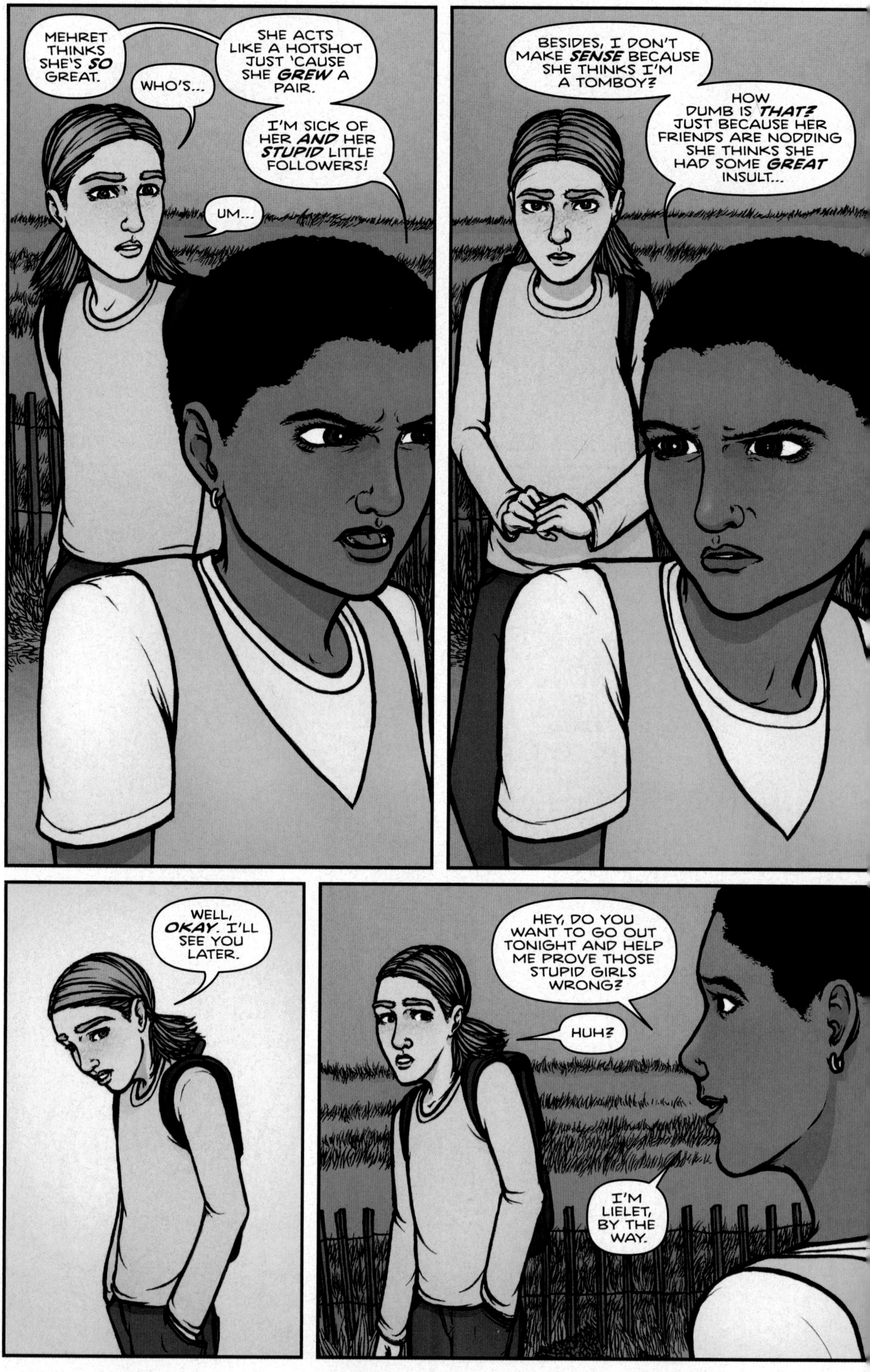
MEHRET THINKS SHE'S SO GREAT.
WHO'S...
SHE ACTS LIKE A HOTSHOT JUST 'CAUSE SHE GREW A PAIR.
I'M SICK OF HER AND HER STUPID LITTLE FOLLOWERS!
UM...
BESIDES, I DON'T MAKE SENSE BECAUSE SHE THINKS I'M A TOMBOY?
HOW DUMB IS THAT? JUST BECAUSE HER FRIENDS ARE NODDING SHE THINKS SHE HAD SOME GREAT INSULT...
WELL, OKAY. I'LL SEE YOU LATER.
HEY, DO YOU WANT TO GO OUT TONIGHT AND HELP ME PROVE THOSE STUPID GIRLS WRONG?
HUH?
I'M LIELET, BY THE WAY.

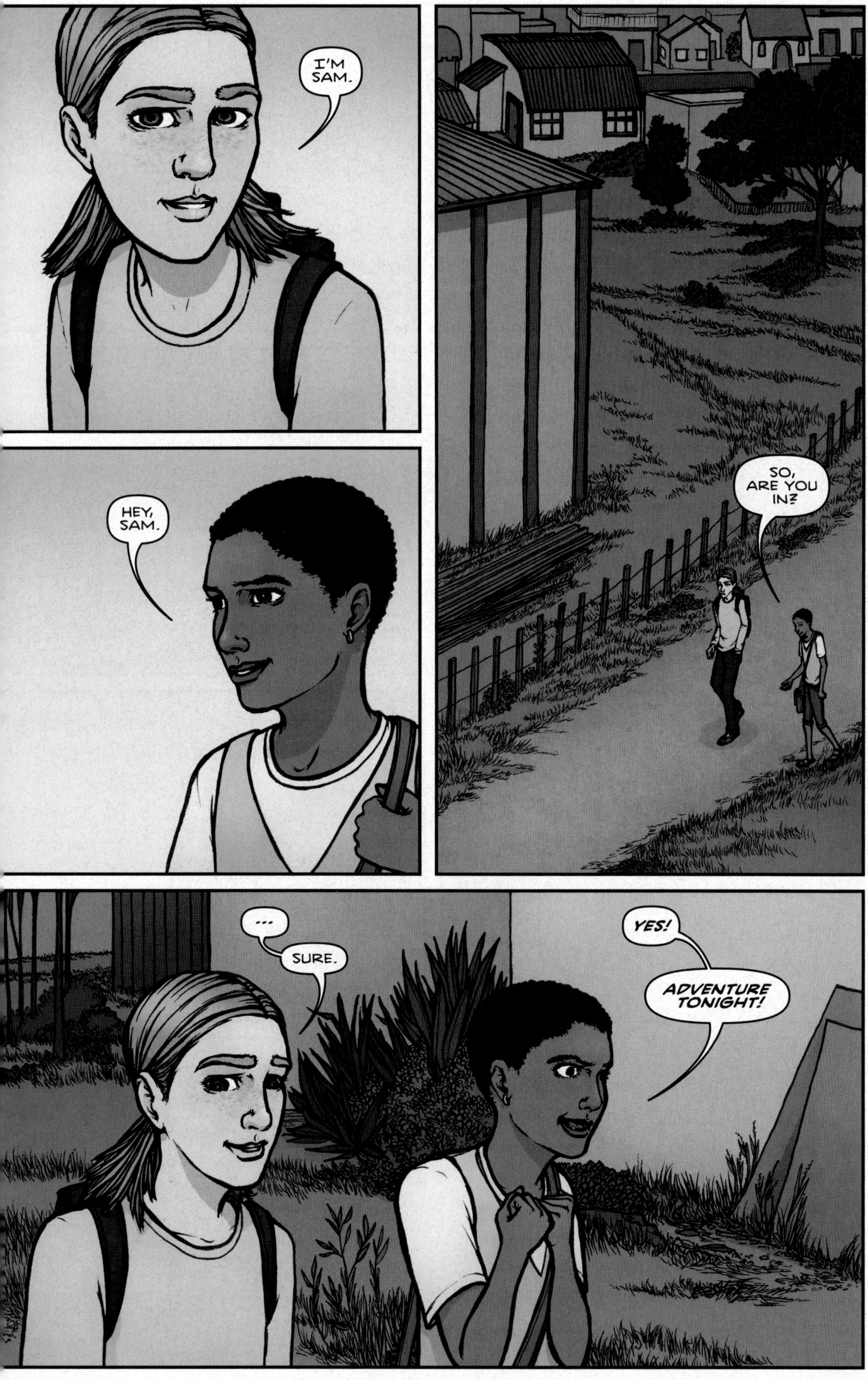
I'M SAM.
HEY, SAM.
SO, ARE YOU IN?
...
SURE.
YES!
ADVENTURE TONIGHT!

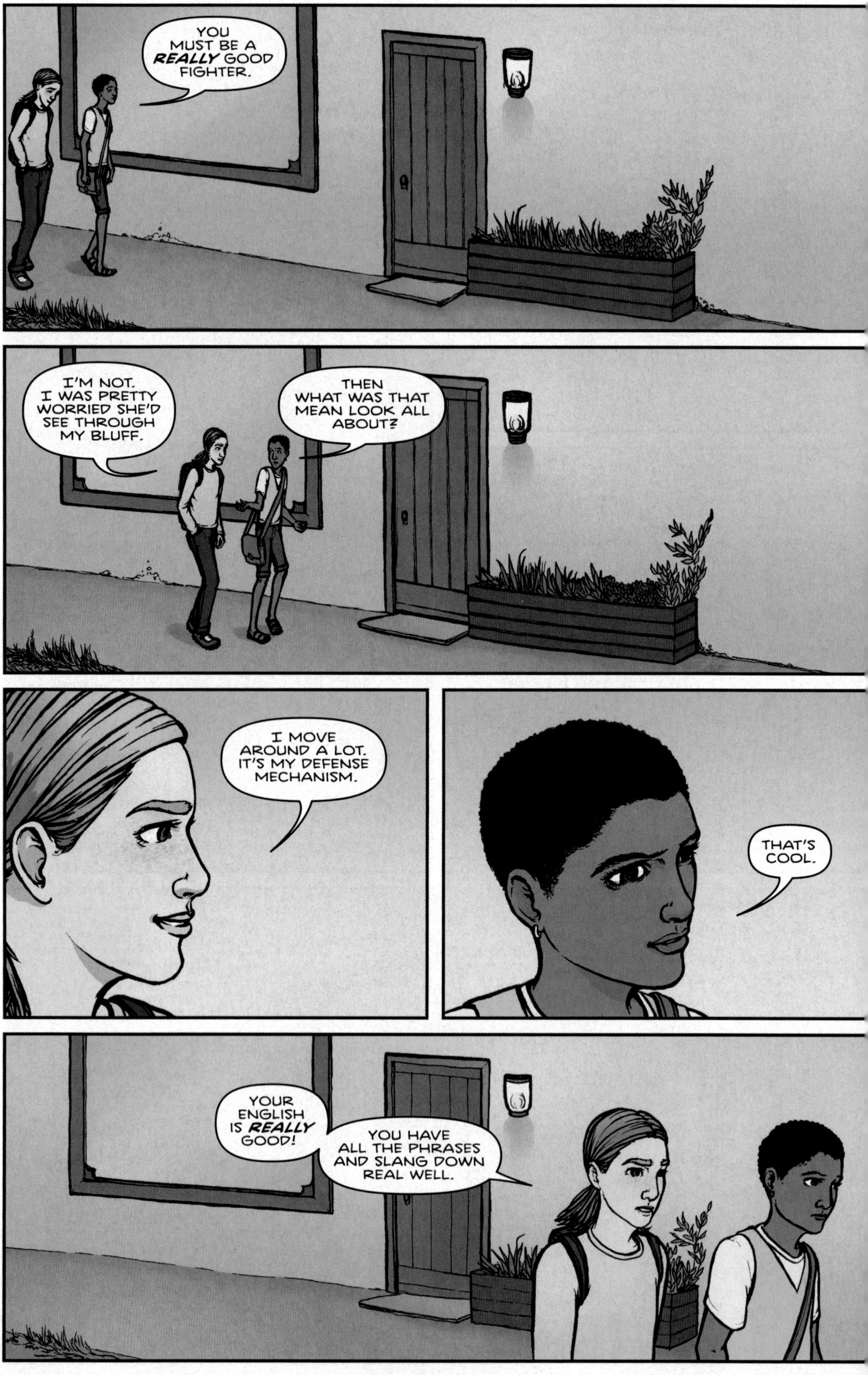
YOU MUST BE A REALLY GOOD FIGHTER.
I'M NOT. I WAS PRETTY WORRIED SHE'D SEE THROUGH MY BLUFF.
THEN WHAT WAS THAT MEAN LOOK ALL ABOUT?
I MOVE AROUND A LOT. IT'S MY DEFENSE MECHANISM.
THAT'S COOL.
YOUR ENGLISH IS REALLY GOOD!
YOU HAVE ALL THE PHRASES AND SLANG DOWN REAL WELL.

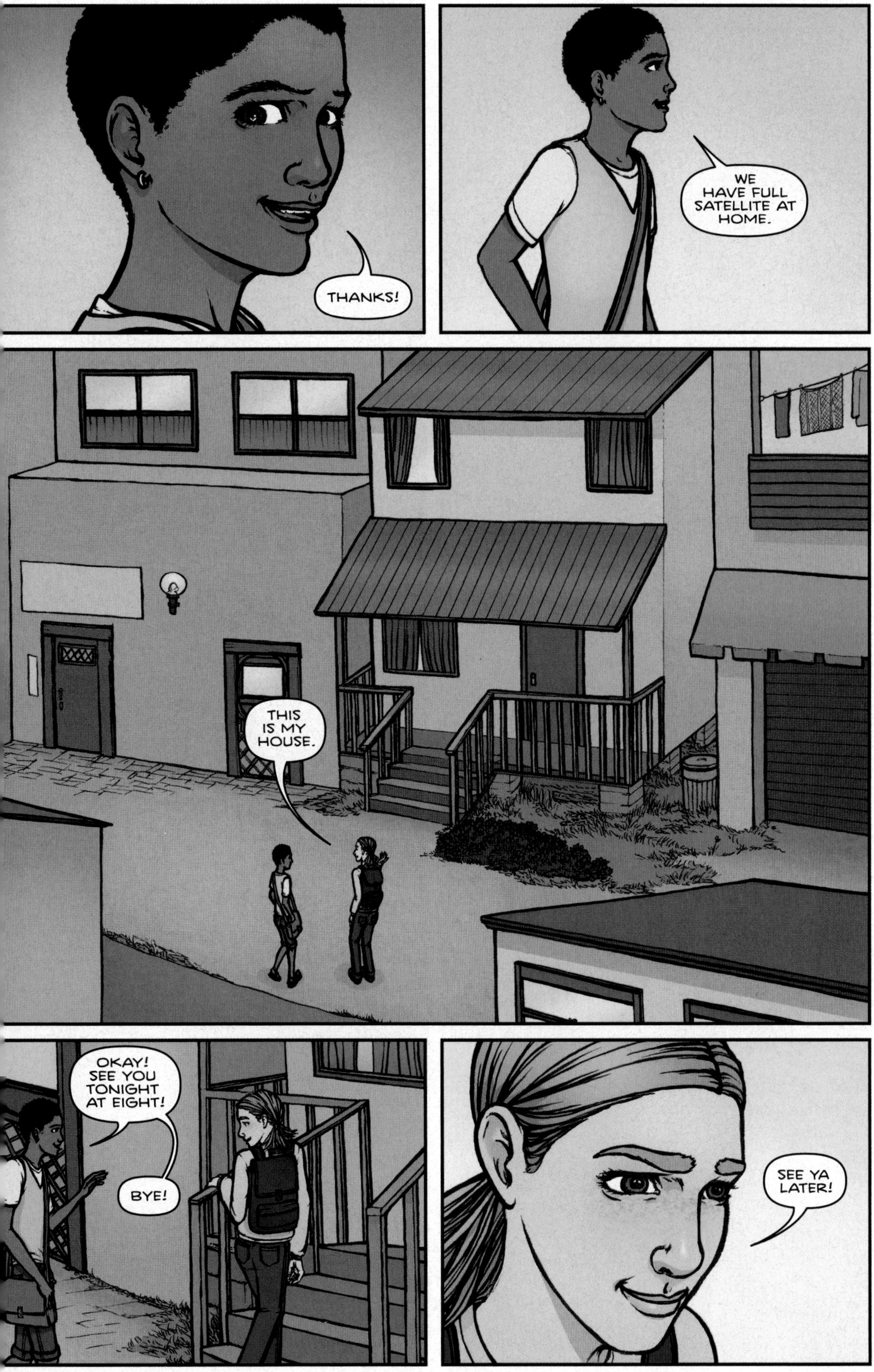
THANKS!
WE HAVE FULL SATELLITE AT HOME.
THIS IS MY HOUSE.
OKAY! SEE YOU TONIGHT AT EIGHT!
BYE!
SEE YA LATER!

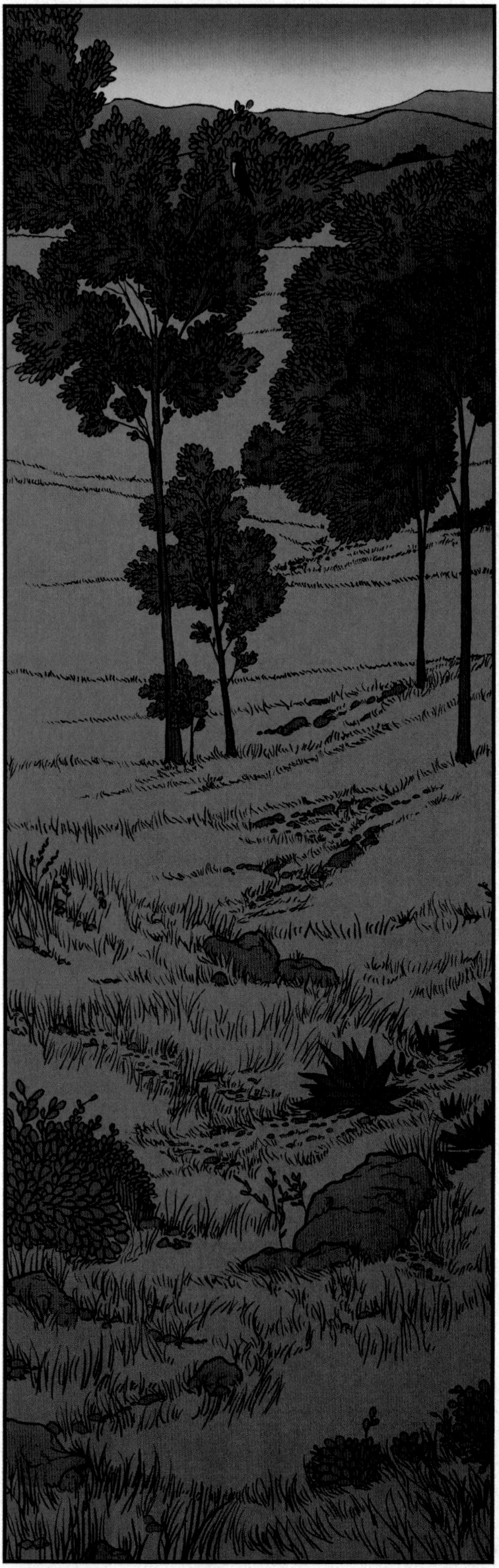

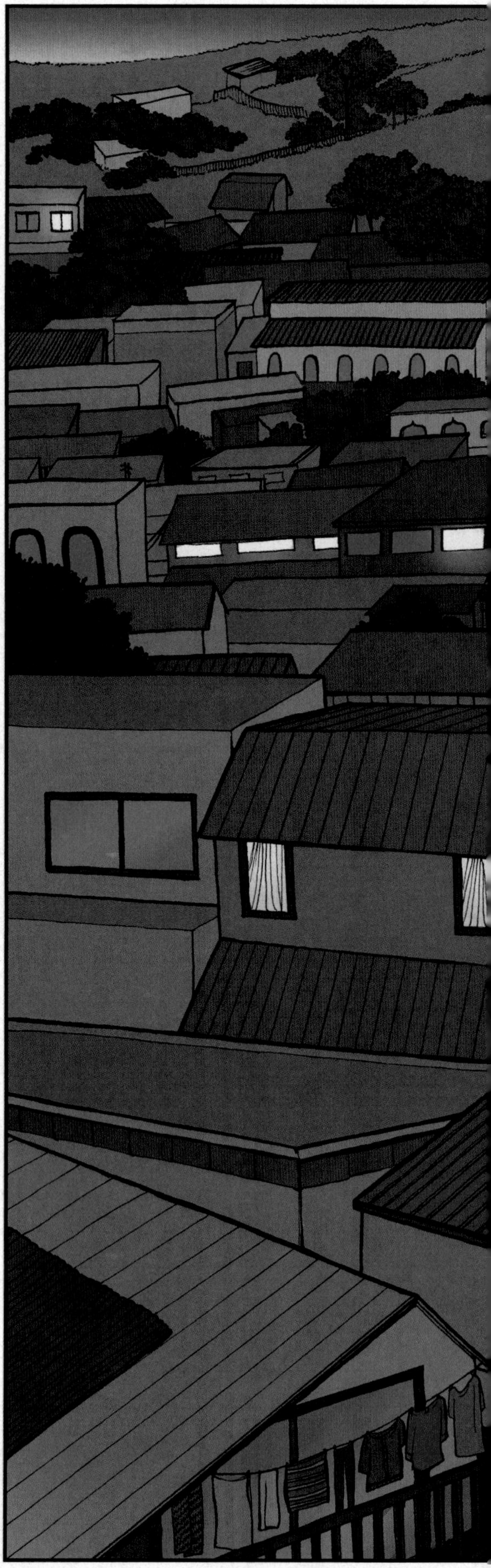

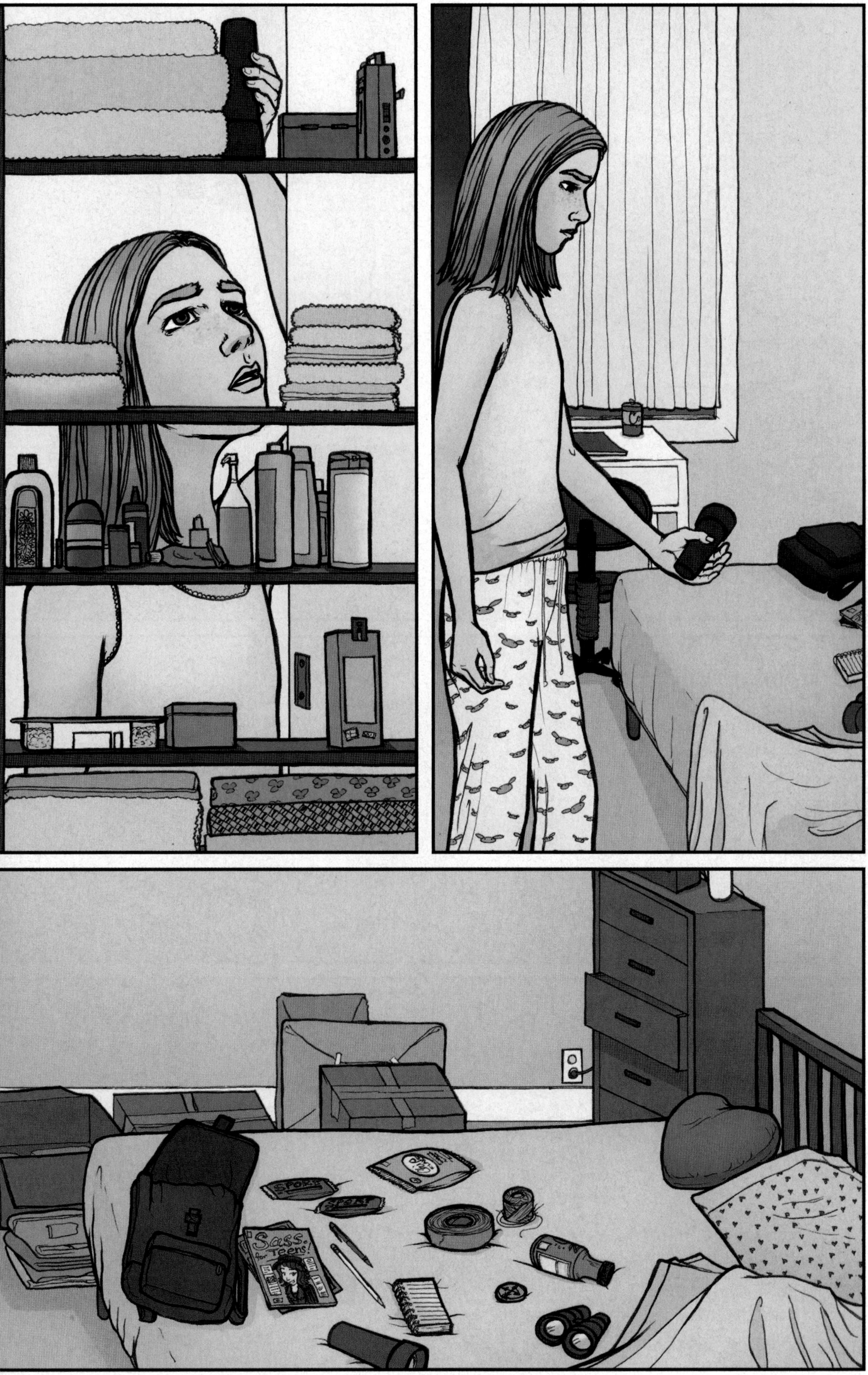
Sass. for Teens!

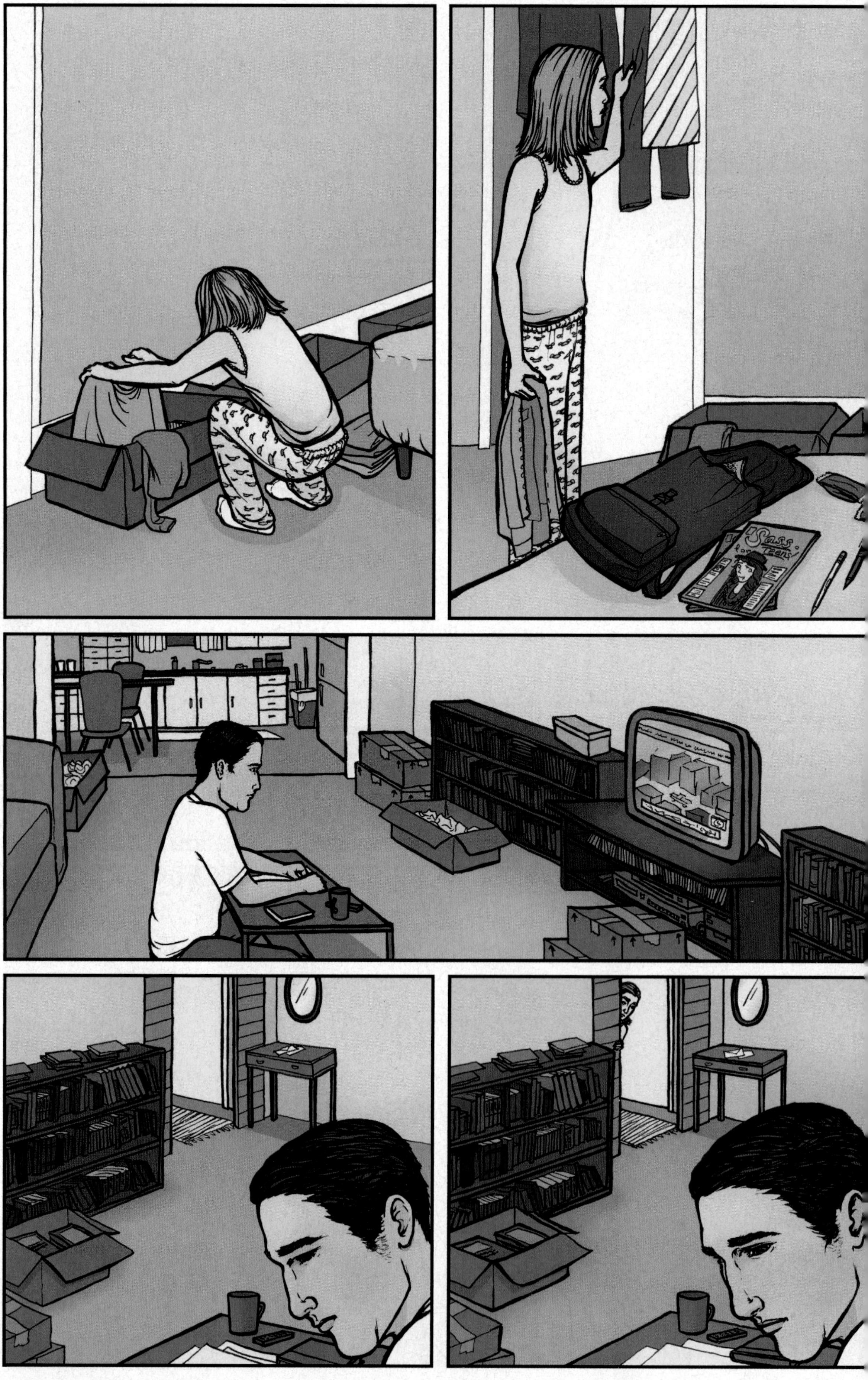
Sass
Teens

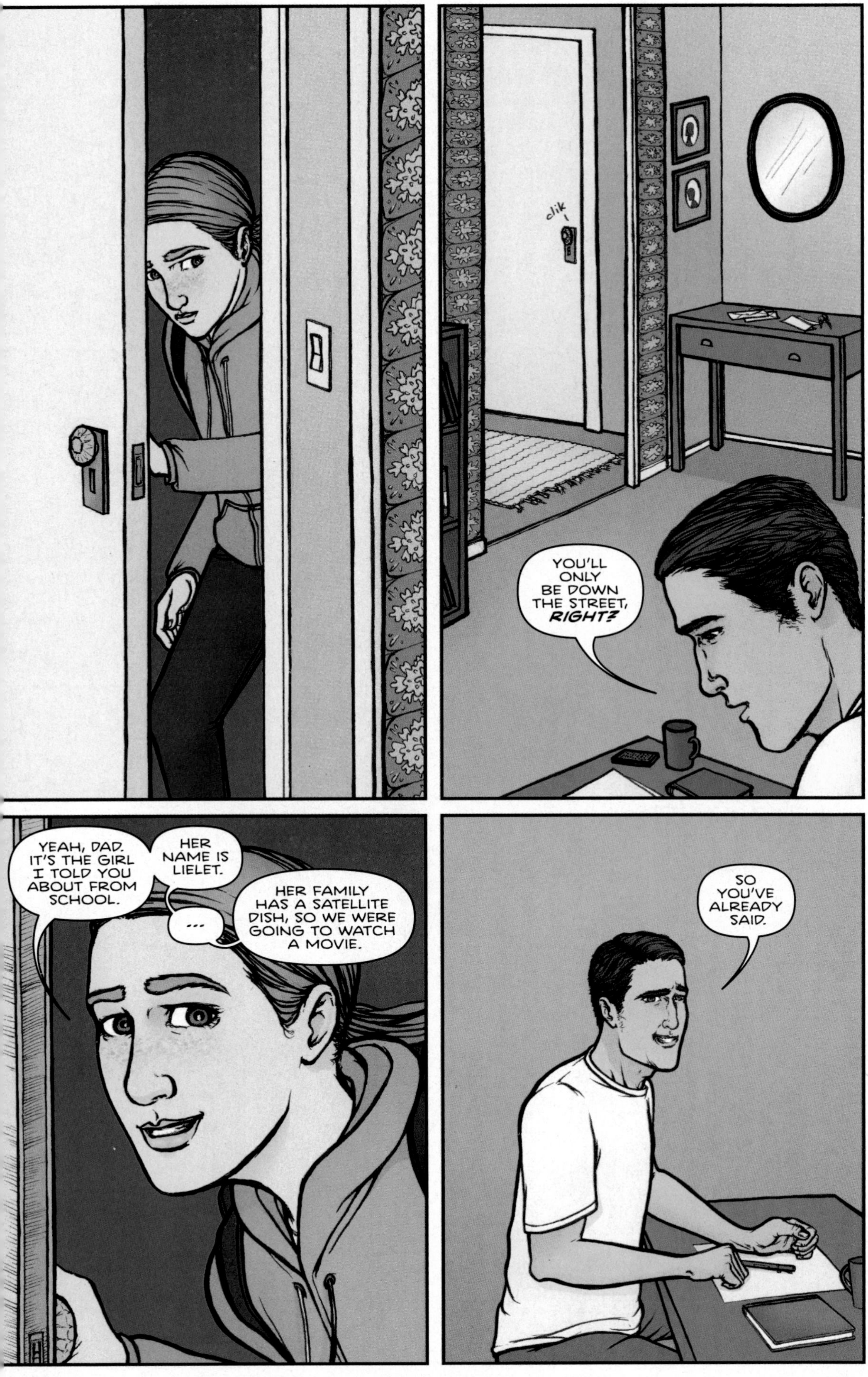
clik
YOU'LL ONLY BE DOWN THE STREET, RIGHT?
YEAH, DAD. IT'S THE GIRL I TOLD YOU ABOUT FROM SCHOOL.
HER NAME IS LIELET.
...
HER FAMILY HAS A SATELLITE DISH, SO WE WERE GOING TO WATCH A MOVIE.
SO YOU'VE ALREADY SAID.

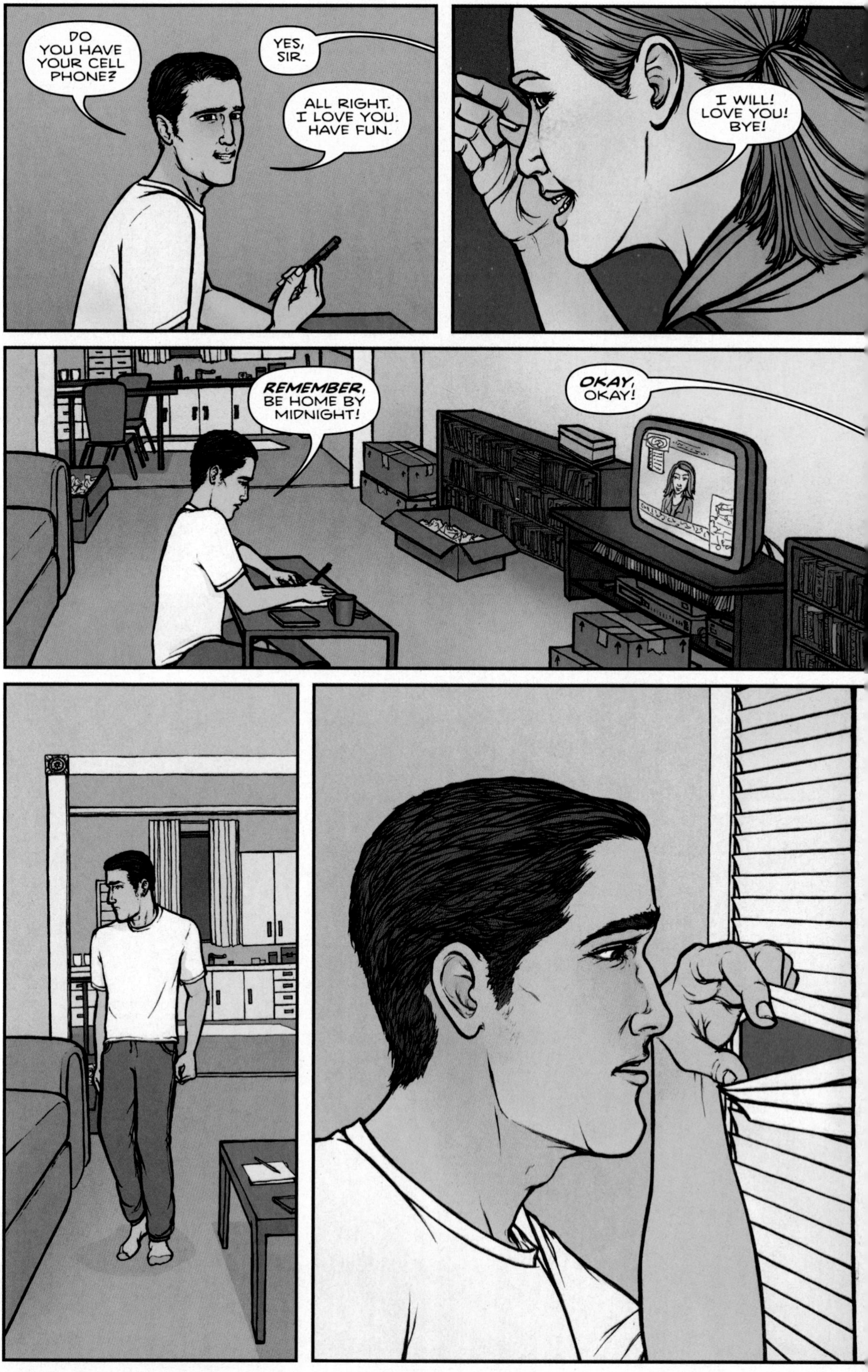
DO YOU HAVE YOUR CELL PHONE?
YES, SIR.
ALL RIGHT. I LOVE YOU. HAVE FUN.
I WILL! LOVE YOU! BYE!
REMEMBER, BE HOME BY MIDNIGHT!
OKAY, OKAY!

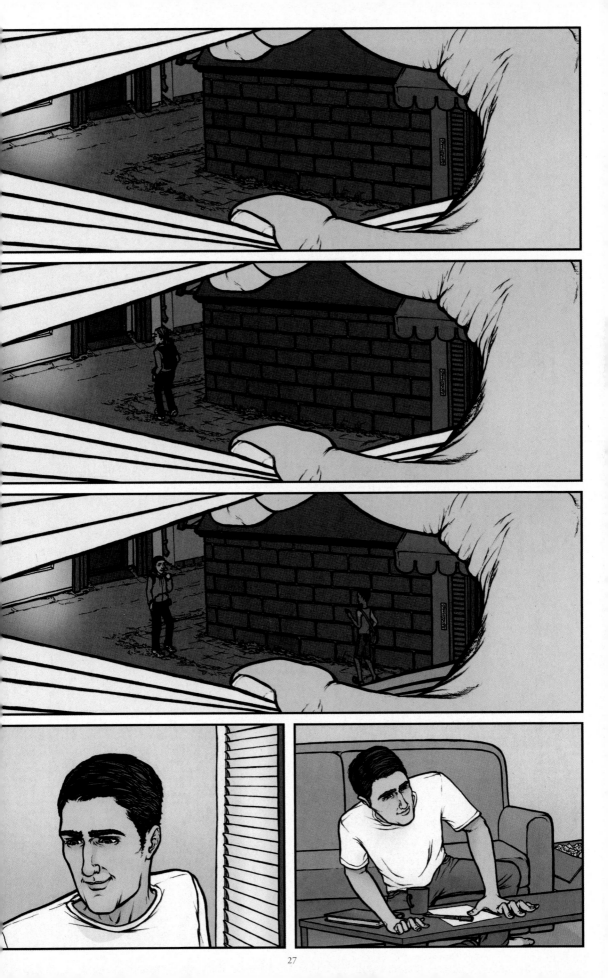

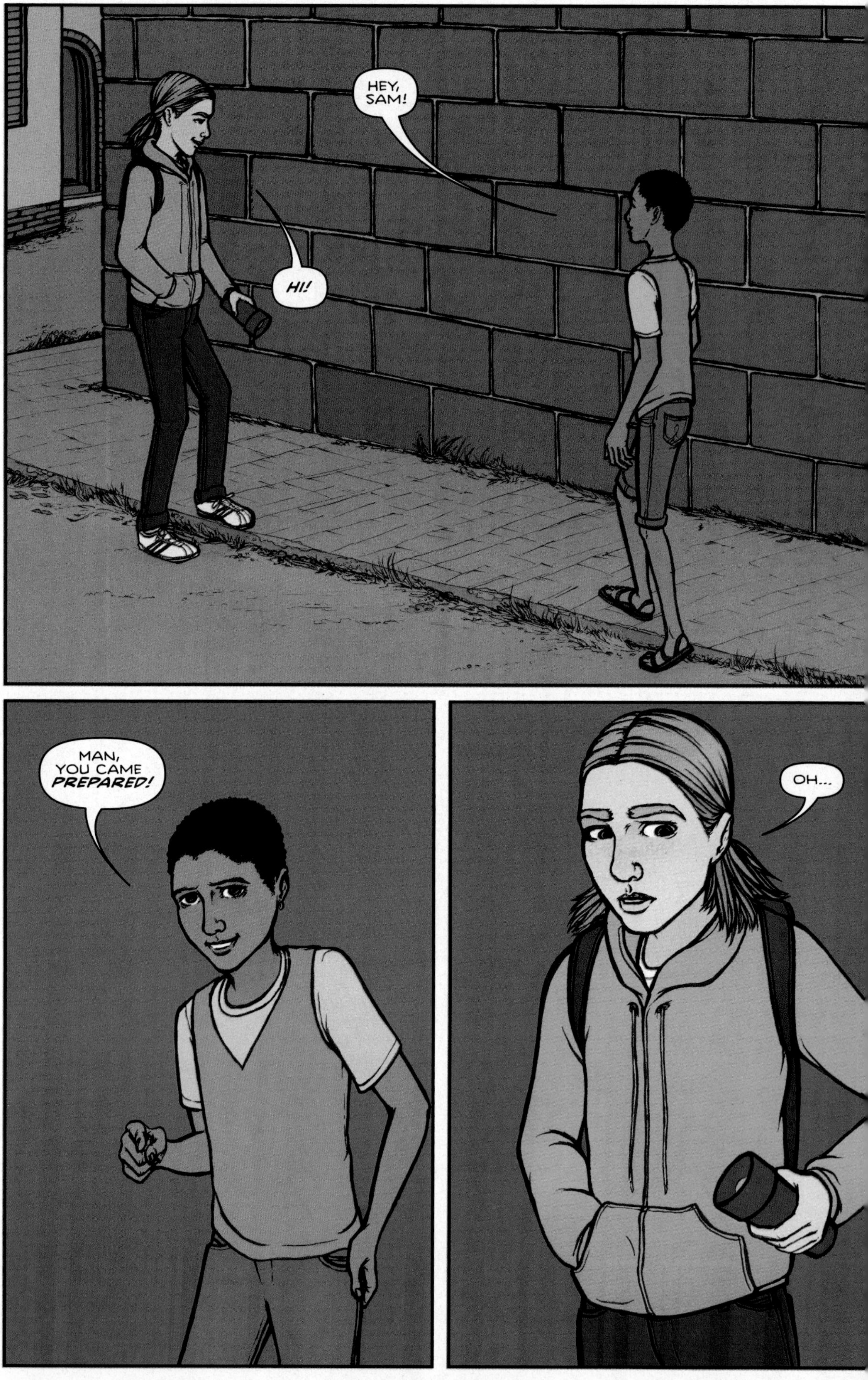
HEY, SAM!
HI!
MAN, YOU CAME PREPARED!
OH...

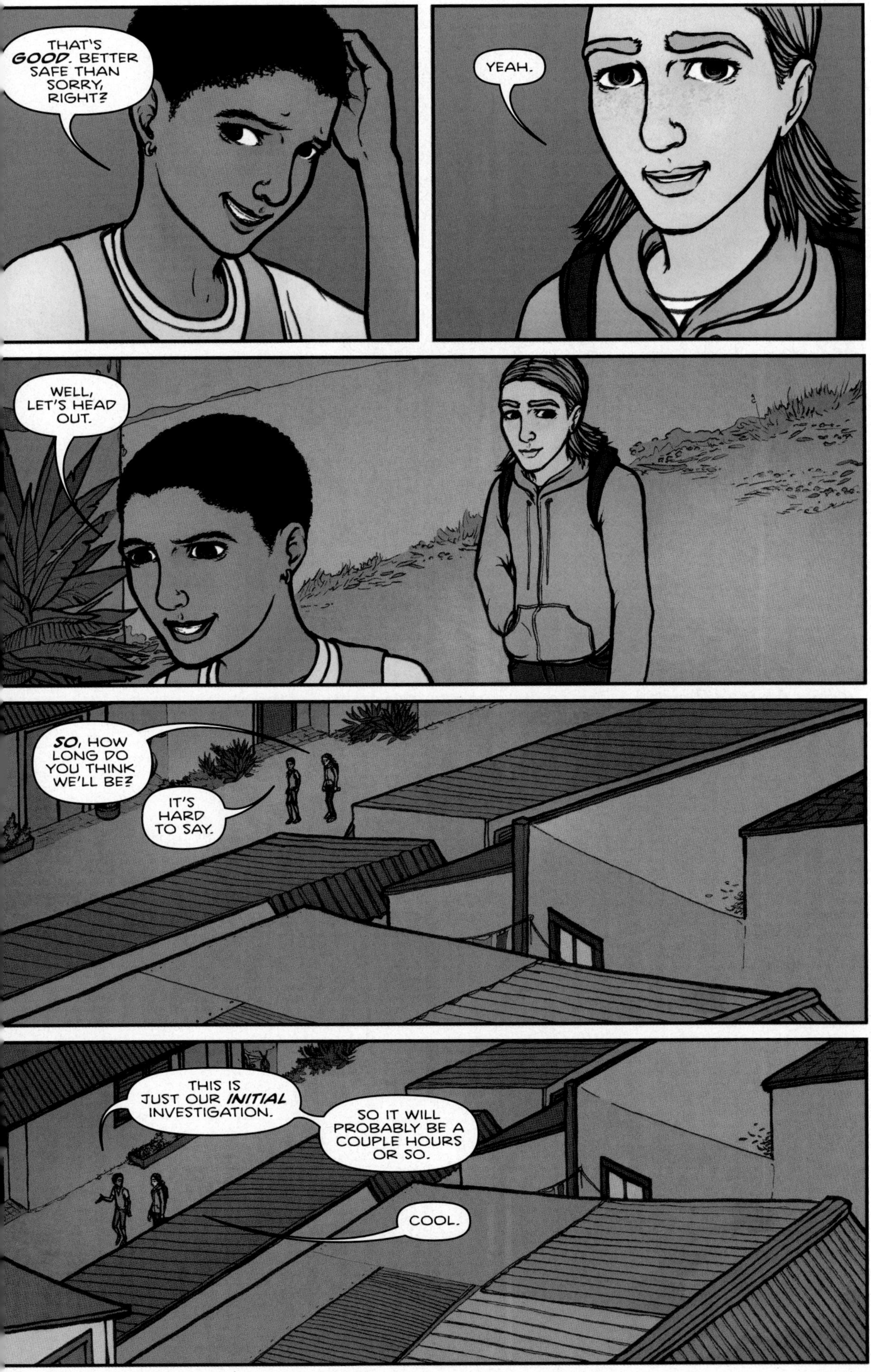
THAT'S *GOOD*. BETTER SAFE THAN SORRY, RIGHT?
YEAH.
WELL, LET'S HEAD OUT.
SO, HOW LONG DO YOU THINK WE'LL BE?
IT'S HARD TO SAY.
THIS IS JUST OUR *INITIAL* INVESTIGATION.
SO IT WILL PROBABLY BE A COUPLE HOURS OR SO.
COOL.

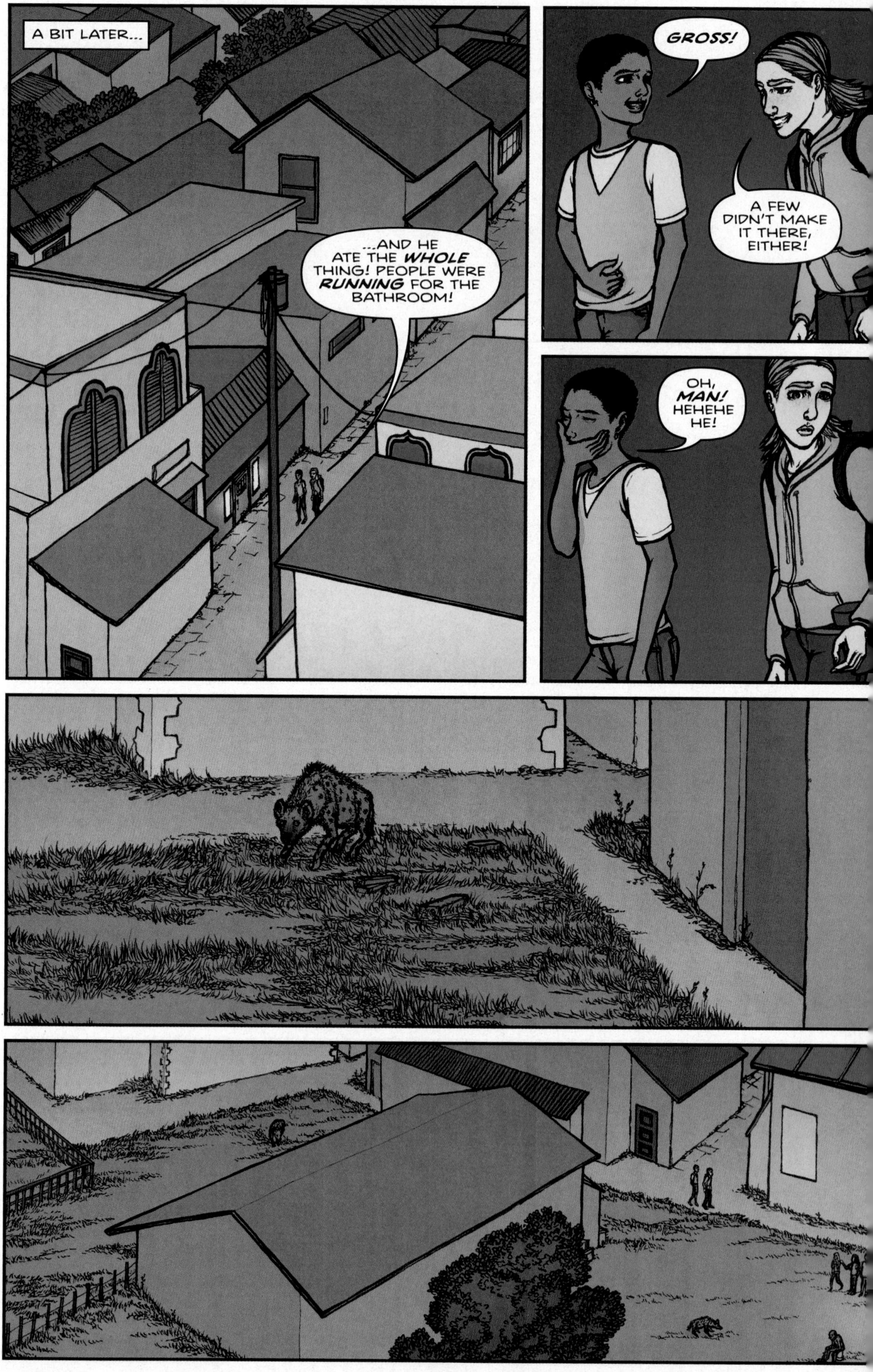
A BIT LATER...
...AND HE ATE THE WHOLE THING! PEOPLE WERE RUNNING FOR THE BATHROOM!
GROSS!
A FEW DIDN'T MAKE IT THERE, EITHER!
OH, MAN! HEHEHE HE!

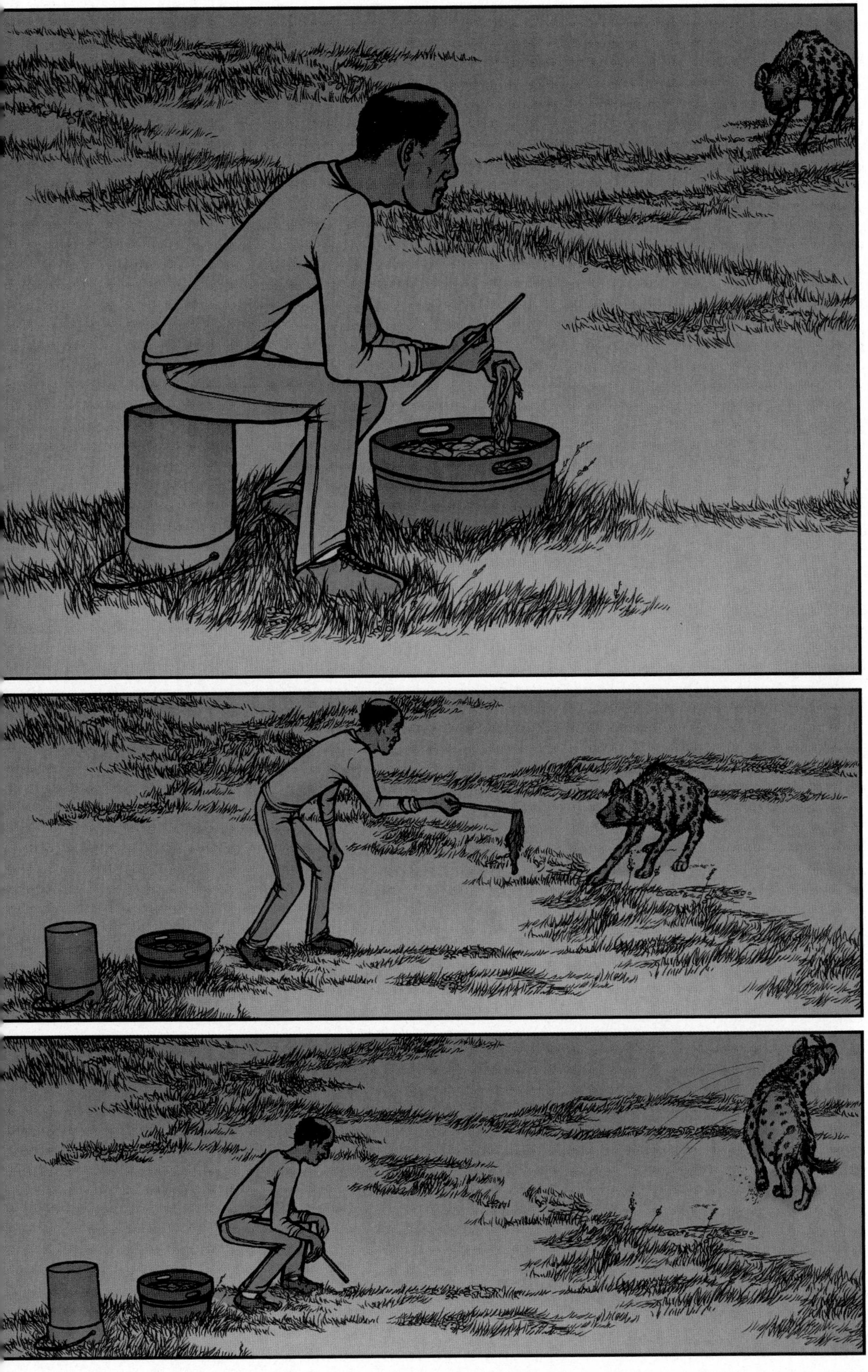

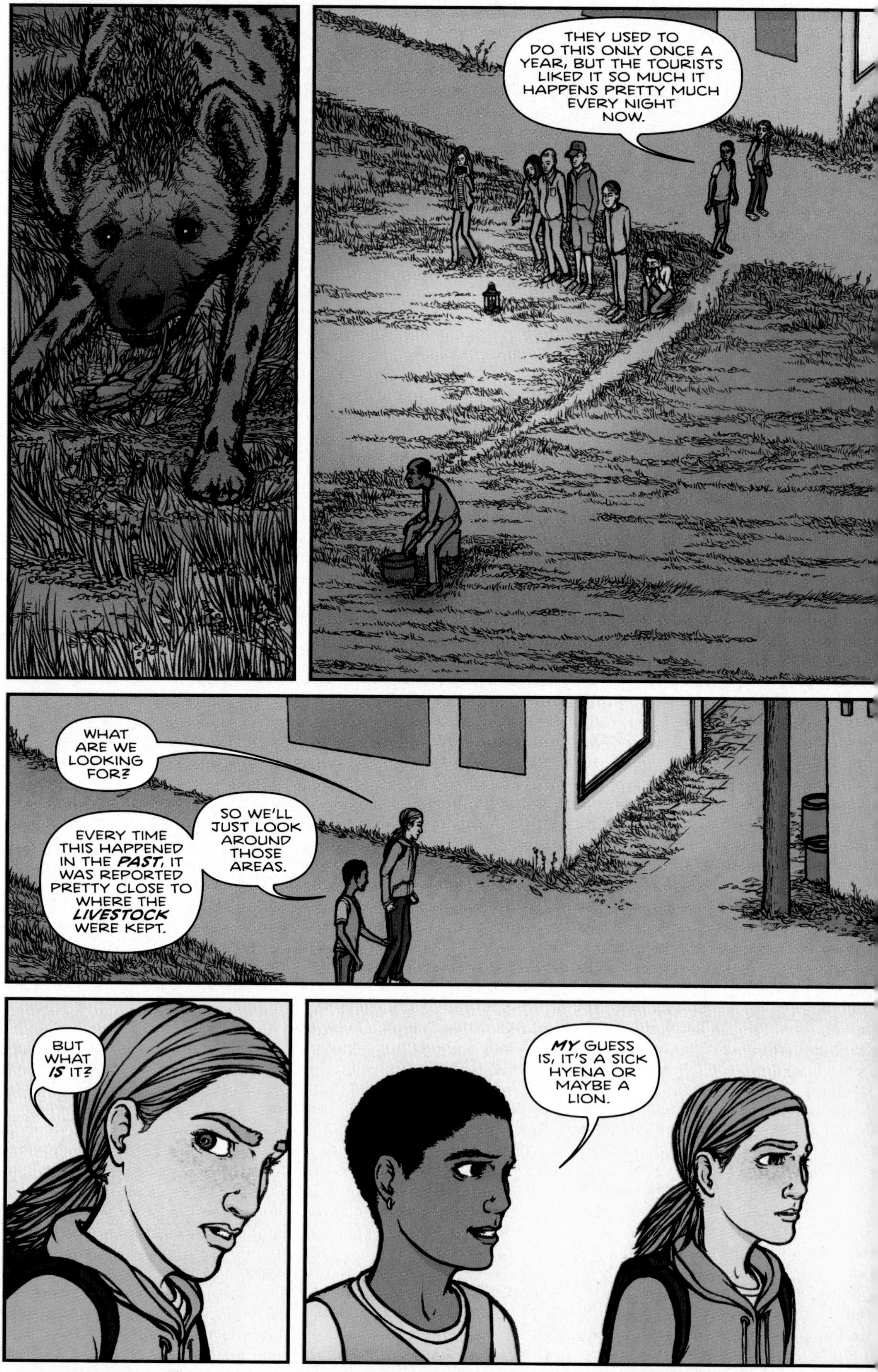
THEY USED TO DO THIS ONLY ONCE A YEAR, BUT THE TOURISTS LIKED IT SO MUCH IT HAPPENS PRETTY MUCH EVERY NIGHT NOW.
WHAT ARE WE LOOKING FOR?
EVERY TIME THIS HAPPENED IN THE *PAST*, IT WAS REPORTED PRETTY CLOSE TO WHERE THE *LIVESTOCK* WERE KEPT.
SO WE'LL JUST LOOK AROUND THOSE AREAS.
BUT WHAT *IS* IT?
MY GUESS IS, IT'S A SICK HYENA OR MAYBE A LION.

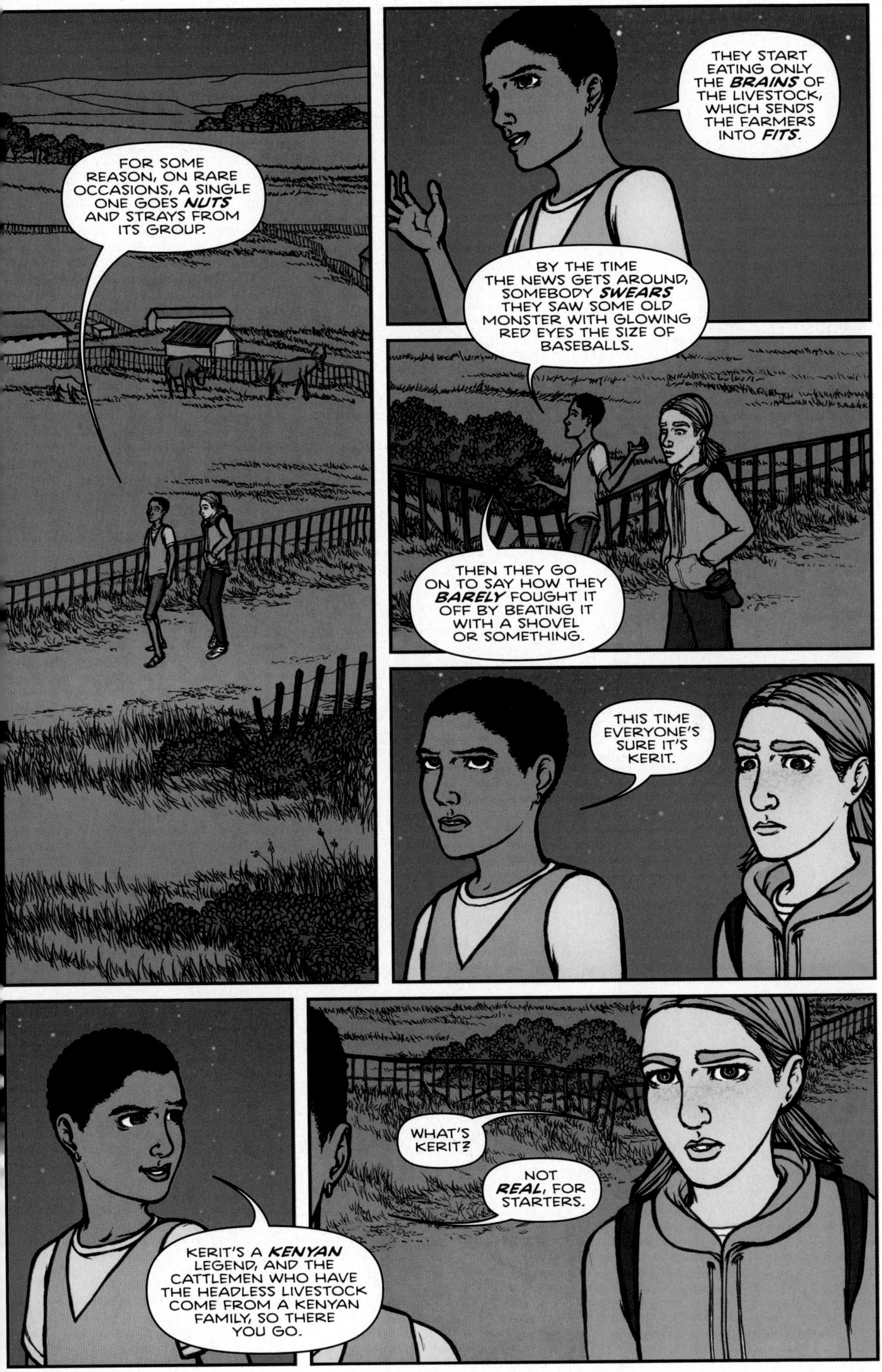
FOR SOME REASON, ON RARE OCCASIONS, A SINGLE ONE GOES NUTS AND STRAYS FROM ITS GROUP.
THEY START EATING ONLY THE BRAINS OF THE LIVESTOCK, WHICH SENDS THE FARMERS INTO FITS.
BY THE TIME THE NEWS GETS AROUND, SOMEBODY SWEARS THEY SAW SOME OLD MONSTER WITH GLOWING RED EYES THE SIZE OF BASEBALLS.
THEN THEY GO ON TO SAY HOW THEY BARELY FOUGHT IT OFF BY BEATING IT WITH A SHOVEL OR SOMETHING.
THIS TIME EVERYONE'S SURE IT'S KERIT.
WHAT'S KERIT?
NOT REAL, FOR STARTERS.
KERIT'S A KENYAN LEGEND, AND THE CATTLEMEN WHO HAVE THE HEADLESS LIVESTOCK COME FROM A KENYAN FAMILY, SO THERE YOU GO.

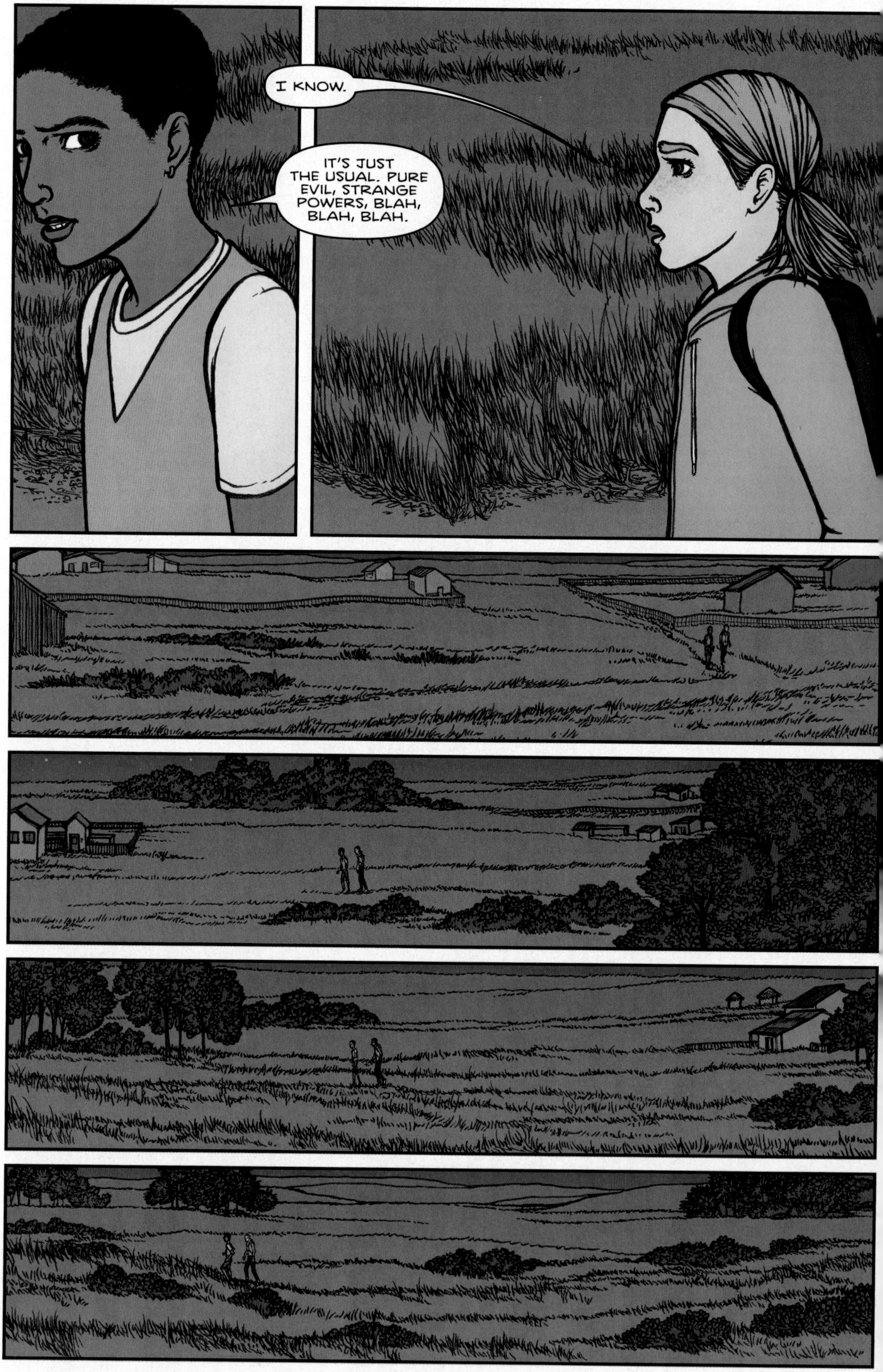
I KNOW.
IT'S JUST THE USUAL. PURE EVIL, STRANGE POWERS, BLAH, BLAH, BLAH.

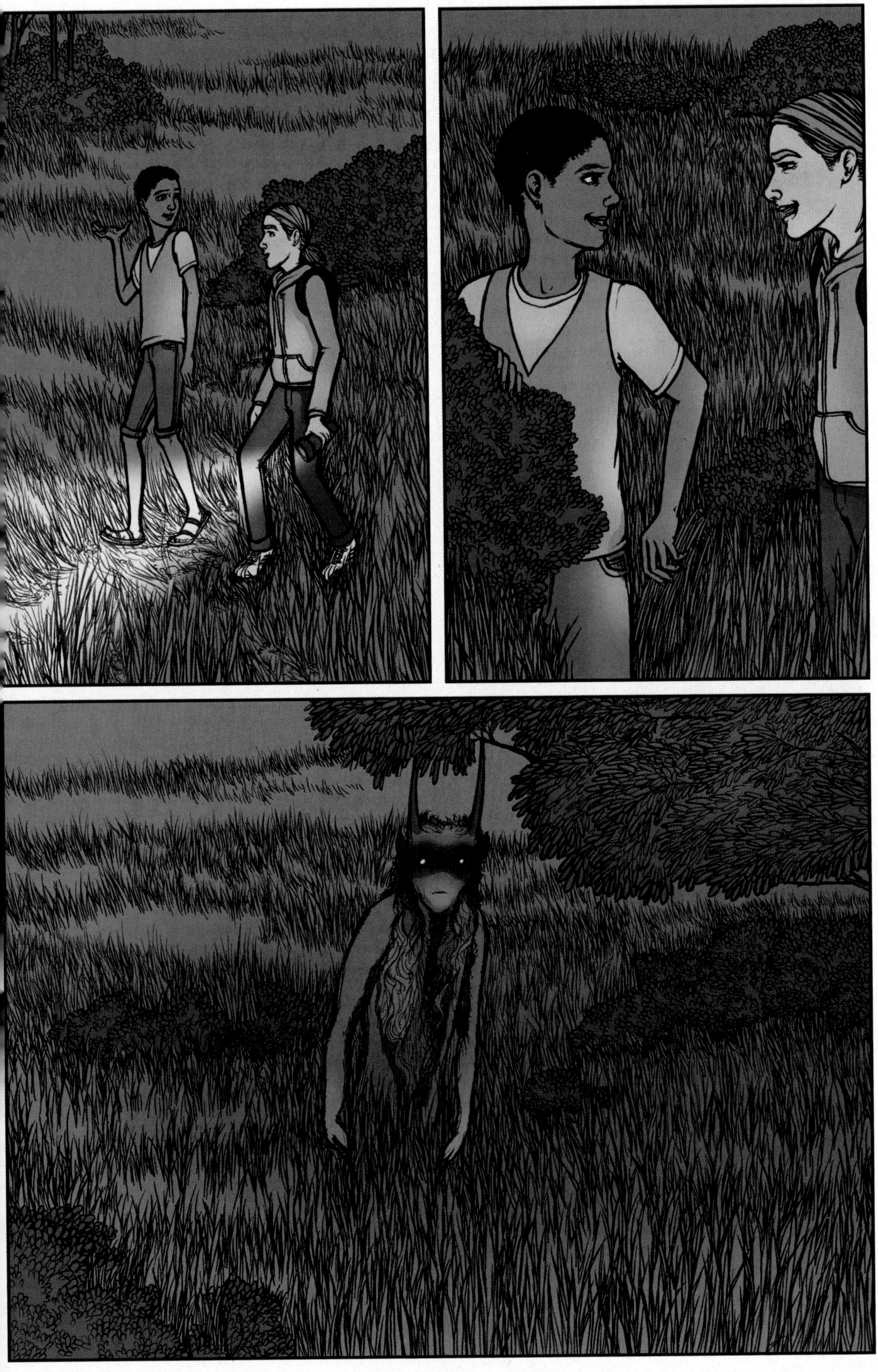

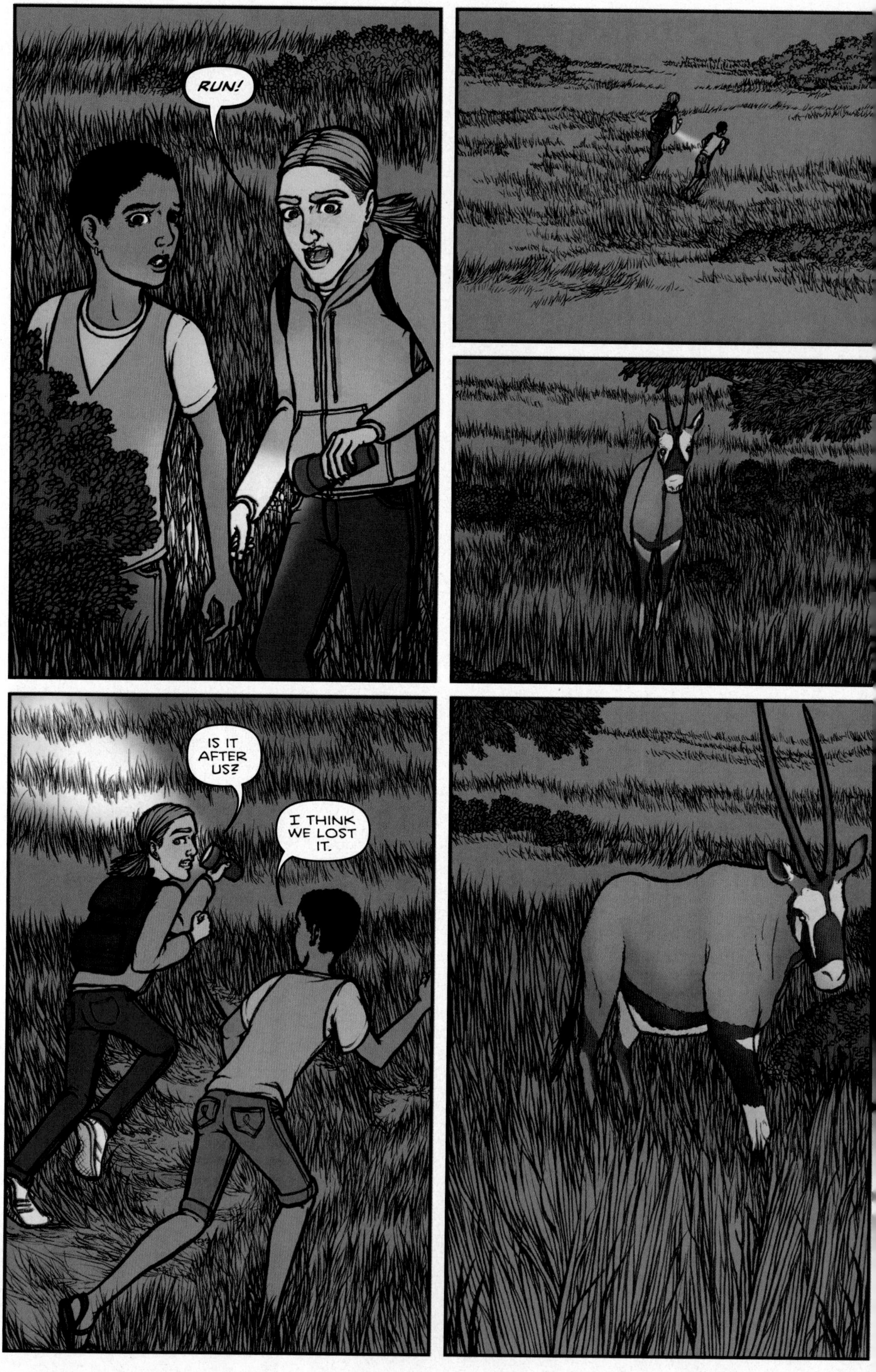
RUN!
IS IT AFTER US?
I THINK WE LOST IT.

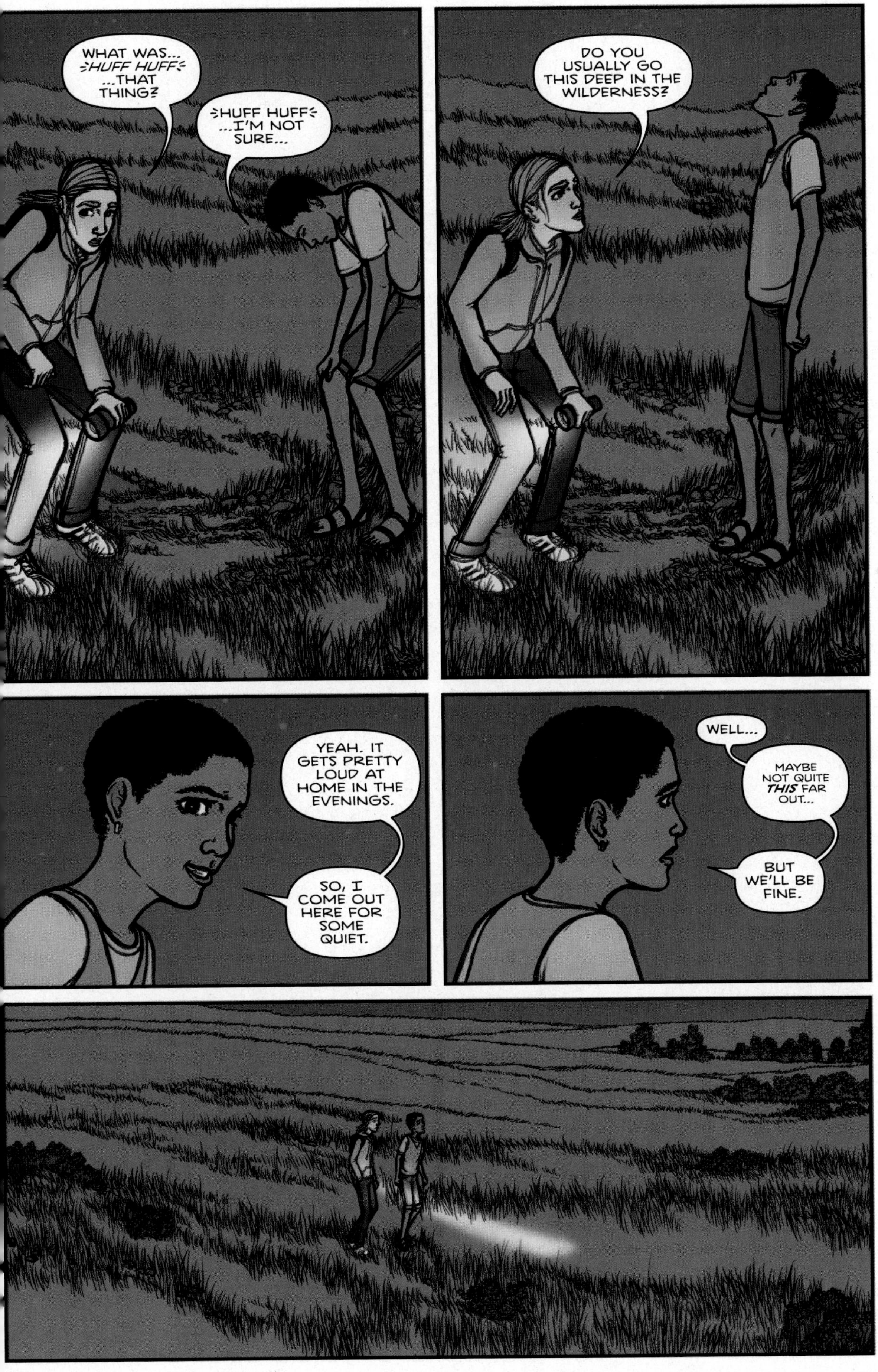
WHAT WAS... ≶HUFF HUFF≶ ...THAT THING?
≶HUFF HUFF≶ ...I'M NOT SURE...
DO YOU USUALLY GO THIS DEEP IN THE WILDERNESS?
YEAH. IT GETS PRETTY LOUD AT HOME IN THE EVENINGS.
SO, I COME OUT HERE FOR SOME QUIET.
WELL...
MAYBE NOT QUITE *THIS* FAR OUT...
BUT WE'LL BE FINE.

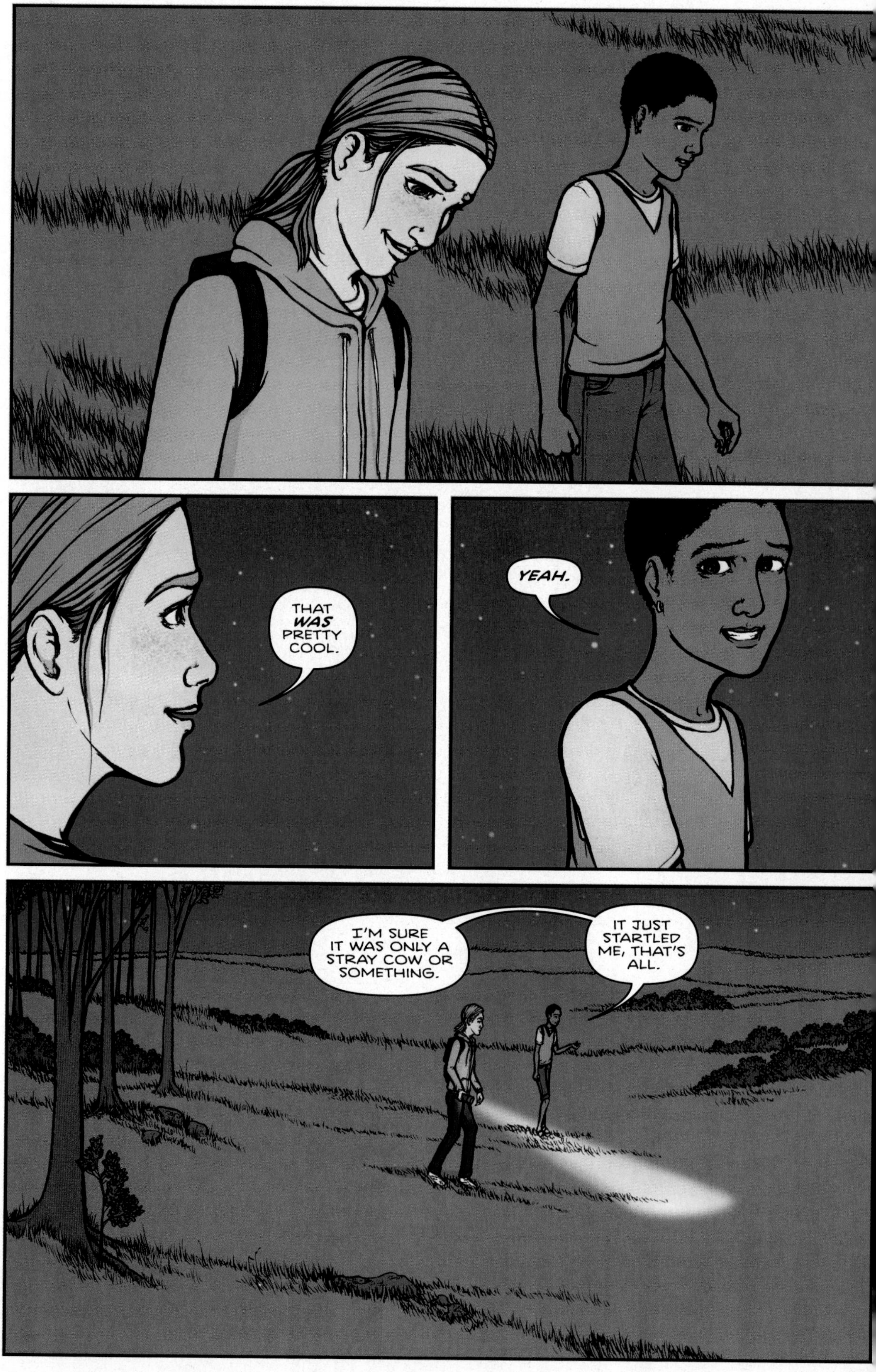
THAT WAS PRETTY COOL.
YEAH.
I'M SURE IT WAS ONLY A STRAY COW OR SOMETHING.
IT JUST STARTLED ME, THAT'S ALL.

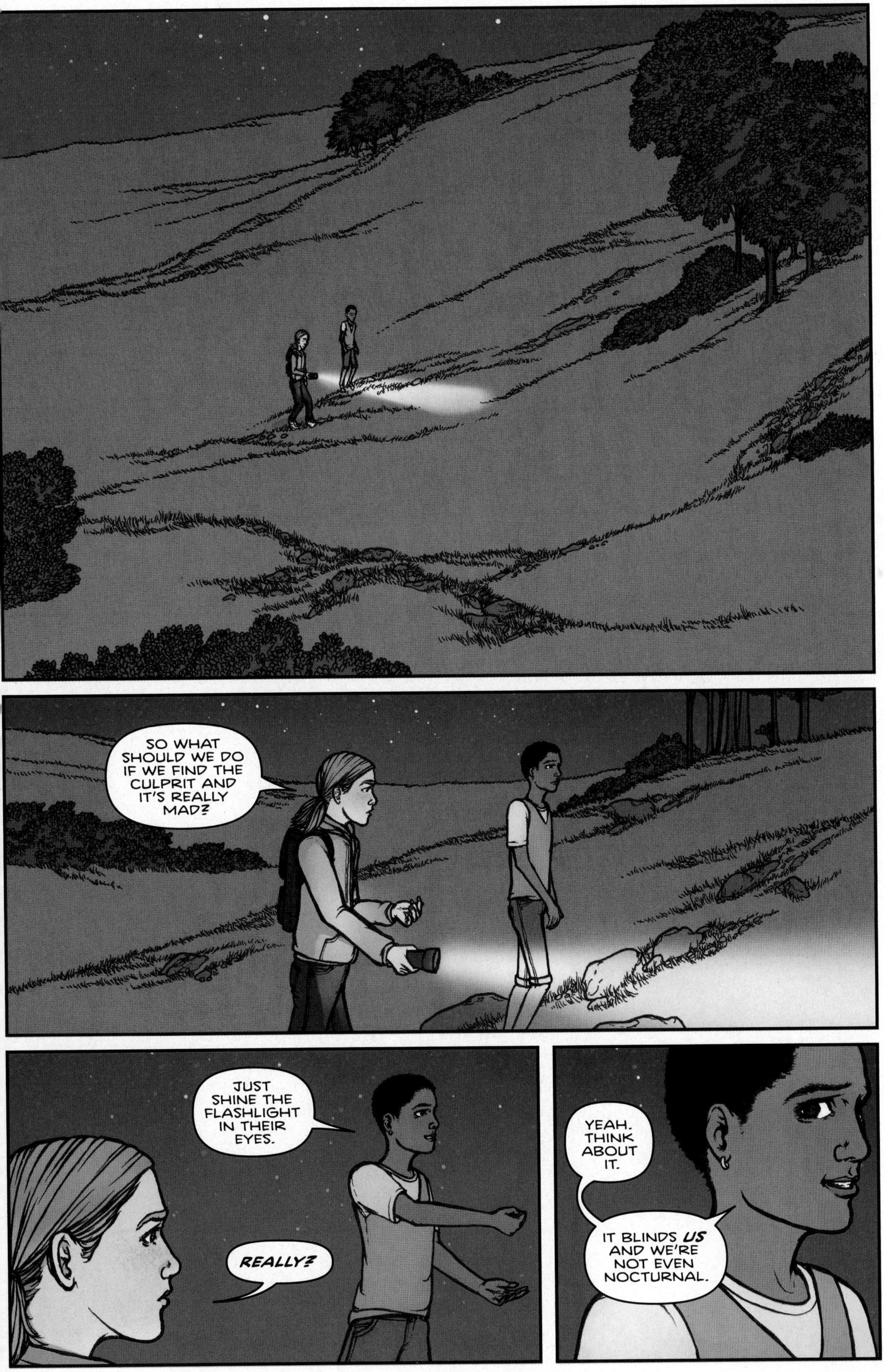
SO WHAT SHOULD WE DO IF WE FIND THE CULPRIT AND IT'S REALLY MAD?
JUST SHINE THE FLASHLIGHT IN THEIR EYES.
REALLY?
YEAH. THINK ABOUT IT.
IT BLINDS US AND WE'RE NOT EVEN NOCTURNAL.

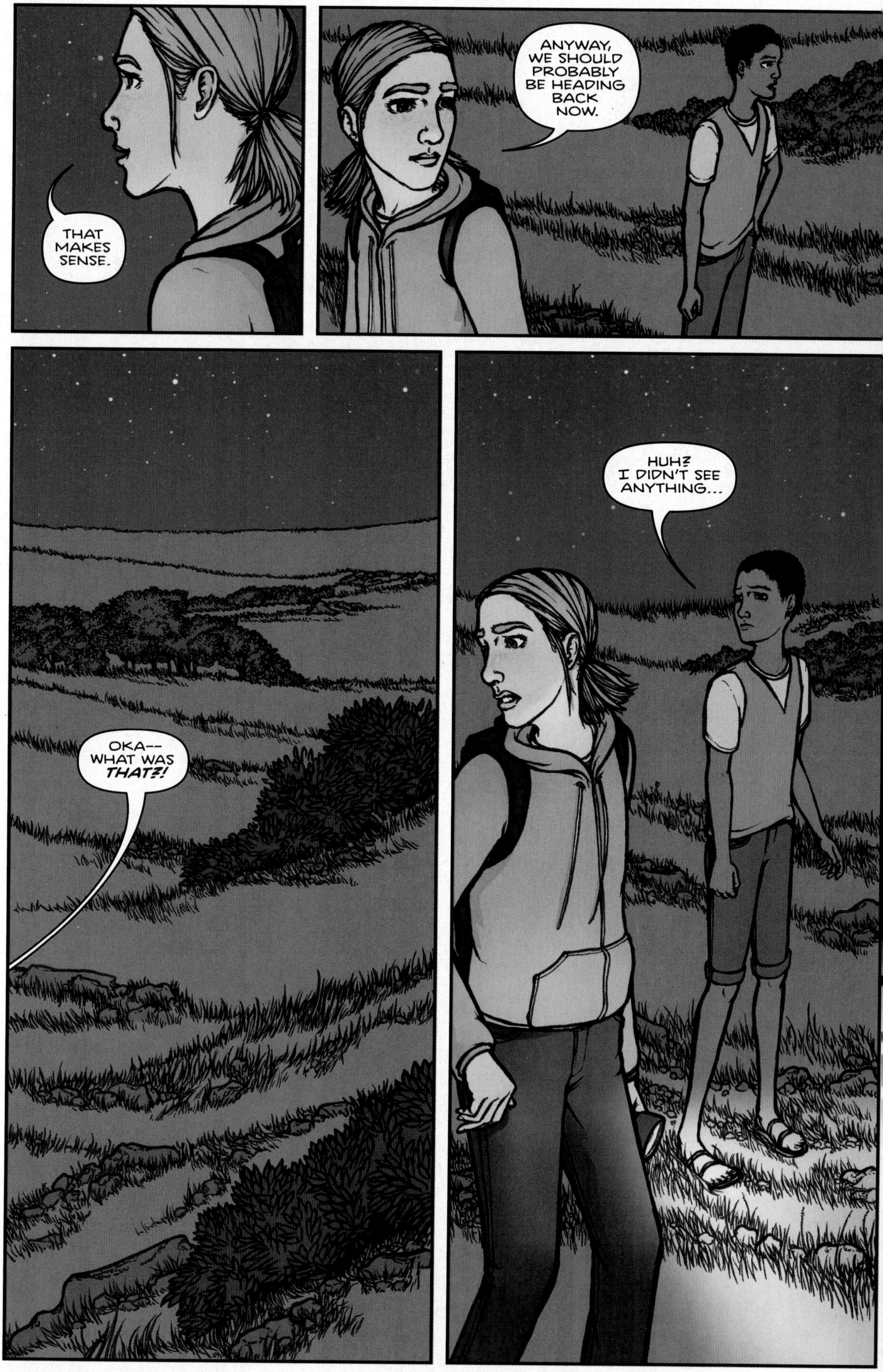
THAT MAKES SENSE.
ANYWAY, WE SHOULD PROBABLY BE HEADING BACK NOW.
OKA-- WHAT WAS *THAT?!*
HUH? I DIDN'T SEE ANYTHING...

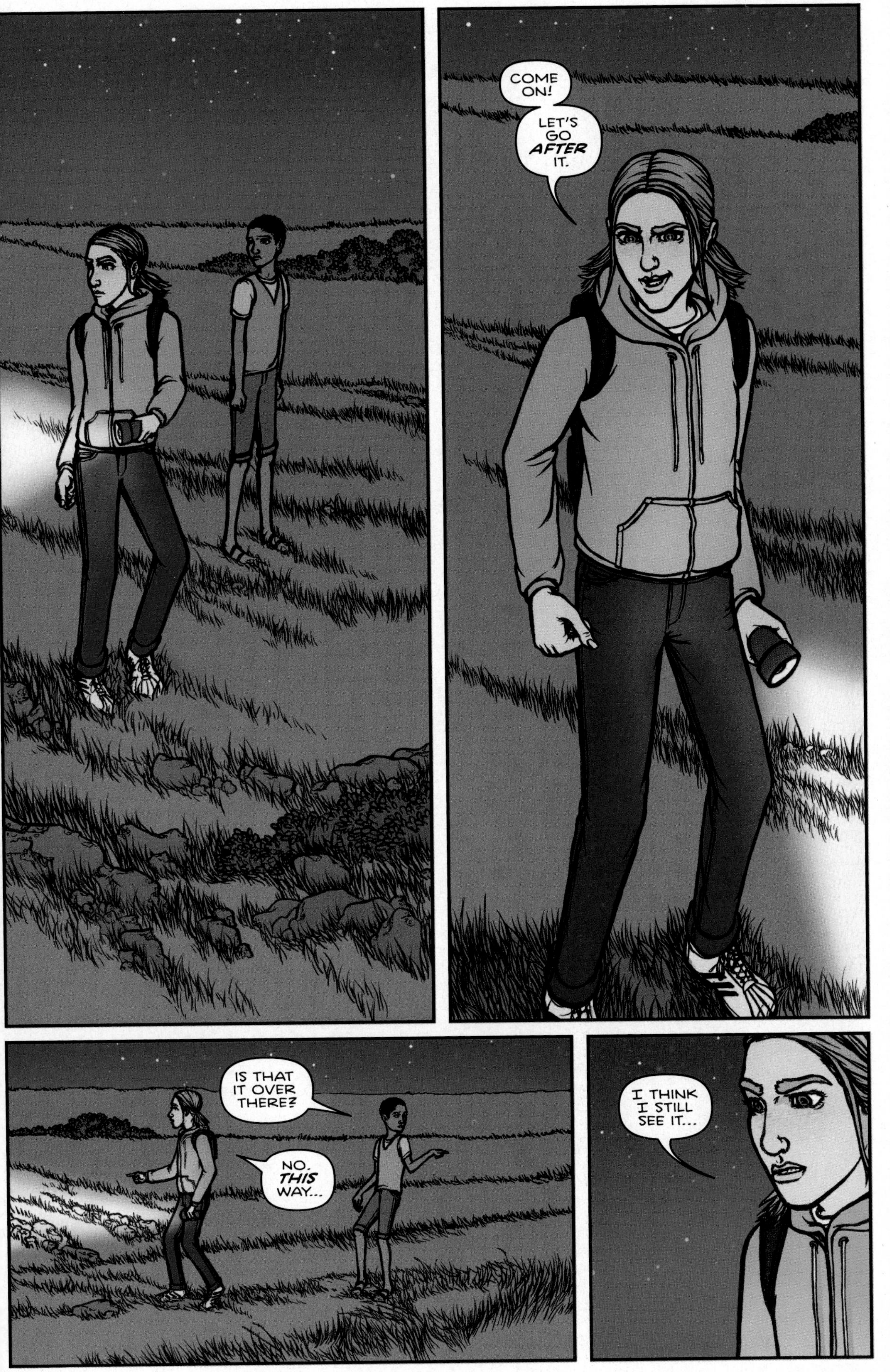
COME ON!
LET'S GO AFTER IT.
IS THAT IT OVER THERE?
NO. THIS WAY...
I THINK I STILL SEE IT...

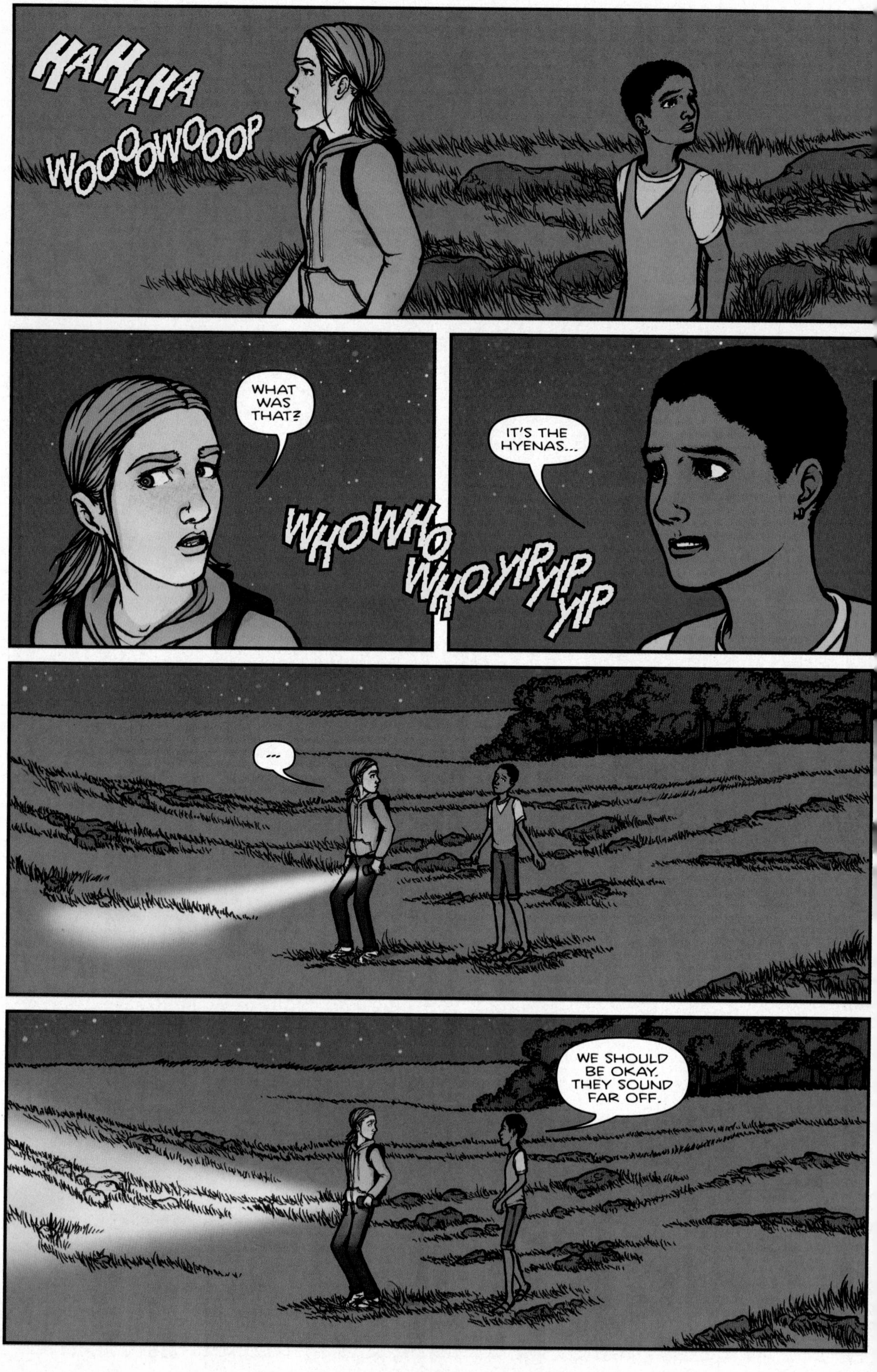
HAHAHAHA
WOOOOWOOOP
WHAT WAS THAT?
IT'S THE HYENAS...
WHOWHO WHOYIPYIPYIP
...
WE SHOULD BE OKAY. THEY SOUND FAR OFF.

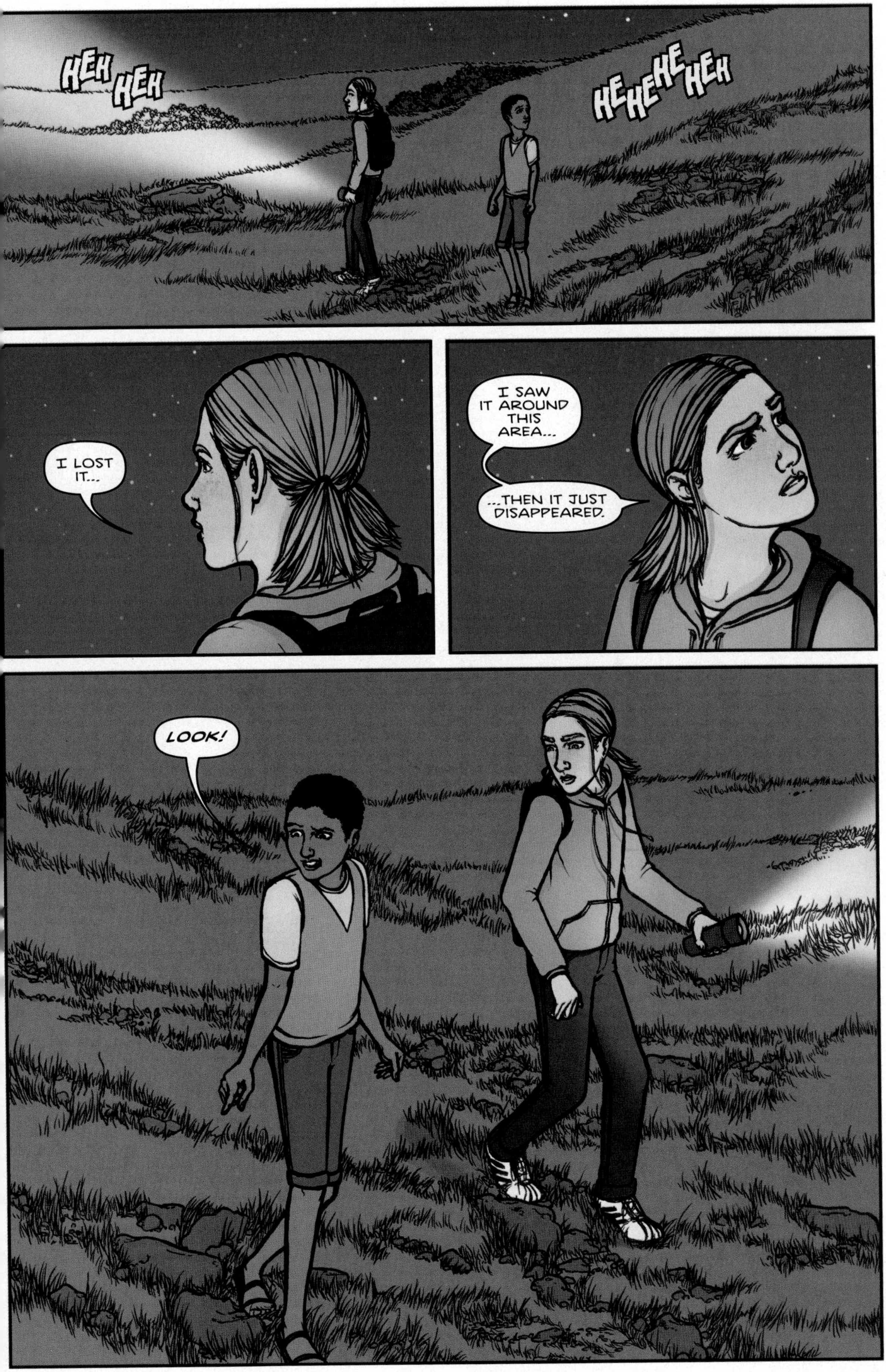
HEH HEH
HEHEHEHEH
I LOST IT...
I SAW IT AROUND THIS AREA...
...THEN IT JUST DISAPPEARED.
LOOK!

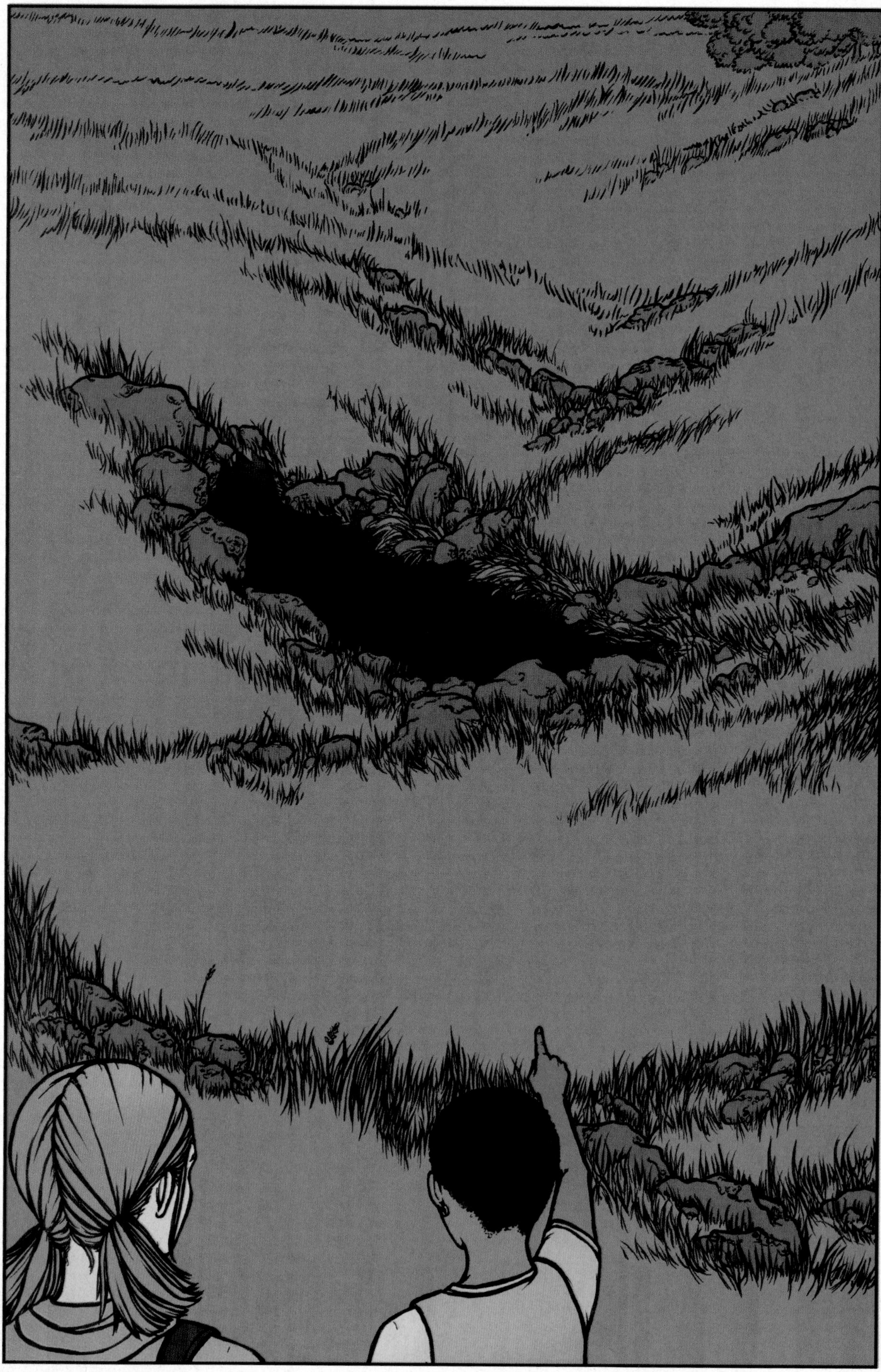

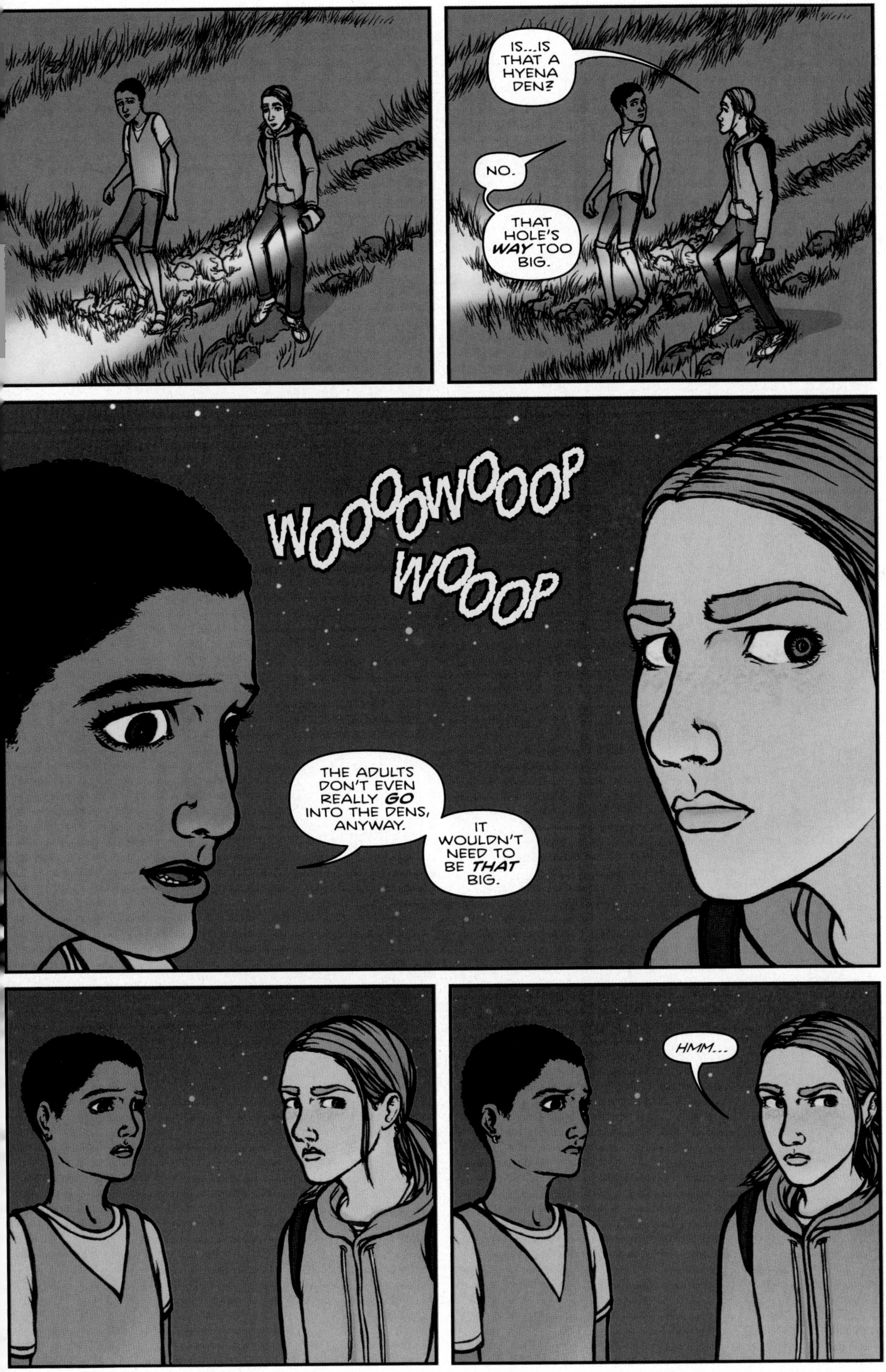
IS...IS THAT A HYENA DEN?
NO.
THAT HOLE'S ***WAY*** TOO BIG.
WOOOOWOOOP WOOOP
THE ADULTS DON'T EVEN REALLY ***GO*** INTO THE DENS, ANYWAY.
IT WOULDN'T NEED TO BE ***THAT*** BIG.
HMM...

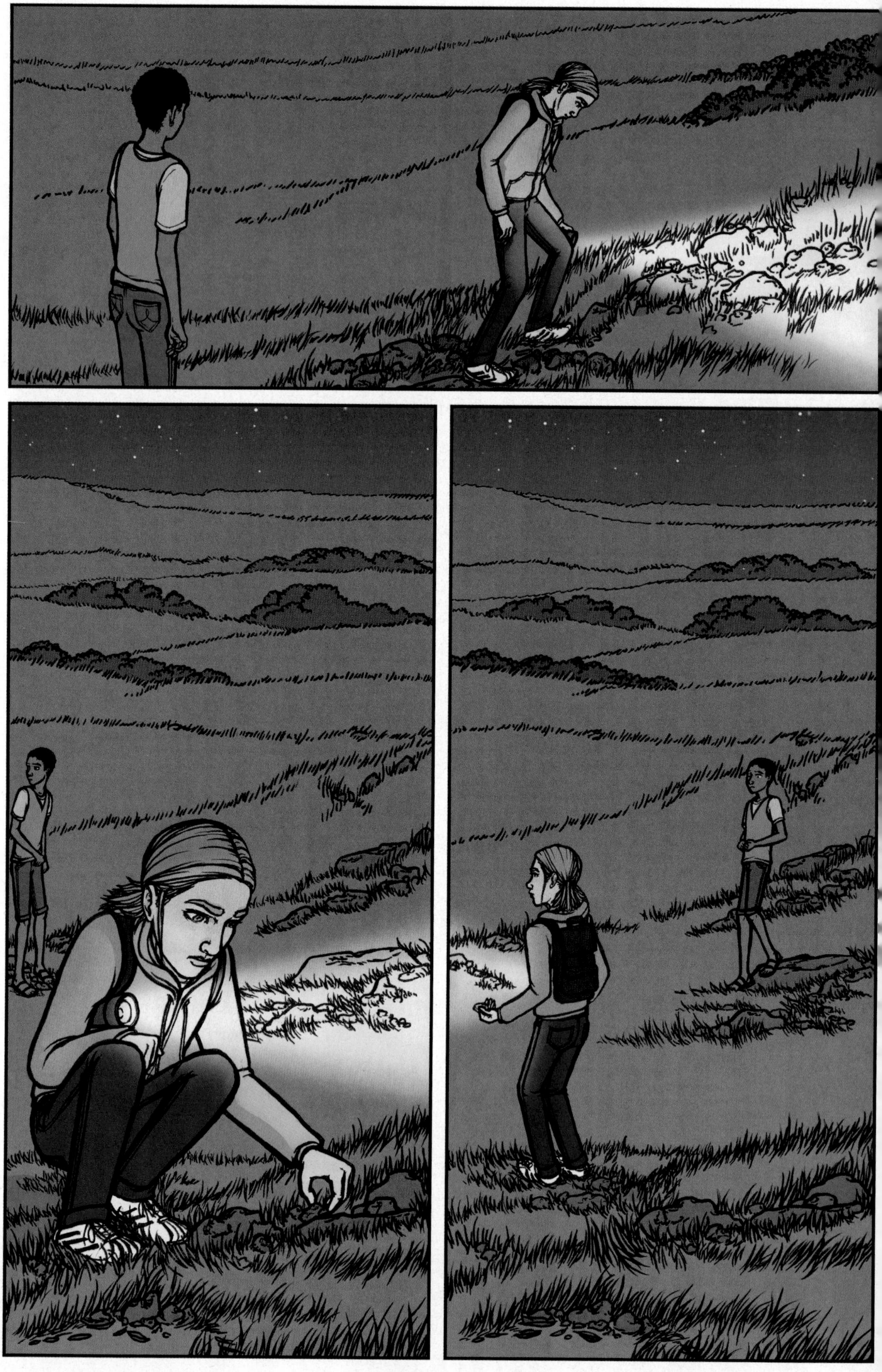

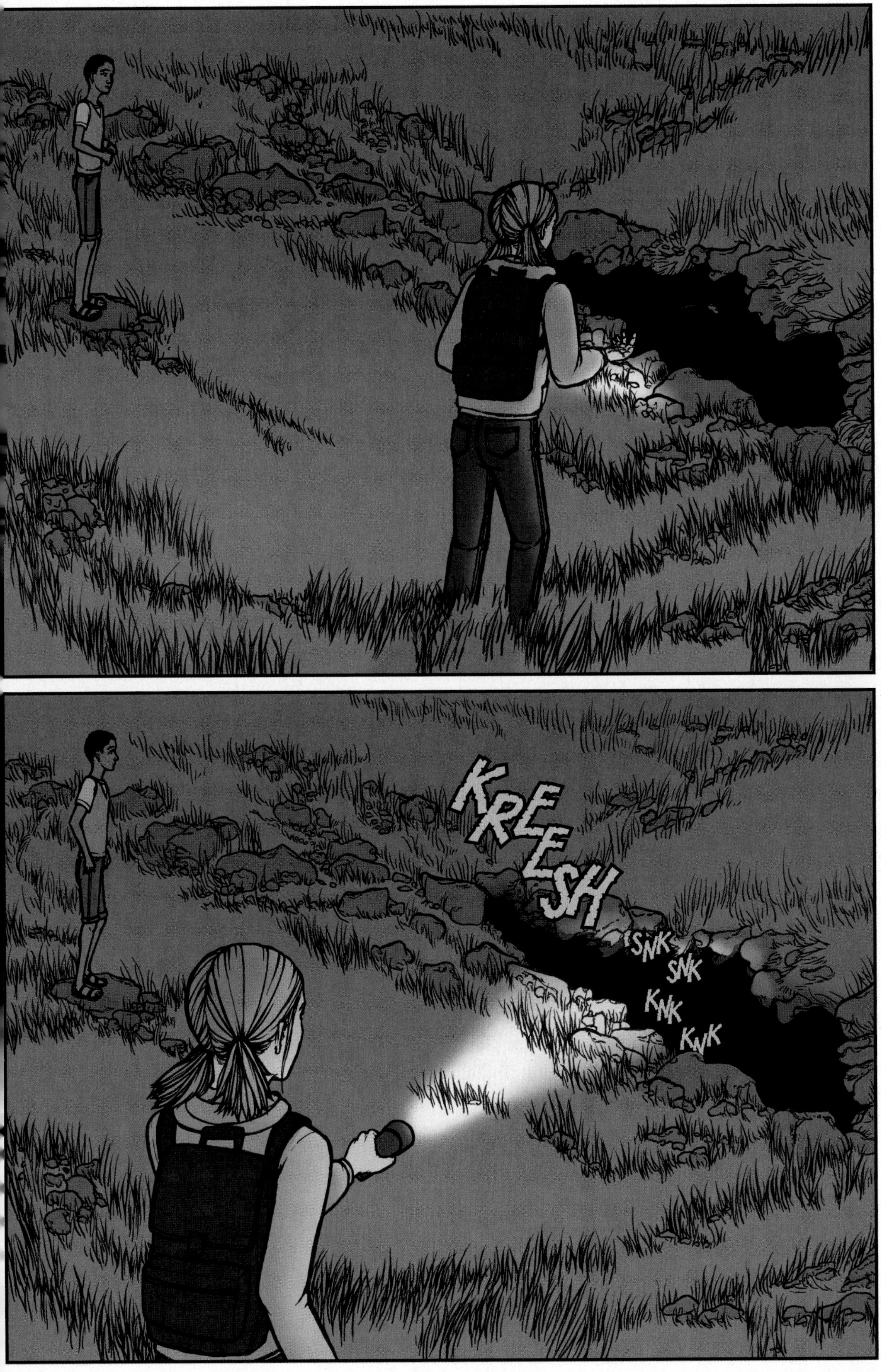
KREESH
SNK
SNK
KNK
KNK

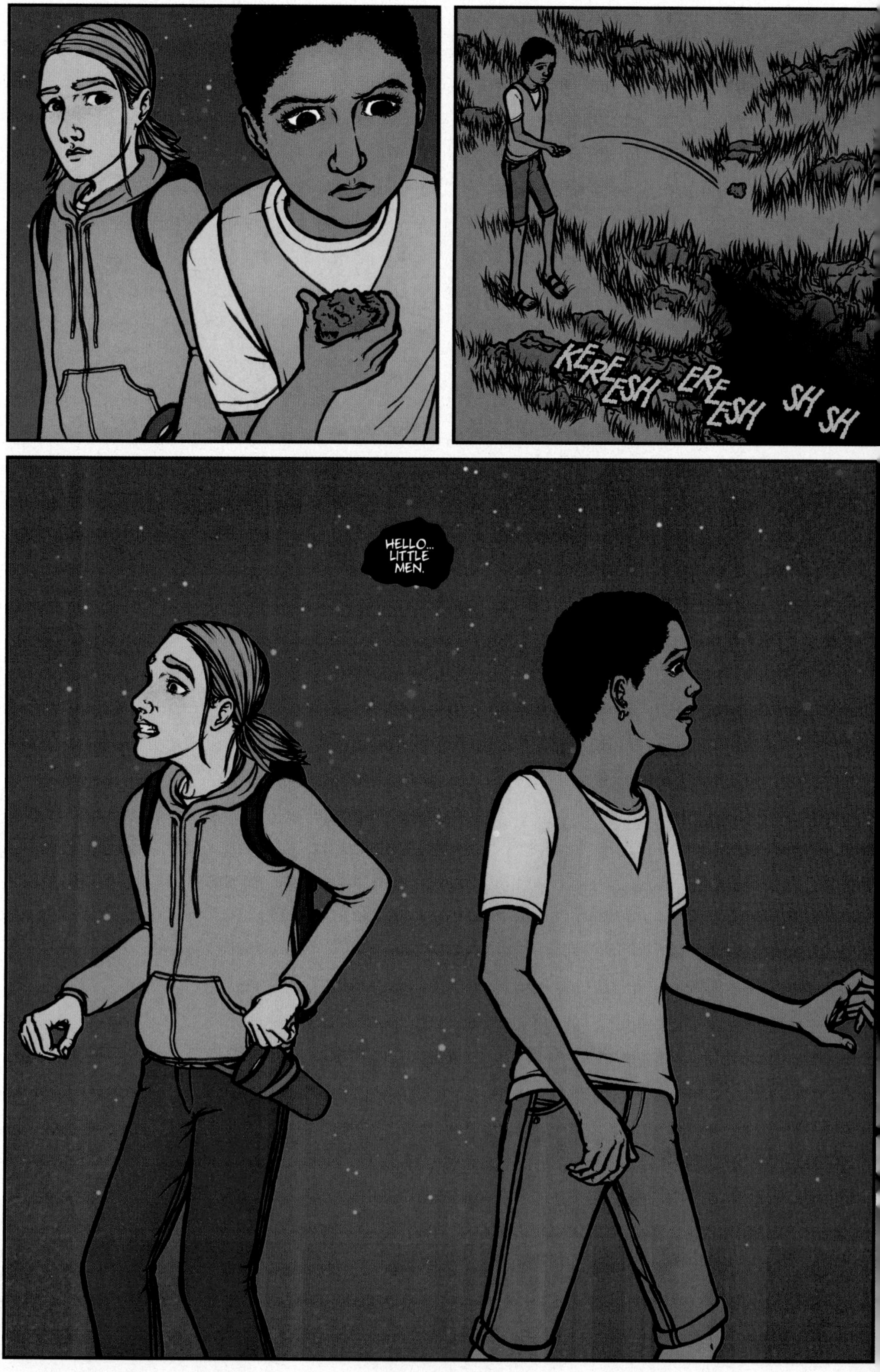
KEREESH
EREESH
SH SH
HELLO... LITTLE MEN.

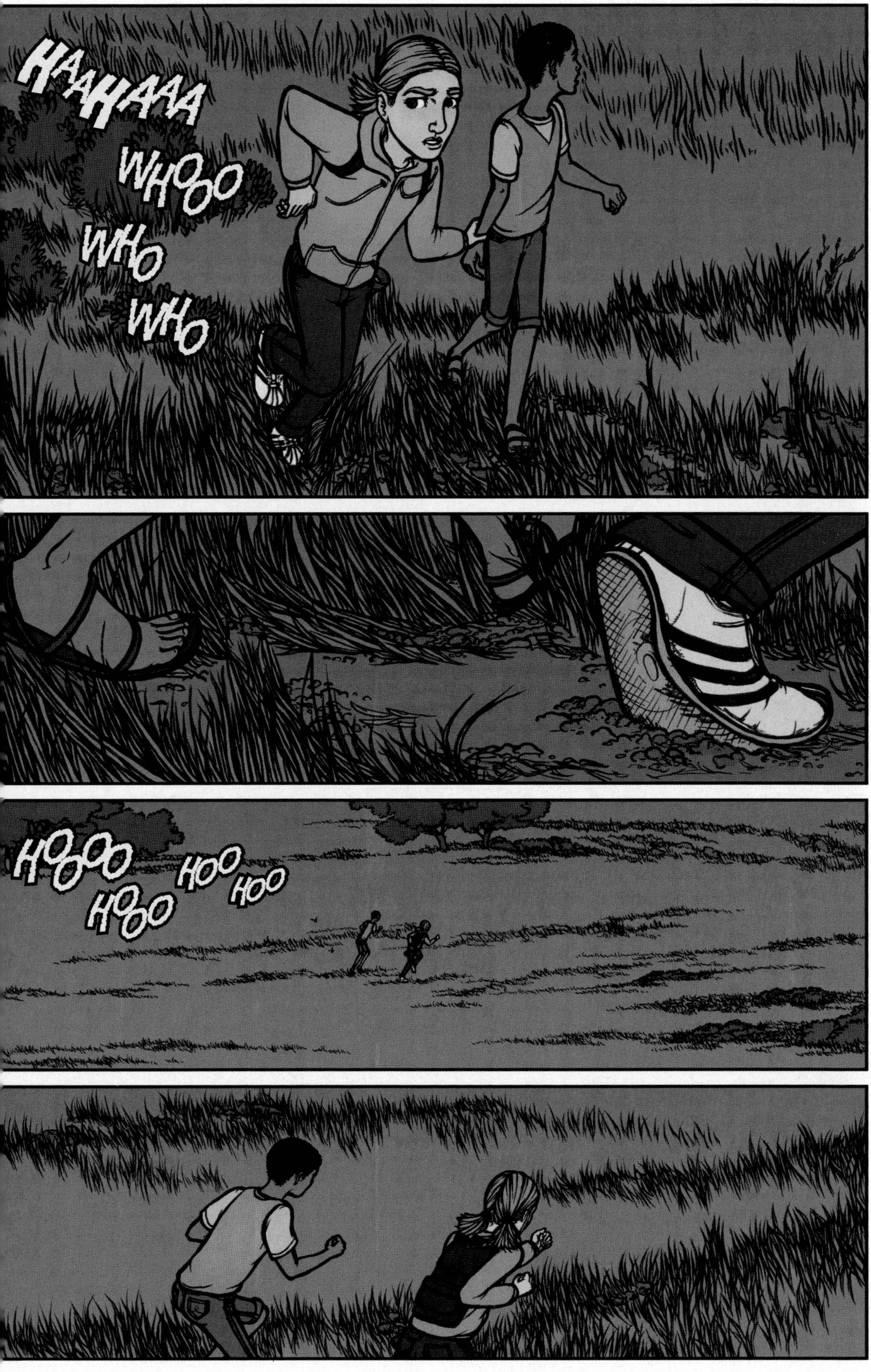
HAAHAAA
WHOOO
WHO
WHO
HOOOO
HOOO
HOO
HOO

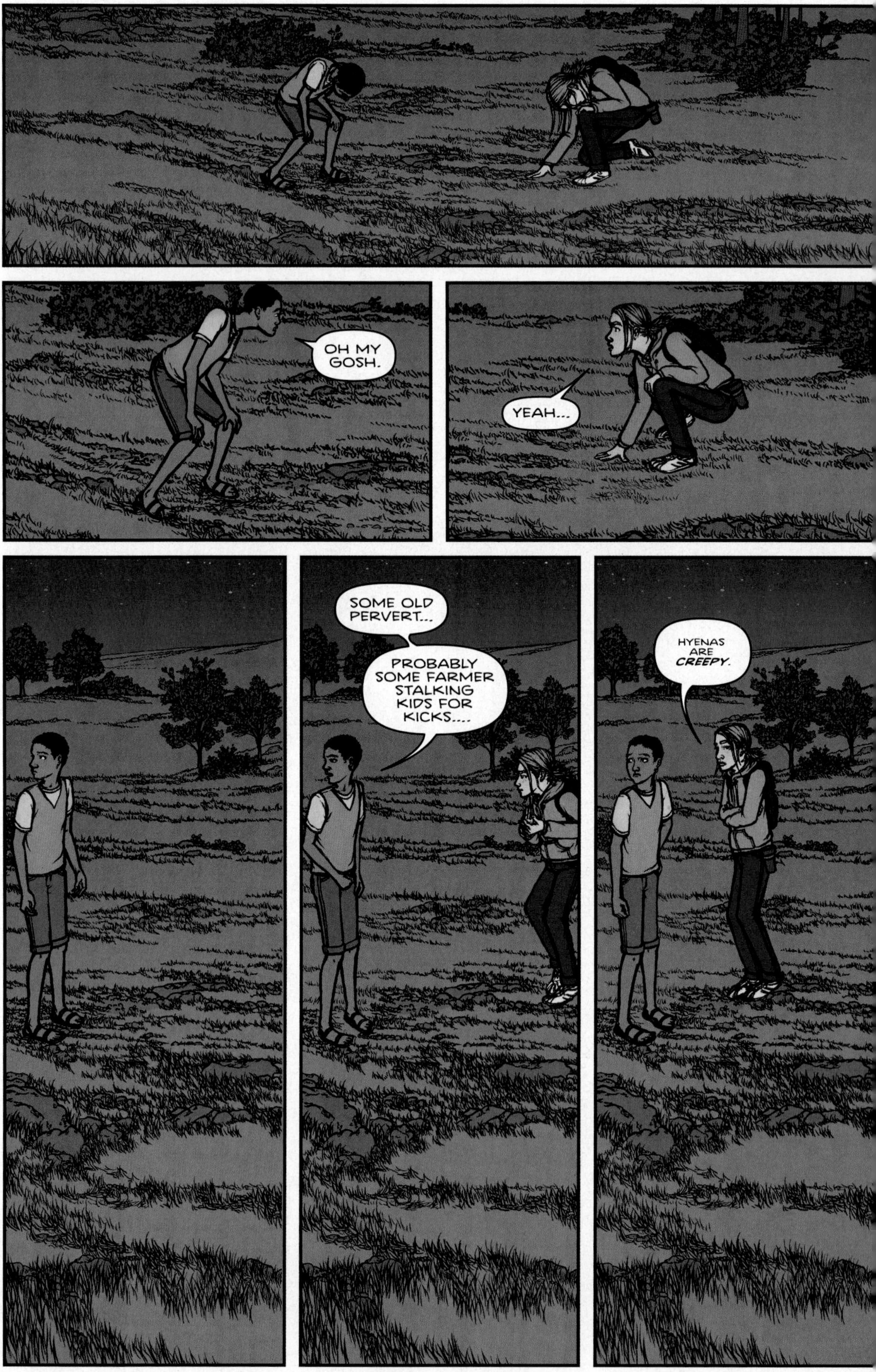
OH MY GOSH.
YEAH...
SOME OLD PERVERT...
PROBABLY SOME FARMER STALKING KIDS FOR KICKS....
HYENAS ARE CREEPY.

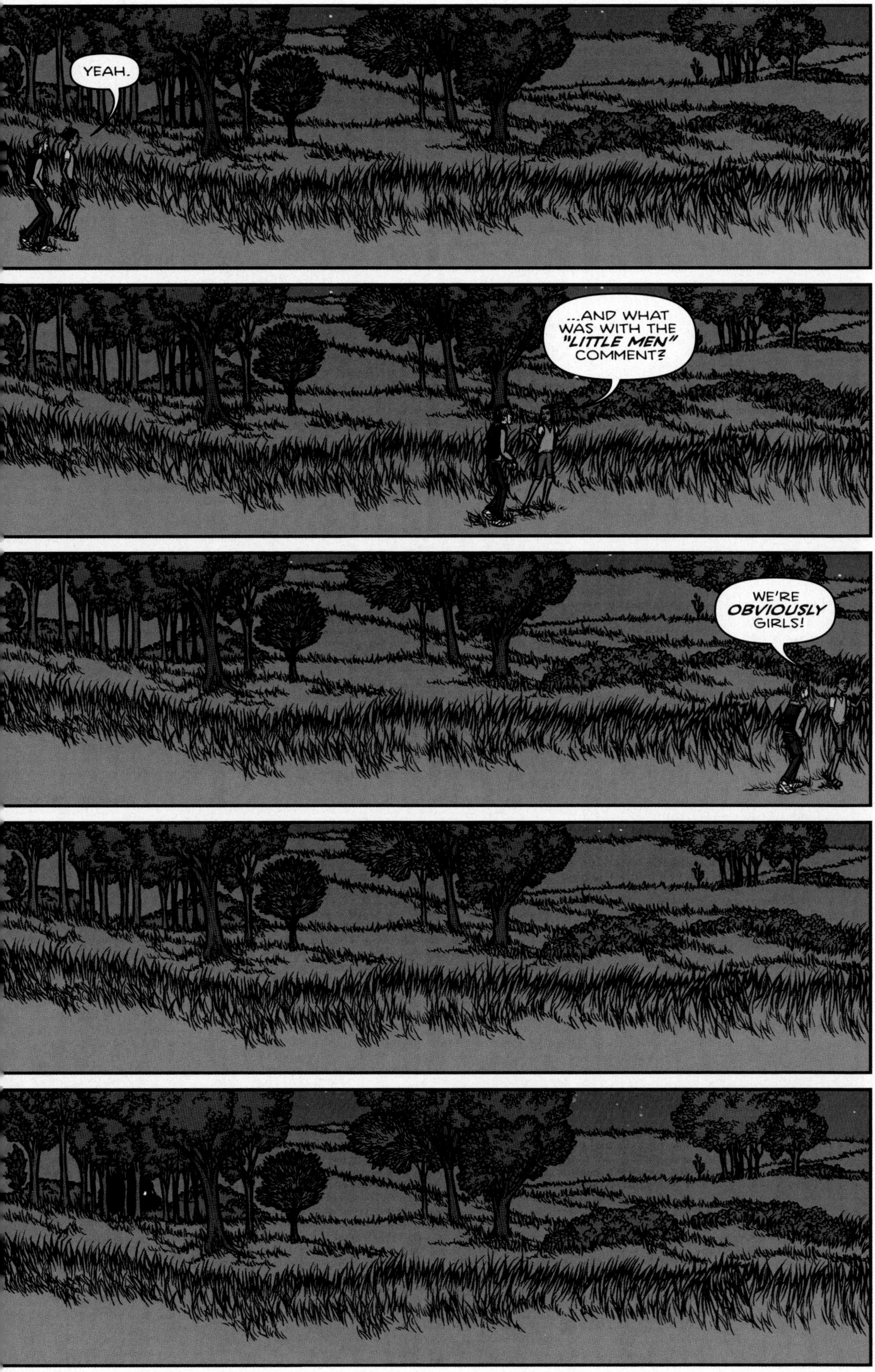
YEAH.
...AND WHAT WAS WITH THE "LITTLE MEN" COMMENT?
WE'RE OBVIOUSLY GIRLS!

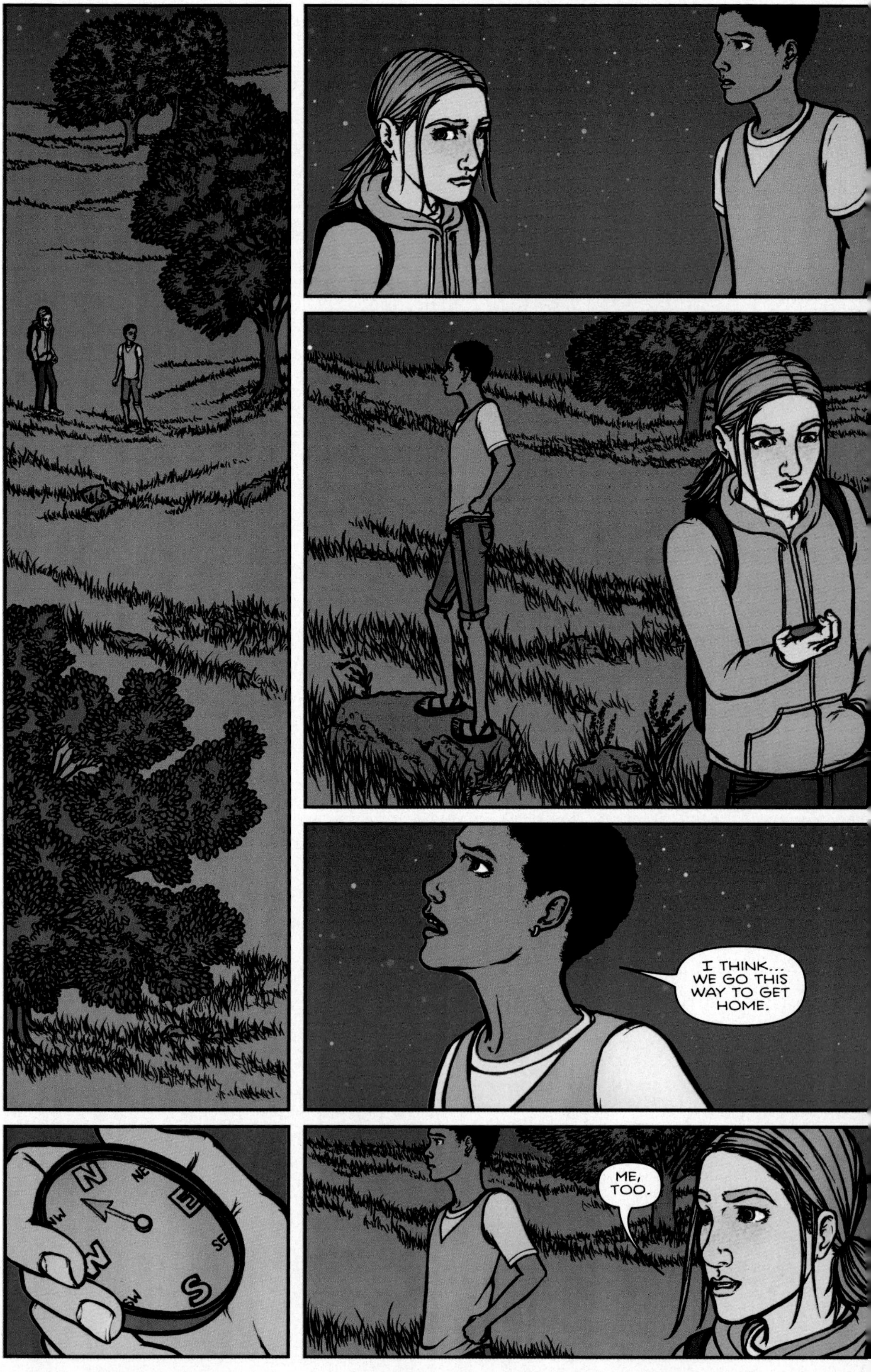
I THINK... WE GO THIS WAY TO GET HOME.
ME, TOO.
N
NE
E
SE
S
SW
W
NW

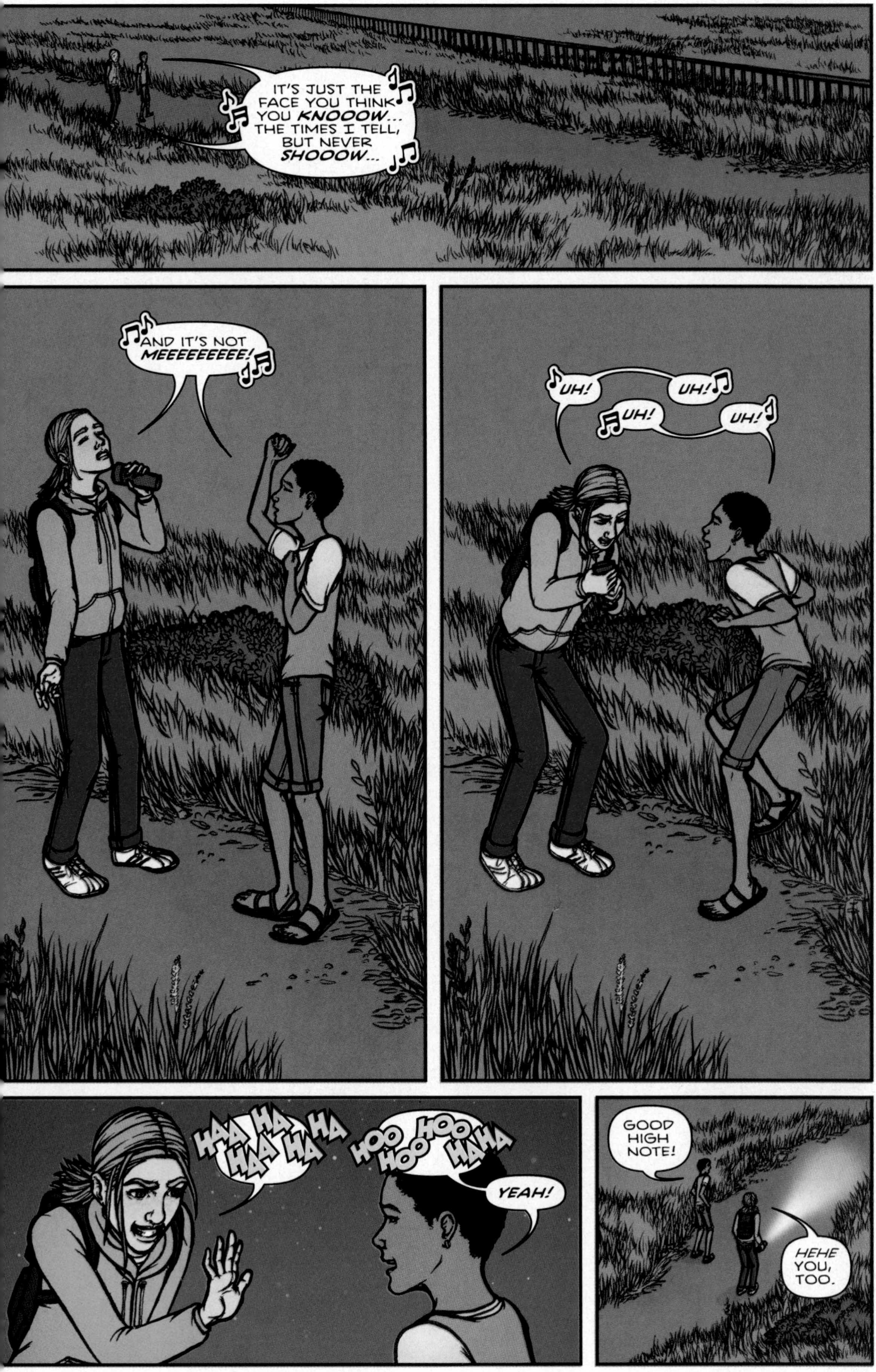
IT'S JUST THE FACE YOU THINK YOU KNOOOW... THE TIMES I TELL, BUT NEVER SHOOOW...
AND IT'S NOT MEEEEEEEEE!
UH!
UH!
UH!
UH!
HA HA HA HA HA HA
HOO HOO HOO HOO HA HA
YEAH!
GOOD HIGH NOTE!
HEHE YOU, TOO.

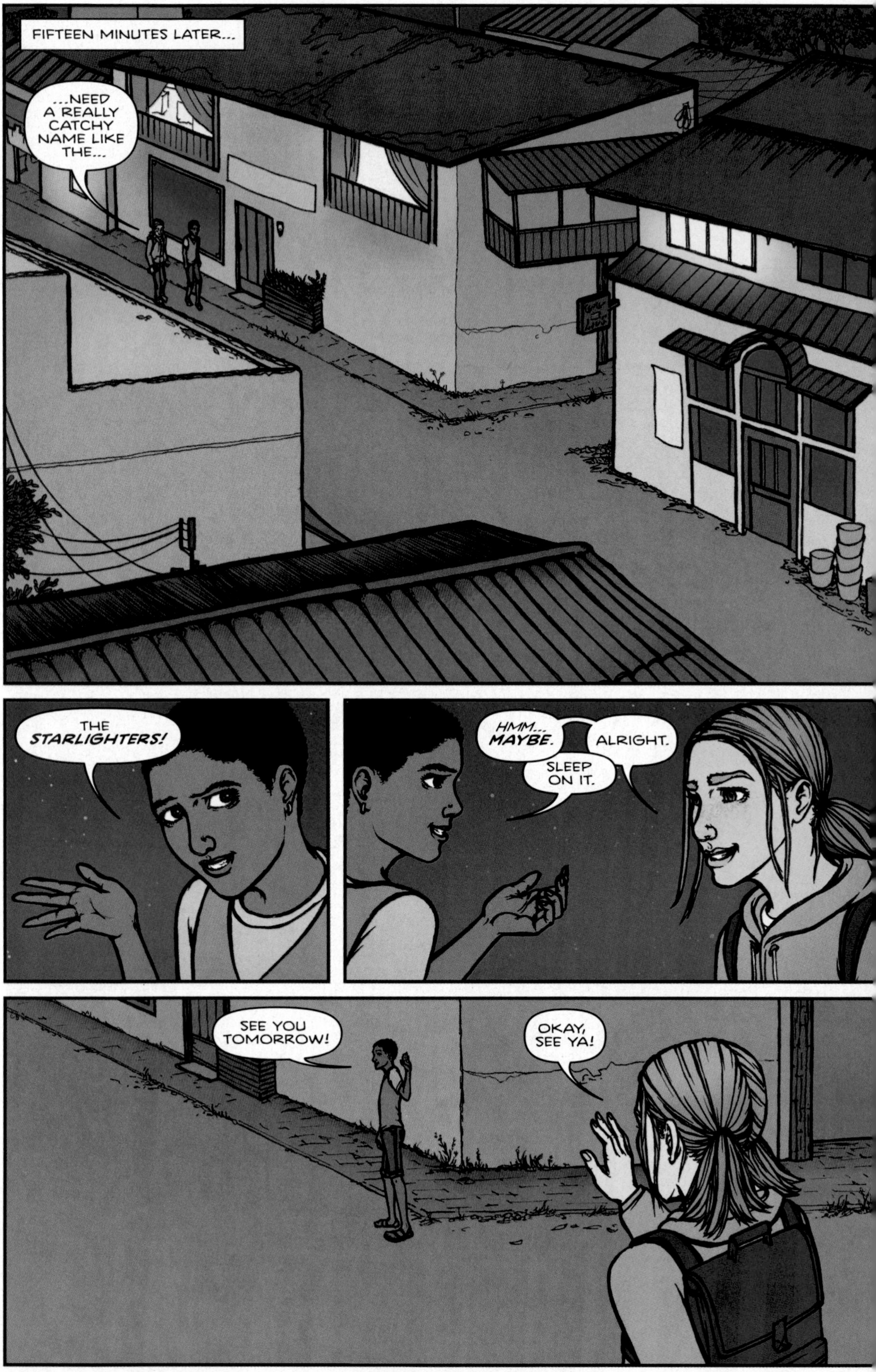
FIFTEEN MINUTES LATER...
...NEED A REALLY CATCHY NAME LIKE THE...
THE STARLIGHTERS!
HMM... MAYBE.
ALRIGHT.
SLEEP ON IT.
SEE YOU TOMORROW!
OKAY, SEE YA!

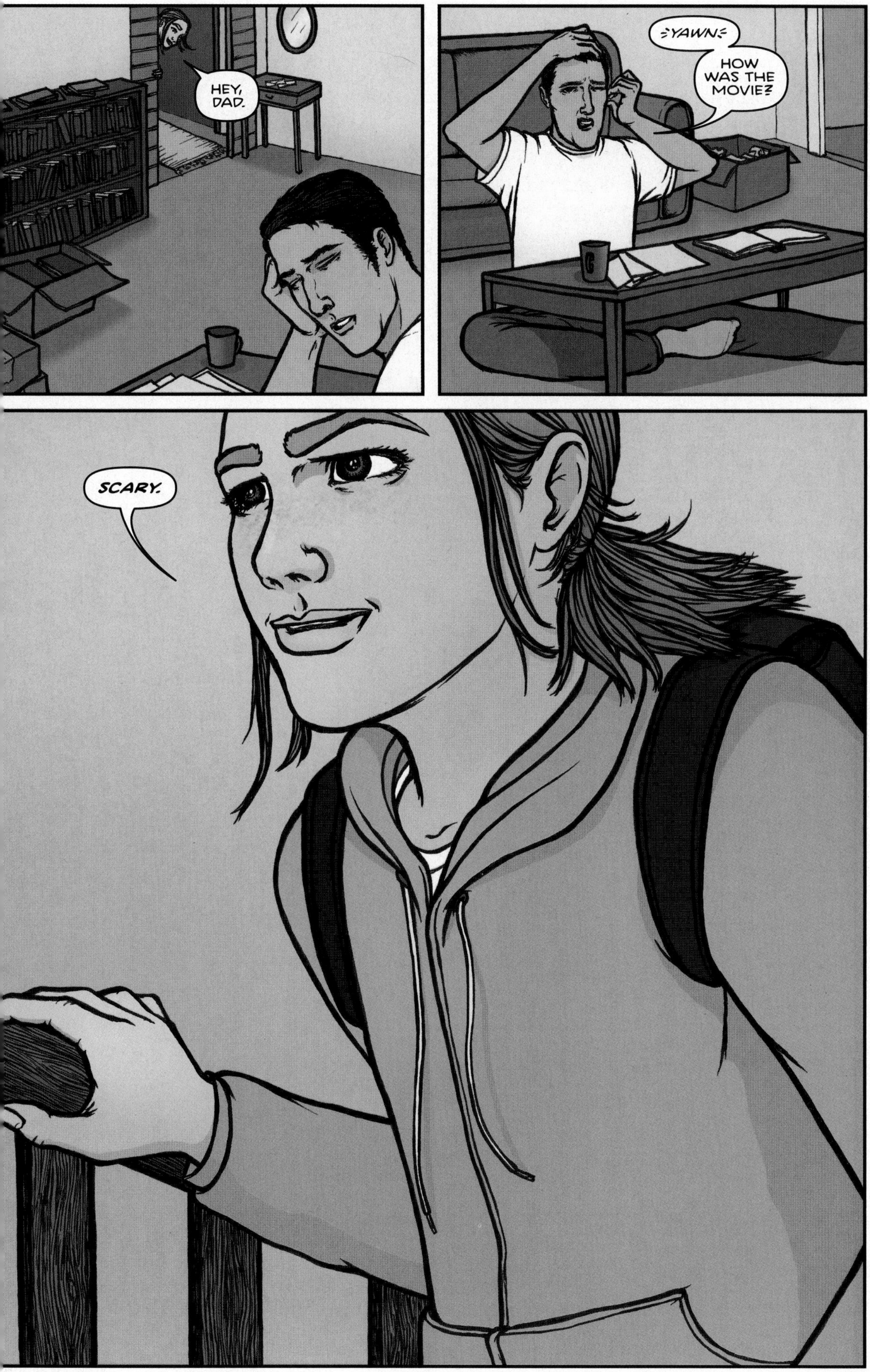
HEY, DAD.
YAWN
HOW WAS THE MOVIE?
SCARY.

ONE WEEK LATER...

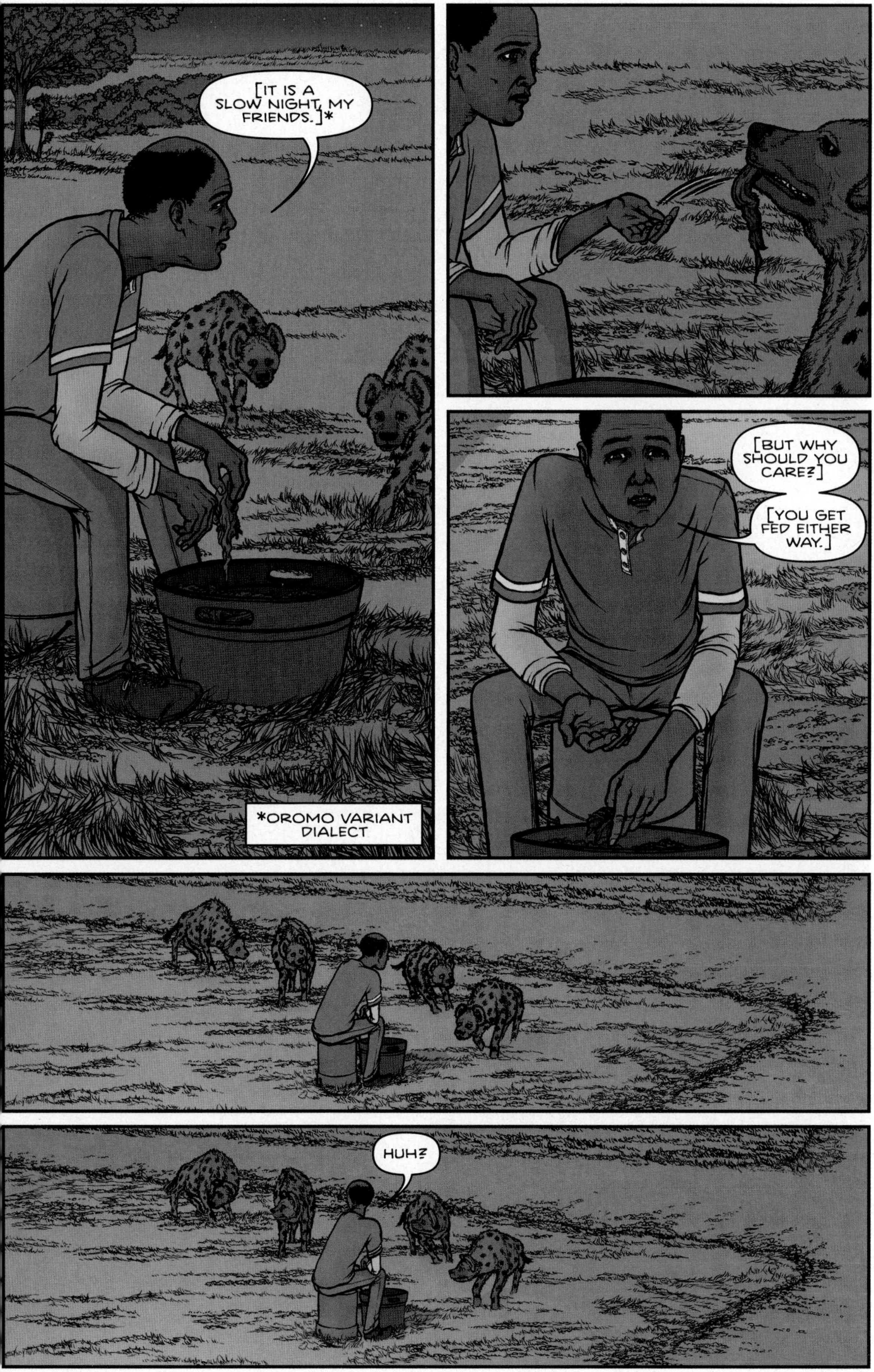
[IT IS A SLOW NIGHT, MY FRIENDS.]*
*OROMO VARIANT DIALECT
[BUT WHY SHOULD YOU CARE?]
[YOU GET FED EITHER WAY.]
HUH?

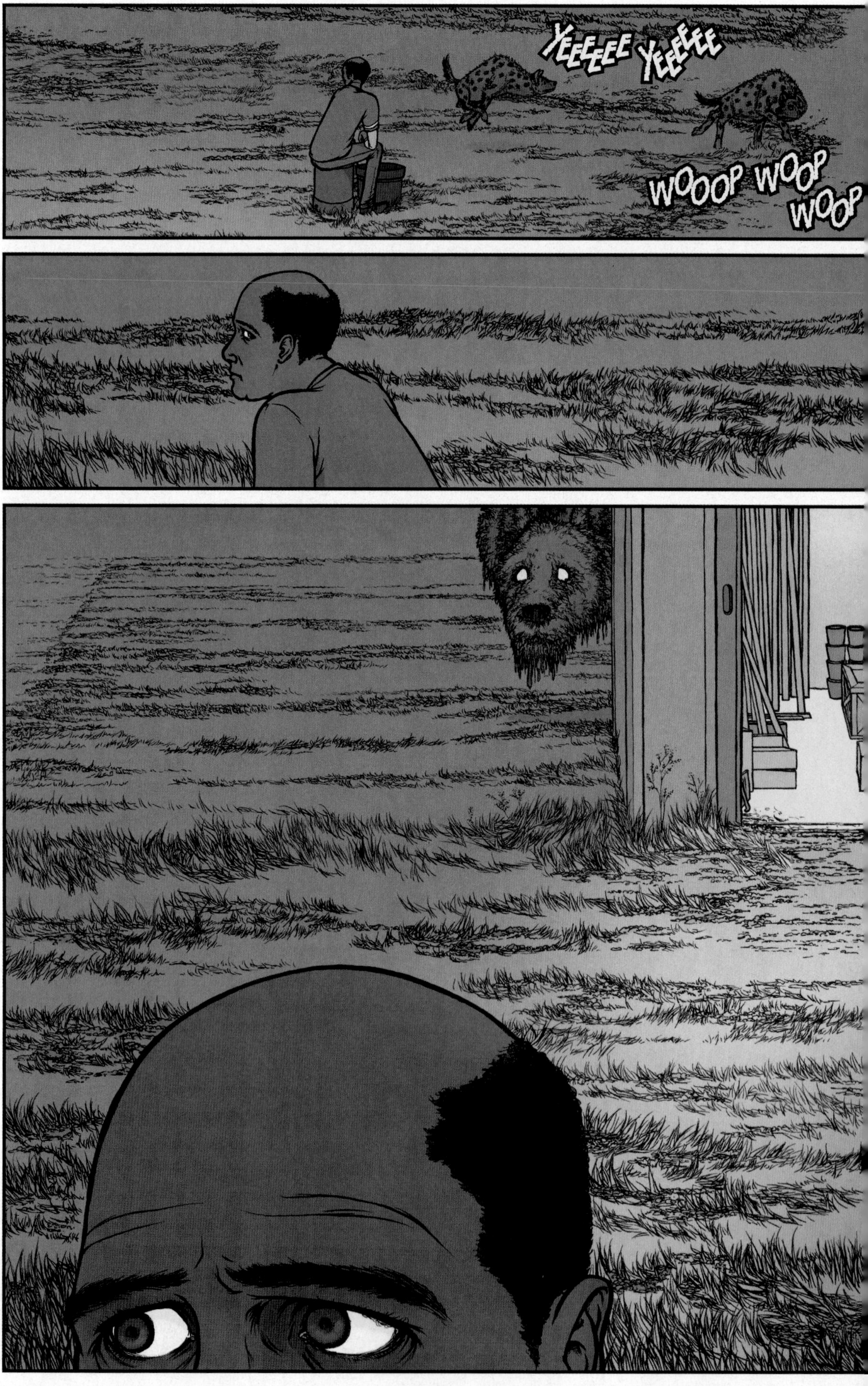
YEEEEEE YEEEEEE
WOOOP WOOP WOOP

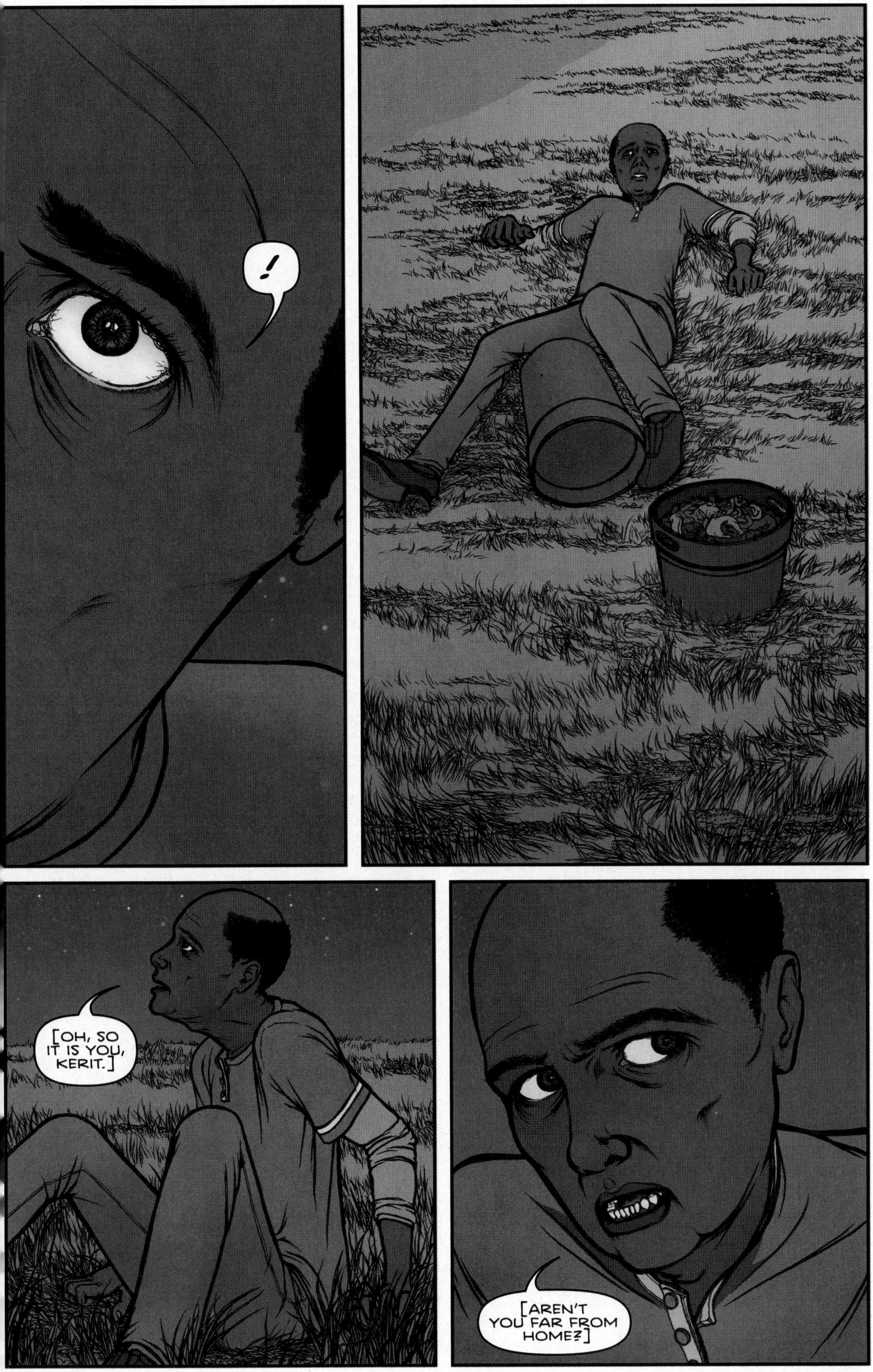
!
[OH, SO IT IS YOU, KERIT.]
[AREN'T YOU FAR FROM HOME?]

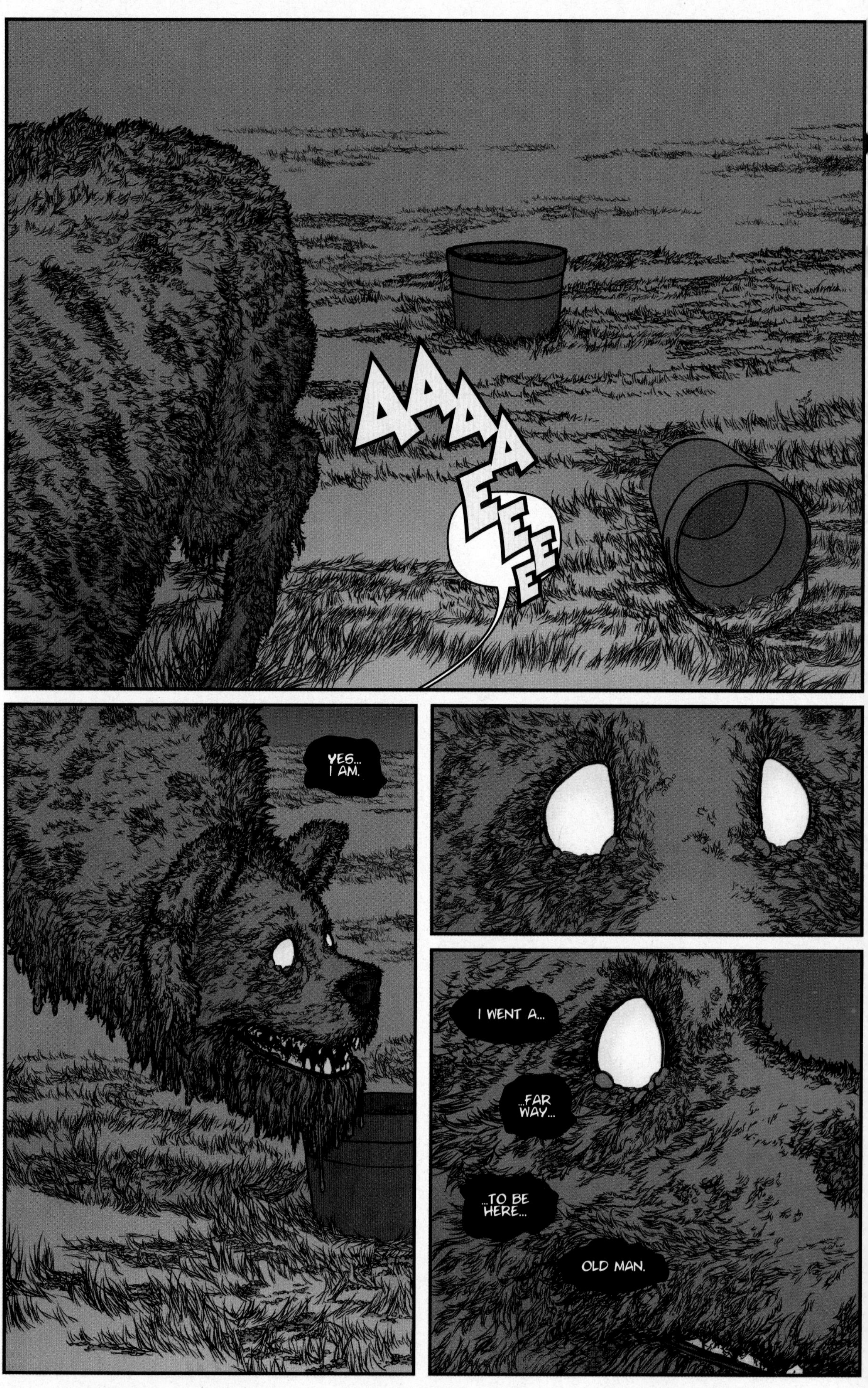
AAAAAEEEEE
YES... I AM.
I WENT A...
...FAR WAY...
...TO BE HERE...
OLD MAN.

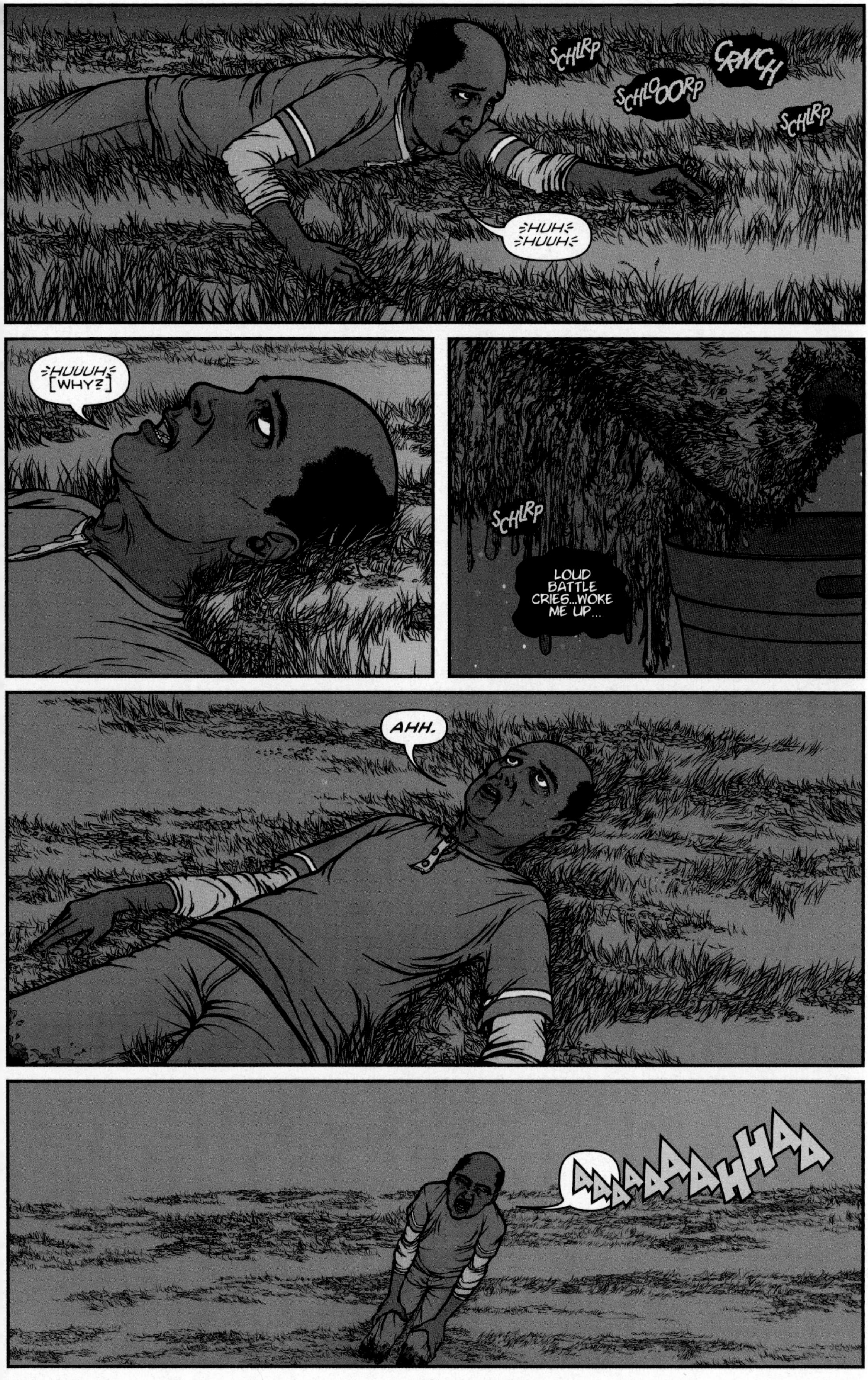
SCHLRP
SCHLOOORP
CRNCH
SCHLRP
HUH HUUH
HUUUH [WHY?]
SCHLRP
LOUD BATTLE CRIES...WOKE ME UP...
AHH.
AAAAAAAHHAA

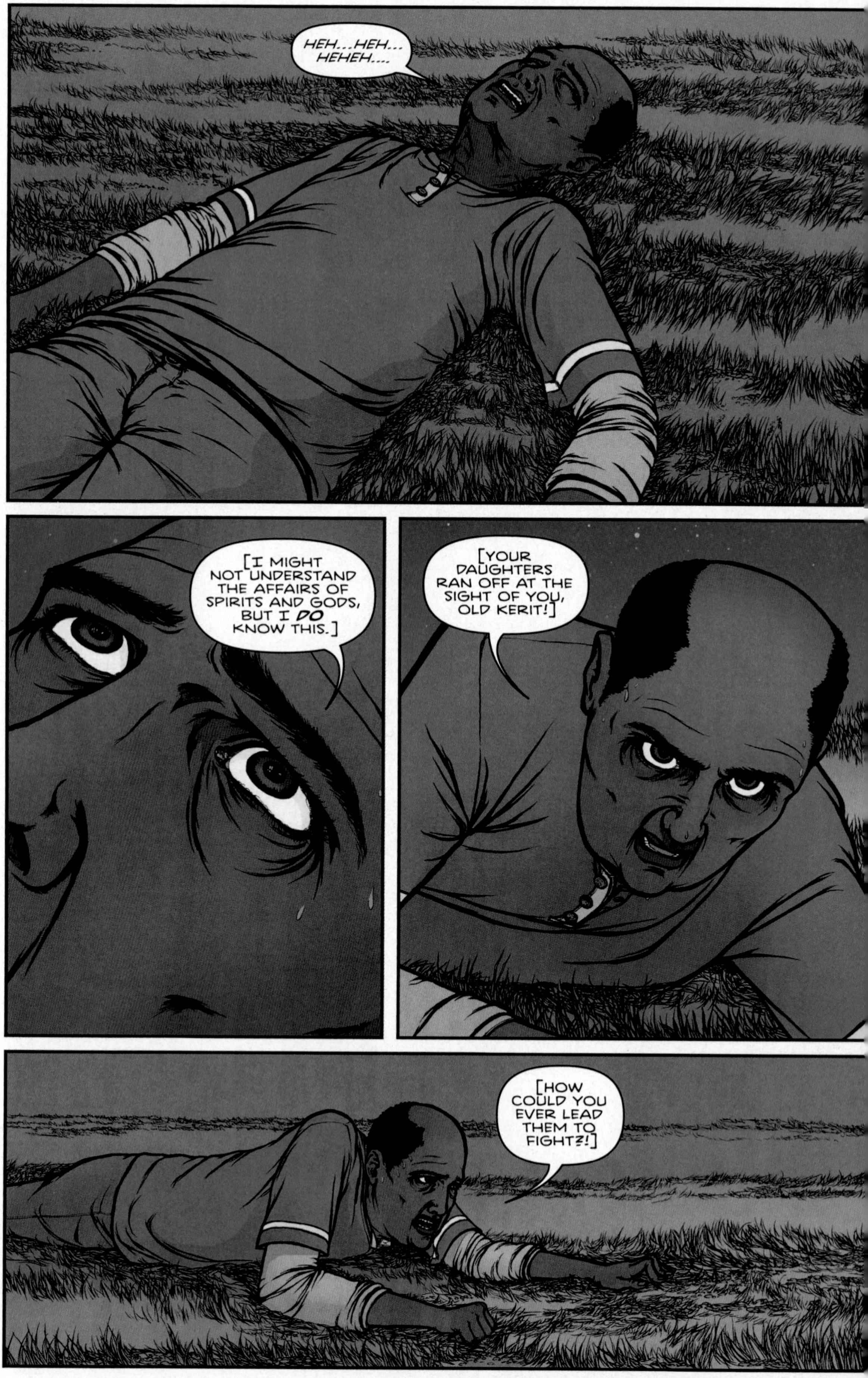
HEH...HEH... HEHEH....
[I MIGHT NOT UNDERSTAND THE AFFAIRS OF SPIRITS AND GODS, BUT I *DO* KNOW THIS.]
[YOUR DAUGHTERS RAN OFF AT THE SIGHT OF YOU, OLD KERIT!]
[HOW COULD YOU EVER LEAD THEM TO FIGHT?!]

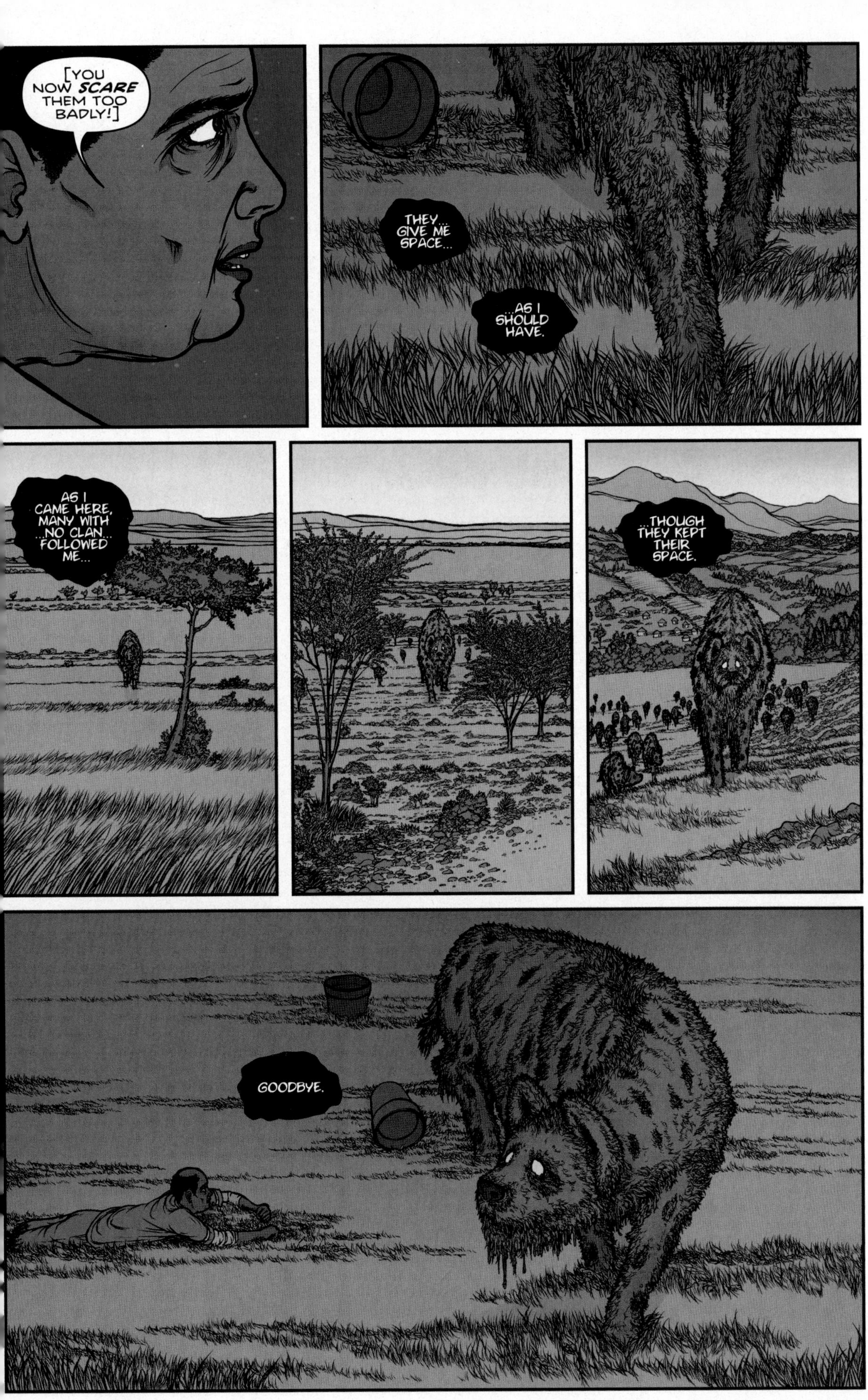
[YOU NOW SCARE THEM TOO BADLY!]
THEY... GIVE ME SPACE...
...AS I SHOULD HAVE.
AS I CAME HERE, MANY WITH ...NO CLAN... FOLLOWED ME...
...THOUGH THEY KEPT THEIR SPACE.
GOODBYE.

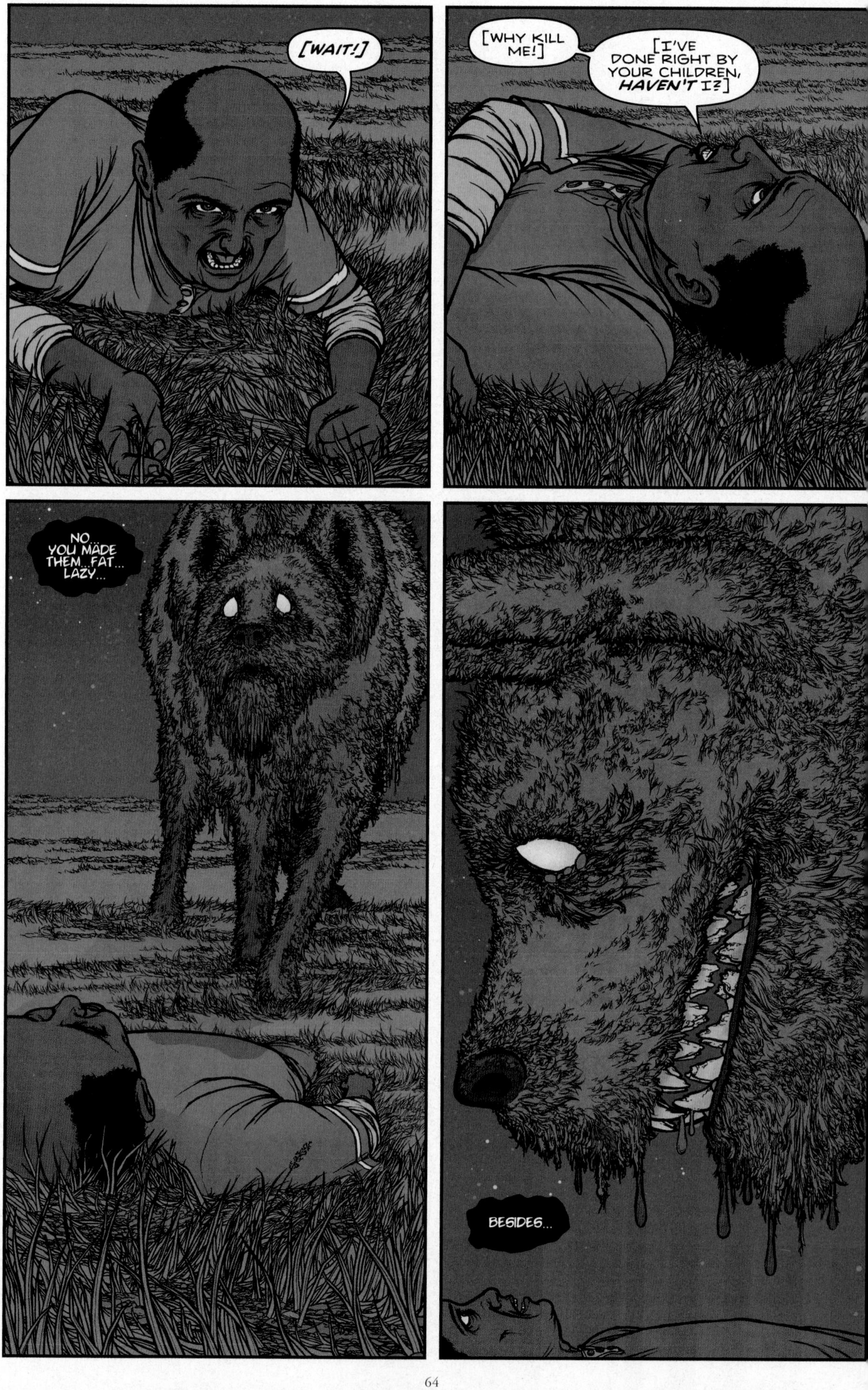
[WAIT!]
[WHY KILL ME!]
[I'VE DONE RIGHT BY YOUR CHILDREN, HAVEN'T I?]
NO... YOU MÄDE THEM...FAT... LAZY...
BESIDES...

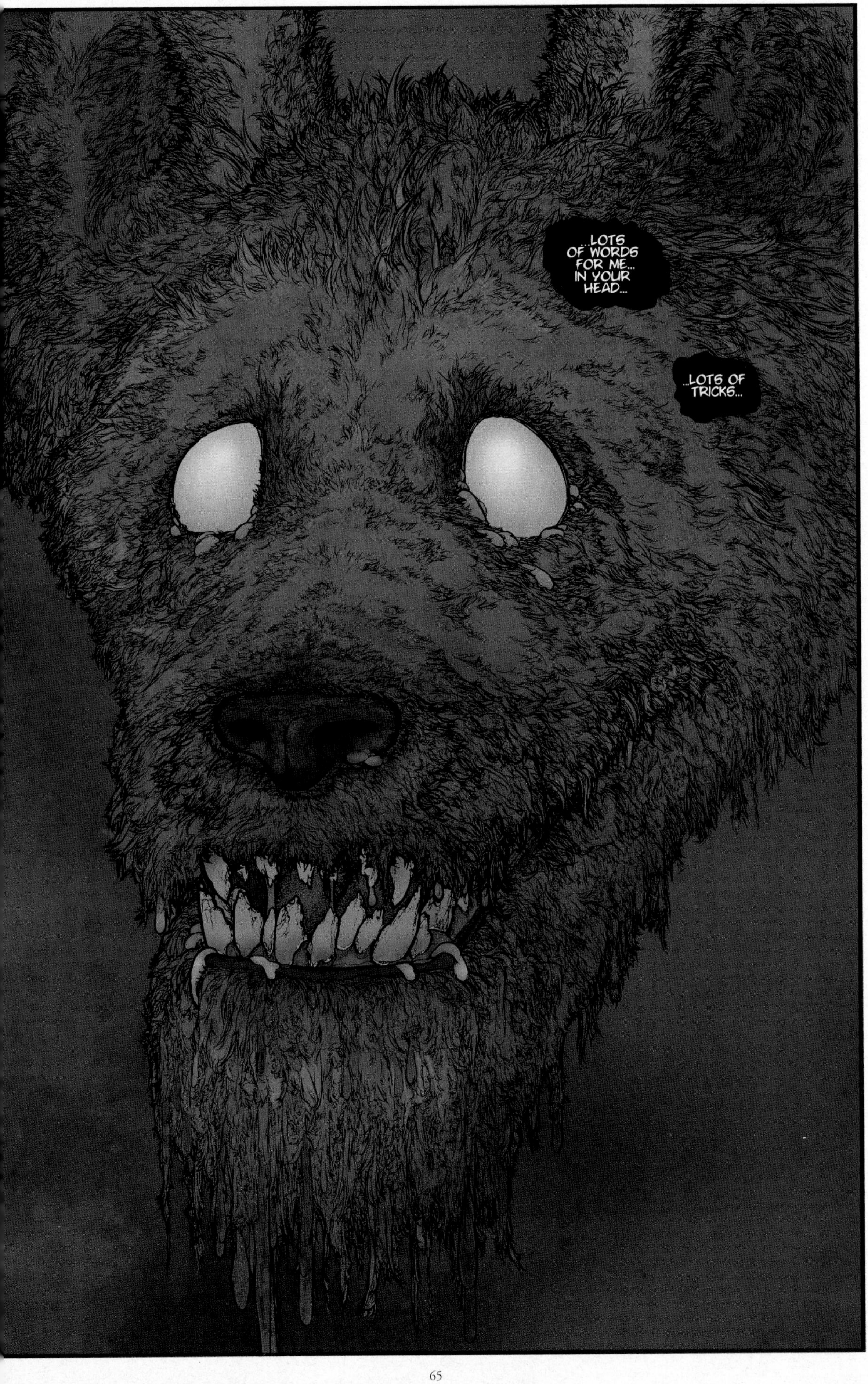
...LOTS OF WORDS FOR ME... IN YOUR HEAD...
...LOTS OF TRICKS...

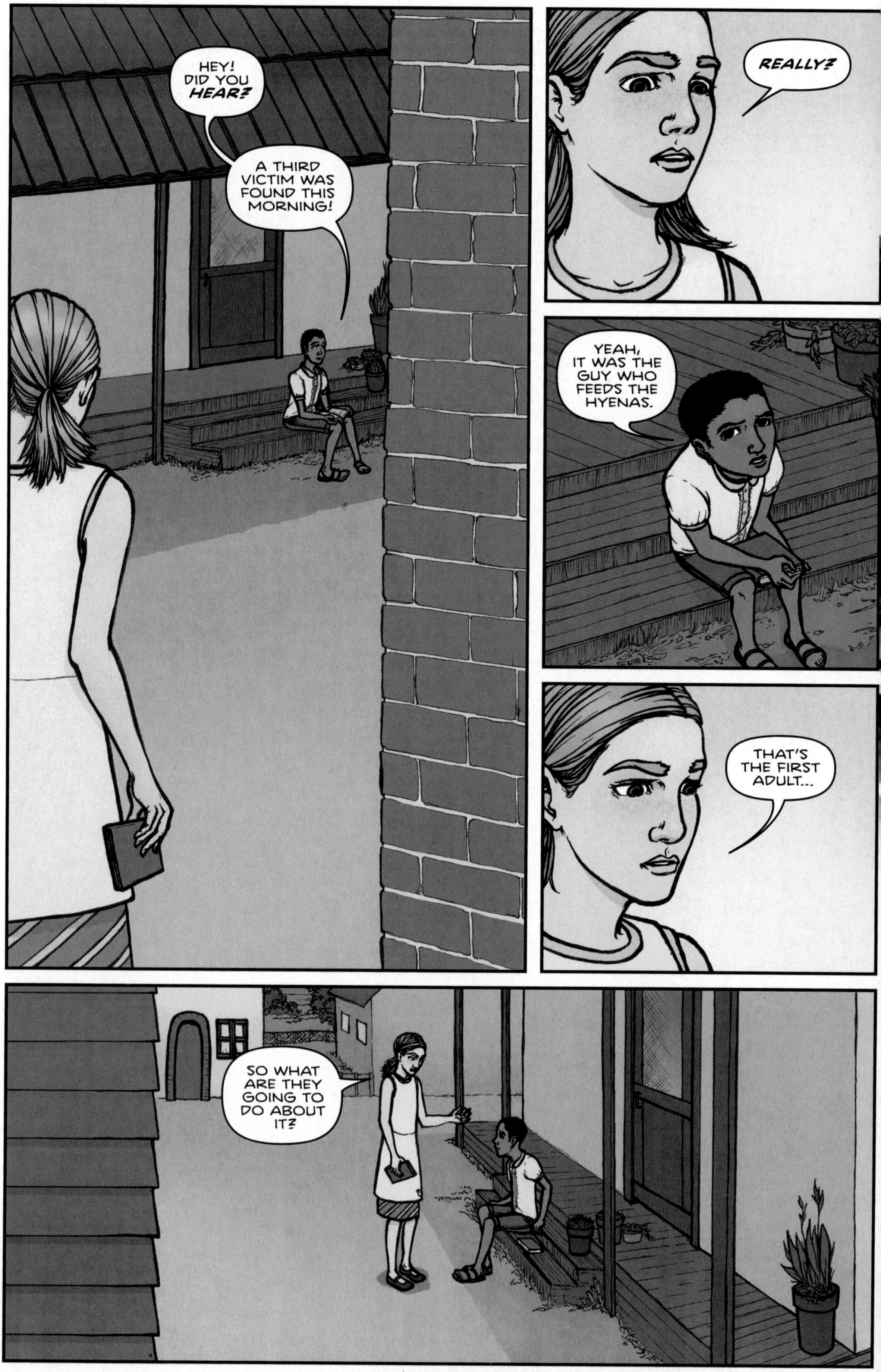
HEY! DID YOU *HEAR?*
A THIRD VICTIM WAS FOUND THIS MORNING!
REALLY?
YEAH, IT WAS THE GUY WHO FEEDS THE HYENAS.
THAT'S THE FIRST ADULT...
SO WHAT ARE THEY GOING TO DO ABOUT IT?

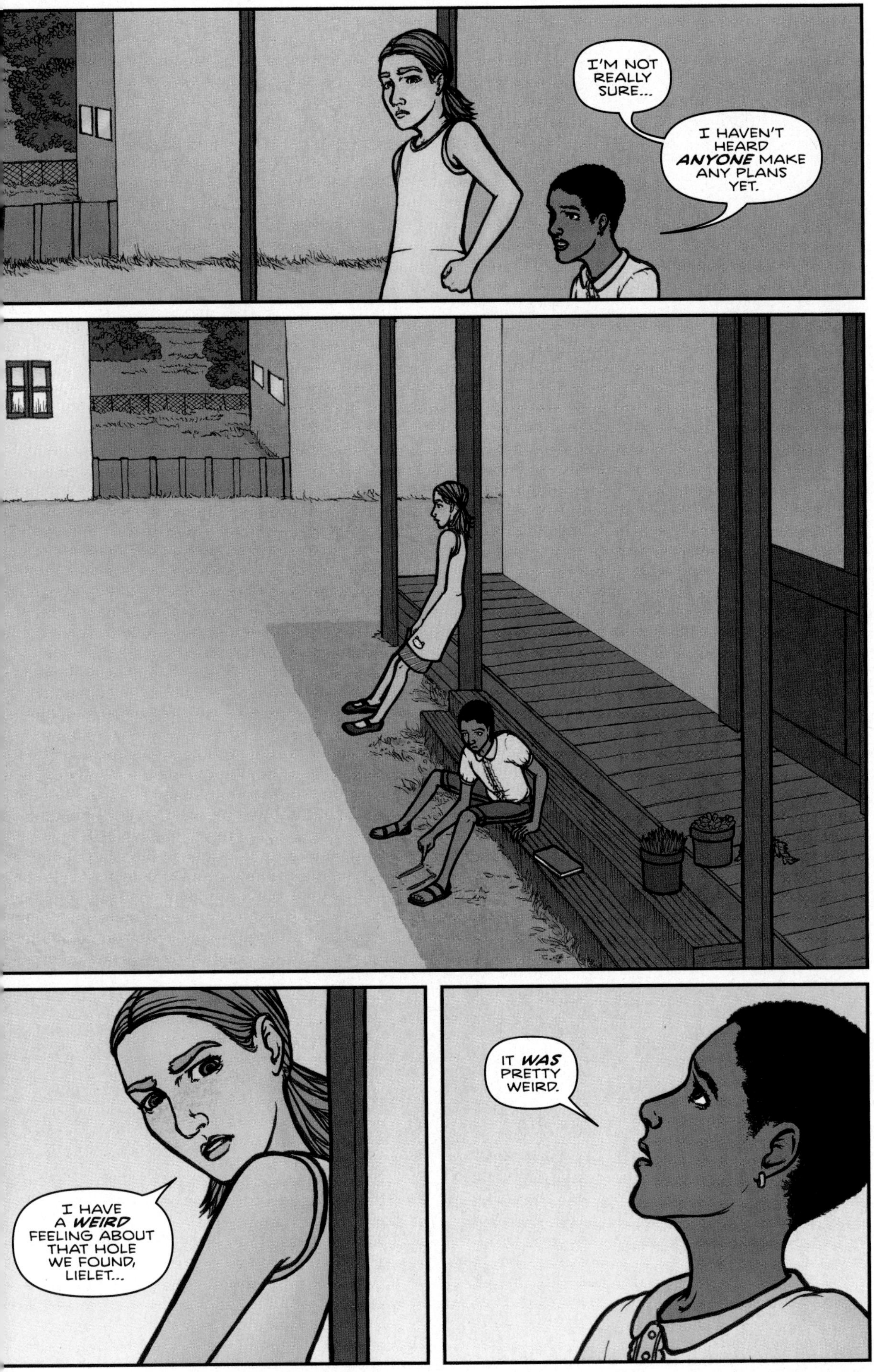
I'M NOT REALLY SURE...
I HAVEN'T HEARD ANYONE MAKE ANY PLANS YET.
I HAVE A WEIRD FEELING ABOUT THAT HOLE WE FOUND, LIELET...
IT WAS PRETTY WEIRD.

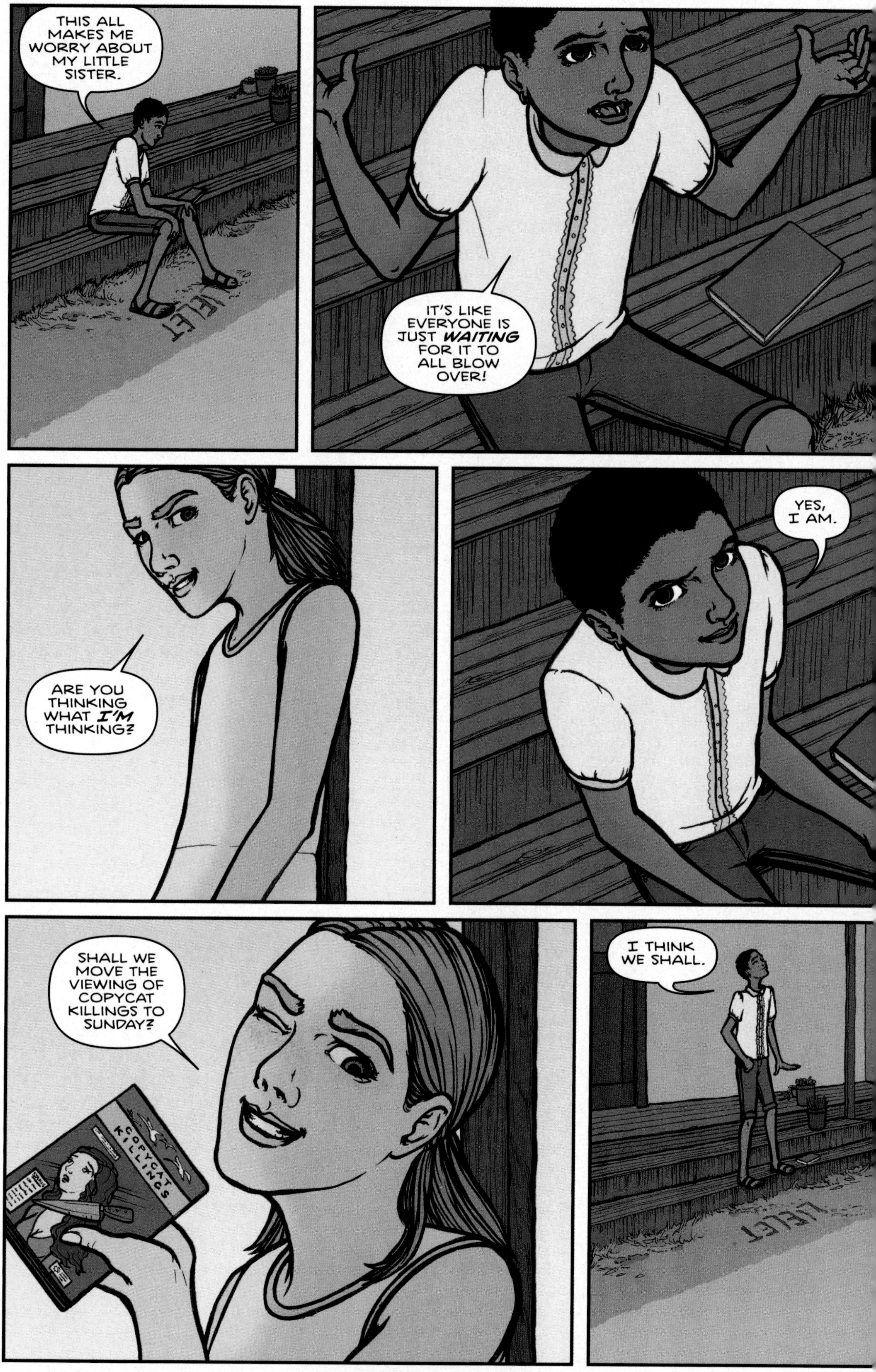
THIS ALL MAKES ME WORRY ABOUT MY LITTLE SISTER.
IT'S LIKE EVERYONE IS JUST *WAITING* FOR IT TO ALL BLOW OVER!
ARE YOU THINKING WHAT *I'M* THINKING?
YES, I AM.
SHALL WE MOVE THE VIEWING OF COPYCAT KILLINGS TO SUNDAY?
COPYCAT KILLINGS
I THINK WE SHALL.

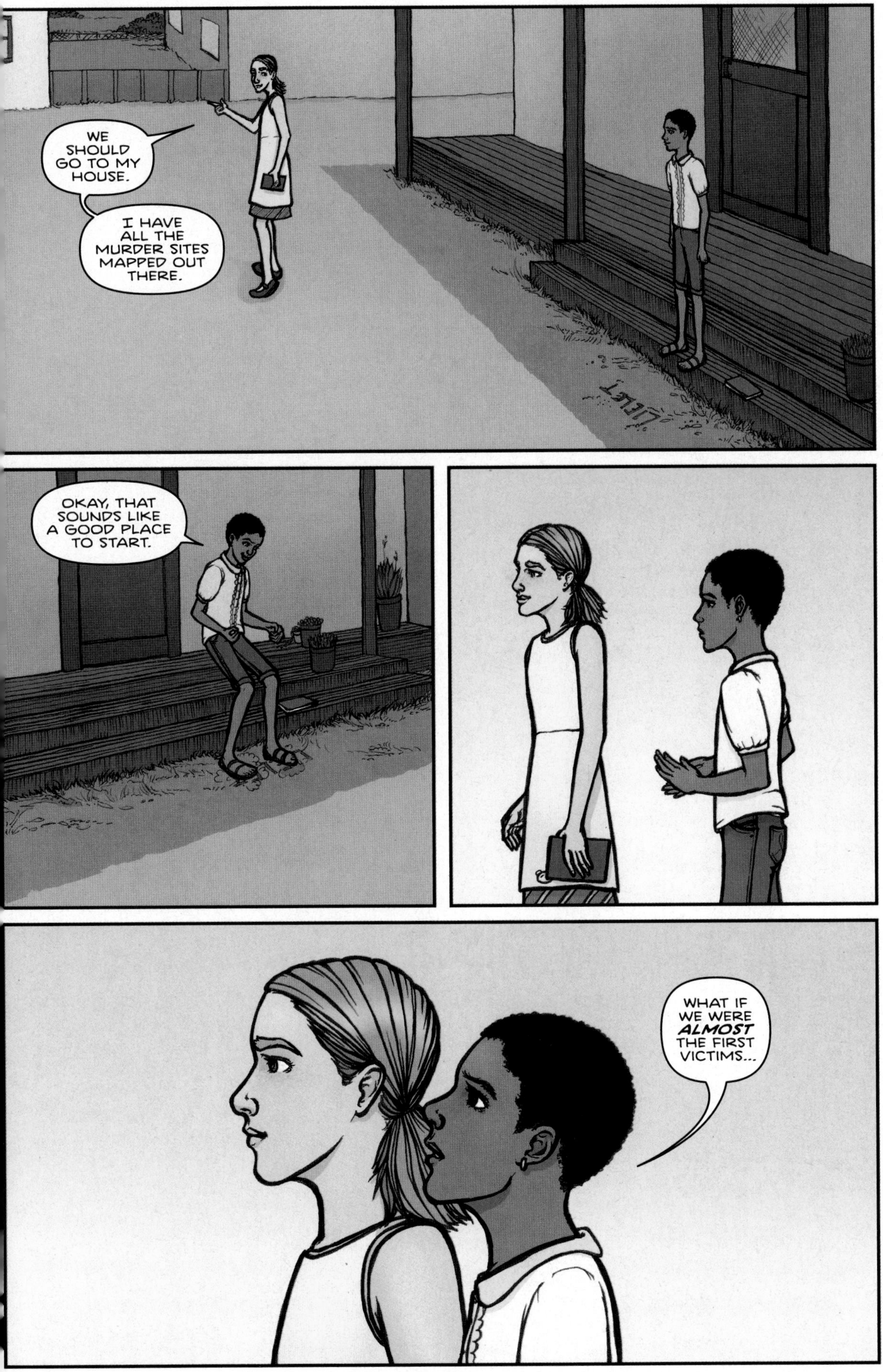
WE SHOULD GO TO MY HOUSE.
I HAVE ALL THE MURDER SITES MAPPED OUT THERE.
OKAY, THAT SOUNDS LIKE A GOOD PLACE TO START.
WHAT IF WE WERE ALMOST THE FIRST VICTIMS...

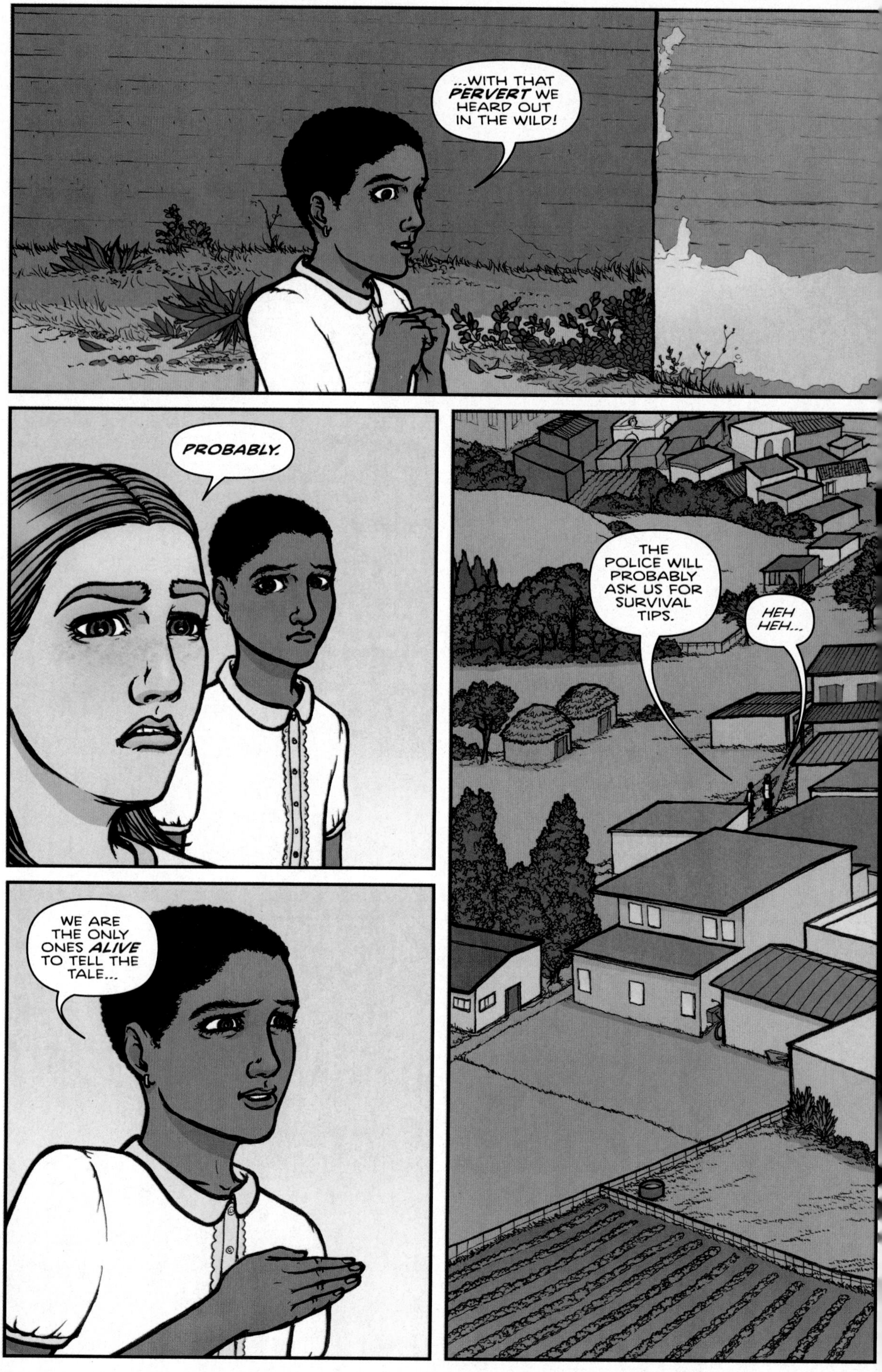
...WITH THAT *PERVERT* WE HEARD OUT IN THE WILD!
PROBABLY.
THE POLICE WILL PROBABLY ASK US FOR SURVIVAL TIPS.
HEH HEH...
WE ARE THE ONLY ONES *ALIVE* TO TELL THE TALE...

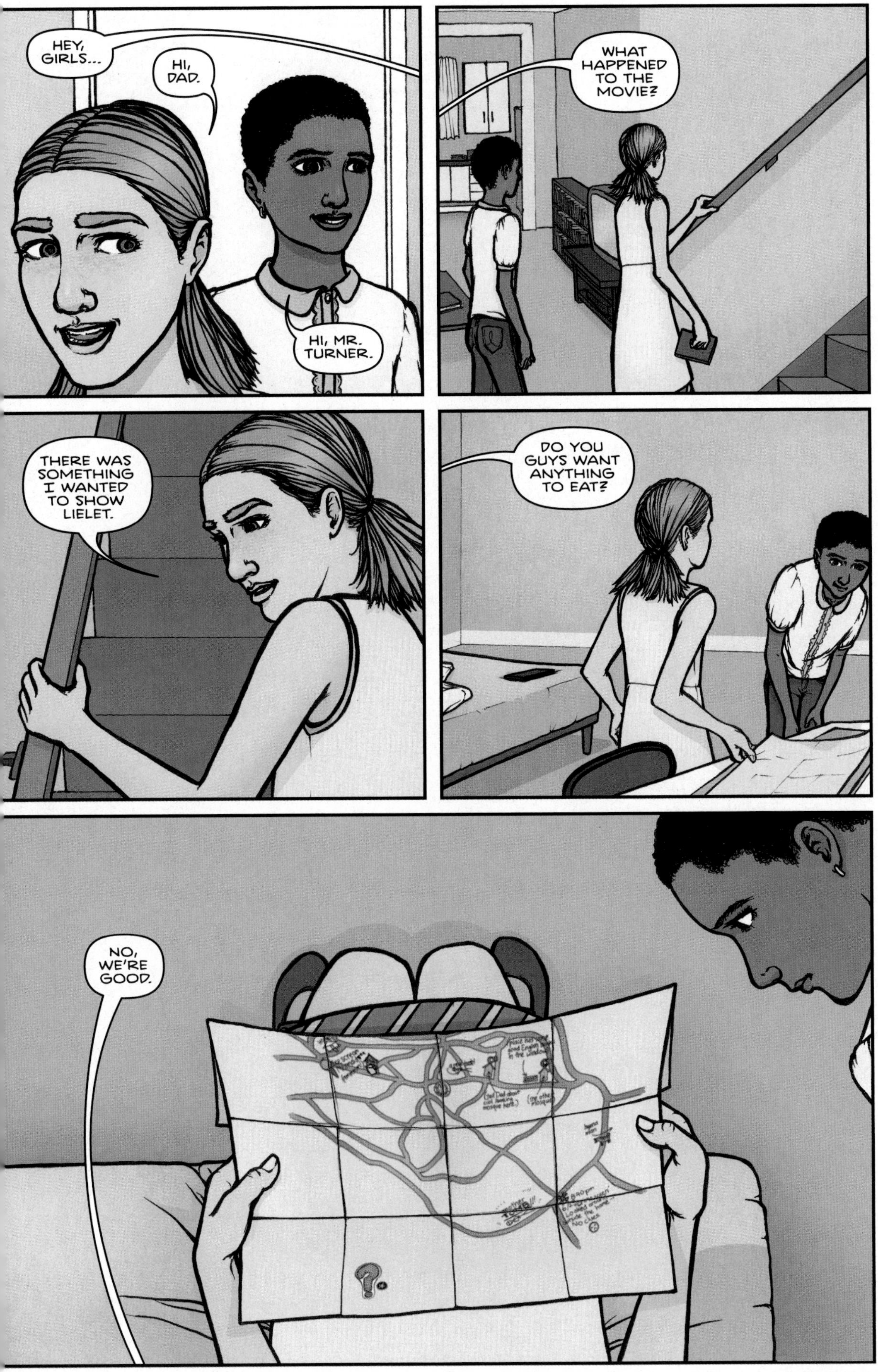
HEY, GIRLS...
HI, DAD.
HI, MR. TURNER.
WHAT HAPPENED TO THE MOVIE?
THERE WAS SOMETHING I WANTED TO SHOW LIELET.
DO YOU GUYS WANT ANYTHING TO EAT?
NO, WE'RE GOOD.

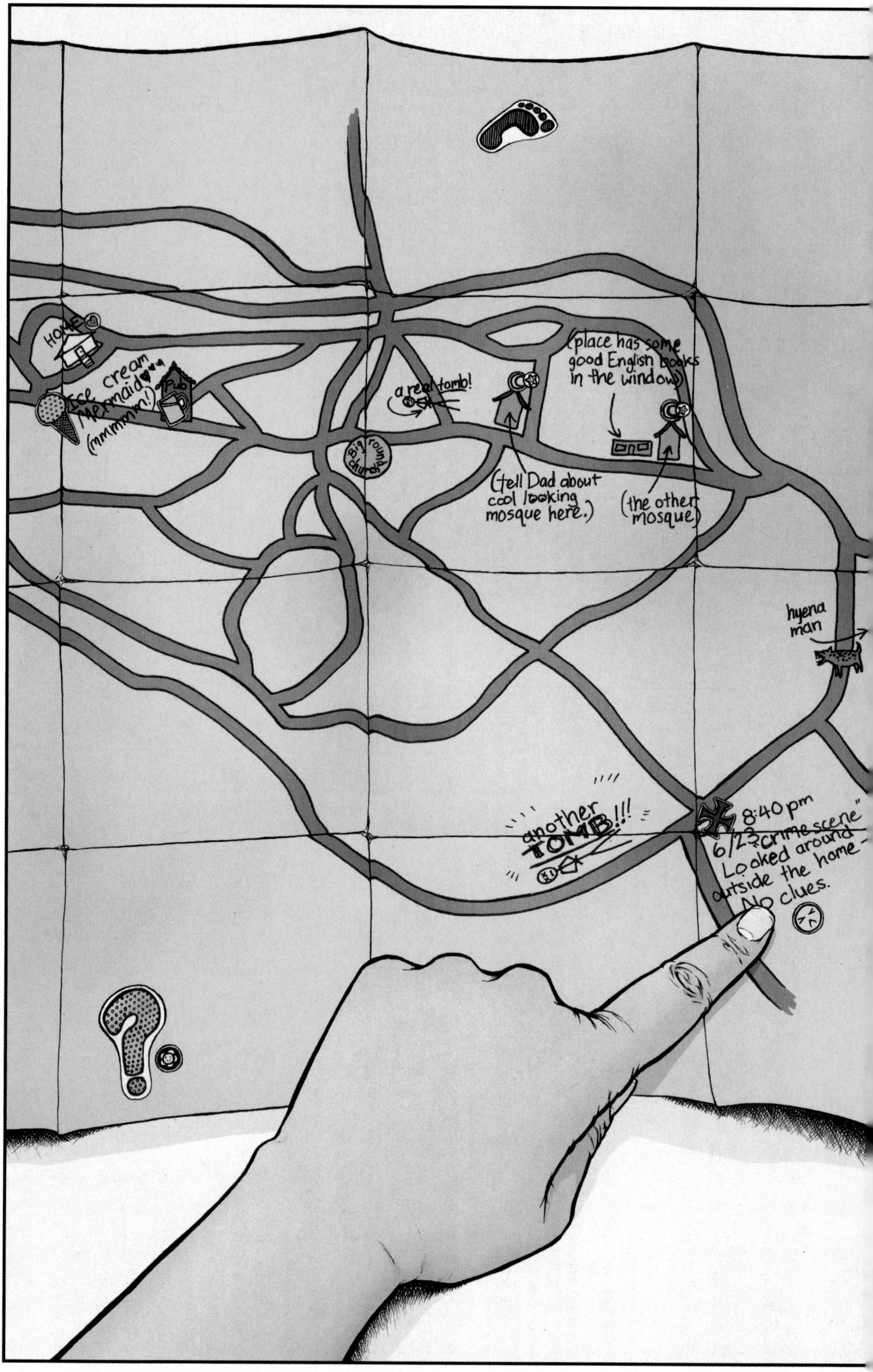
HOME
Ice cream Mermaid
(mmmmm!)
Pub
a real tomb!
Big round church
(place has some good English books in the window)
(tell Dad about cool looking mosque here.)
(the other mosque)
hyena man
another TOMB!!!
8:40 pm
6/23 "crime scene"
Looked around outside the home -
No clues.

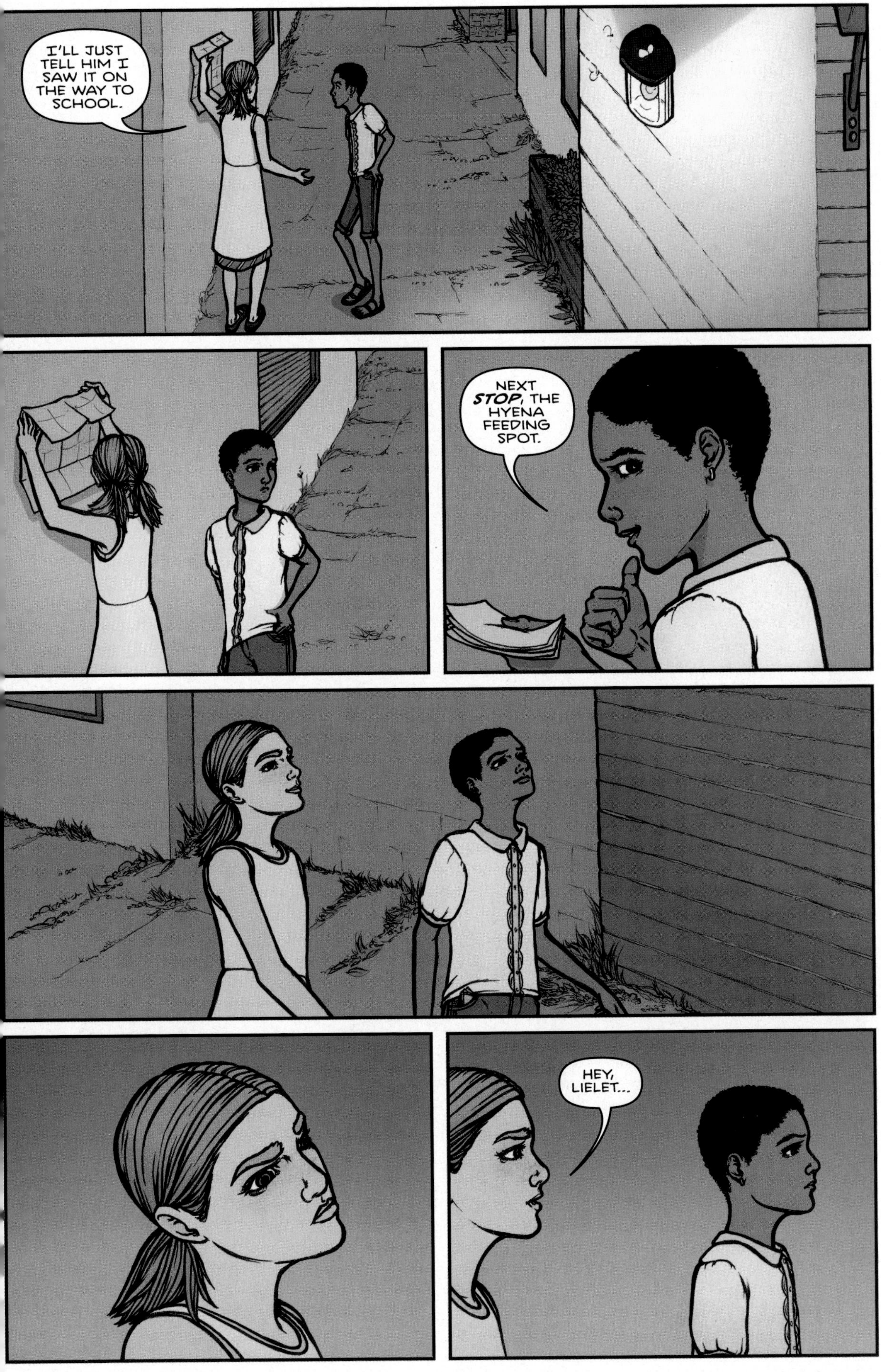
I'LL JUST TELL HIM I SAW IT ON THE WAY TO SCHOOL.
NEXT STOP, THE HYENA FEEDING SPOT.
HEY, LIELET...

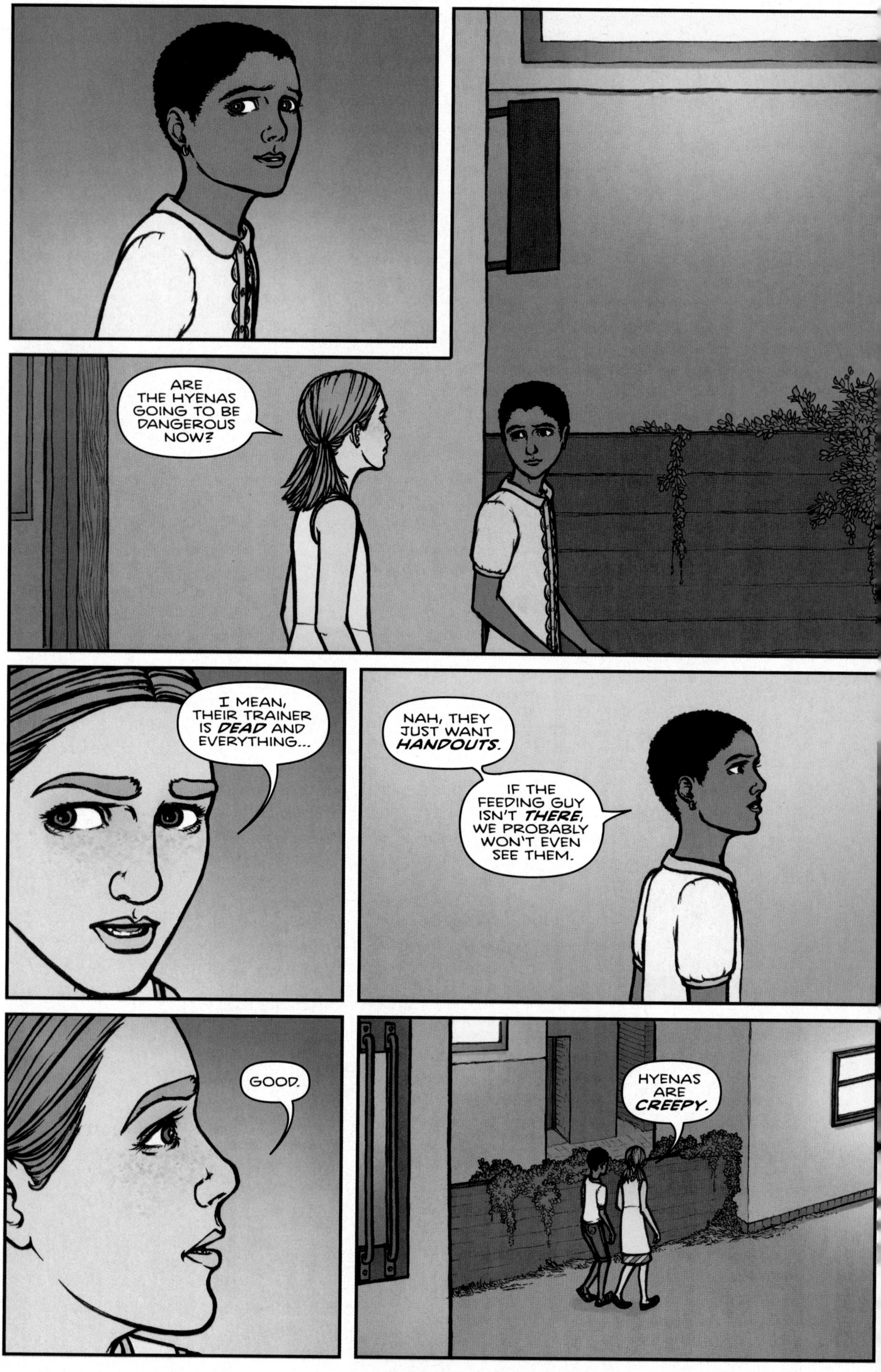
ARE THE HYENAS GOING TO BE DANGEROUS NOW?
I MEAN, THEIR TRAINER IS DEAD AND EVERYTHING...
NAH, THEY JUST WANT HANDOUTS.
IF THE FEEDING GUY ISN'T THERE, WE PROBABLY WON'T EVEN SEE THEM.
GOOD.
HYENAS ARE CREEPY.

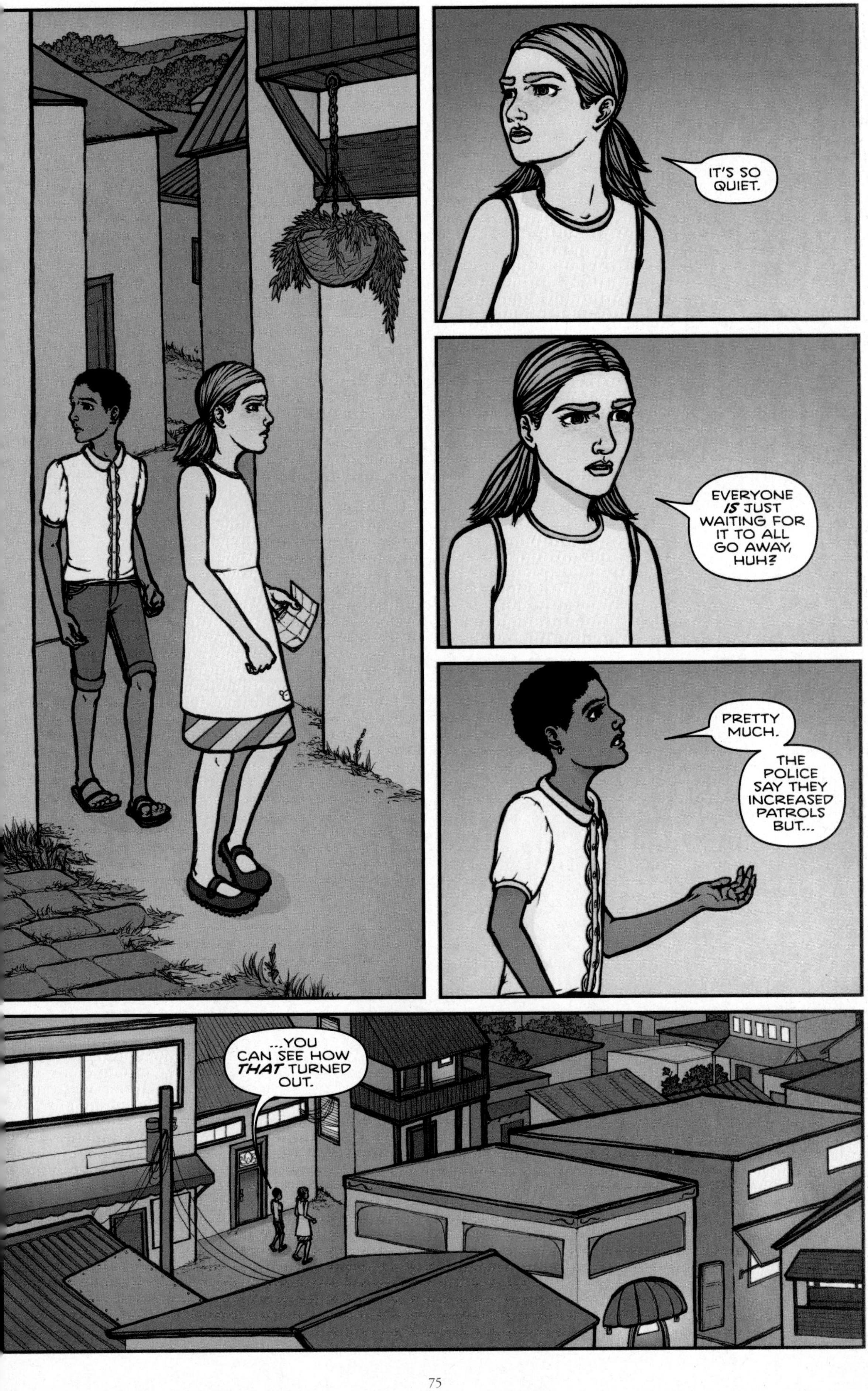

IT'S SO QUIET.
EVERYONE *IS* JUST WAITING FOR IT TO ALL GO AWAY, HUH?
PRETTY MUCH.
THE POLICE SAY THEY INCREASED PATROLS BUT...
...YOU CAN SEE HOW *THAT* TURNED OUT.

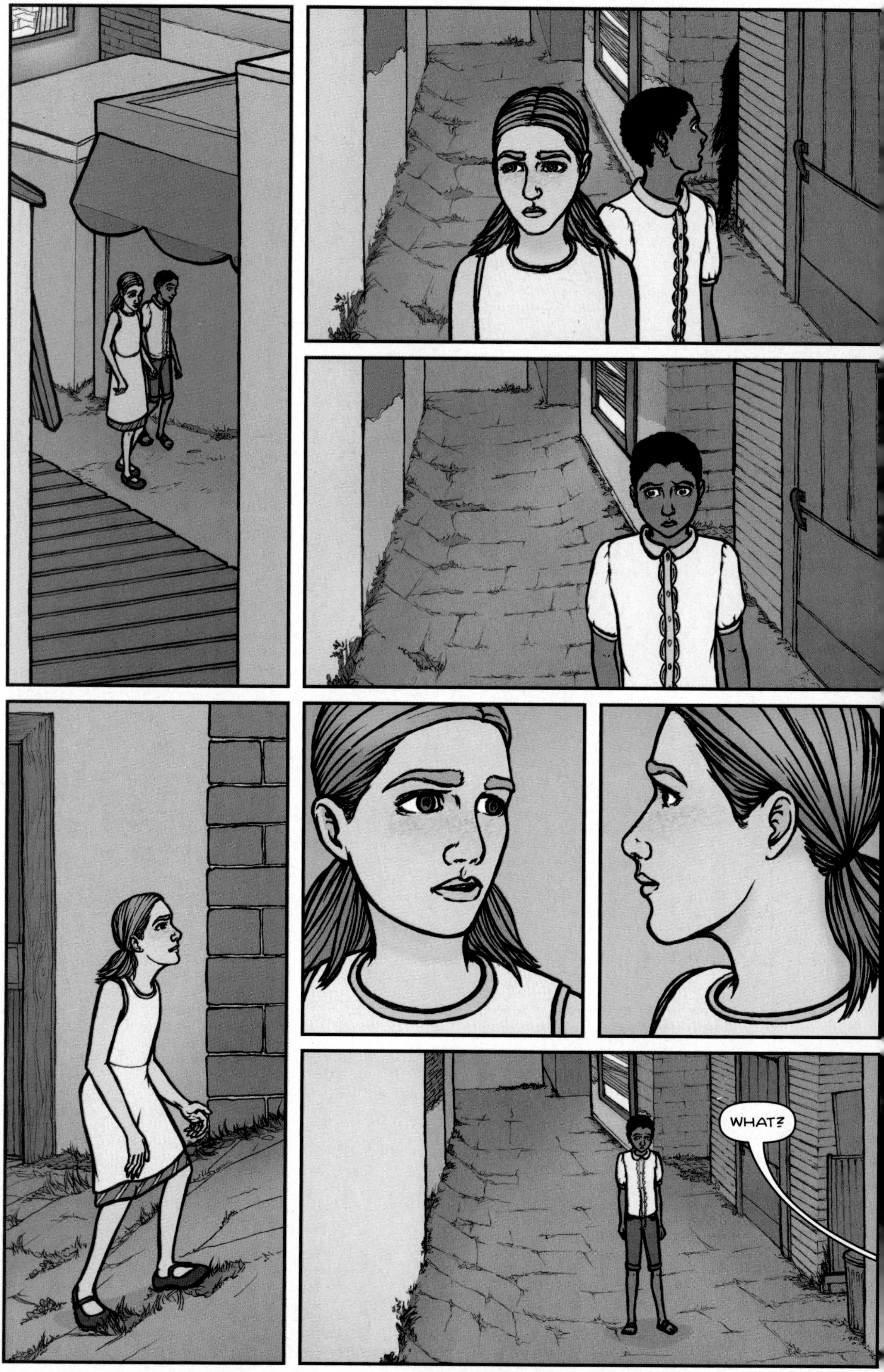
WHAT?

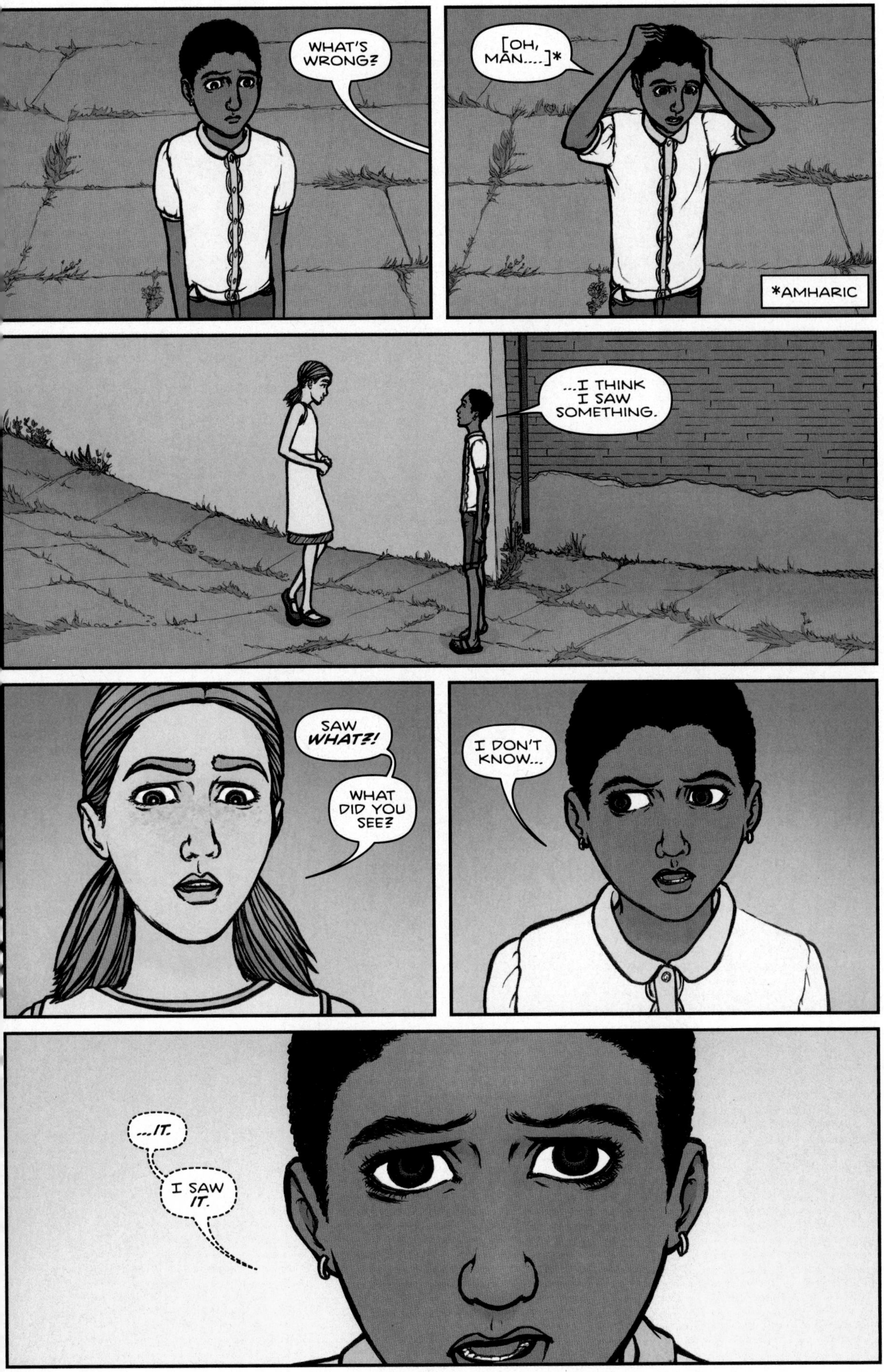
WHAT'S WRONG?
[OH, MAN....]*
*AMHARIC
...I THINK I SAW SOMETHING.
SAW *WHAT?!*
WHAT DID YOU SEE?
I DON'T KNOW...
...*IT.*
I SAW *IT.*

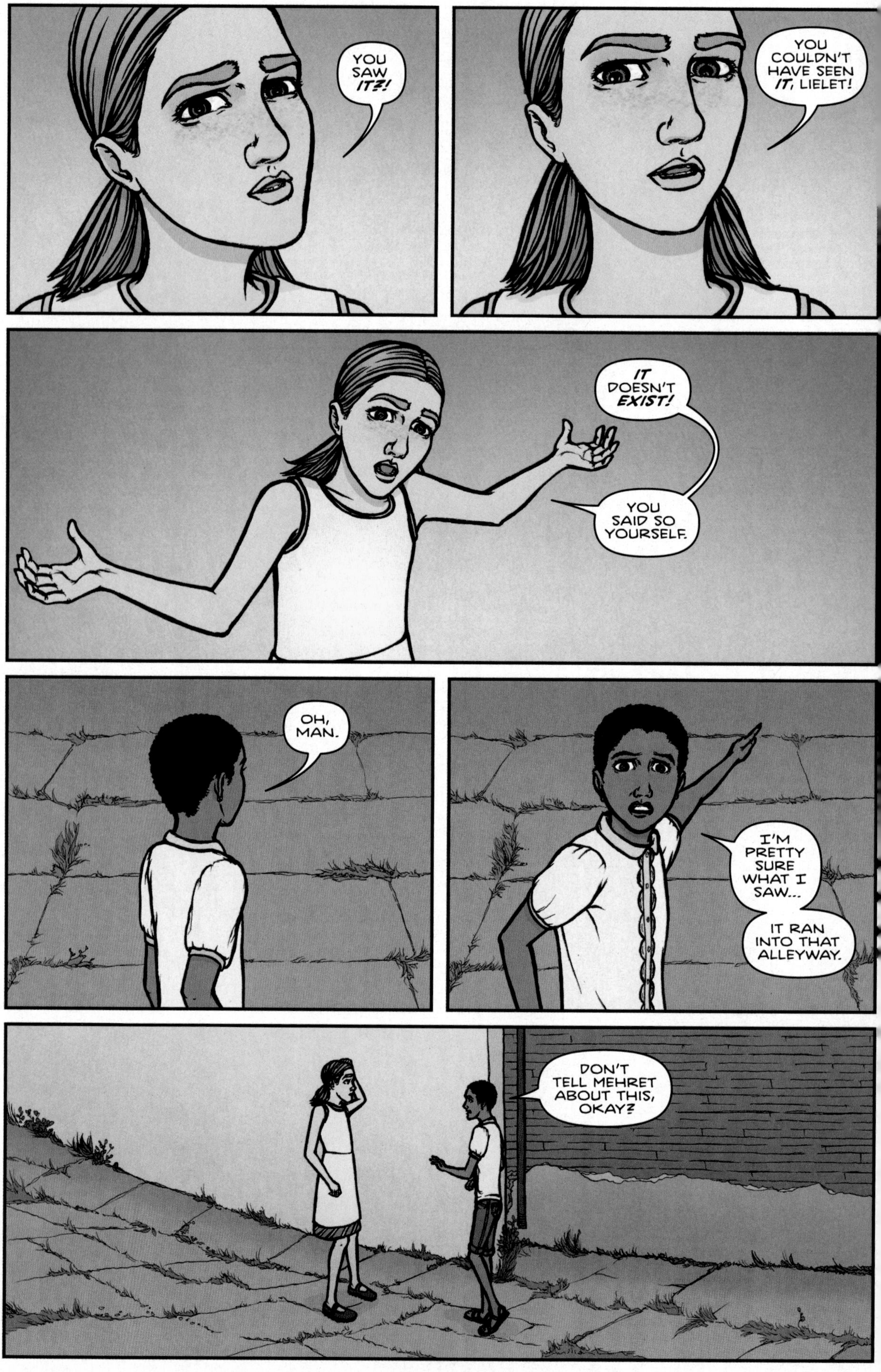
YOU SAW *IT?!*
YOU COULDN'T HAVE SEEN *IT*, LIELET!
IT DOESN'T *EXIST!*
YOU SAID SO YOURSELF.
OH, MAN.
I'M PRETTY SURE WHAT I SAW...
IT RAN INTO THAT ALLEYWAY.
DON'T TELL MEHRET ABOUT THIS, OKAY?

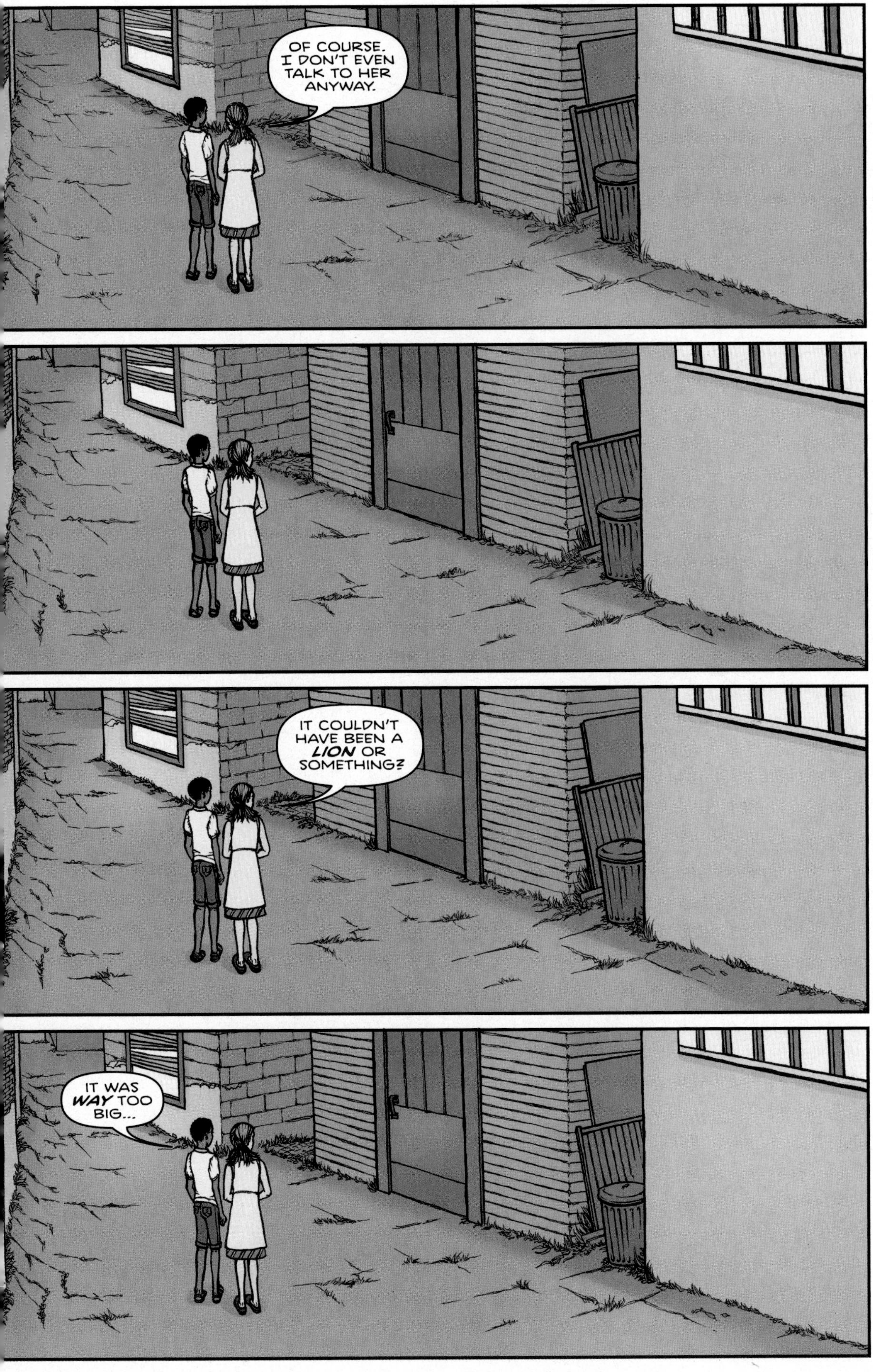
OF COURSE. I DON'T EVEN TALK TO HER ANYWAY.
IT COULDN'T HAVE BEEN A *LION* OR SOMETHING?
IT WAS *WAY* TOO BIG...

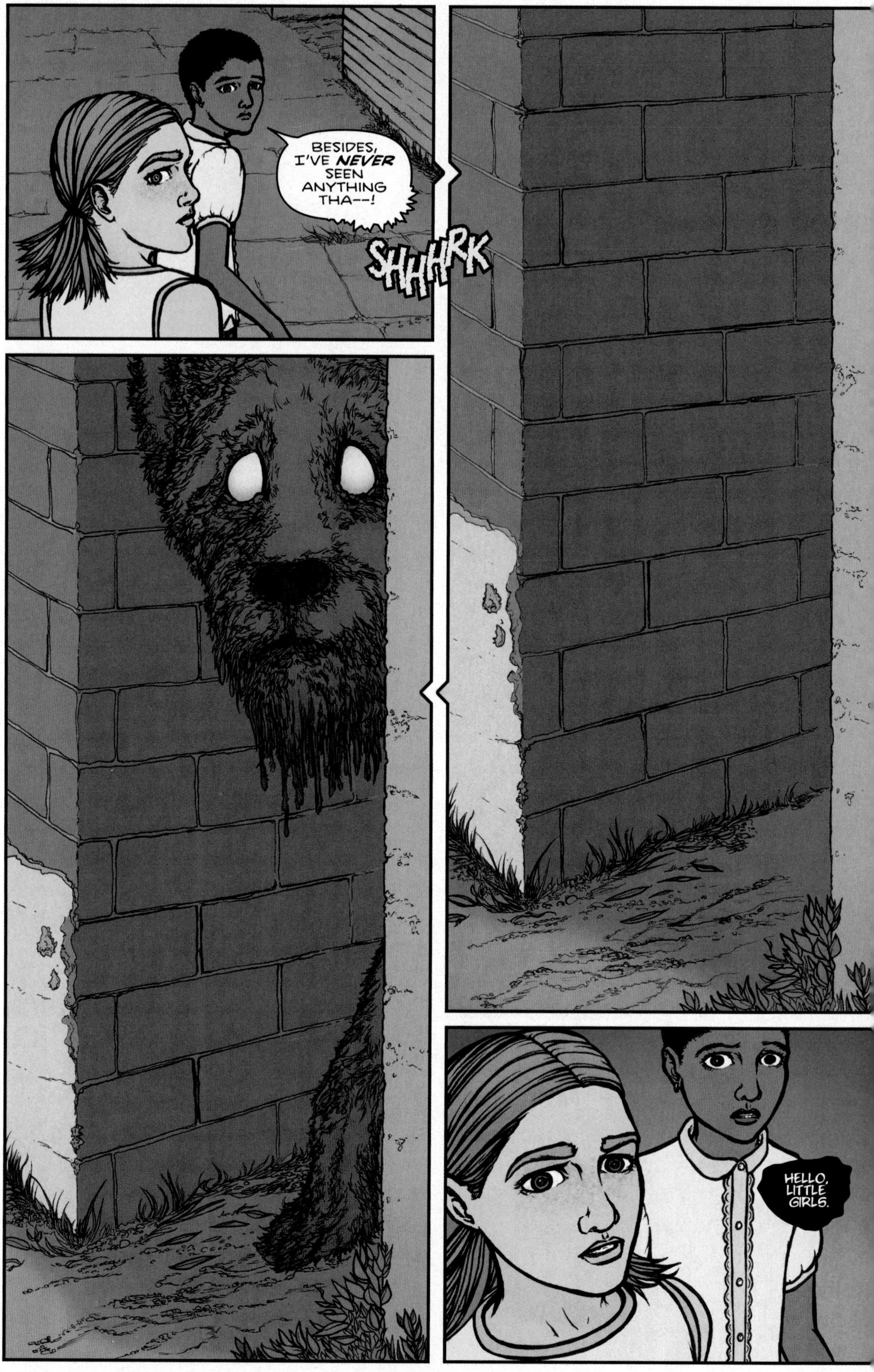
BESIDES, I'VE NEVER SEEN ANYTHING THA--!
SHHHRK
HELLO, LITTLE GIRLS.

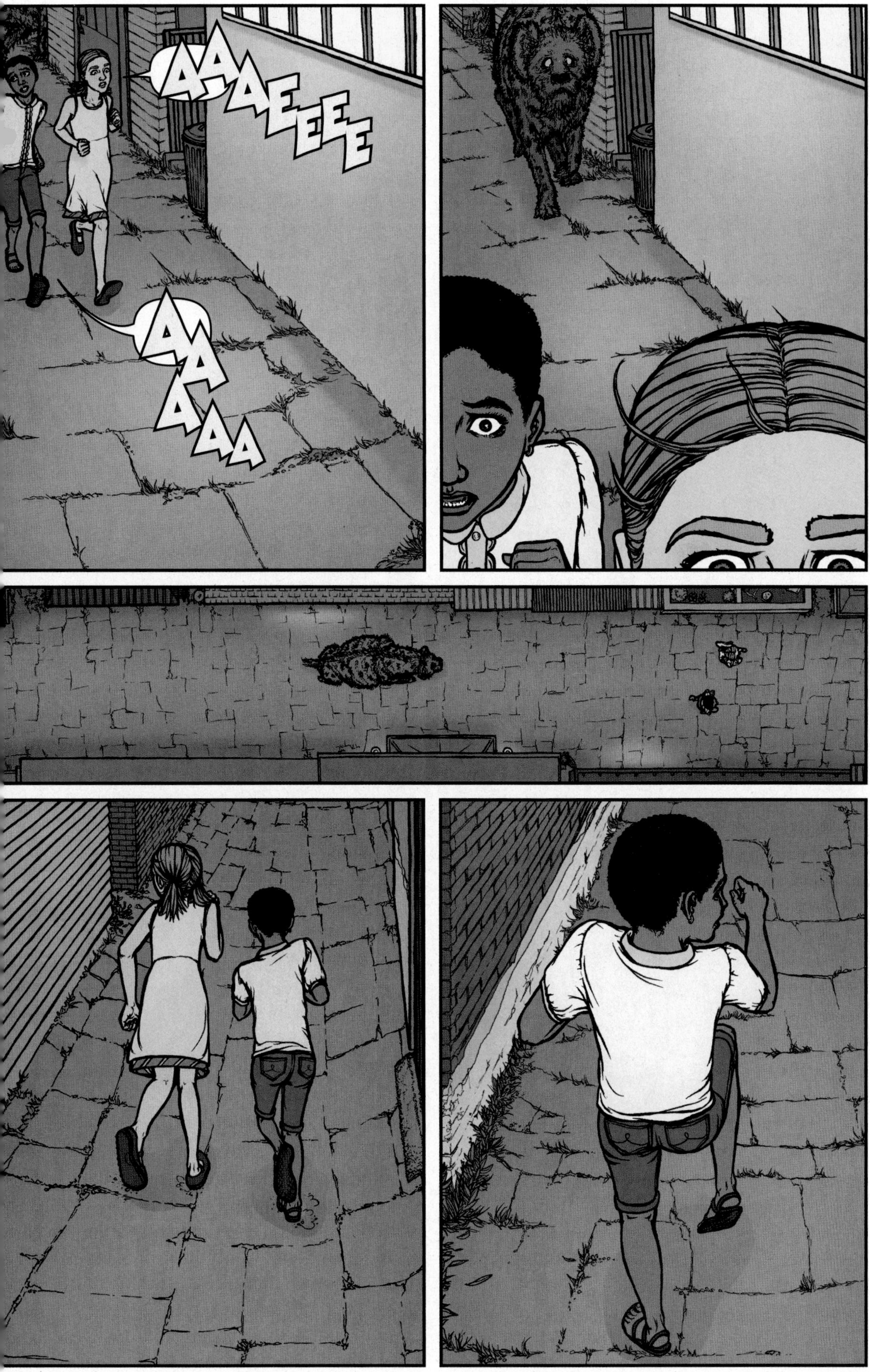
AAAEEEE
AAAAA

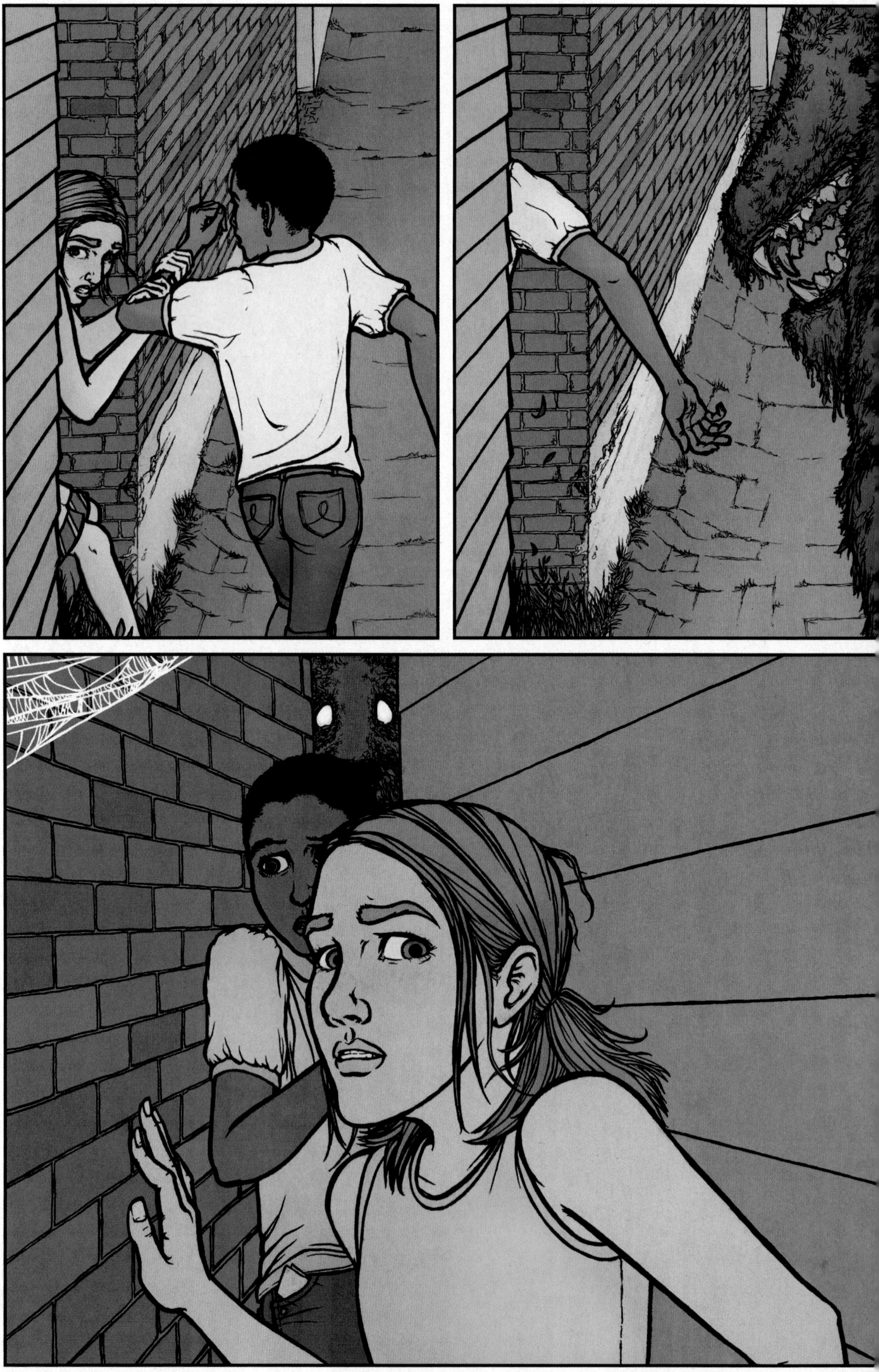

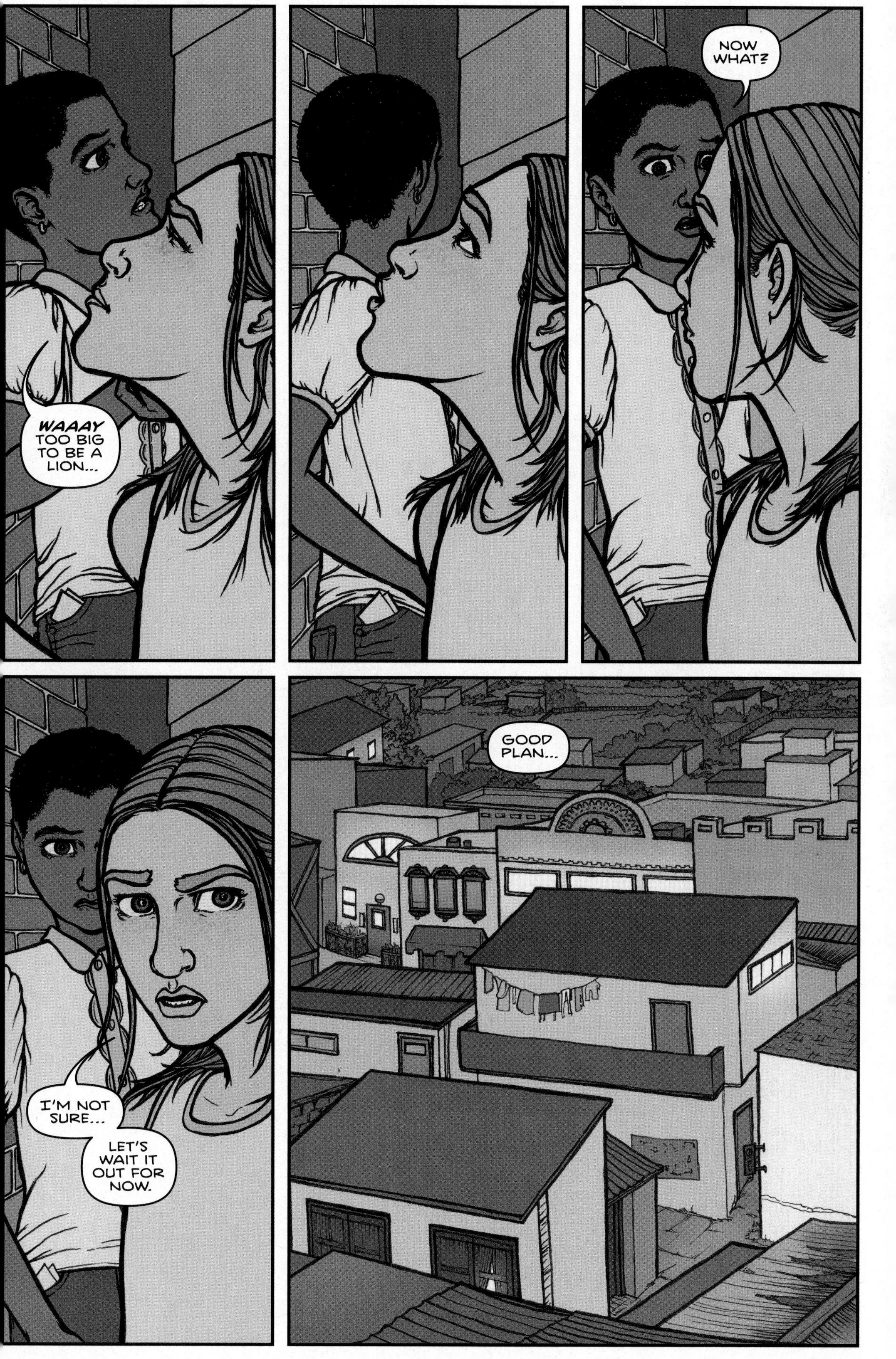
WAAAY TOO BIG TO BE A LION...
NOW WHAT?
I'M NOT SURE...
LET'S WAIT IT OUT FOR NOW.
GOOD PLAN...

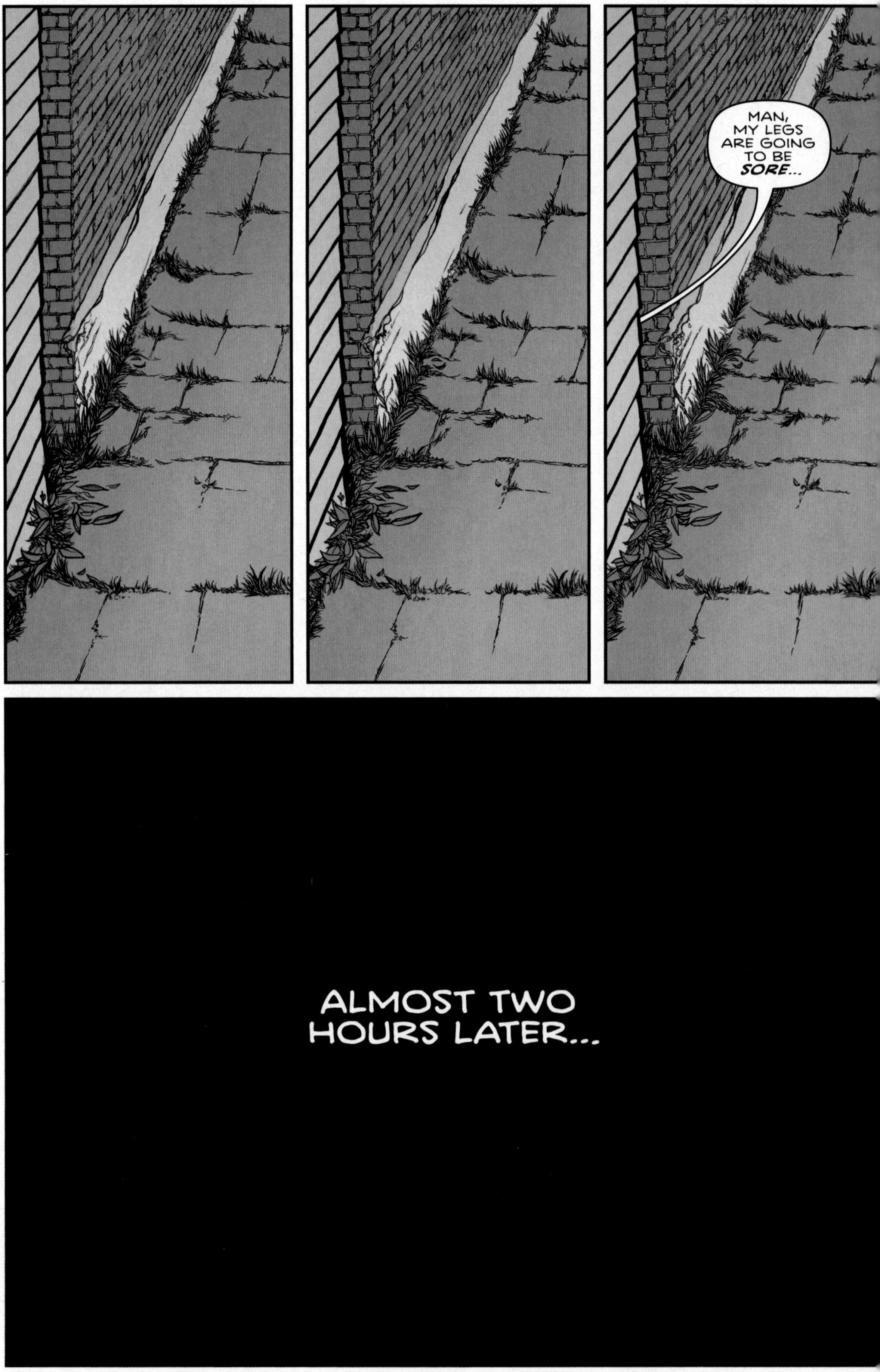
MAN, MY LEGS ARE GOING TO BE *SORE*...
ALMOST TWO HOURS LATER...

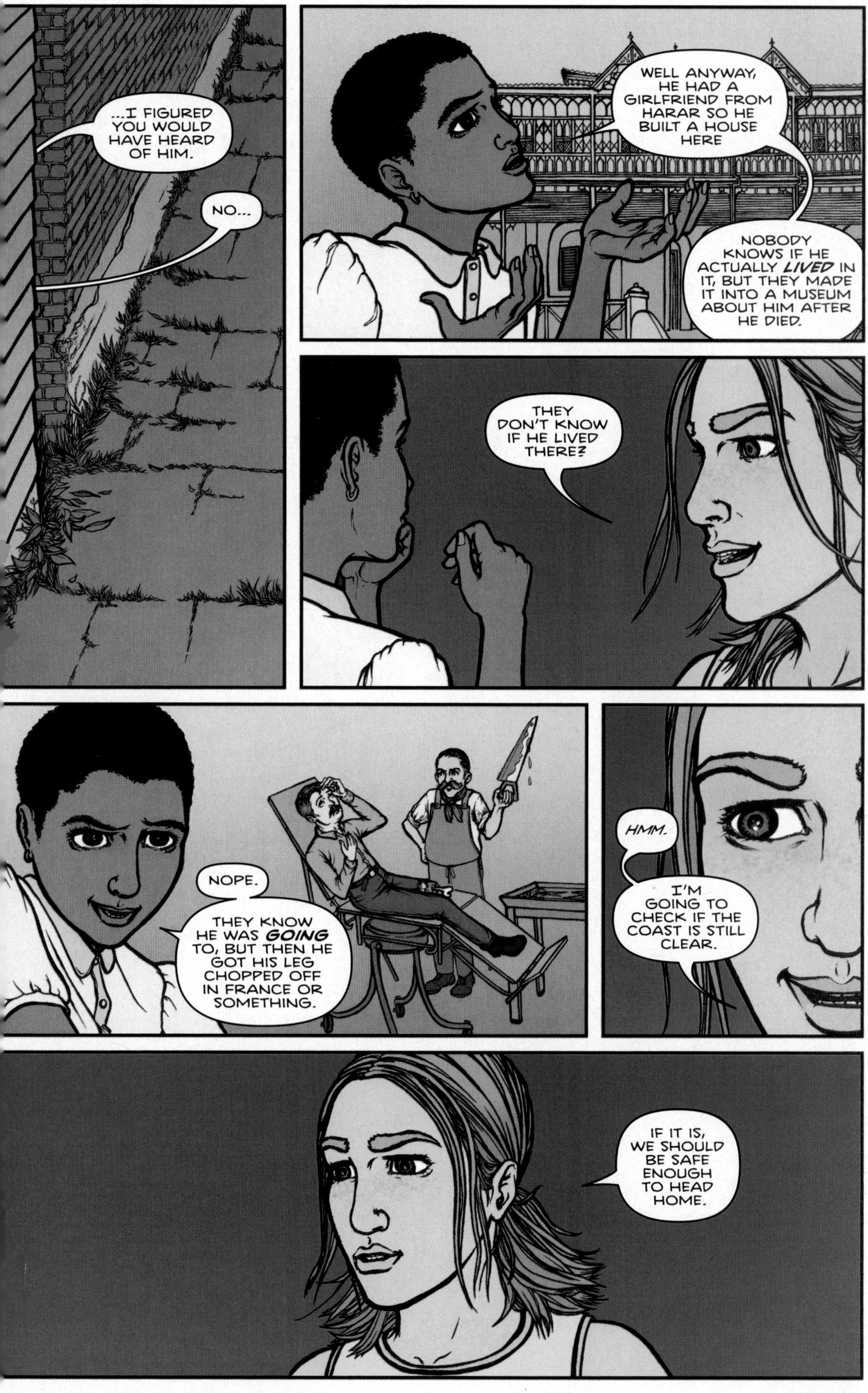
...I FIGURED YOU WOULD HAVE HEARD OF HIM.
NO...
WELL ANYWAY, HE HAD A GIRLFRIEND FROM HARAR SO HE BUILT A HOUSE HERE
NOBODY KNOWS IF HE ACTUALLY LIVED IN IT, BUT THEY MADE IT INTO A MUSEUM ABOUT HIM AFTER HE DIED.
THEY DON'T KNOW IF HE LIVED THERE?
NOPE.
THEY KNOW HE WAS GOING TO, BUT THEN HE GOT HIS LEG CHOPPED OFF IN FRANCE OR SOMETHING.
HMM.
I'M GOING TO CHECK IF THE COAST IS STILL CLEAR.
IF IT IS, WE SHOULD BE SAFE ENOUGH TO HEAD HOME.

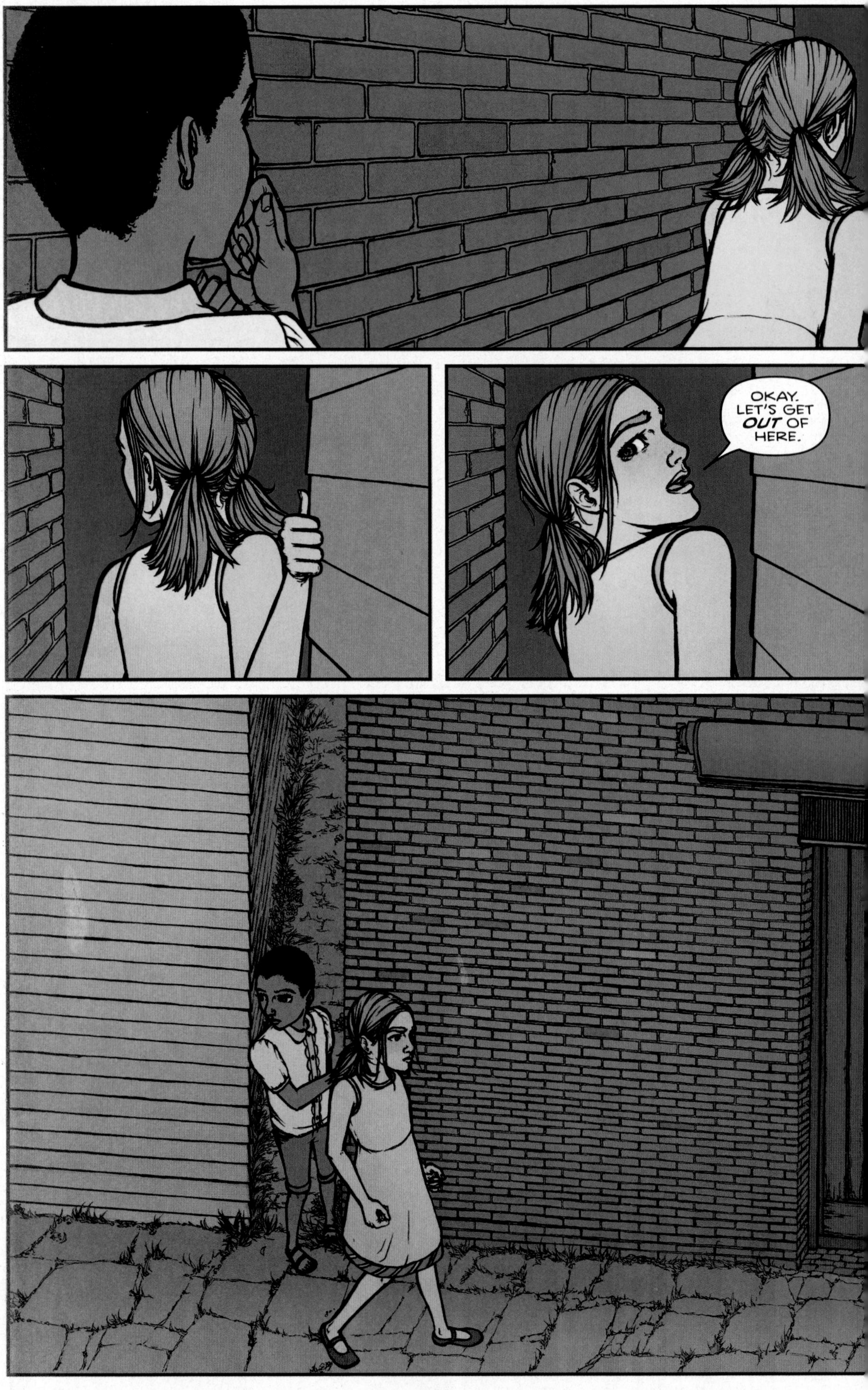
OKAY. LET'S GET OUT OF HERE.

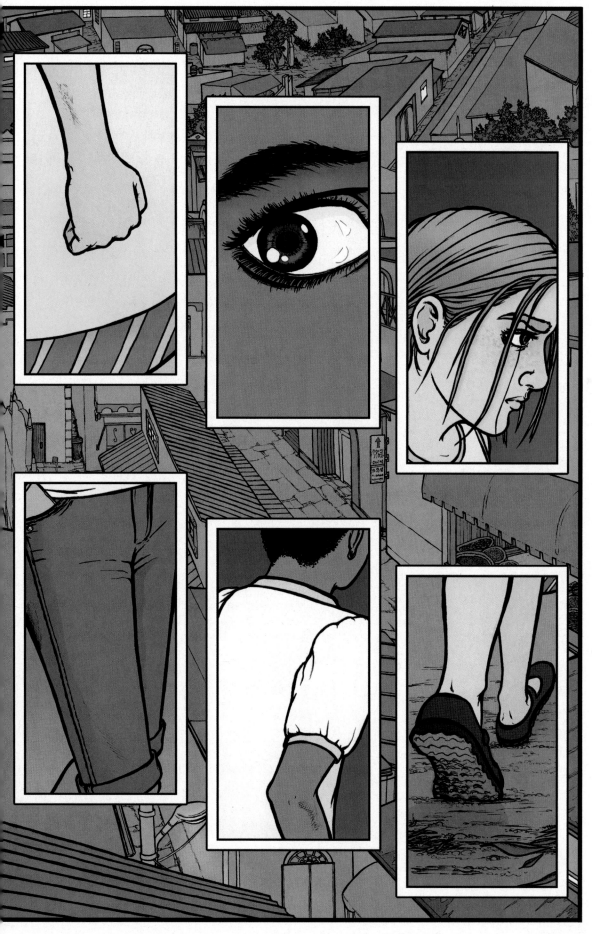

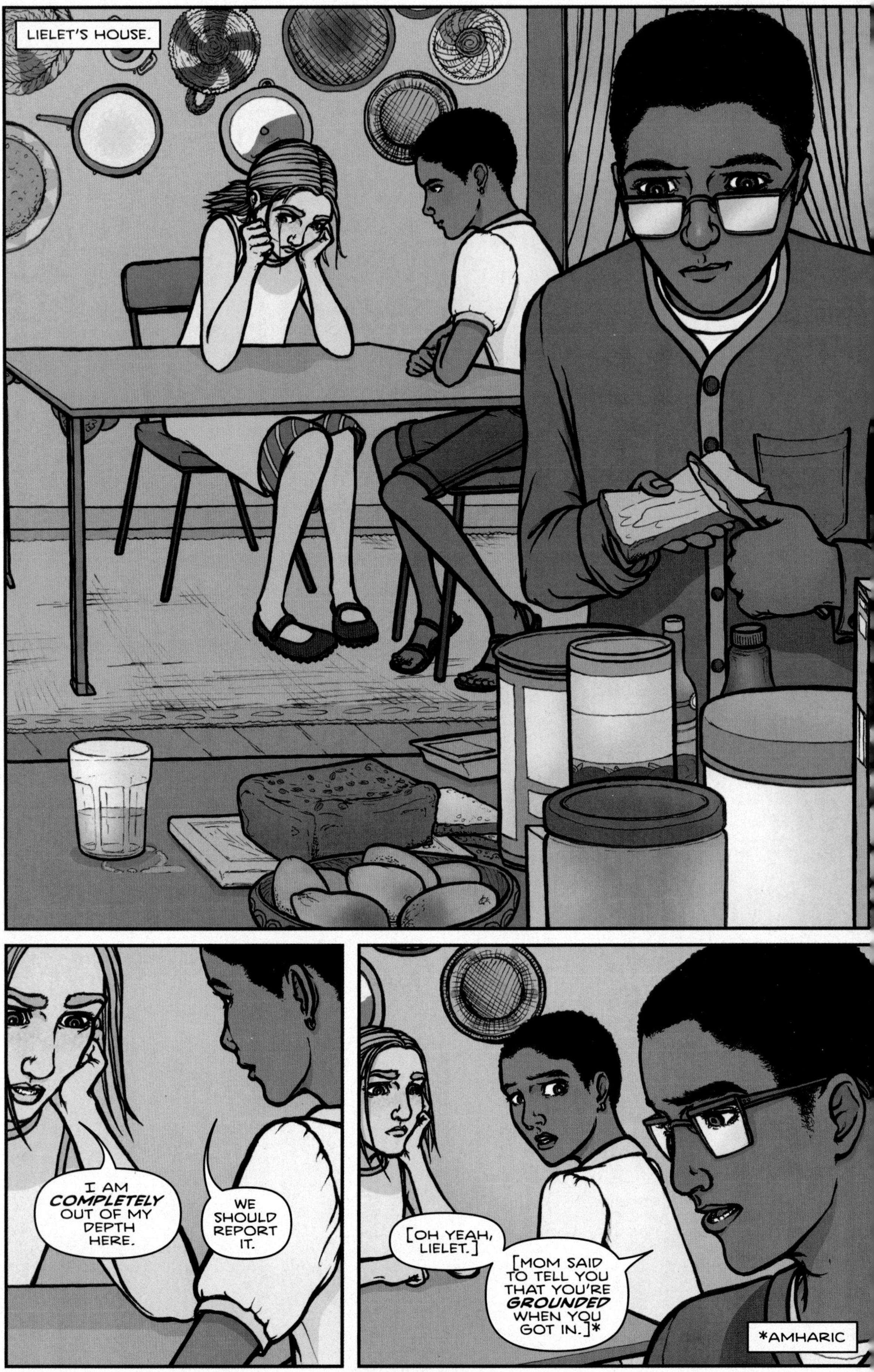
LIELET'S HOUSE.
I AM COMPLETELY OUT OF MY DEPTH HERE.
WE SHOULD REPORT IT.
[OH YEAH, LIELET.]
[MOM SAID TO TELL YOU THAT YOU'RE GROUNDED WHEN YOU GOT IN.]*
*AMHARIC

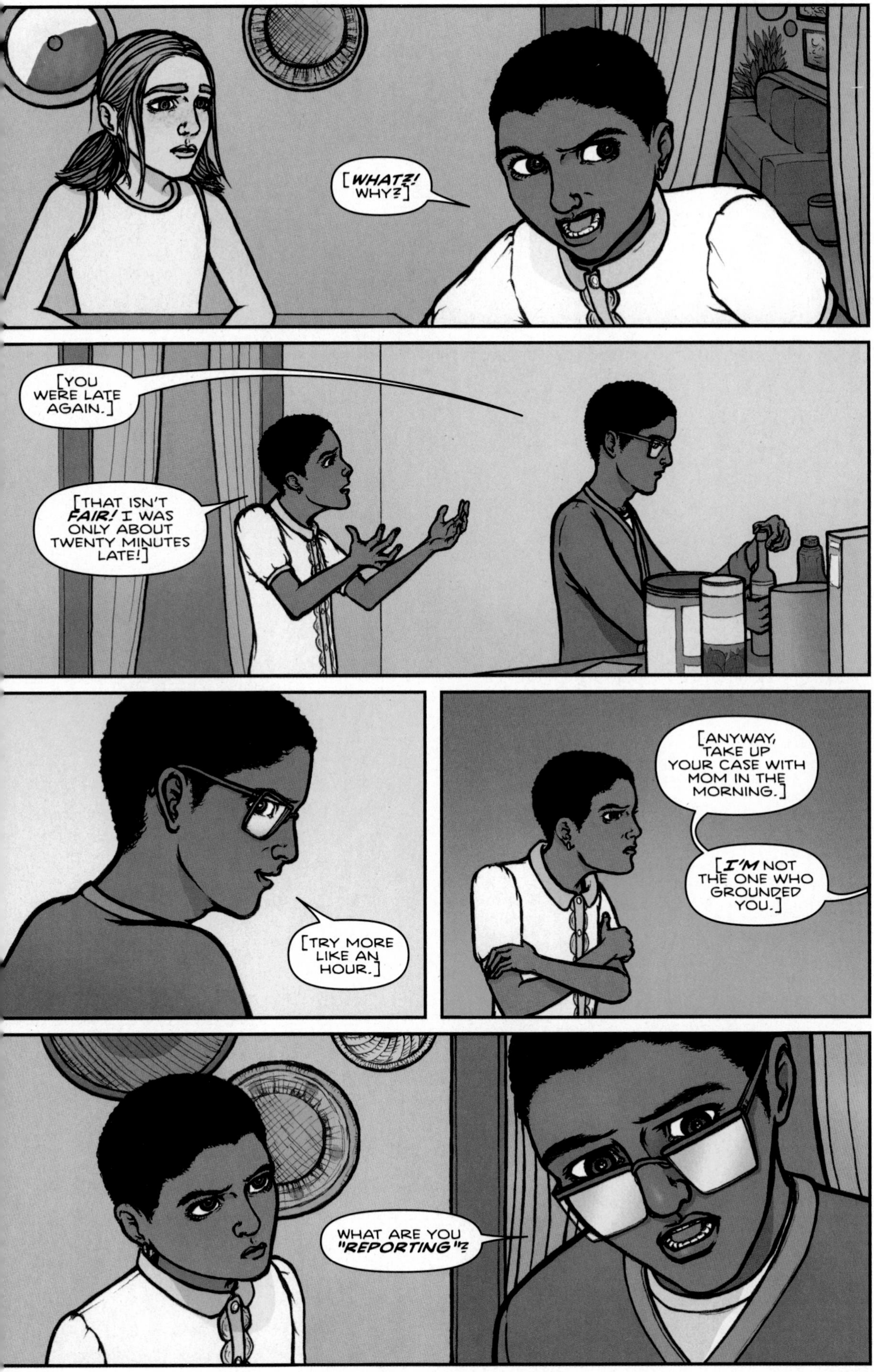
[WHAT?! WHY?]
[YOU WERE LATE AGAIN.]
[THAT ISN'T FAIR! I WAS ONLY ABOUT TWENTY MINUTES LATE!]
[TRY MORE LIKE AN HOUR.]
[ANYWAY, TAKE UP YOUR CASE WITH MOM IN THE MORNING.]
[I'M NOT THE ONE WHO GROUNDED YOU.]
WHAT ARE YOU "REPORTING"?

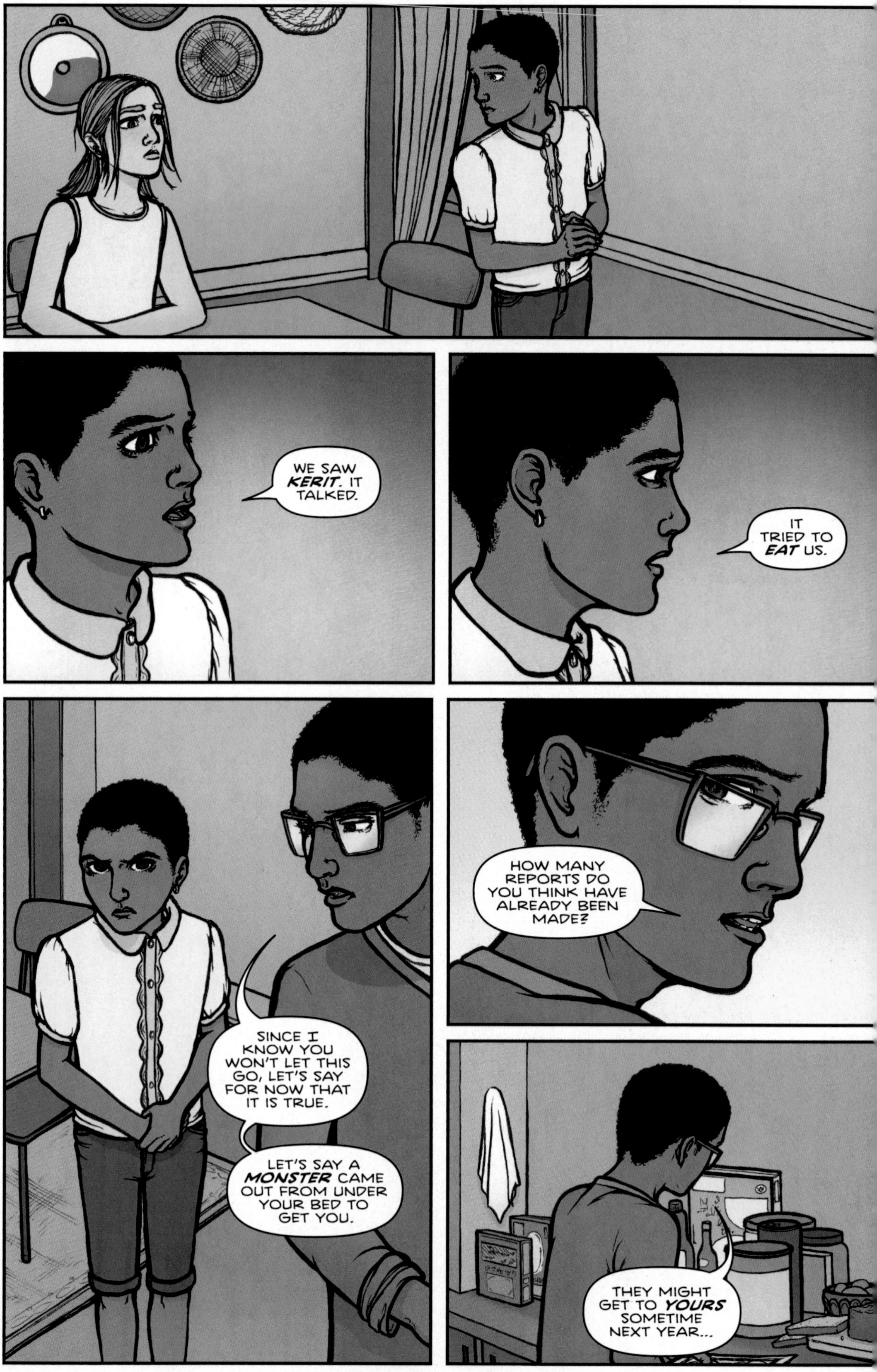
WE SAW KERIT. IT TALKED.
IT TRIED TO EAT US.
SINCE I KNOW YOU WON'T LET THIS GO, LET'S SAY FOR NOW THAT IT IS TRUE.
LET'S SAY A MONSTER CAME OUT FROM UNDER YOUR BED TO GET YOU.
HOW MANY REPORTS DO YOU THINK HAVE ALREADY BEEN MADE?
THEY MIGHT GET TO YOURS SOMETIME NEXT YEAR...

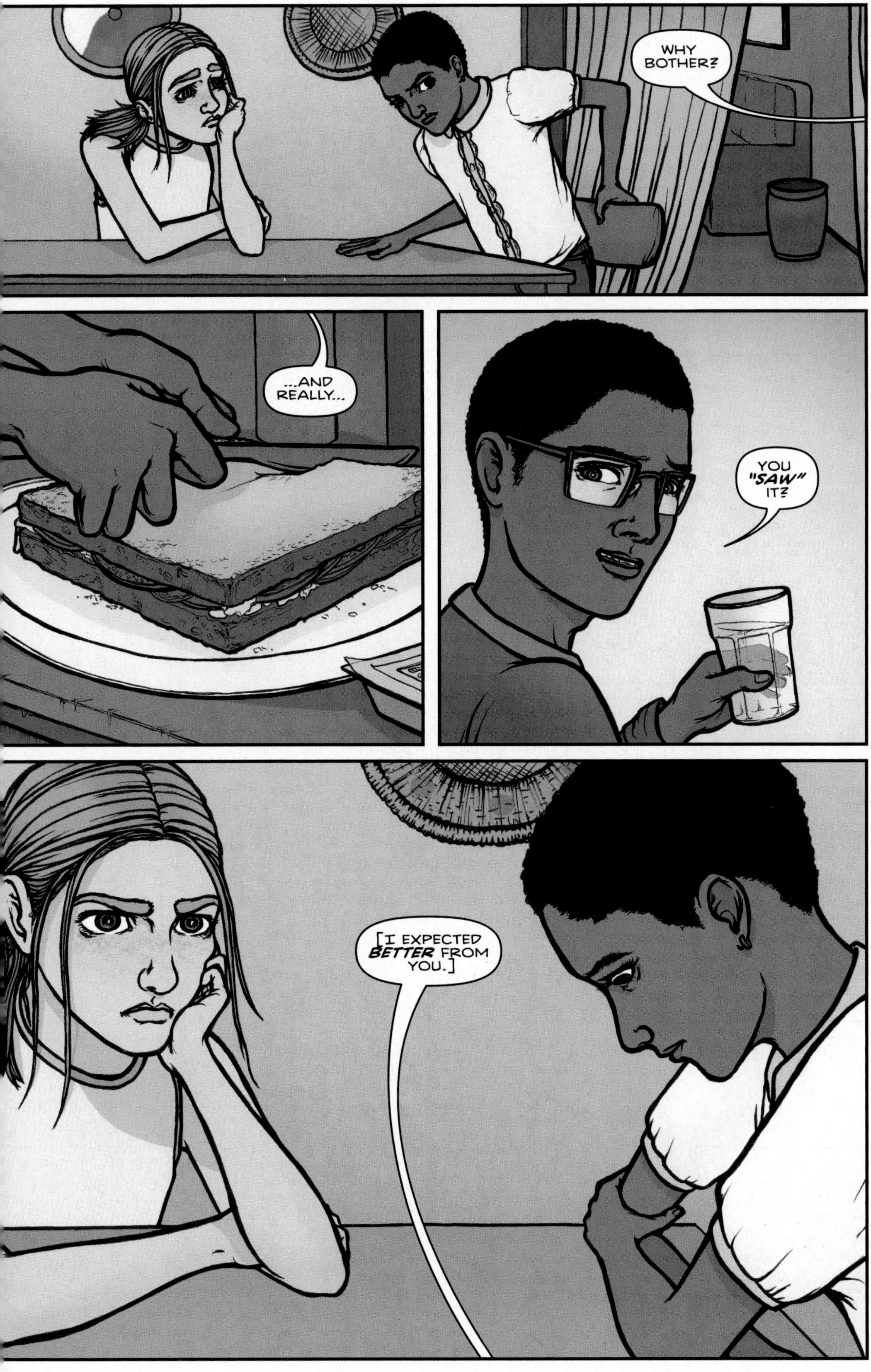
WHY BOTHER?
...AND REALLY...
YOU "SAW" IT?
[I EXPECTED BETTER FROM YOU.]

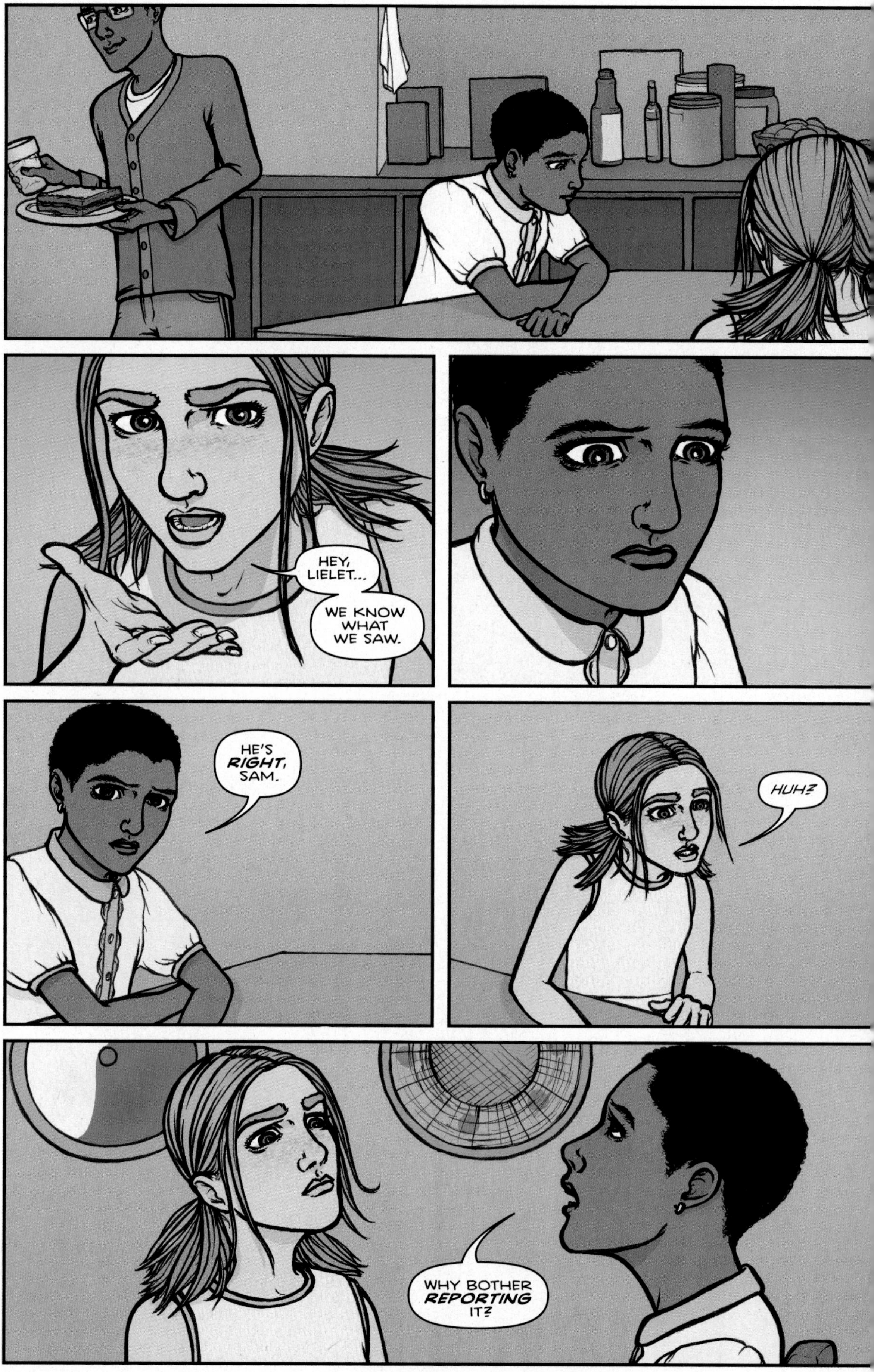
HEY, LIELET...
WE KNOW WHAT WE SAW.
HE'S *RIGHT*, SAM.
HUH?
WHY BOTHER *REPORTING* IT?

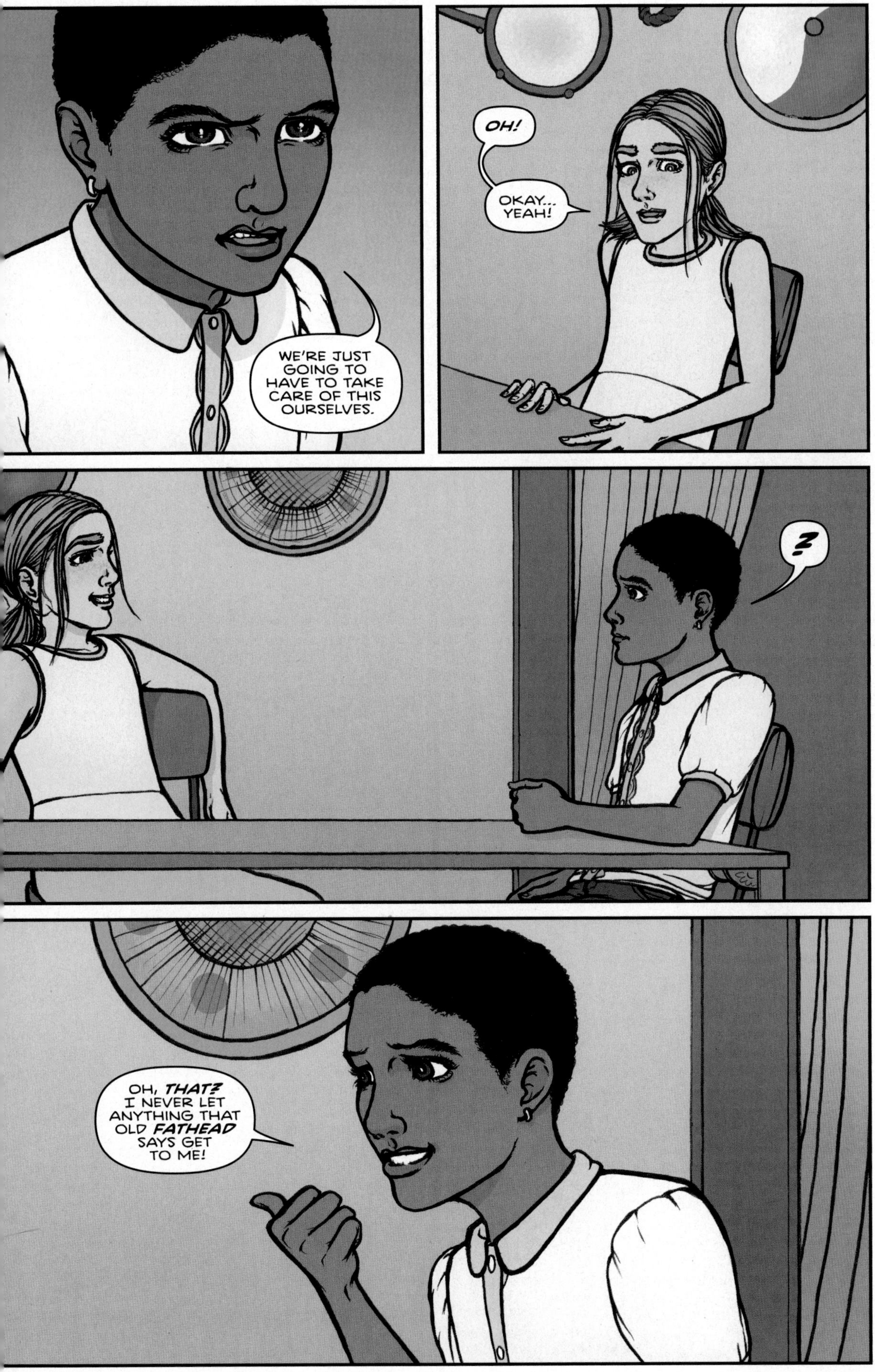
WE'RE JUST GOING TO HAVE TO TAKE CARE OF THIS OURSELVES.
OH!
OKAY... YEAH!
?
OH, THAT? I NEVER LET ANYTHING THAT OLD FATHEAD SAYS GET TO ME!

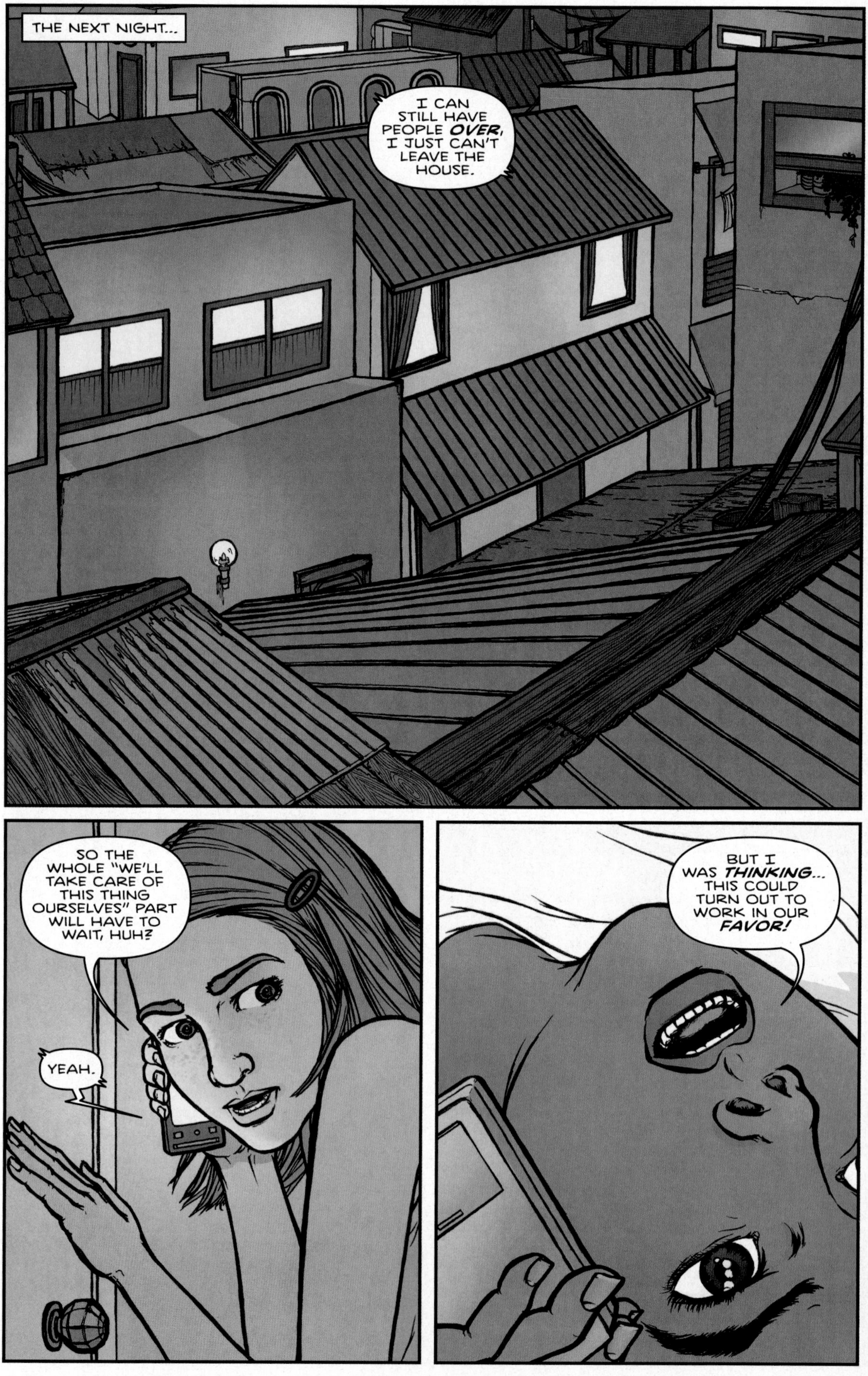
THE NEXT NIGHT...
I CAN STILL HAVE PEOPLE OVER, I JUST CAN'T LEAVE THE HOUSE.
SO THE WHOLE "WE'LL TAKE CARE OF THIS THING OURSELVES" PART WILL HAVE TO WAIT, HUH?
YEAH.
BUT I WAS THINKING... THIS COULD TURN OUT TO WORK IN OUR FAVOR!

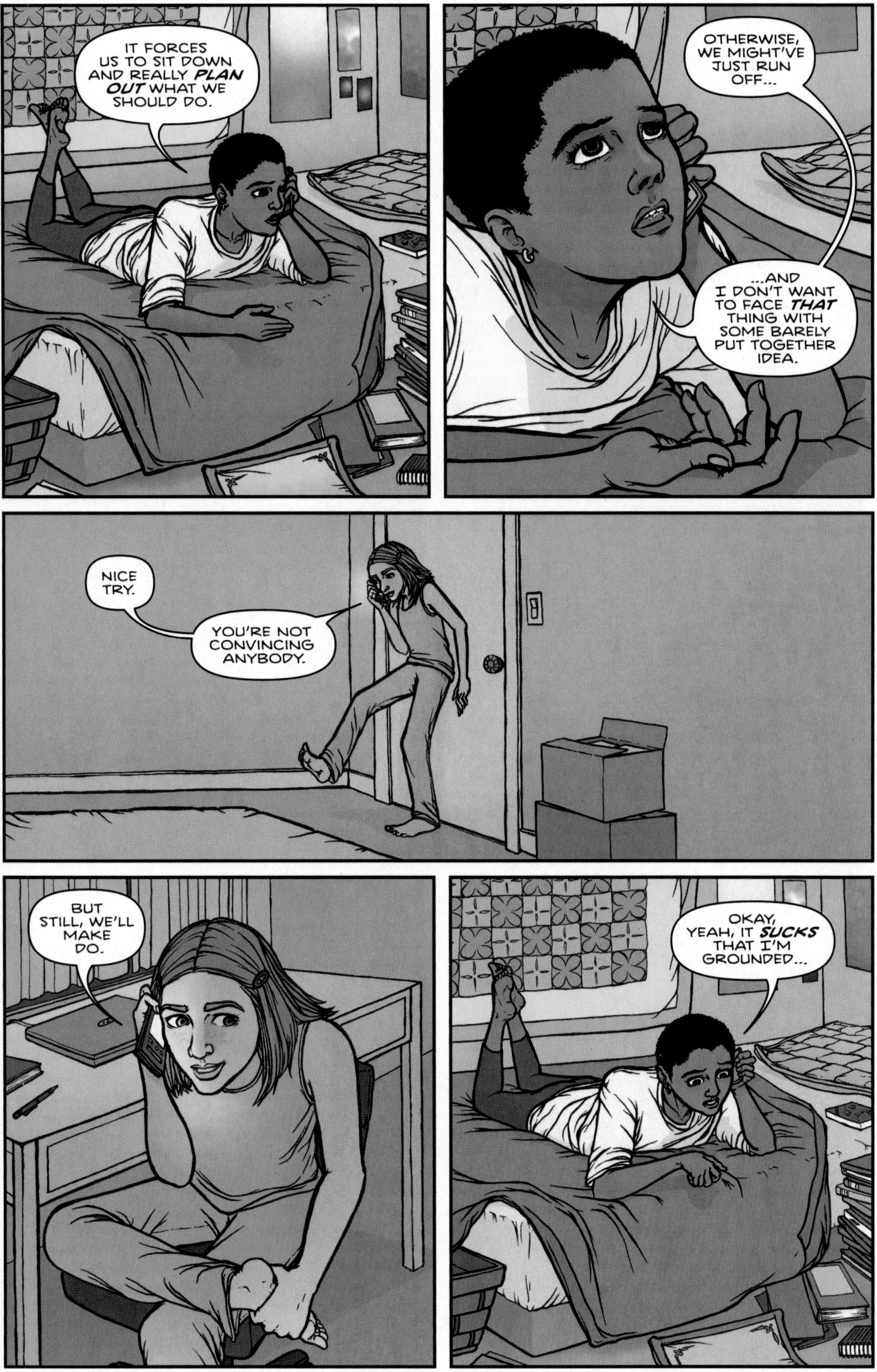
IT FORCES US TO SIT DOWN AND REALLY PLAN OUT WHAT WE SHOULD DO.
OTHERWISE, WE MIGHT'VE JUST RUN OFF...
...AND I DON'T WANT TO FACE THAT THING WITH SOME BARELY PUT TOGETHER IDEA.
NICE TRY.
YOU'RE NOT CONVINCING ANYBODY.
BUT STILL, WE'LL MAKE DO.
OKAY, YEAH, IT SUCKS THAT I'M GROUNDED...

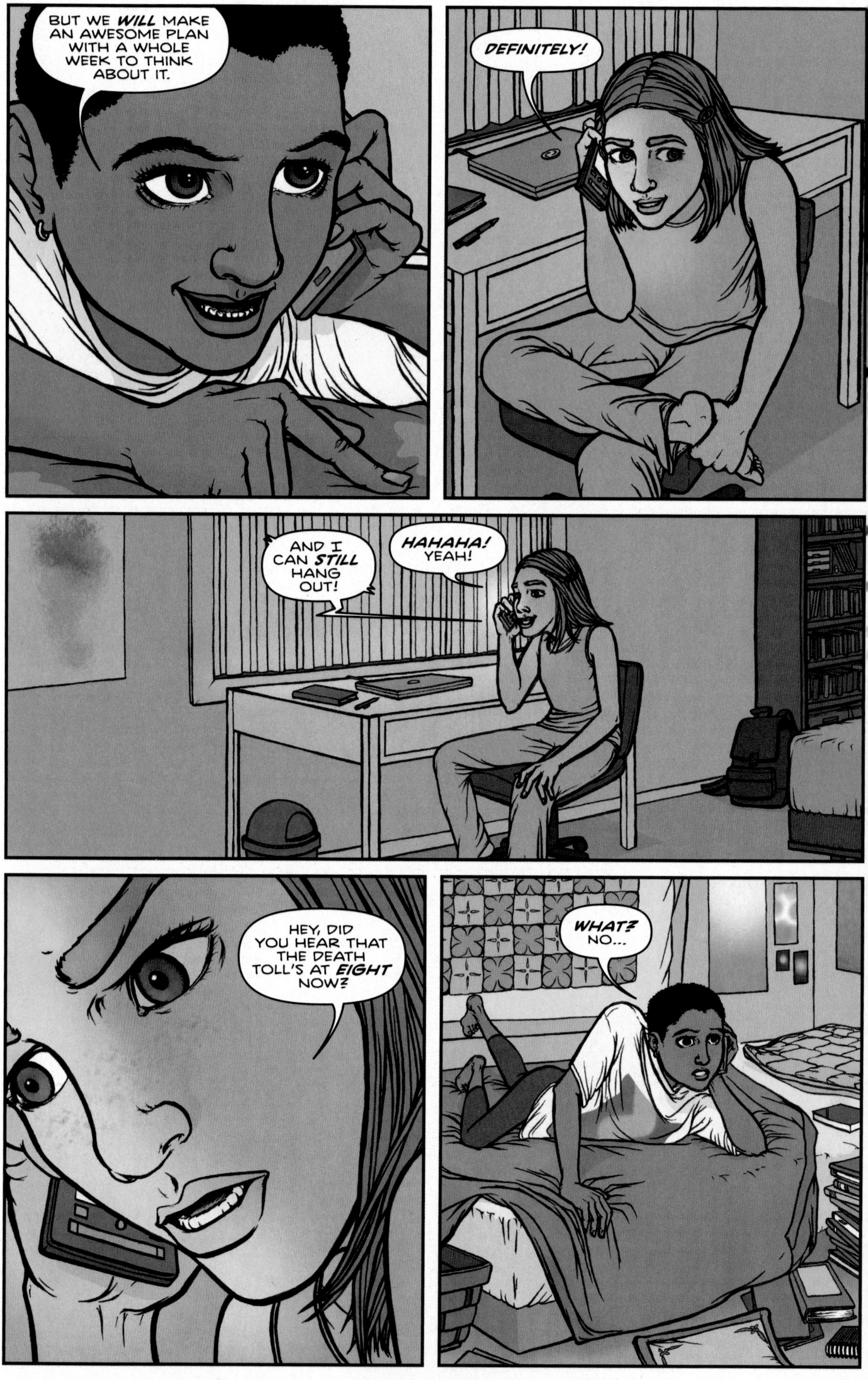
BUT WE WILL MAKE AN AWESOME PLAN WITH A WHOLE WEEK TO THINK ABOUT IT.
DEFINITELY!
AND I CAN STILL HANG OUT!
HAHAHA! YEAH!
HEY, DID YOU HEAR THAT THE DEATH TOLL'S AT EIGHT NOW?
WHAT? NO...

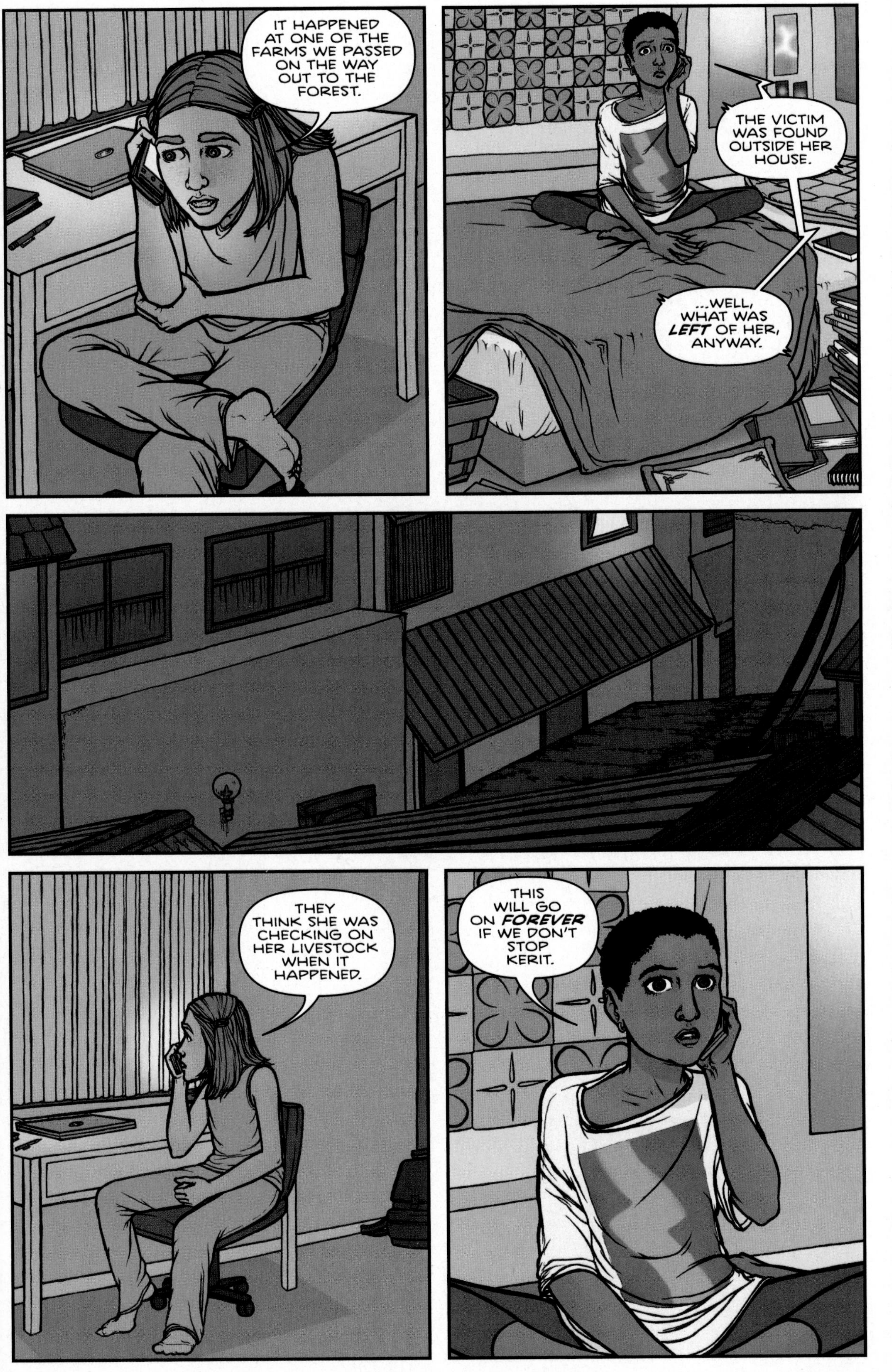
IT HAPPENED AT ONE OF THE FARMS WE PASSED ON THE WAY OUT TO THE FOREST.
THE VICTIM WAS FOUND OUTSIDE HER HOUSE.
...WELL, WHAT WAS *LEFT* OF HER, ANYWAY.
THEY THINK SHE WAS CHECKING ON HER LIVESTOCK WHEN IT HAPPENED.
THIS WILL GO ON *FOREVER* IF WE DON'T STOP KERIT.

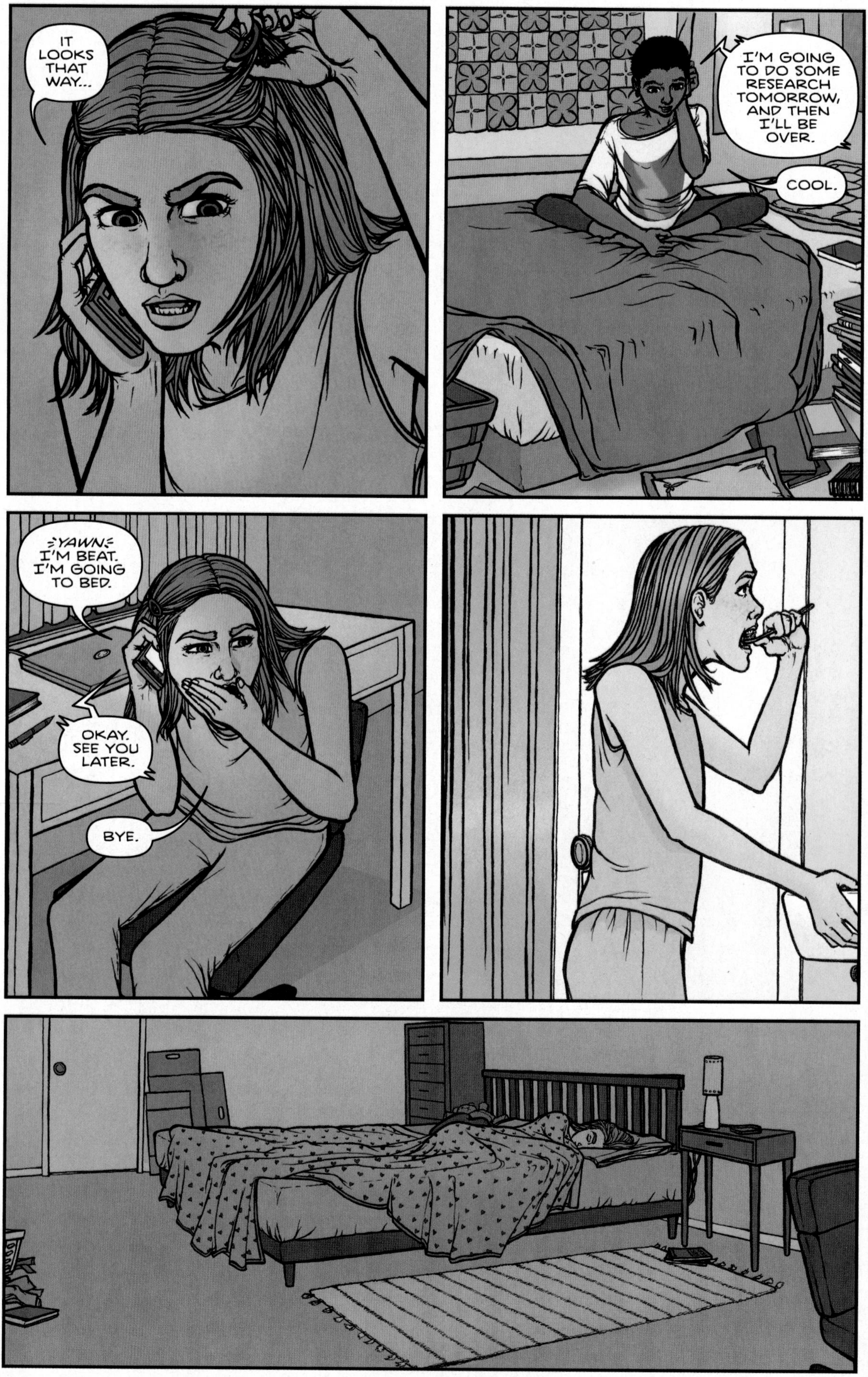
IT LOOKS THAT WAY...
I'M GOING TO DO SOME RESEARCH TOMORROW, AND THEN I'LL BE OVER.
COOL.
YAWN
I'M BEAT. I'M GOING TO BED.
OKAY. SEE YOU LATER.
BYE.

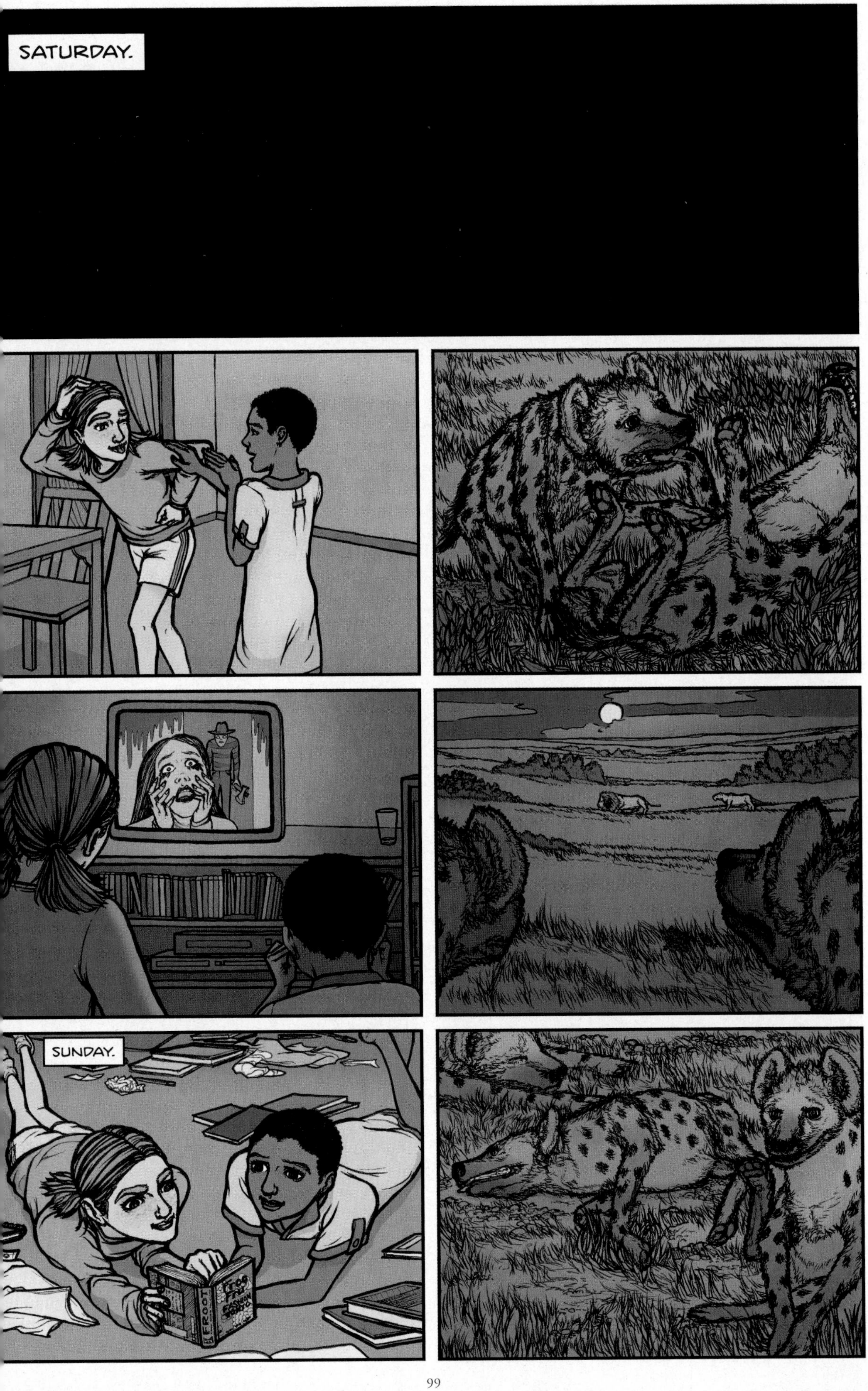
SATURDAY.
SUNDAY.

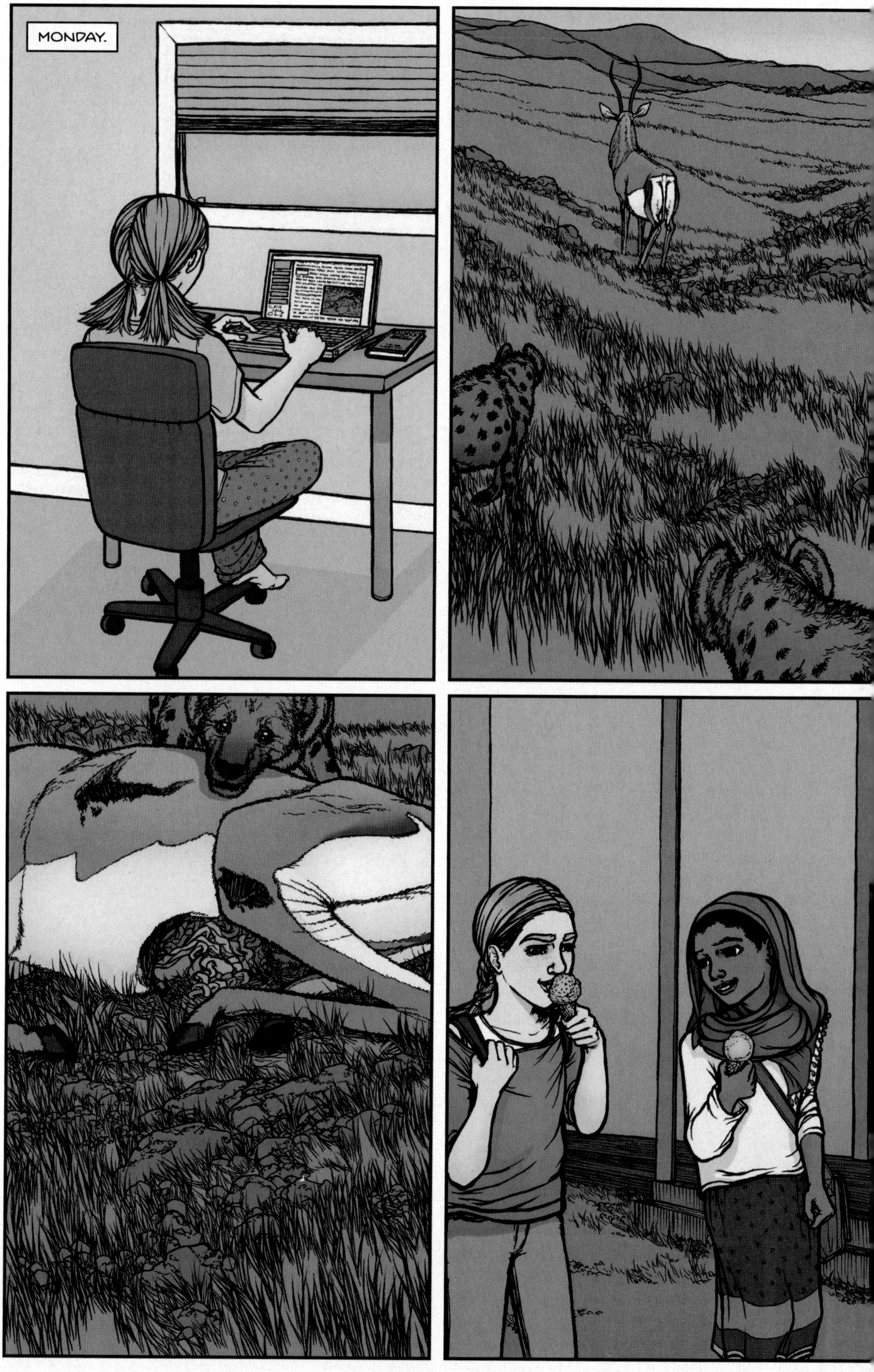
MONDAY.

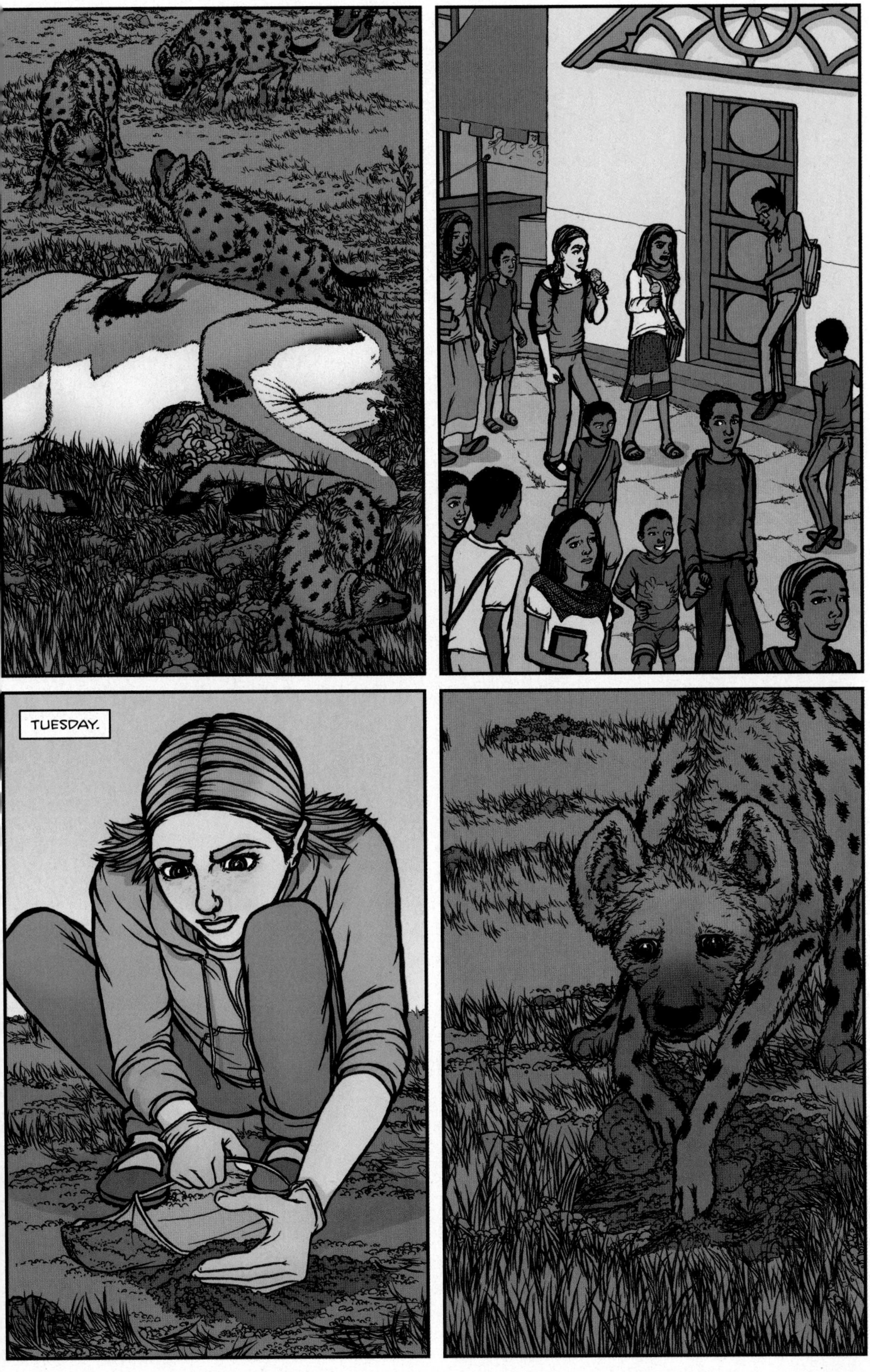
TUESDAY.

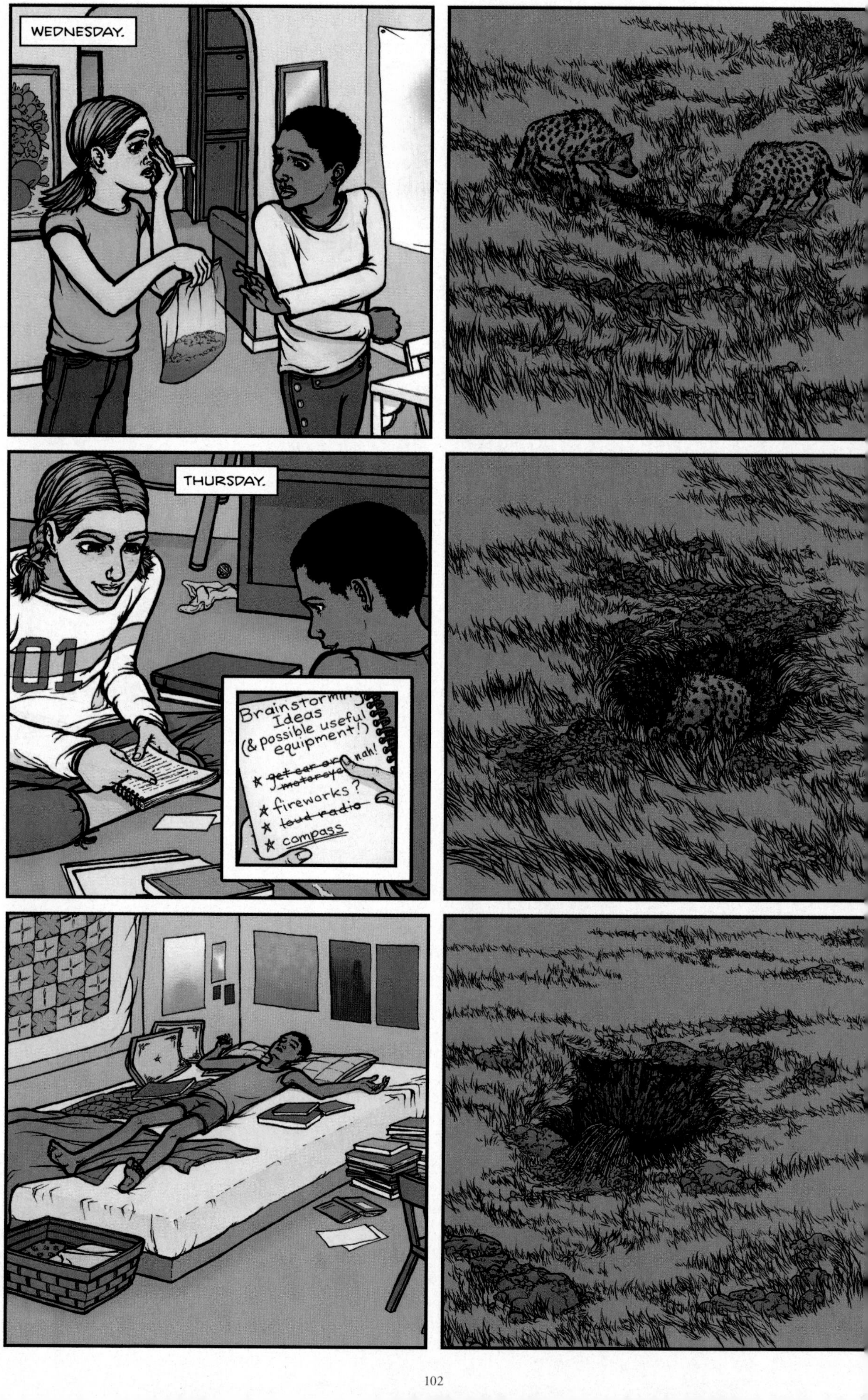
WEDNESDAY.
THURSDAY.
Brainstormin
Ideas
(& possible useful equipment!)
★ ~~get car or~~ nah!
★ fireworks?
★ ~~loud radio~~
★ compass

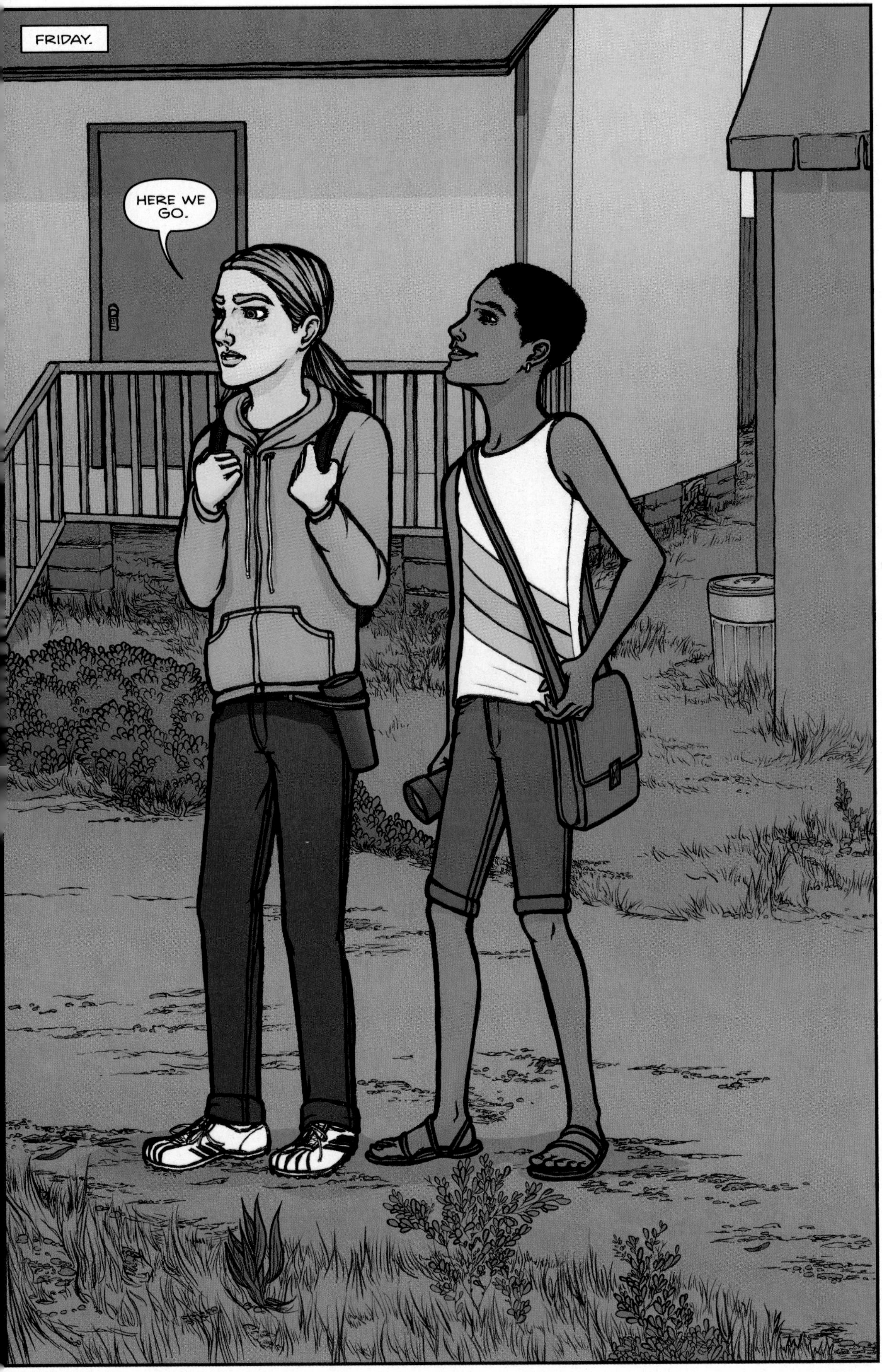
FRIDAY.
HERE WE GO.

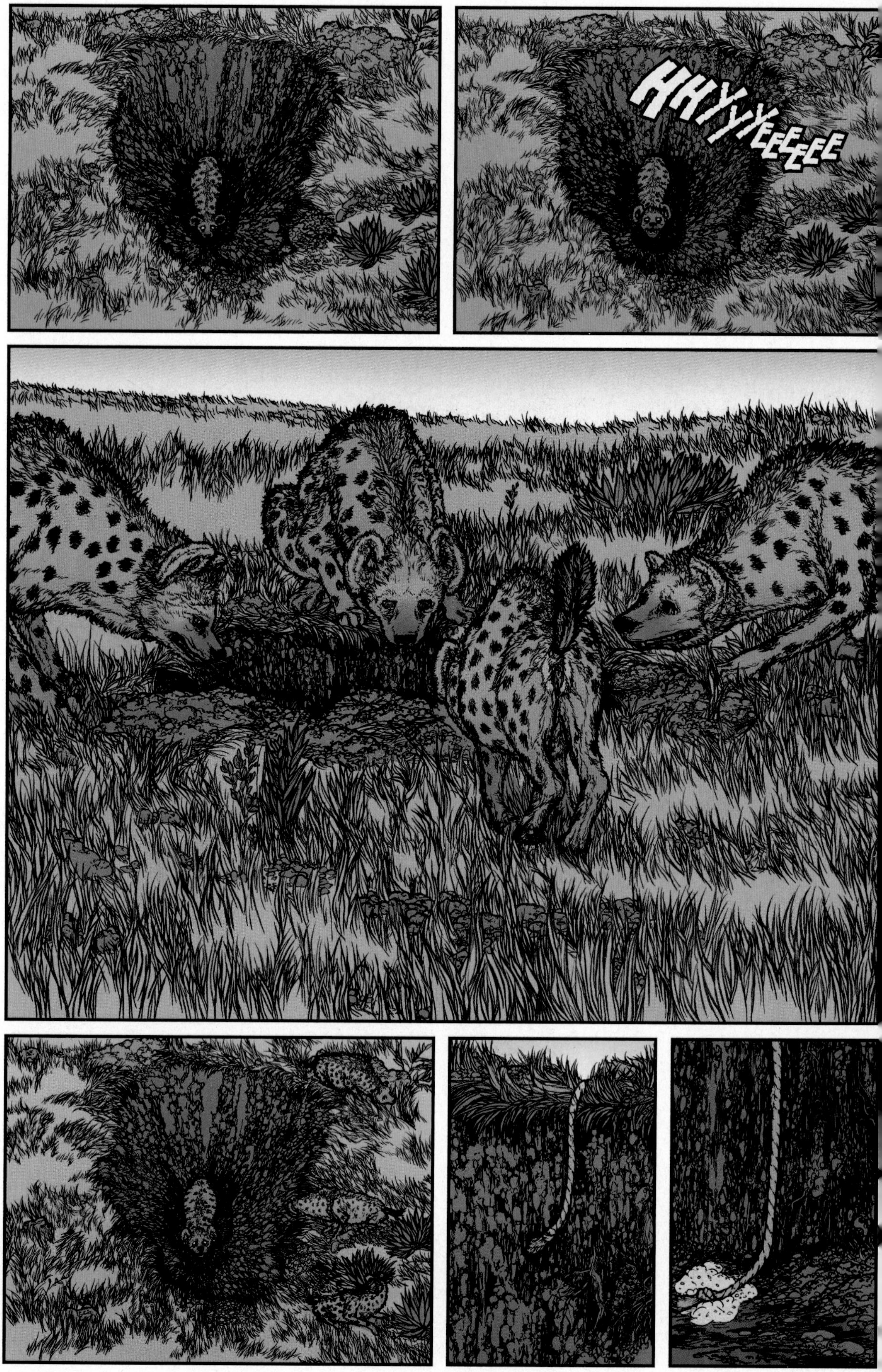
HHYYYYEEEEEE

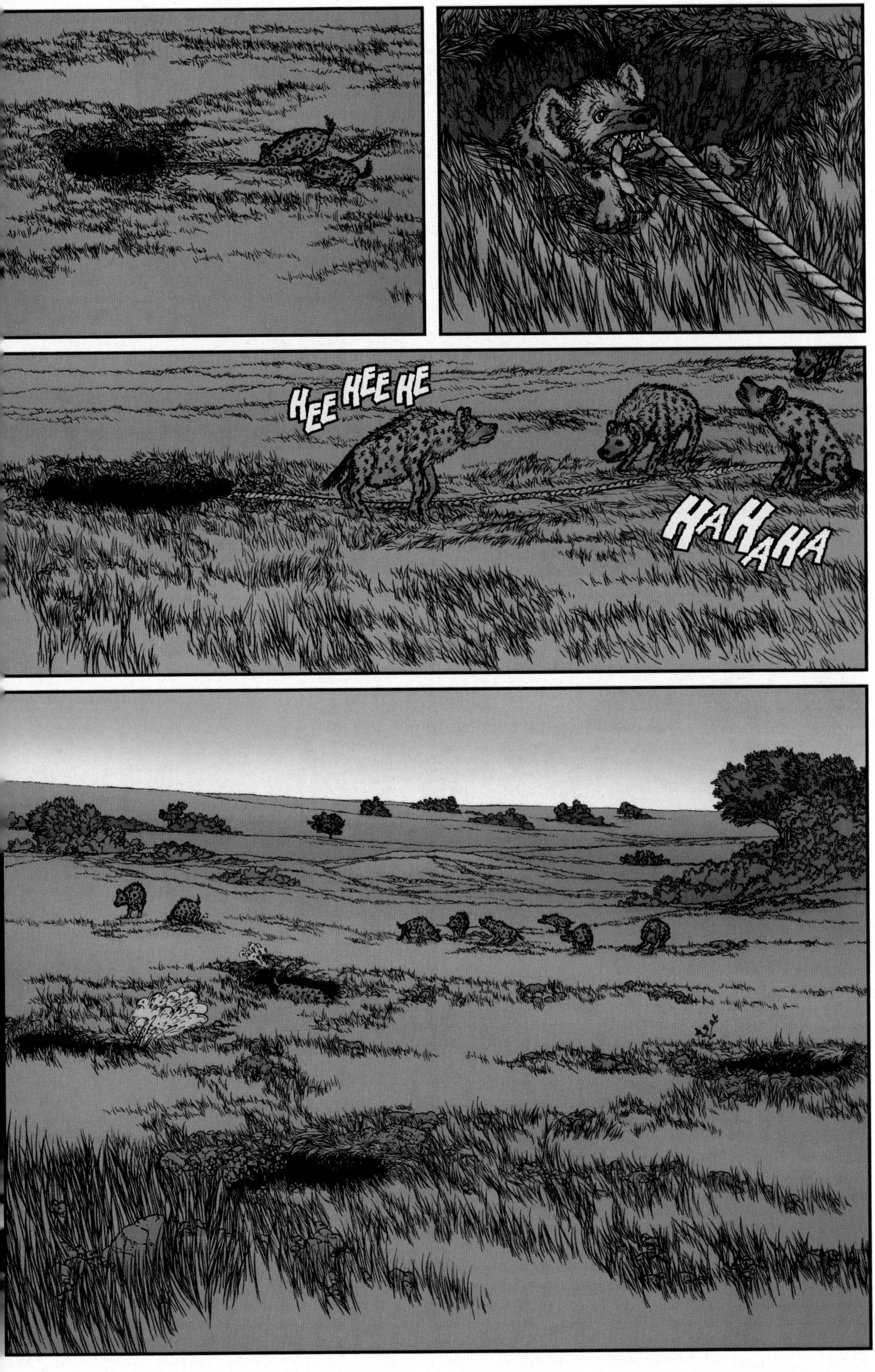
HEE HEE HE
HAHAHAHA

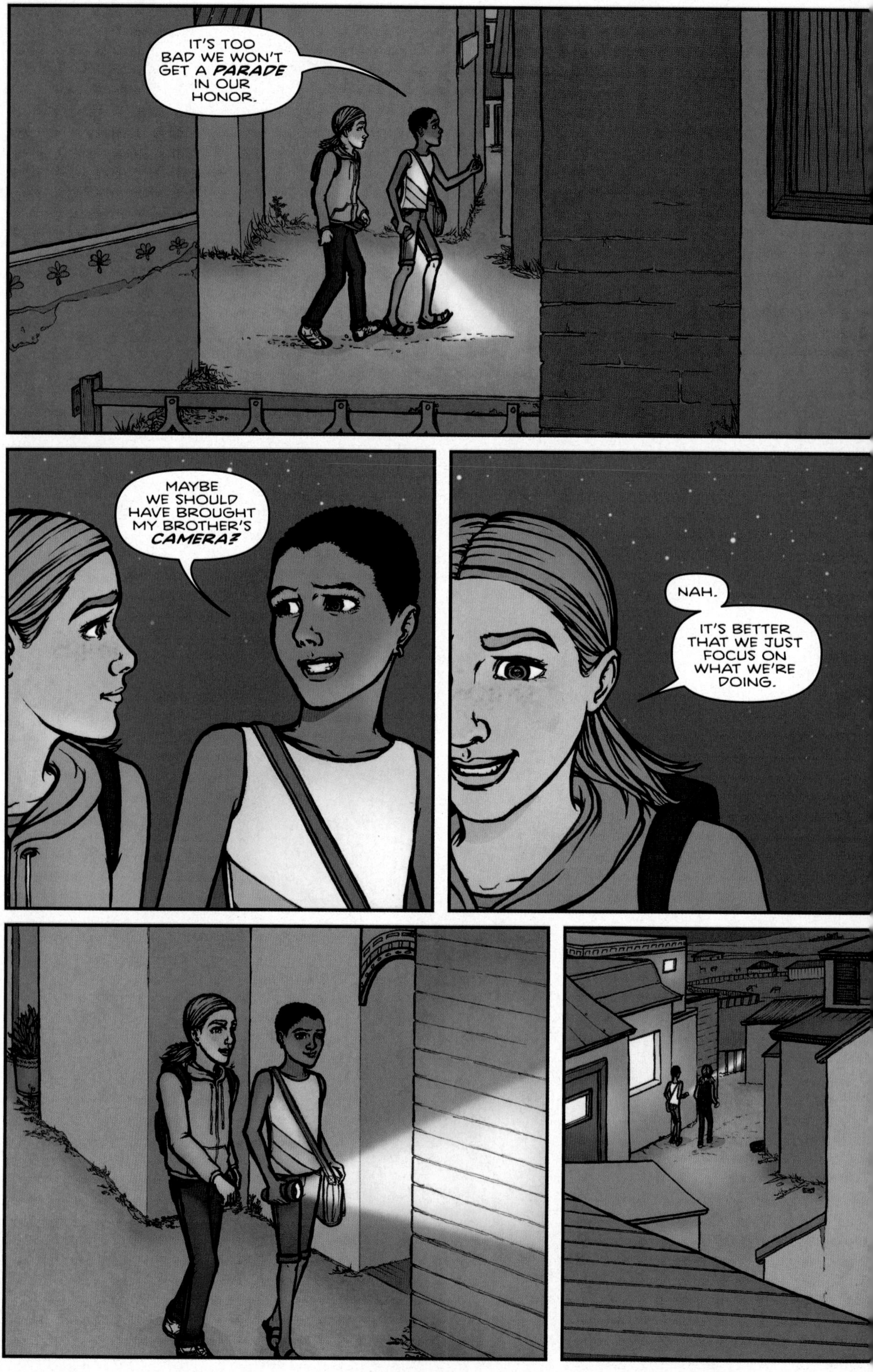
IT'S TOO BAD WE WON'T GET A *PARADE* IN OUR HONOR.
MAYBE WE SHOULD HAVE BROUGHT MY BROTHER'S *CAMERA?*
NAH.
IT'S BETTER THAT WE JUST FOCUS ON WHAT WE'RE DOING.

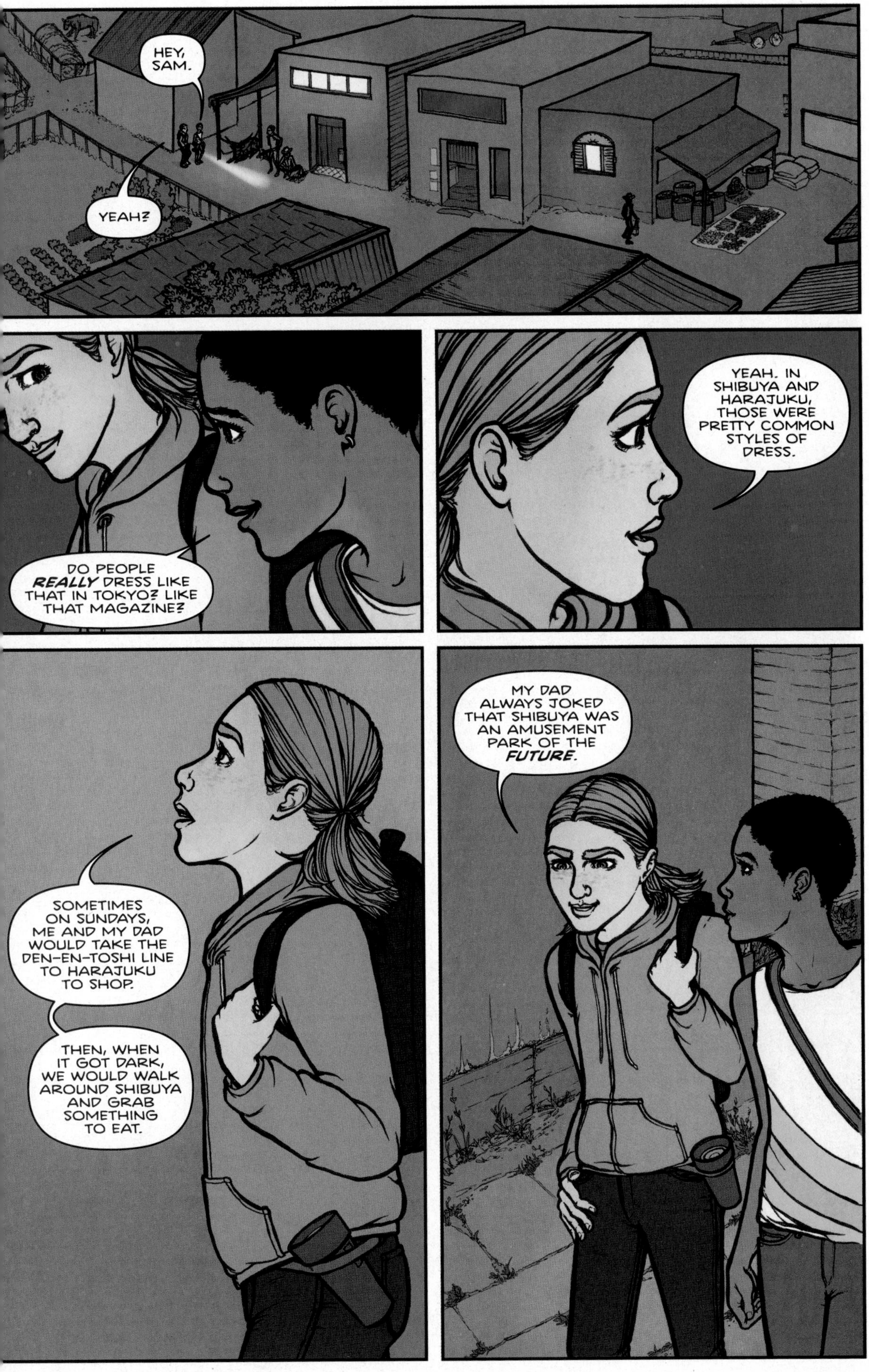
HEY, SAM.
YEAH?
DO PEOPLE *REALLY* DRESS LIKE THAT IN TOKYO? LIKE THAT MAGAZINE?
YEAH. IN SHIBUYA AND HARAJUKU, THOSE WERE PRETTY COMMON STYLES OF DRESS.
SOMETIMES ON SUNDAYS, ME AND MY DAD WOULD TAKE THE DEN-EN-TOSHI LINE TO HARAJUKU TO SHOP.
THEN, WHEN IT GOT DARK, WE WOULD WALK AROUND SHIBUYA AND GRAB SOMETHING TO EAT.
MY DAD ALWAYS JOKED THAT SHIBUYA WAS AN AMUSEMENT PARK OF THE *FUTURE*.

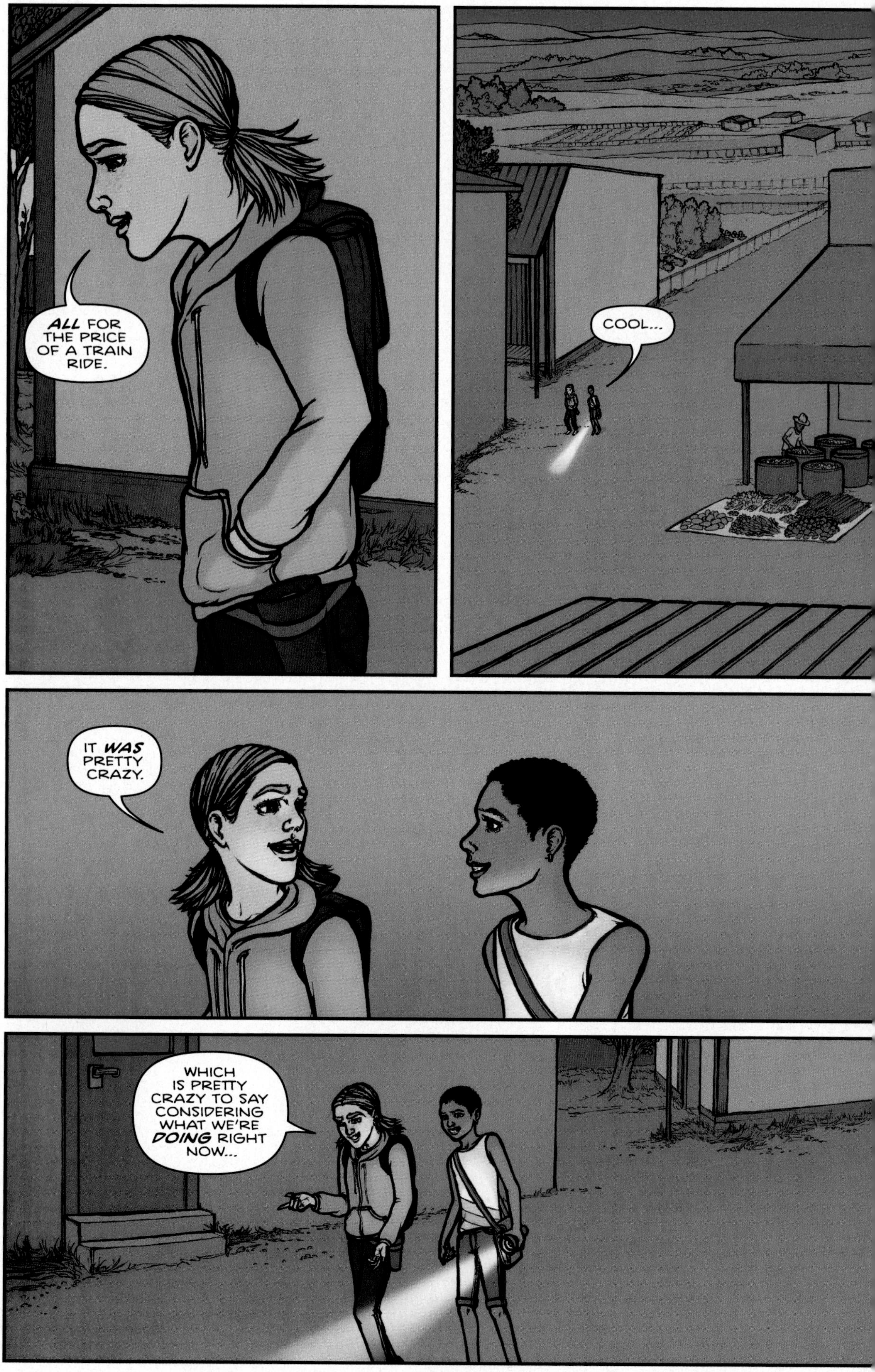
ALL FOR THE PRICE OF A TRAIN RIDE.
COOL...
IT WAS PRETTY CRAZY.
WHICH IS PRETTY CRAZY TO SAY CONSIDERING WHAT WE'RE DOING RIGHT NOW...

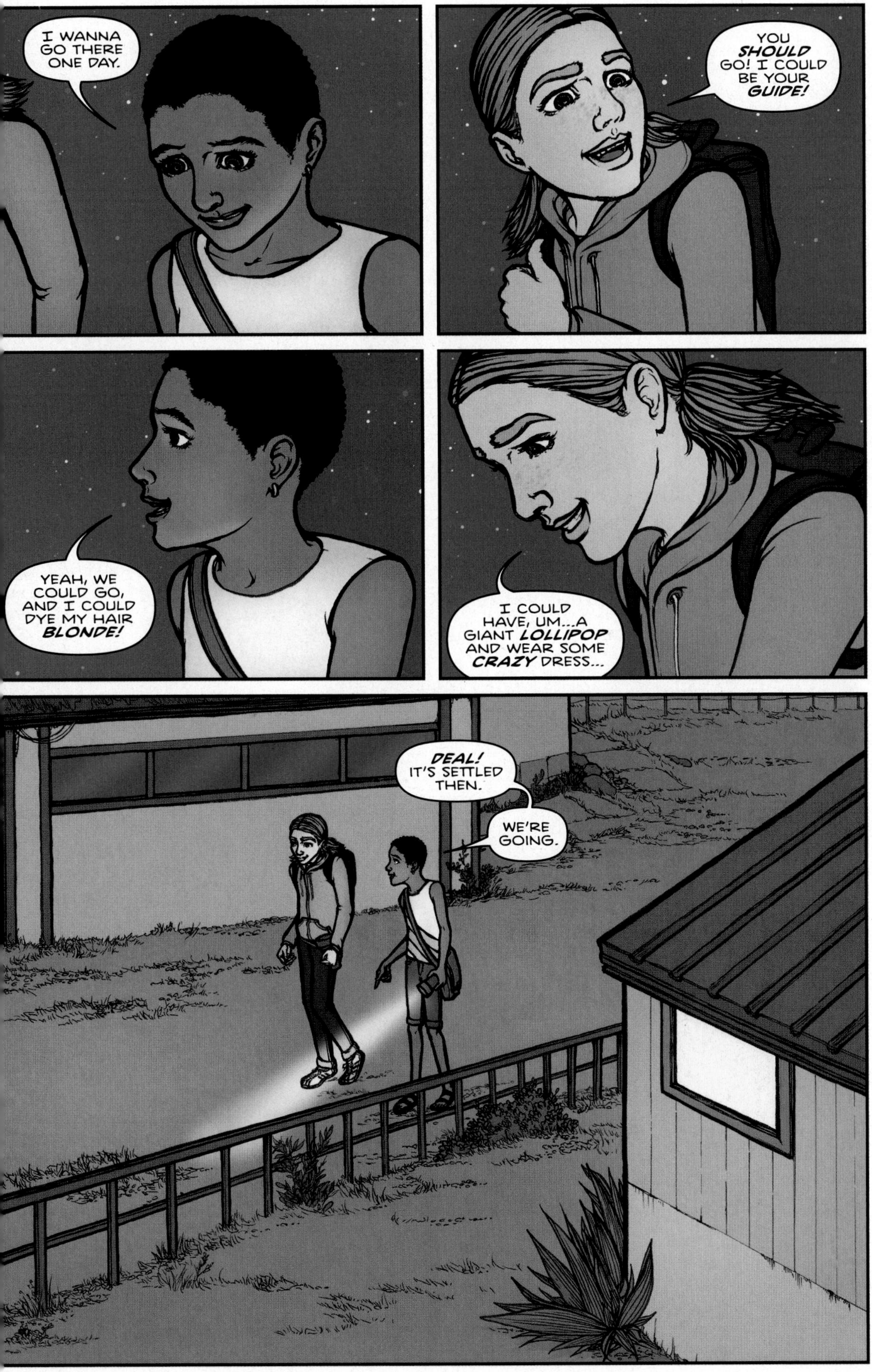
I WANNA GO THERE ONE DAY.
YOU SHOULD GO! I COULD BE YOUR GUIDE!
YEAH, WE COULD GO, AND I COULD DYE MY HAIR BLONDE!
I COULD HAVE, UM...A GIANT LOLLIPOP AND WEAR SOME CRAZY DRESS...
DEAL! IT'S SETTLED THEN.
WE'RE GOING.

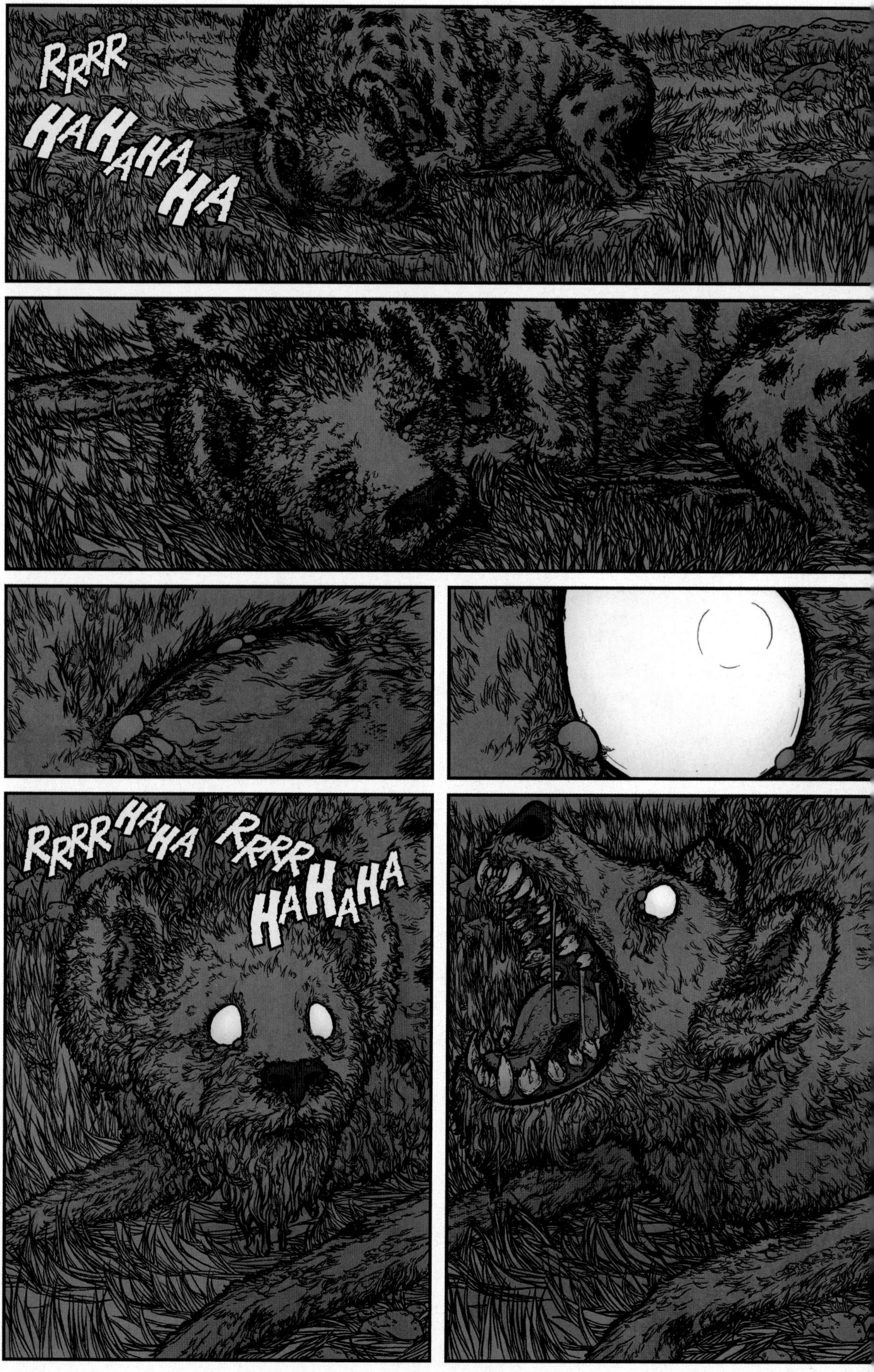
RRRR
HAHAHAHAHA
RRRRHAHA
RRRR
HAHAHA

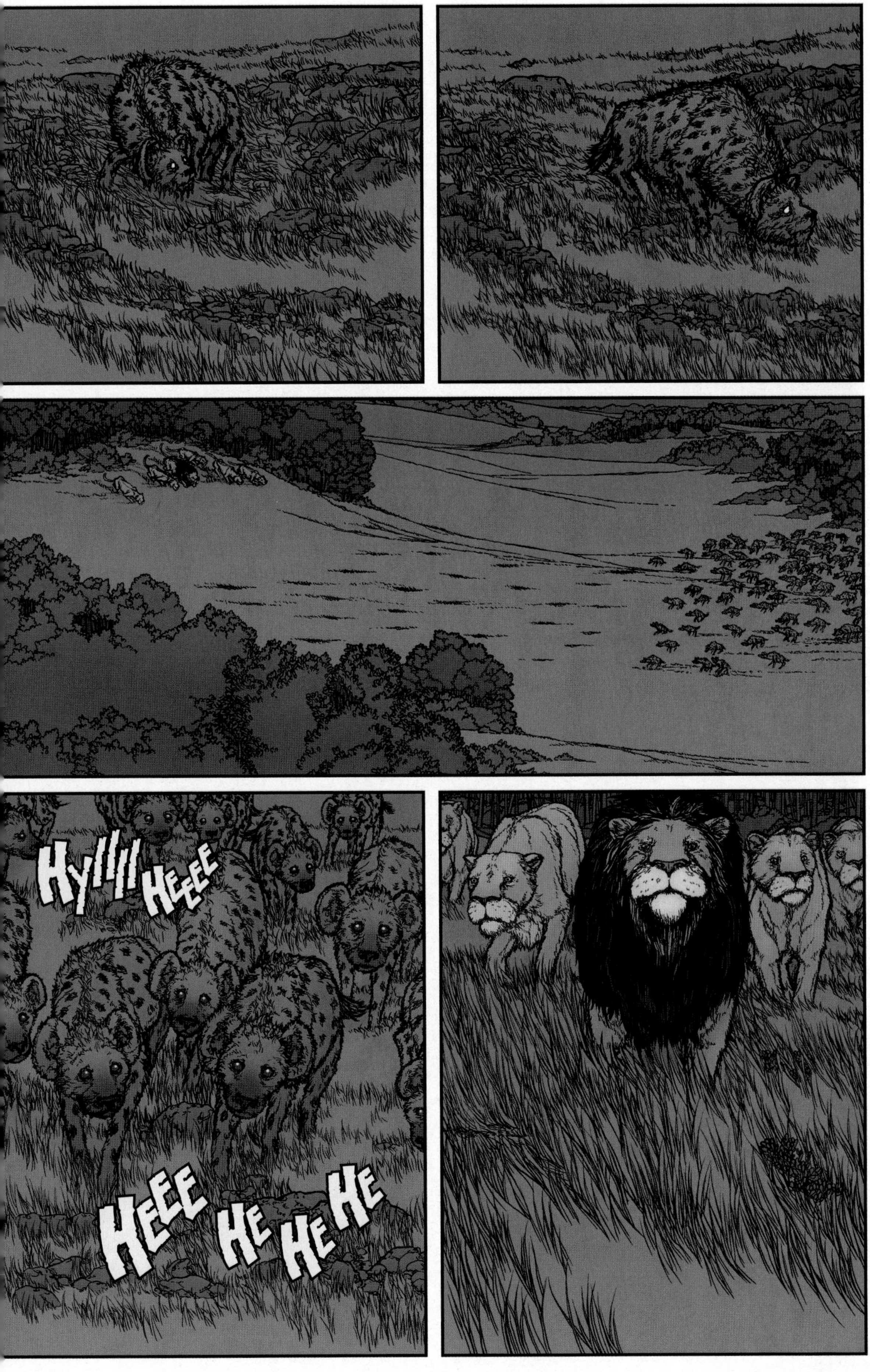
HYIIII HEEEE
HEEE HE HE HE

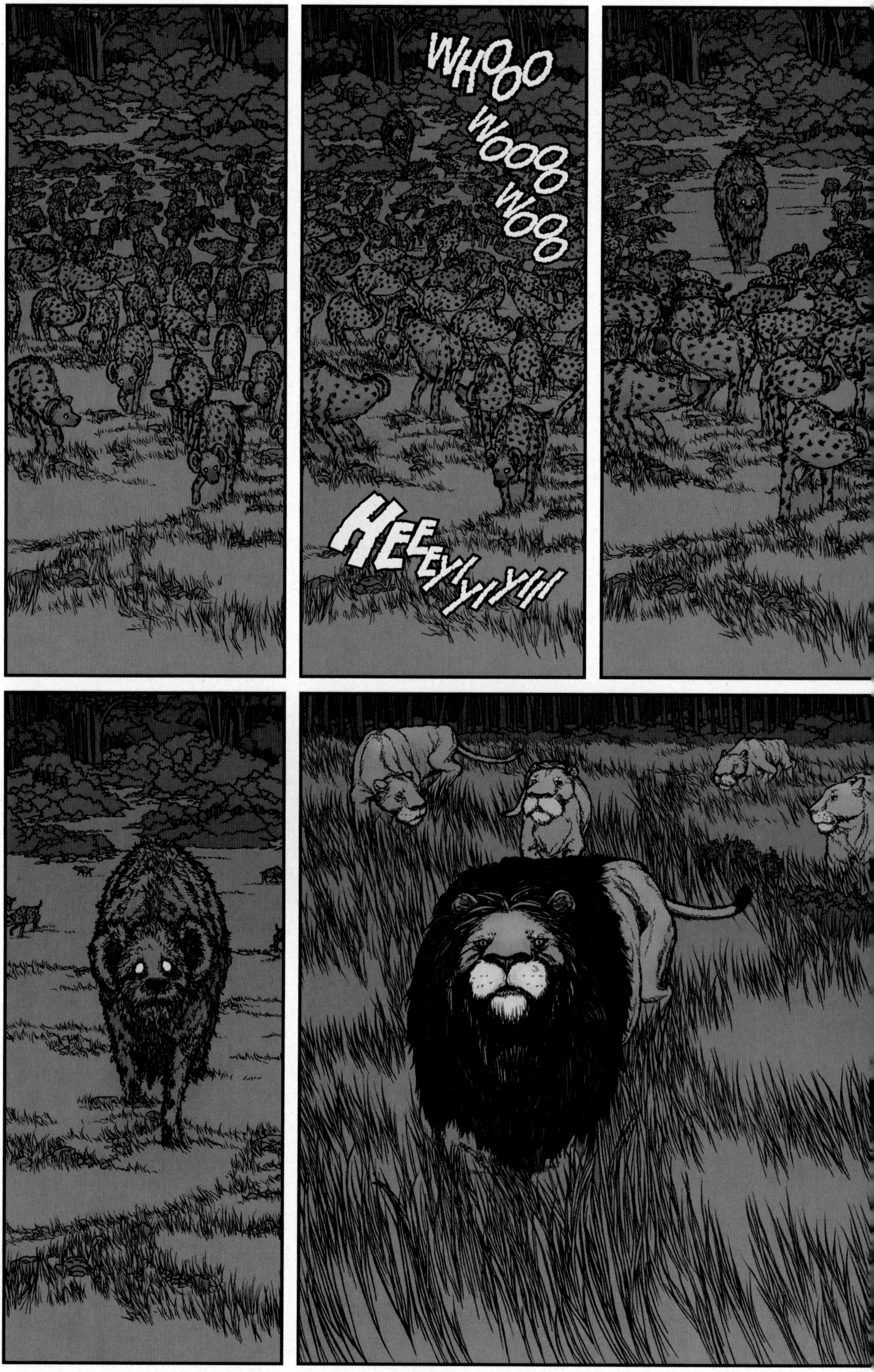
WHOOO
WOOOO
WOOO
HEEEYIIYIIYIII

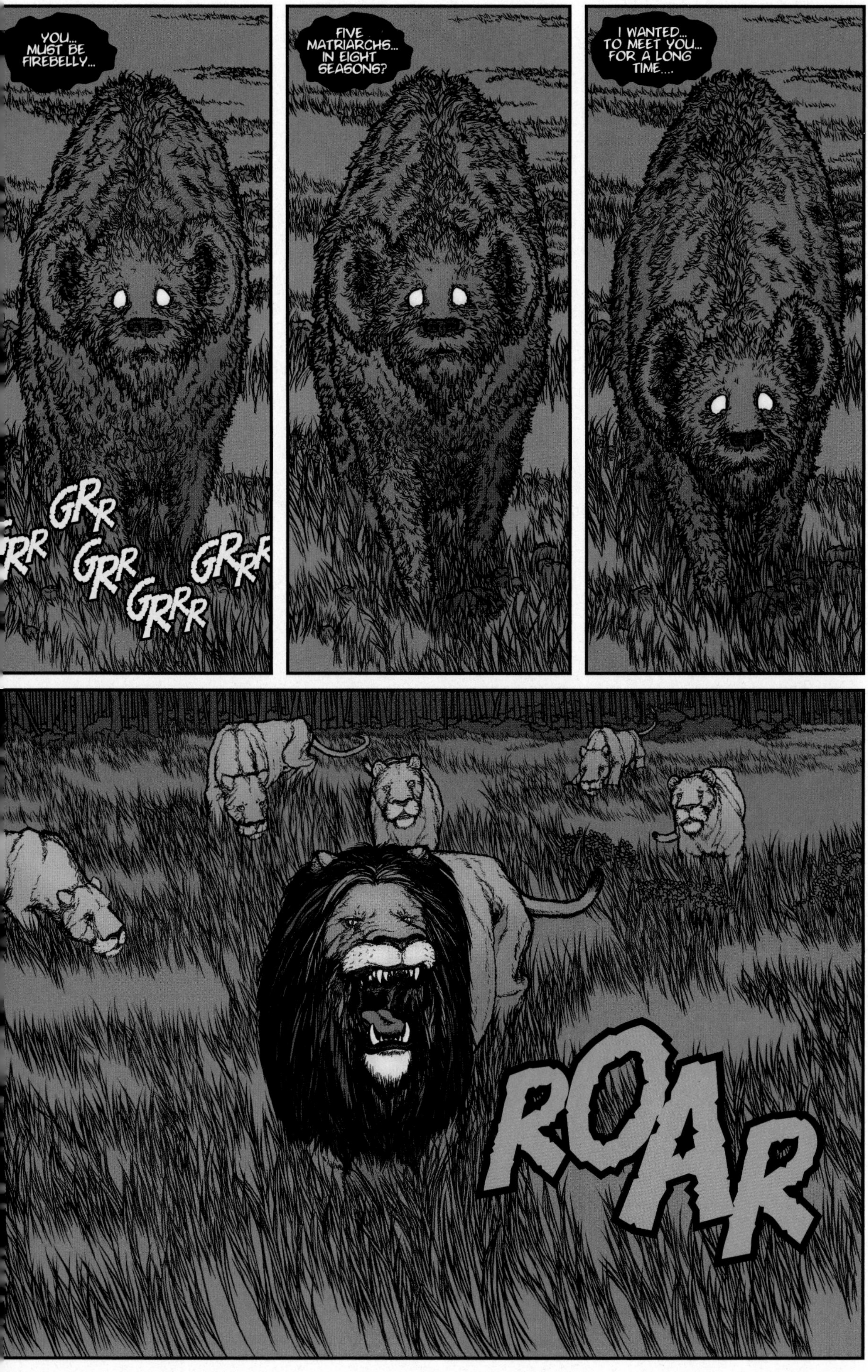
YOU... MUST BE FIREBELLY...
GRR GRR GRR GRRR GRRR
FIVE MATRIARCHS... IN EIGHT SEASONS?
I WANTED... TO MEET YOU... FOR A LONG TIME....
ROAR

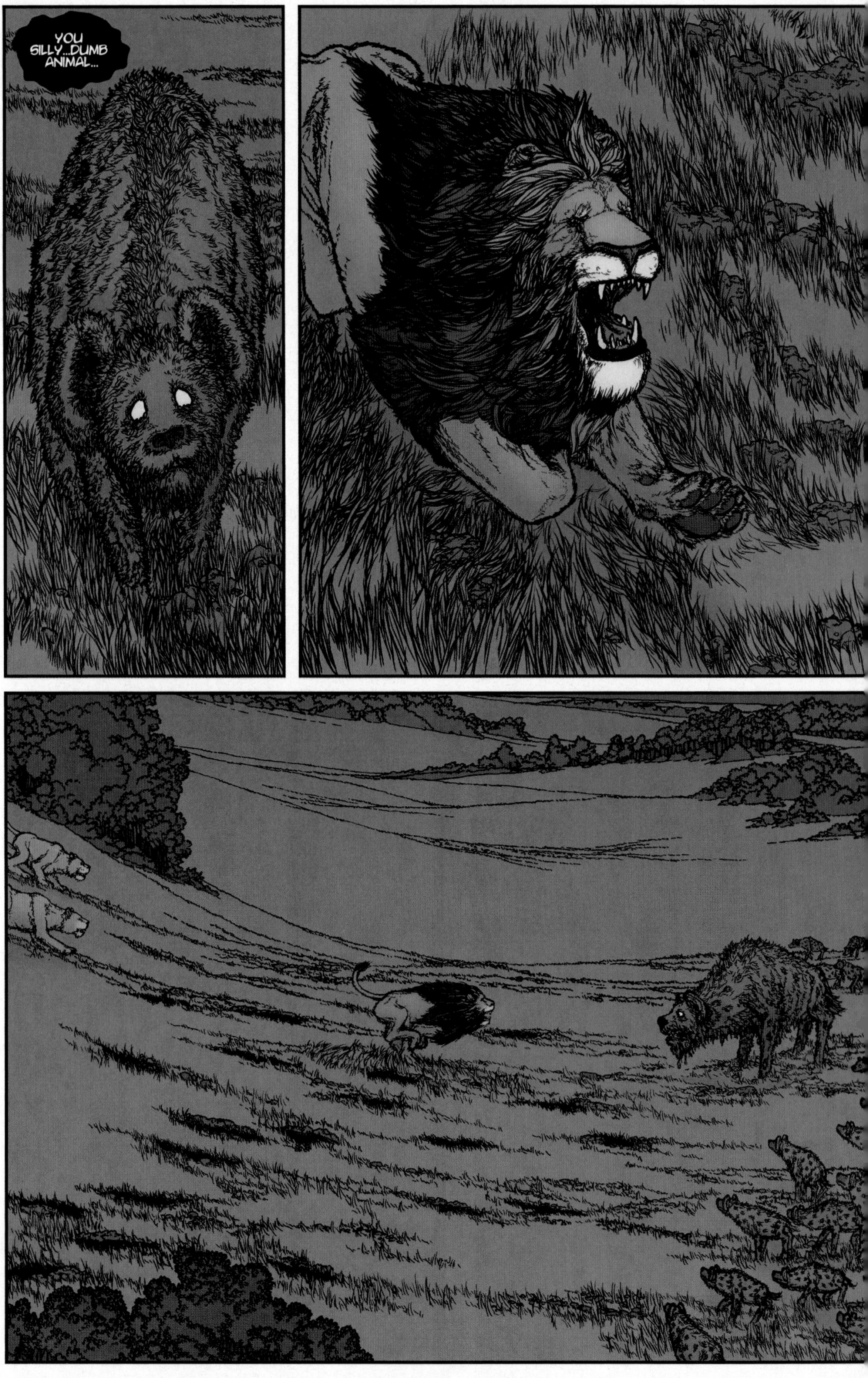
YOU SILLY...DUMB ANIMAL...

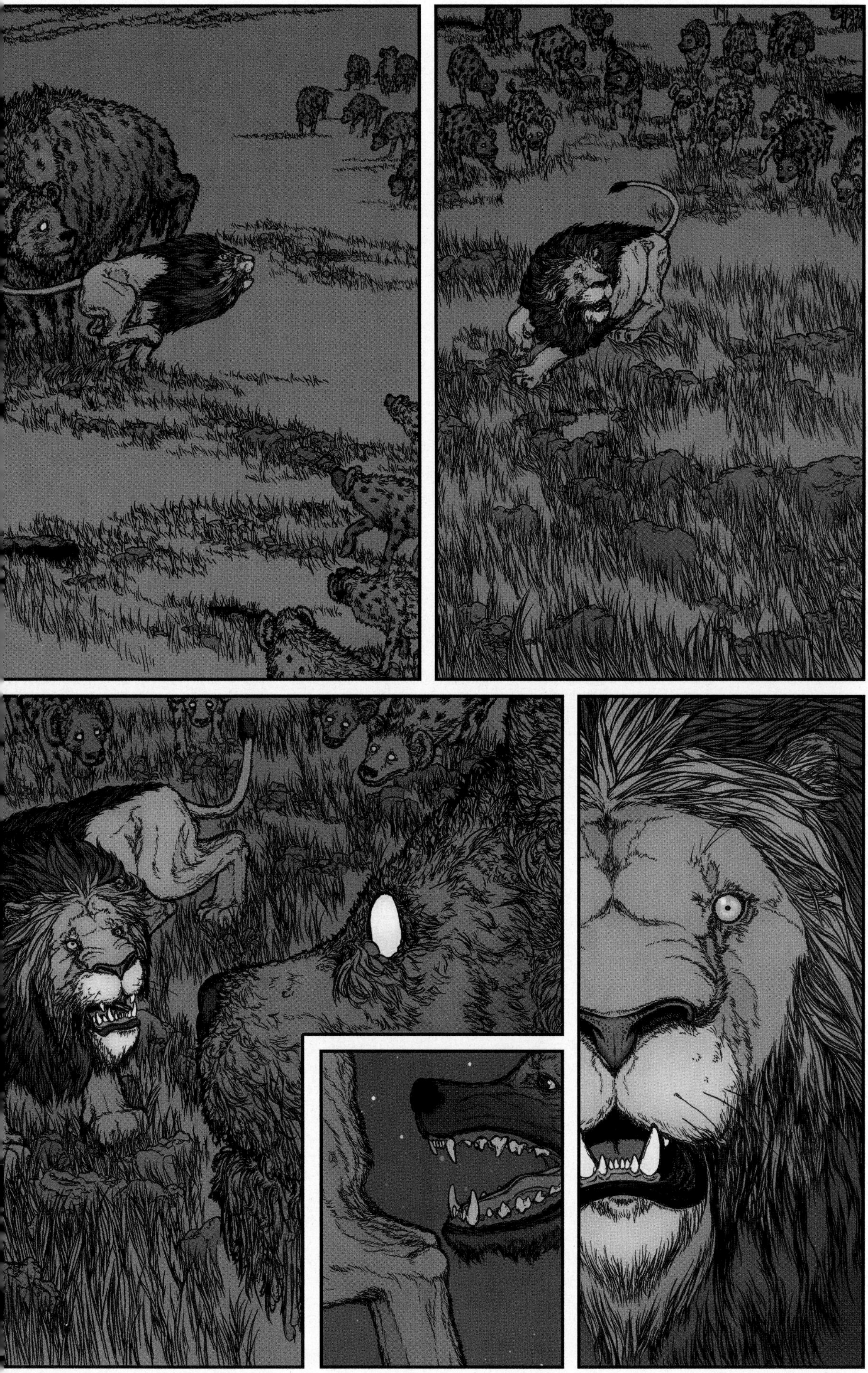

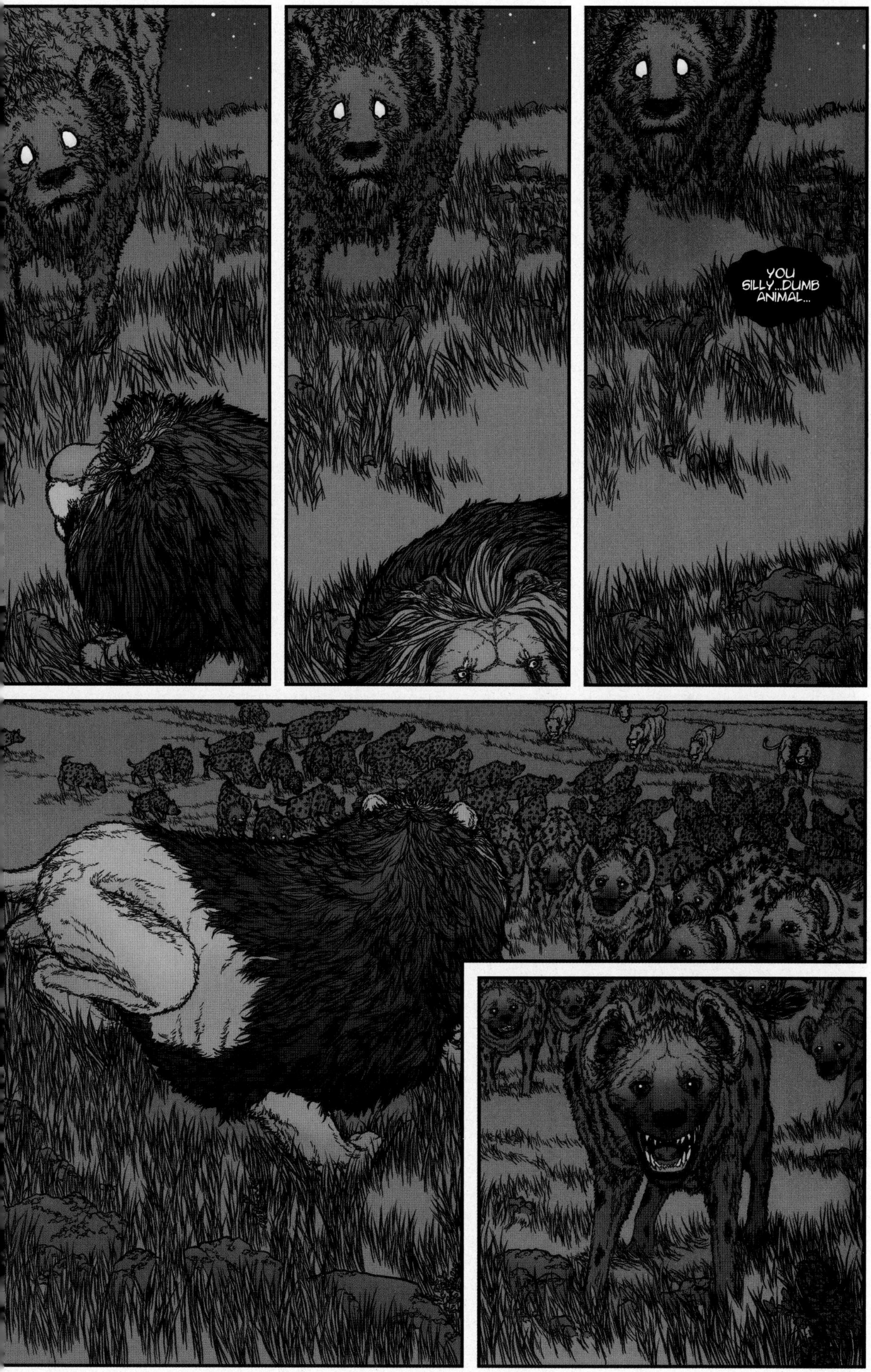
YOU SILLY...DUMB ANIMAL...

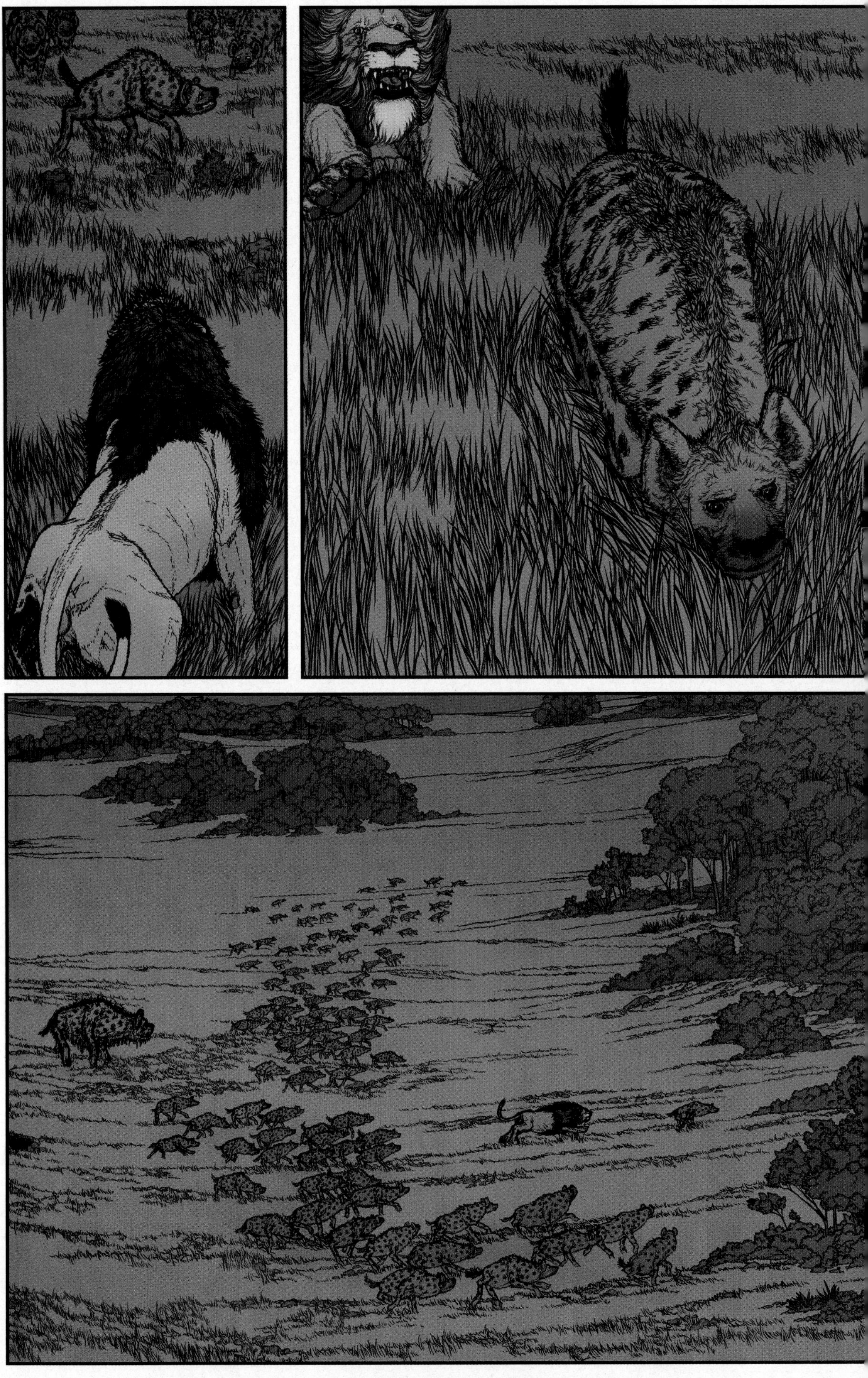

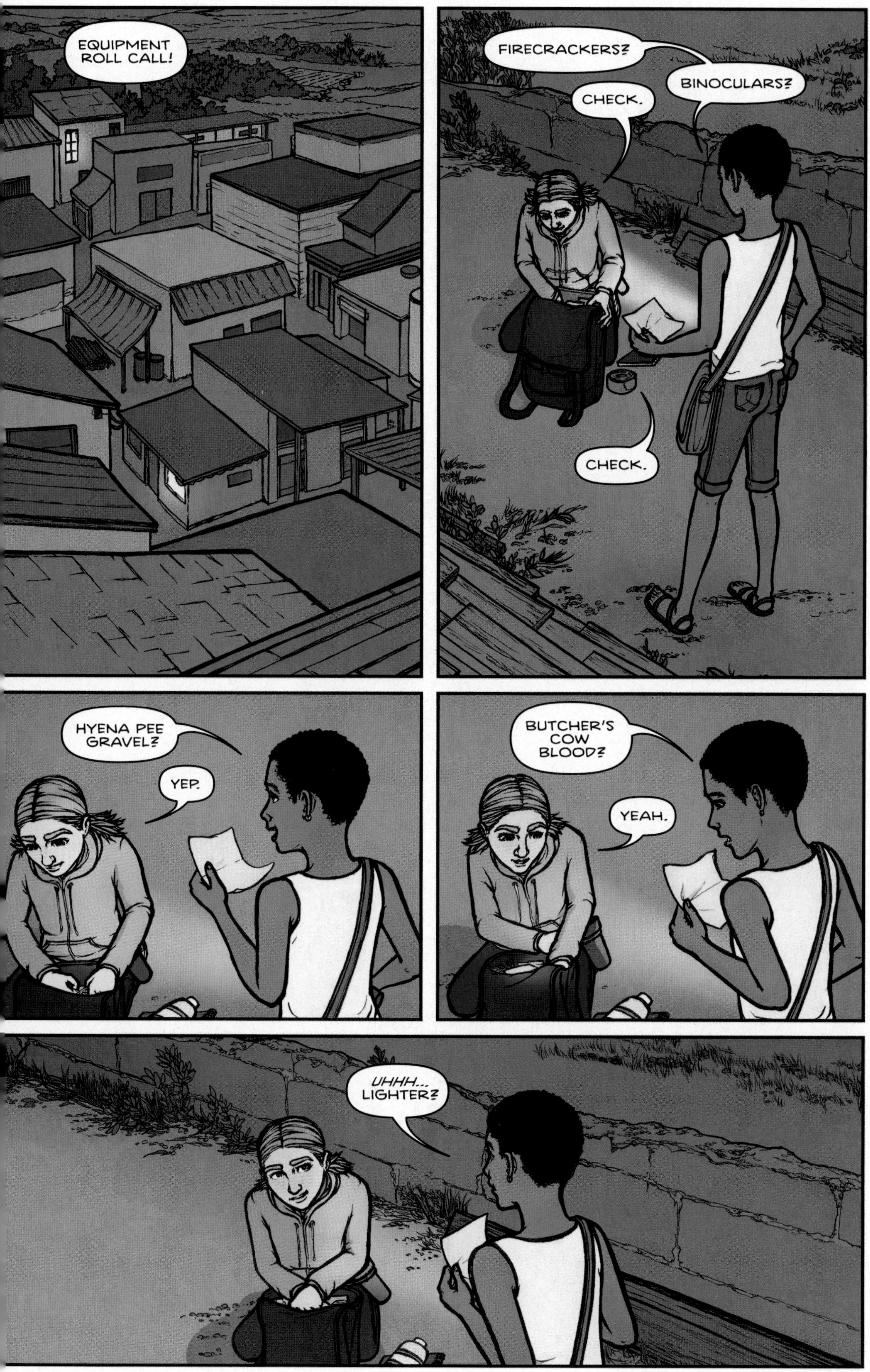
EQUIPMENT ROLL CALL!
FIRECRACKERS?
CHECK.
BINOCULARS?
CHECK.
HYENA PEE GRAVEL?
YEP.
BUTCHER'S COW BLOOD?
YEAH.
UHHH... LIGHTER?

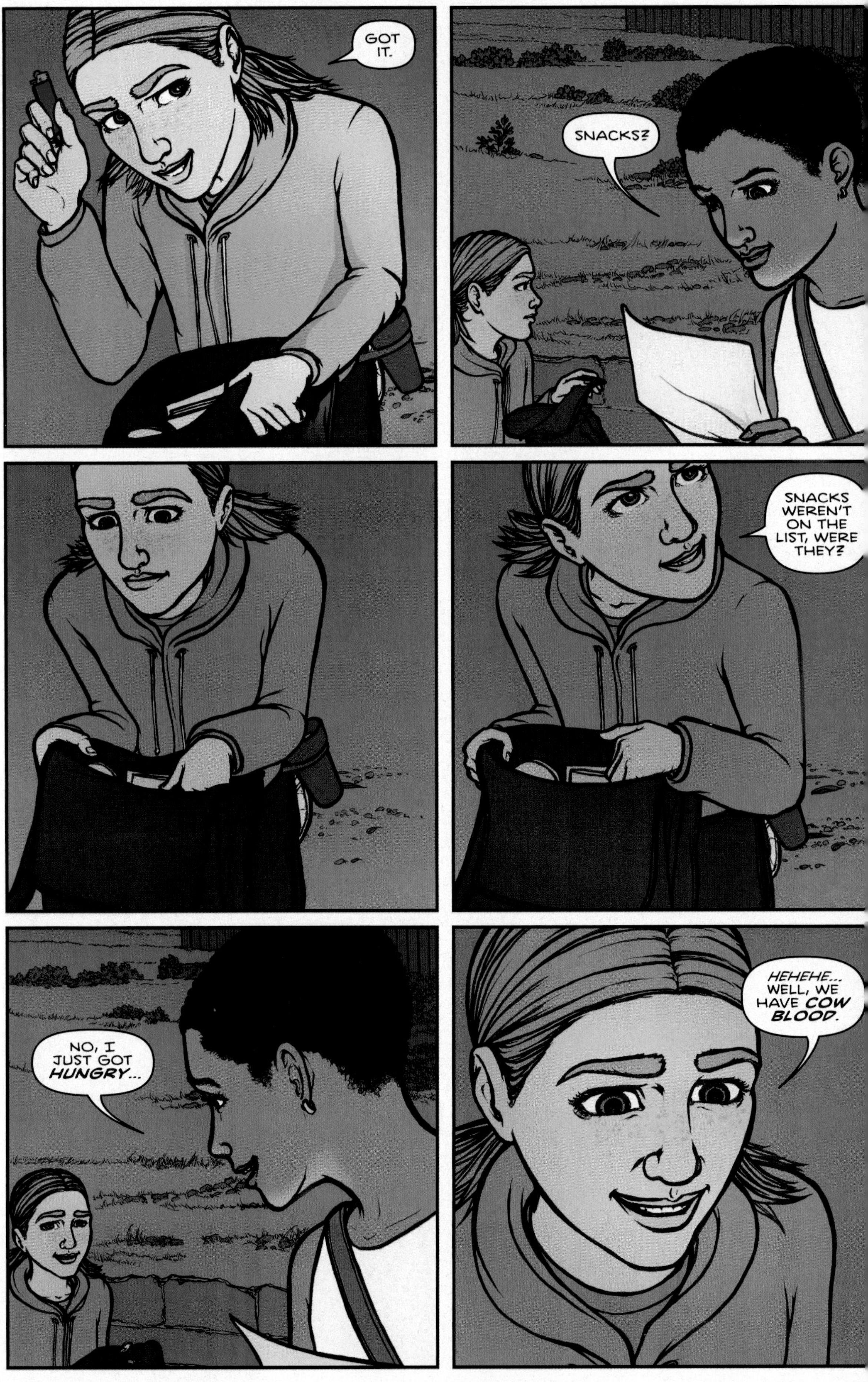
GOT IT.
SNACKS?
SNACKS WEREN'T ON THE LIST, WERE THEY?
NO, I JUST GOT *HUNGRY*...
HEHEHE... WELL, WE HAVE ***COW BLOOD***.

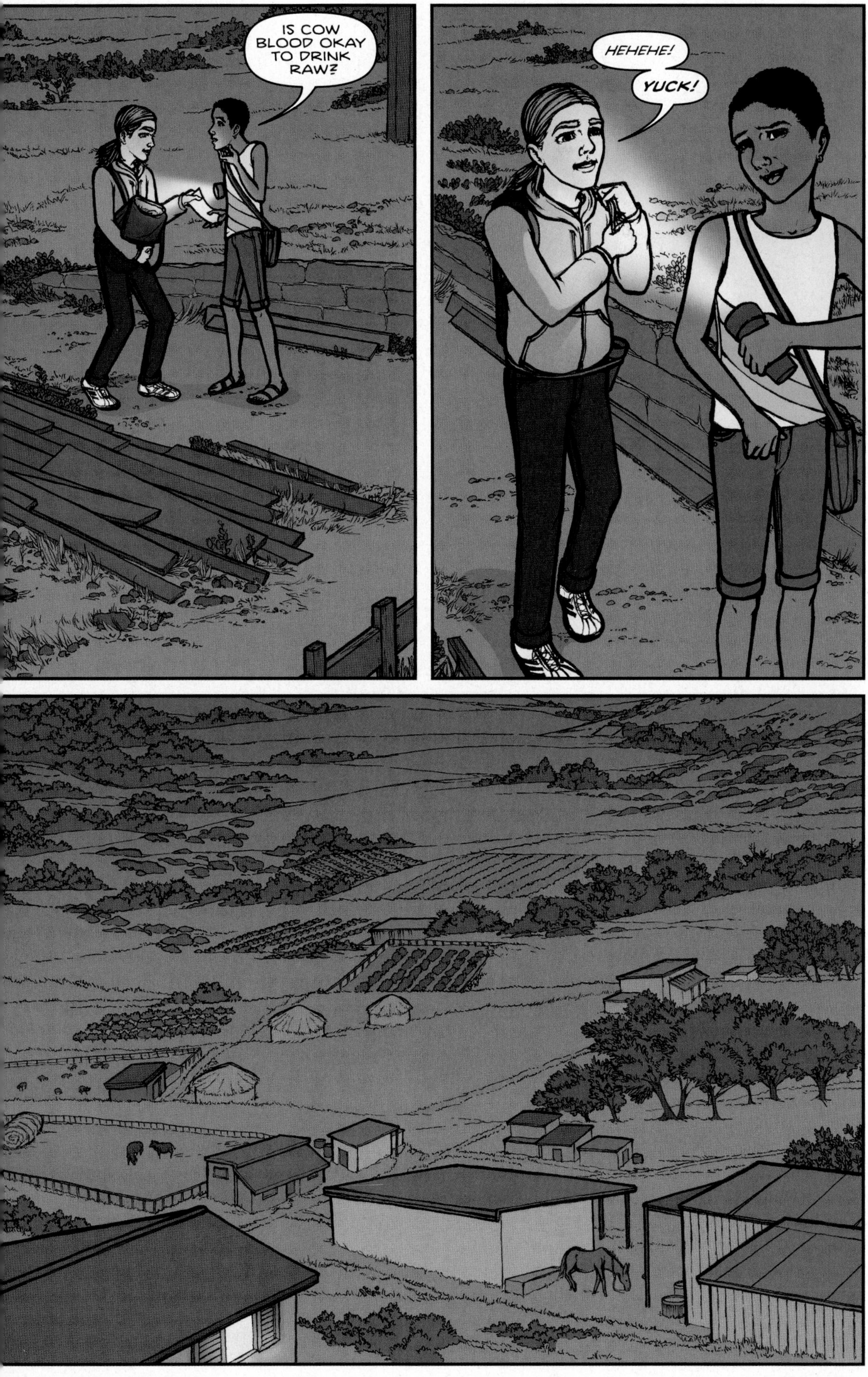
IS COW BLOOD OKAY TO DRINK RAW?
HEHEHE!
YUCK!

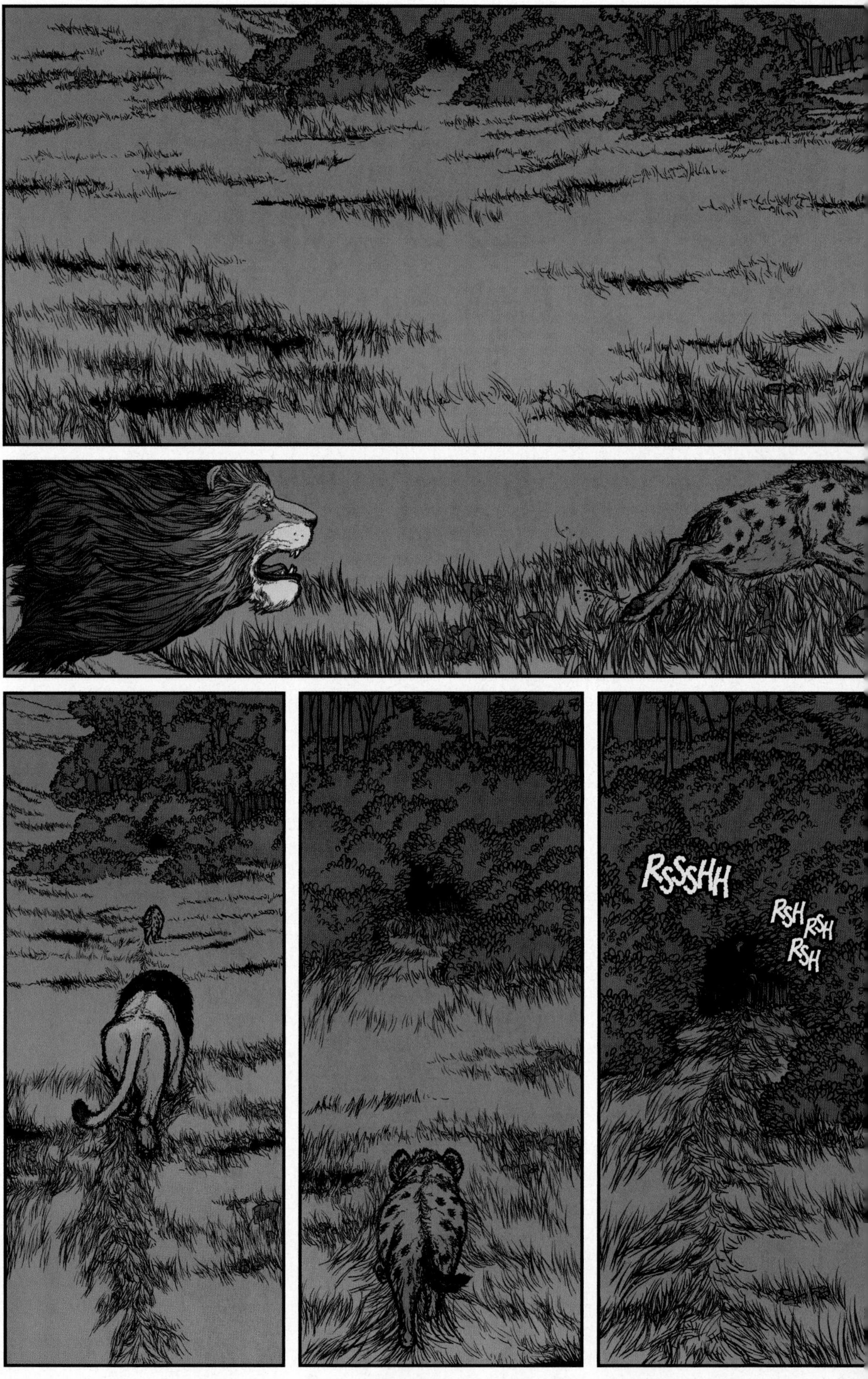

RSSSHH
RSH RSH
RSH

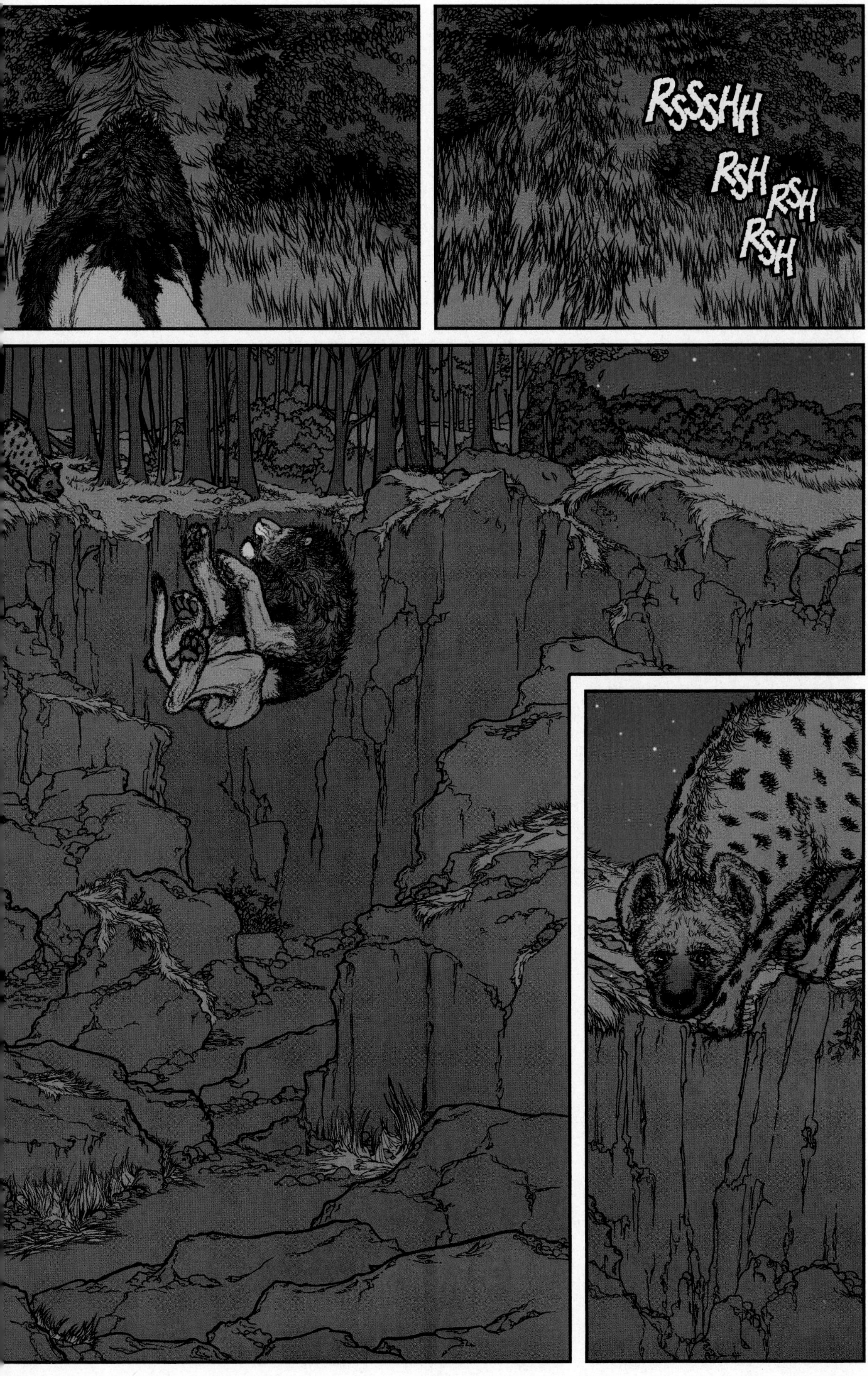
RSSSHH
RSH RSH
RSH

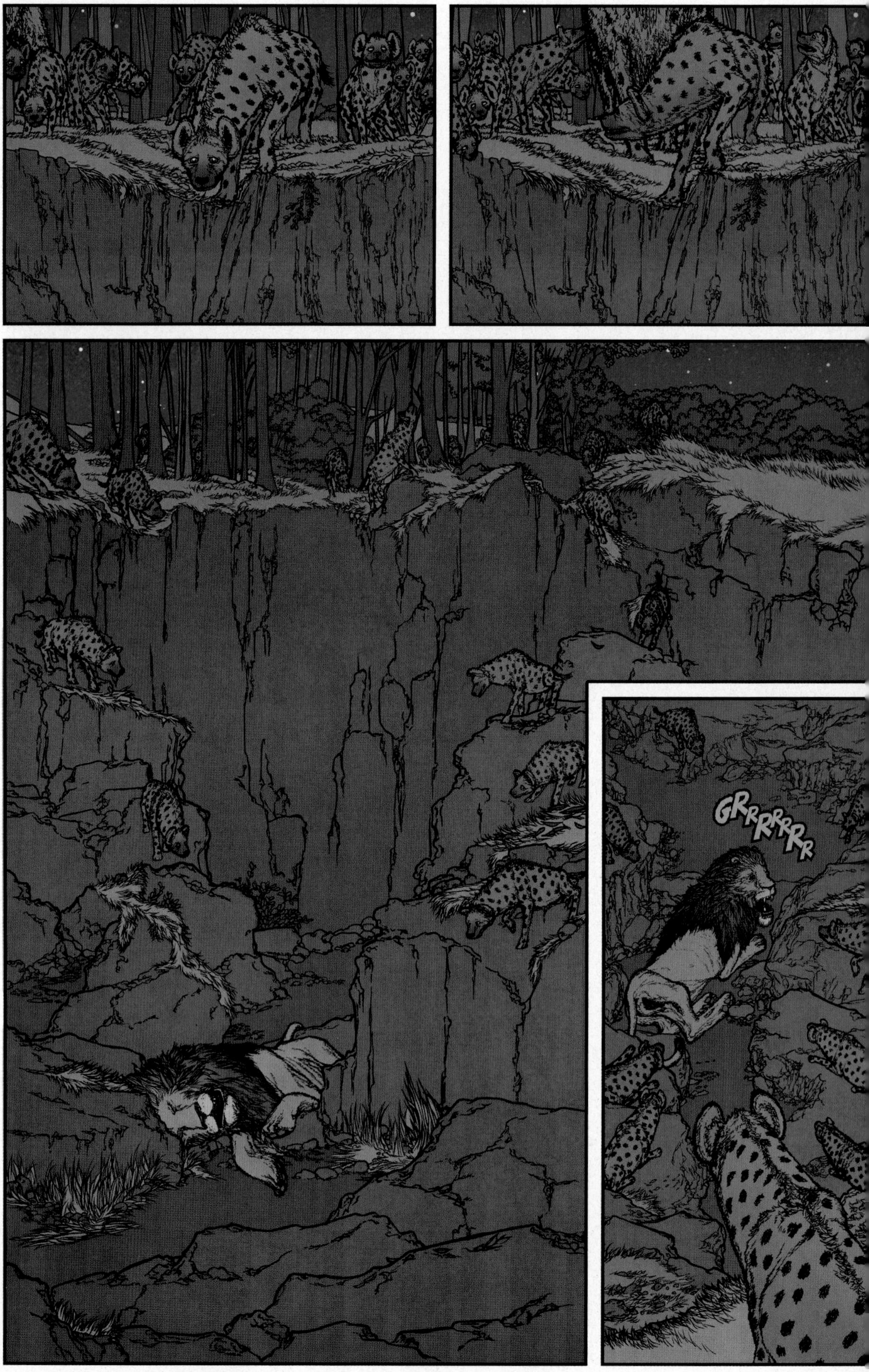
GRRRRRRR

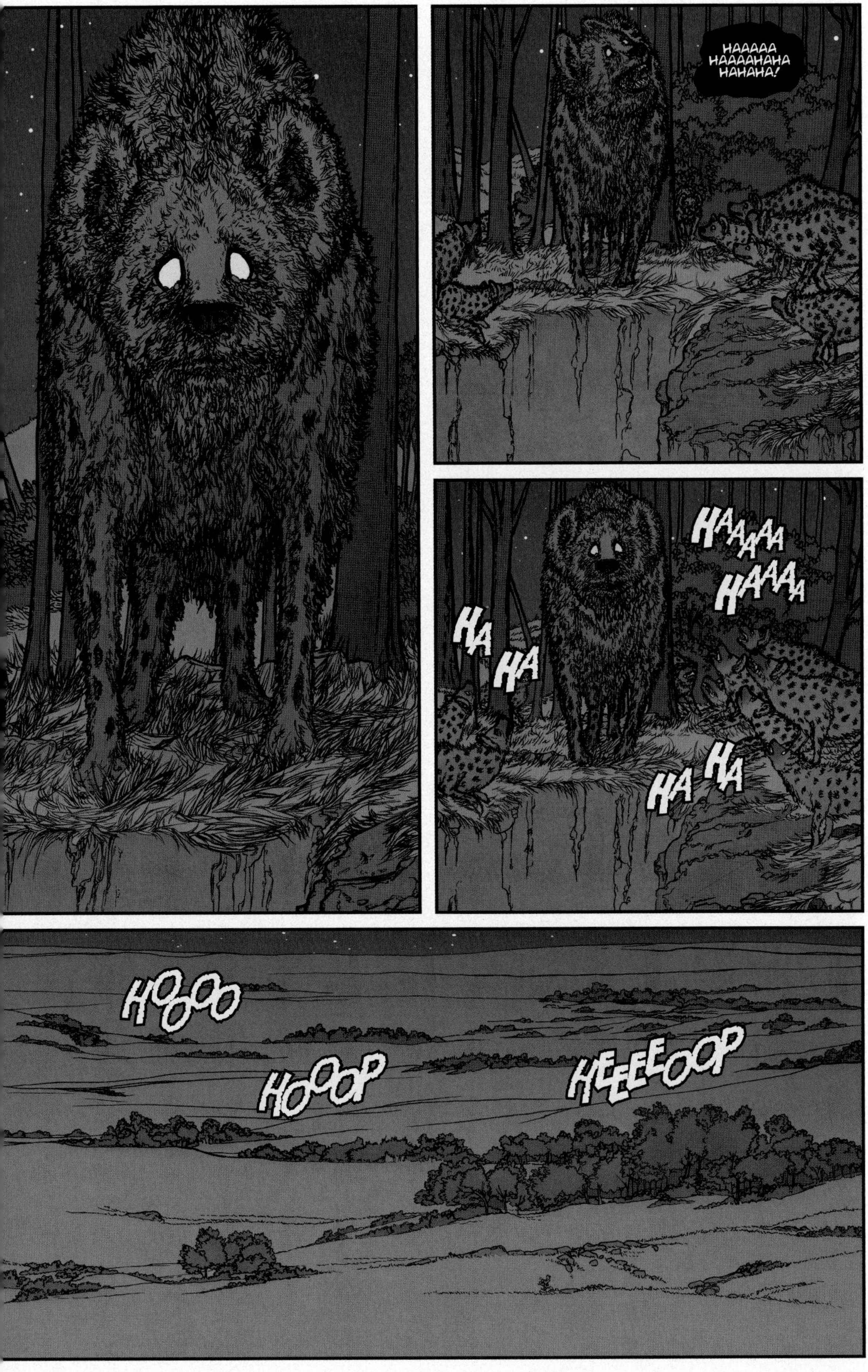
HAAAAA HAAAAHAHA HAHAHA!
HAAAAA
HAAAAA
HA
HA
HA
HA
HOOOO
HOOOP
HEEEEOOP

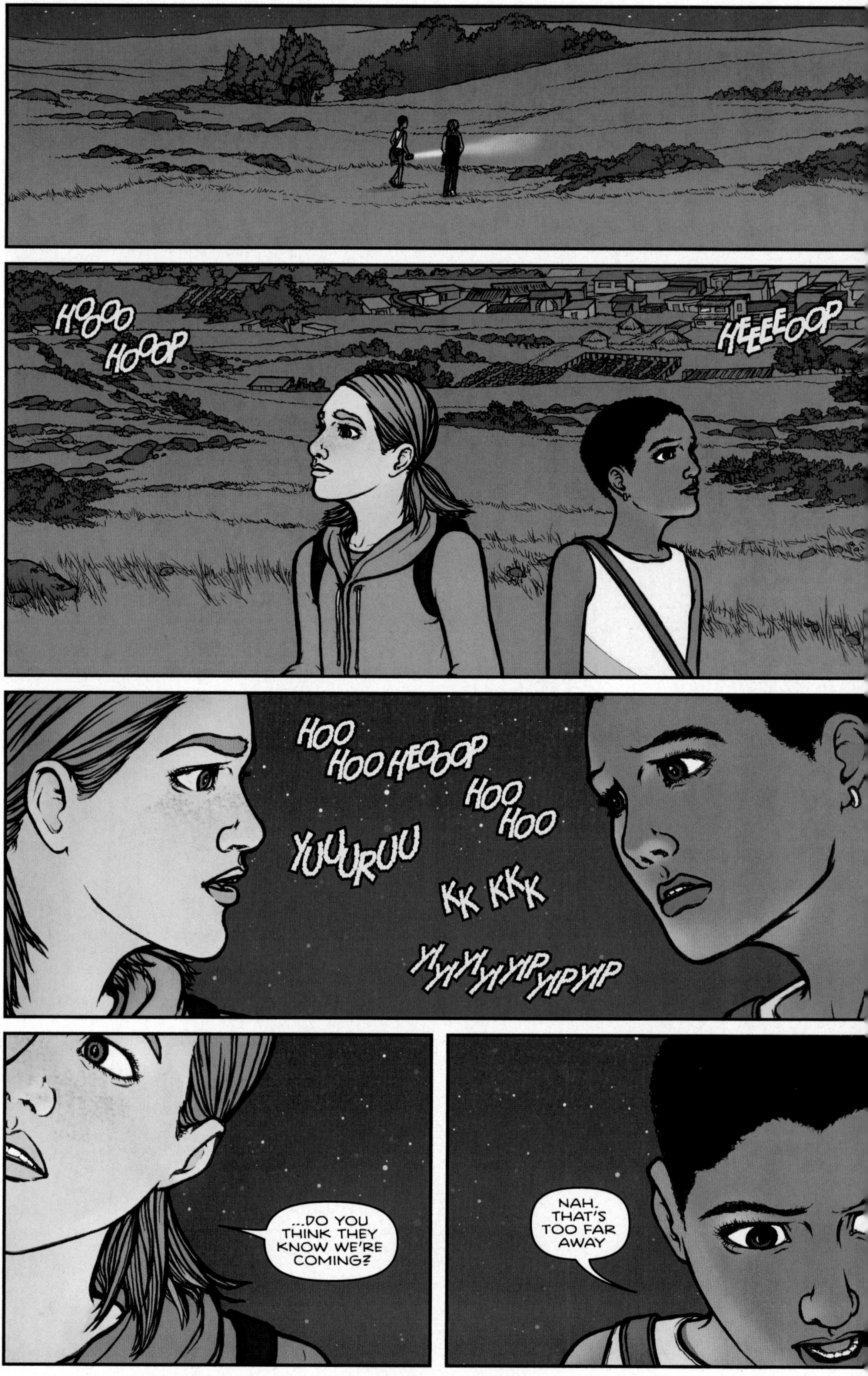
HOOOO HOOOP
HEEEEOOP
HOO HOO HEOOOP
HOO HOO
YUUURUU
KK KKK
YIYIYIYIYIP YIP YIP
...DO YOU THINK THEY KNOW WE'RE COMING?
NAH. THAT'S TOO FAR AWAY

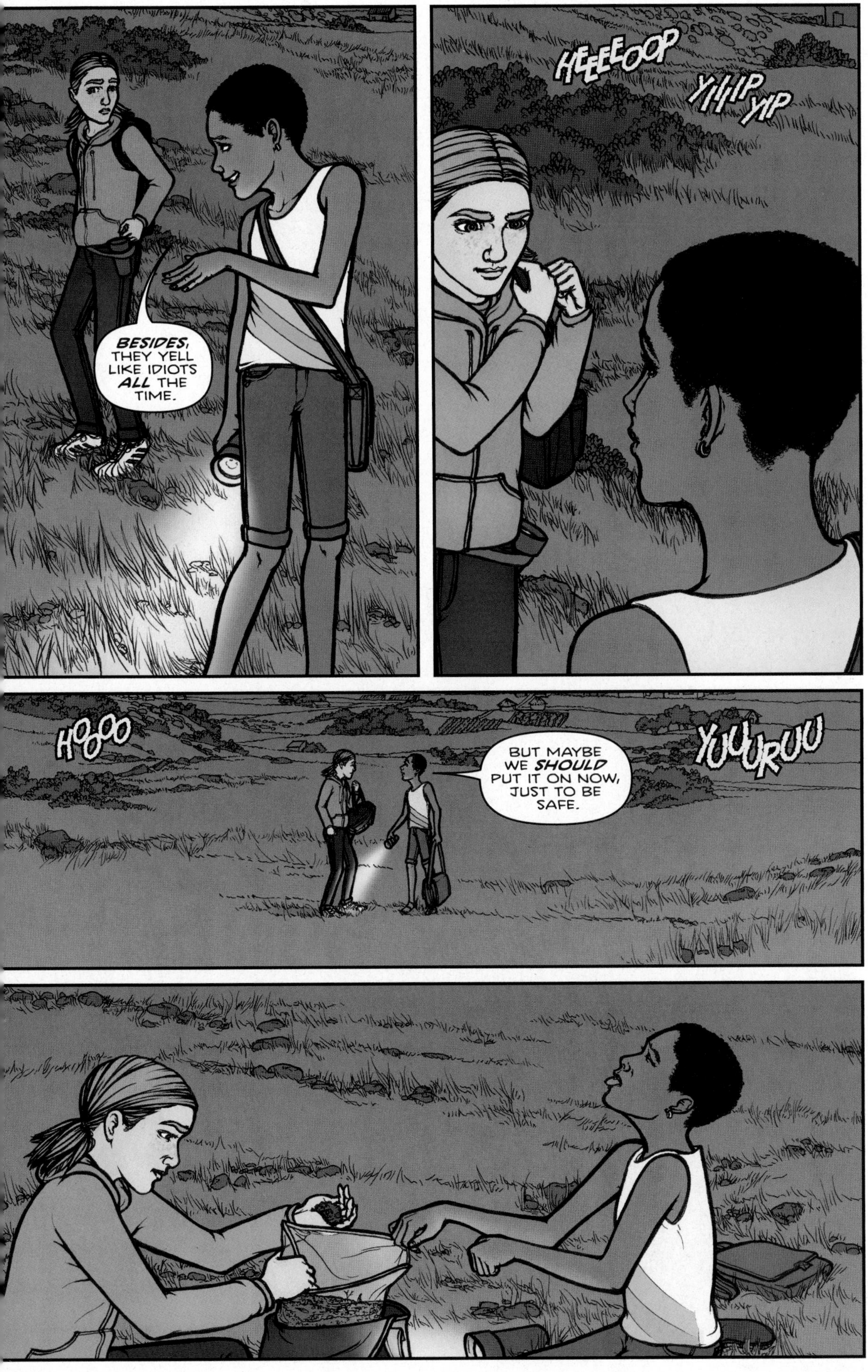

BESIDES, THEY YELL LIKE IDIOTS ALL THE TIME.
HEEEEOOP
YIIIIP YIP
HOOOO
BUT MAYBE WE SHOULD PUT IT ON NOW, JUST TO BE SAFE.
YUUURUU

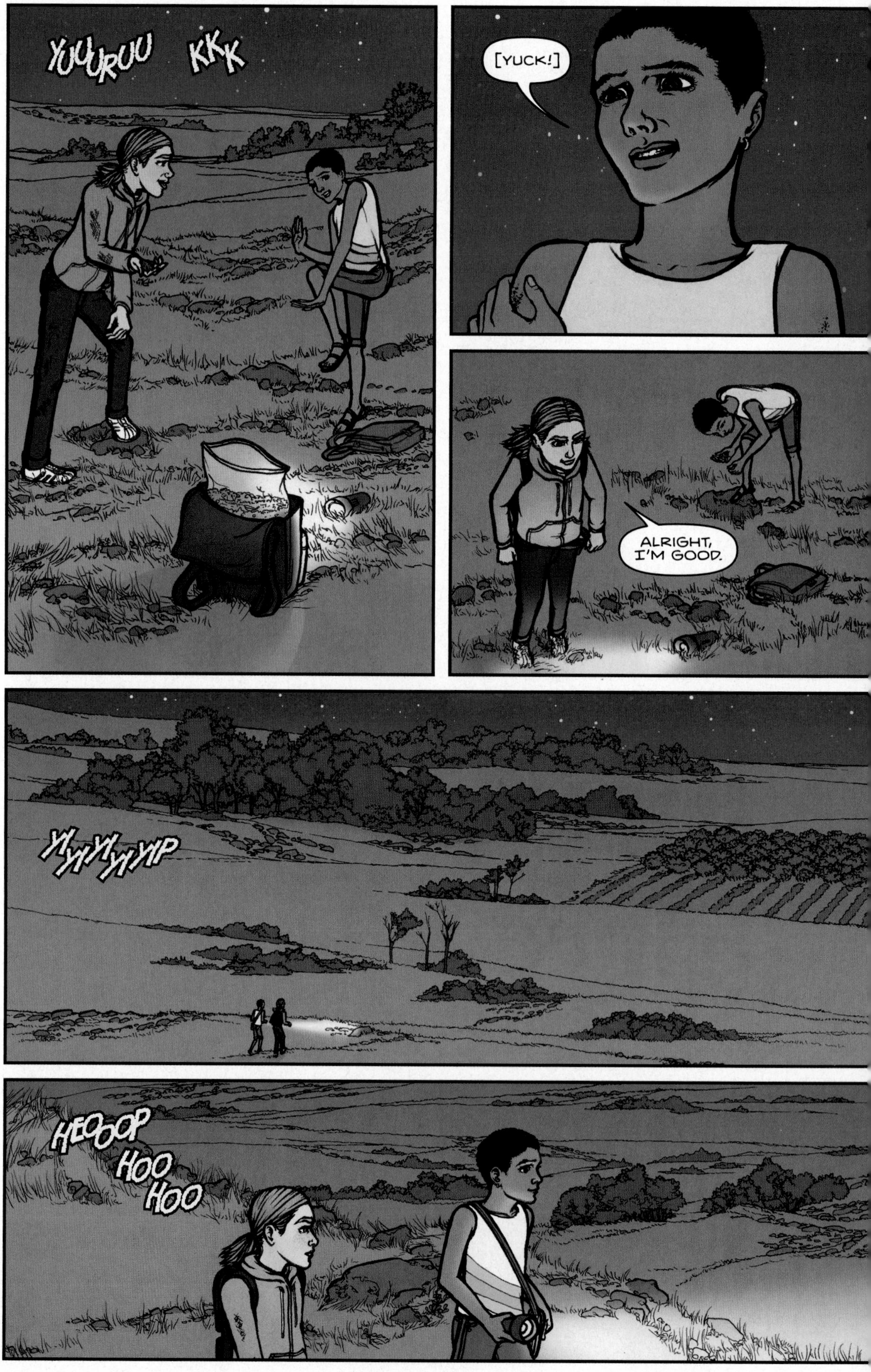
YUUURUU KKK
[YUCK!]
ALRIGHT, I'M GOOD.
YIYIYIYIYIP
HEOOOP HOO HOO

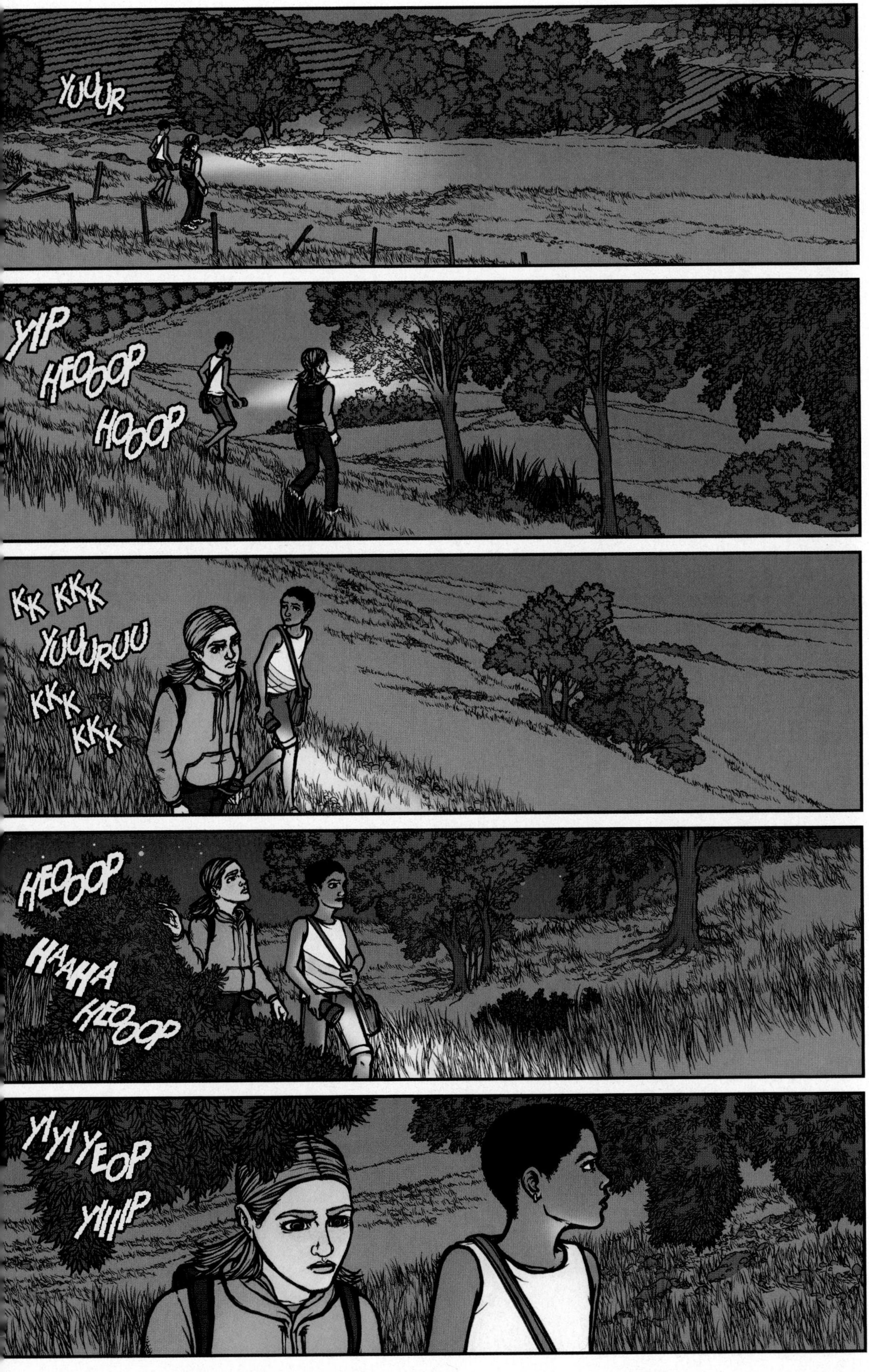
YUUUR
YIP
HEOOOP
HOOOP
KK KKK
YUUURUU
KKK
KKK
HEOOOP
HAAHA
HEOOOP
YIYI YEOP
YIIIIP

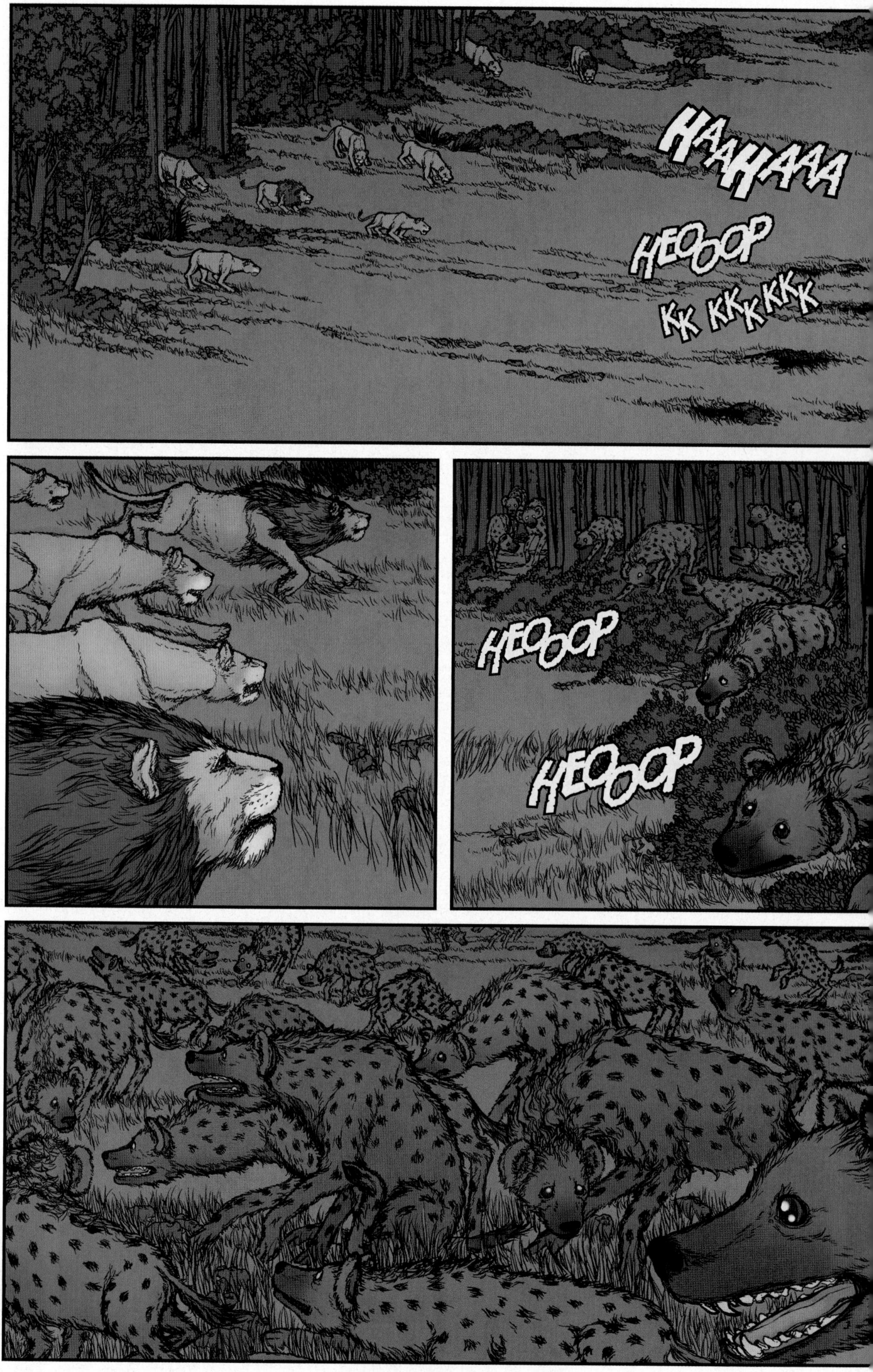
HAAAHAAA
HEOOOP
KK KKKKKK
HEOOOP
HEOOOP

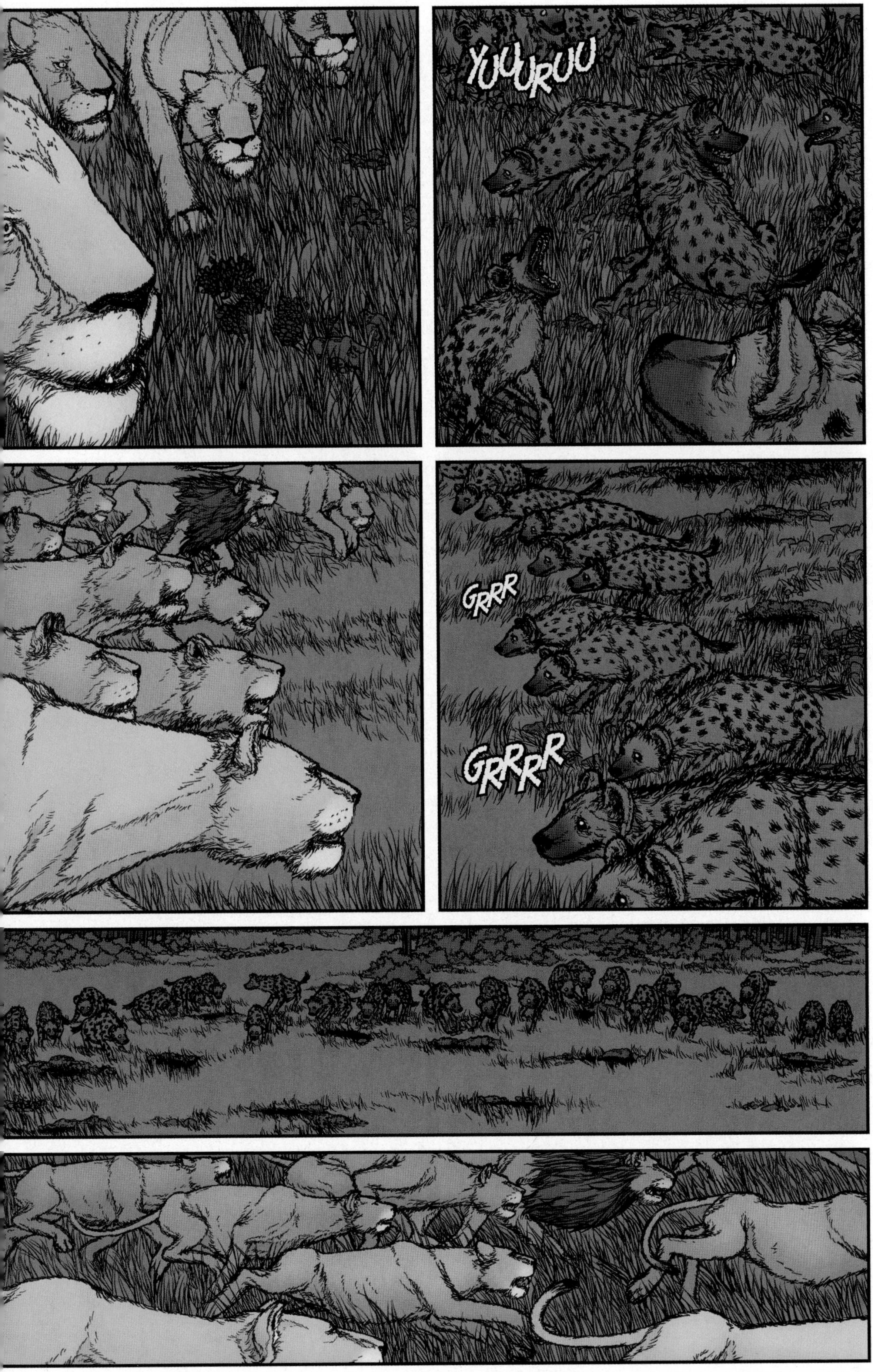
YUUURUU
GRRR
GRRRR

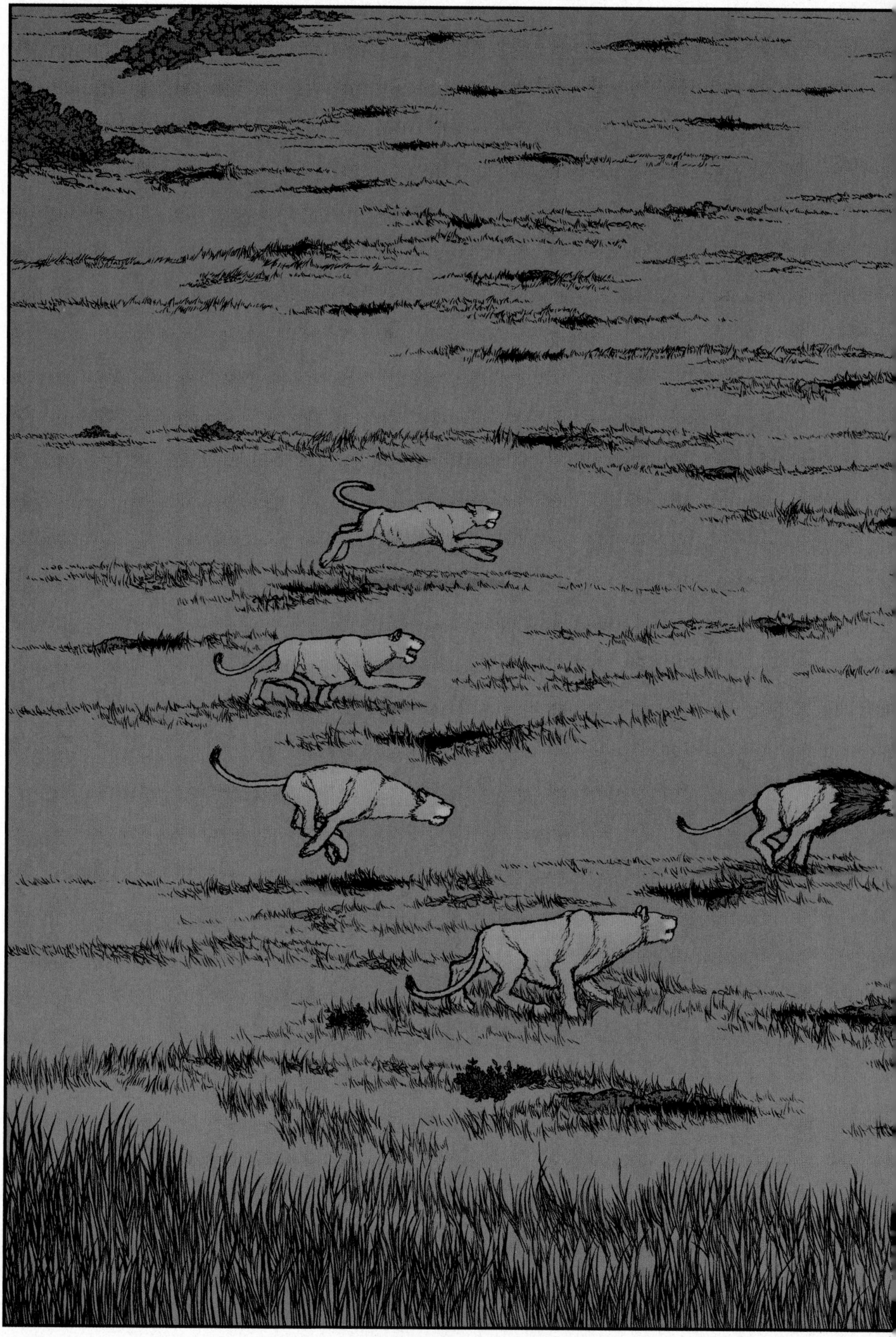

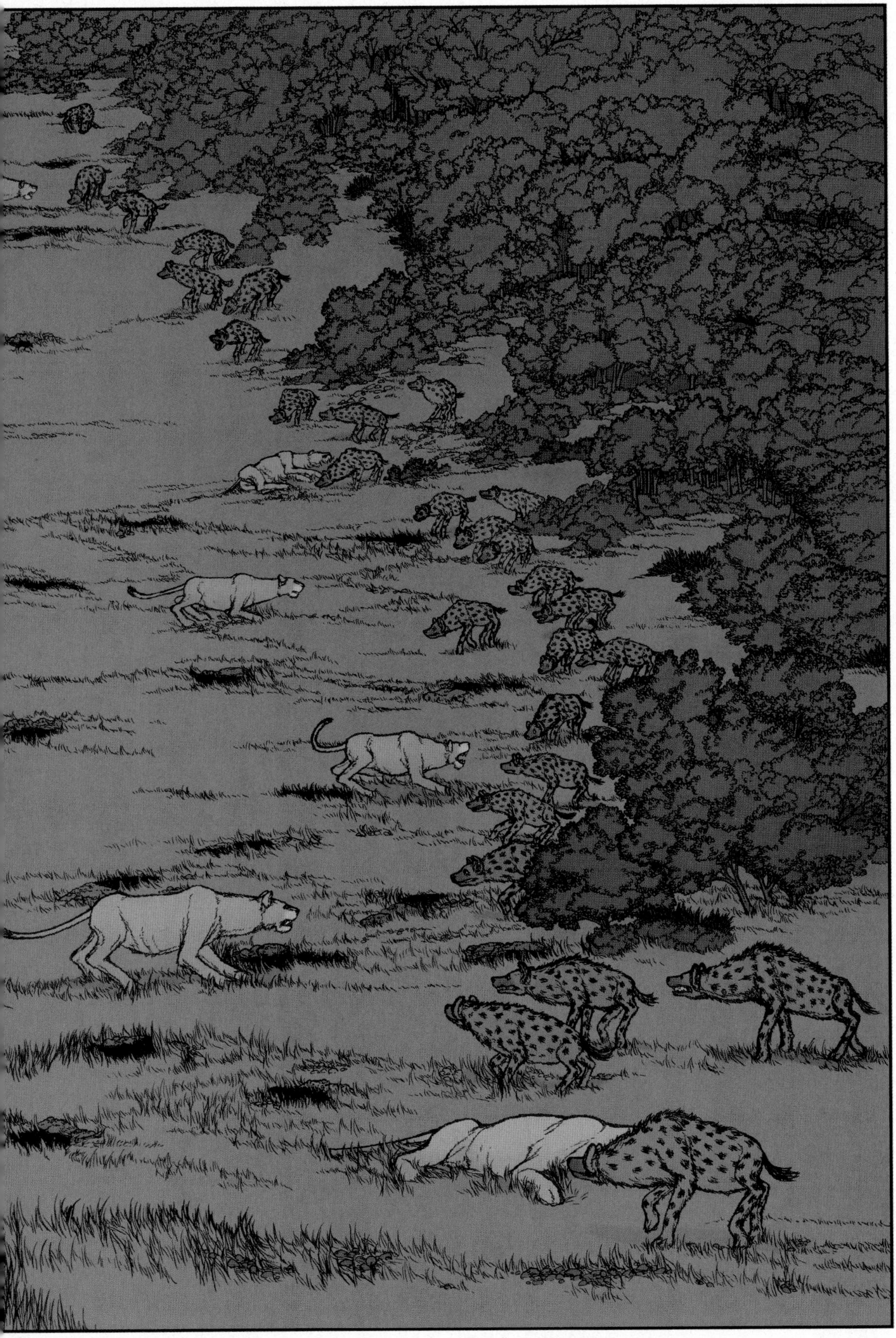

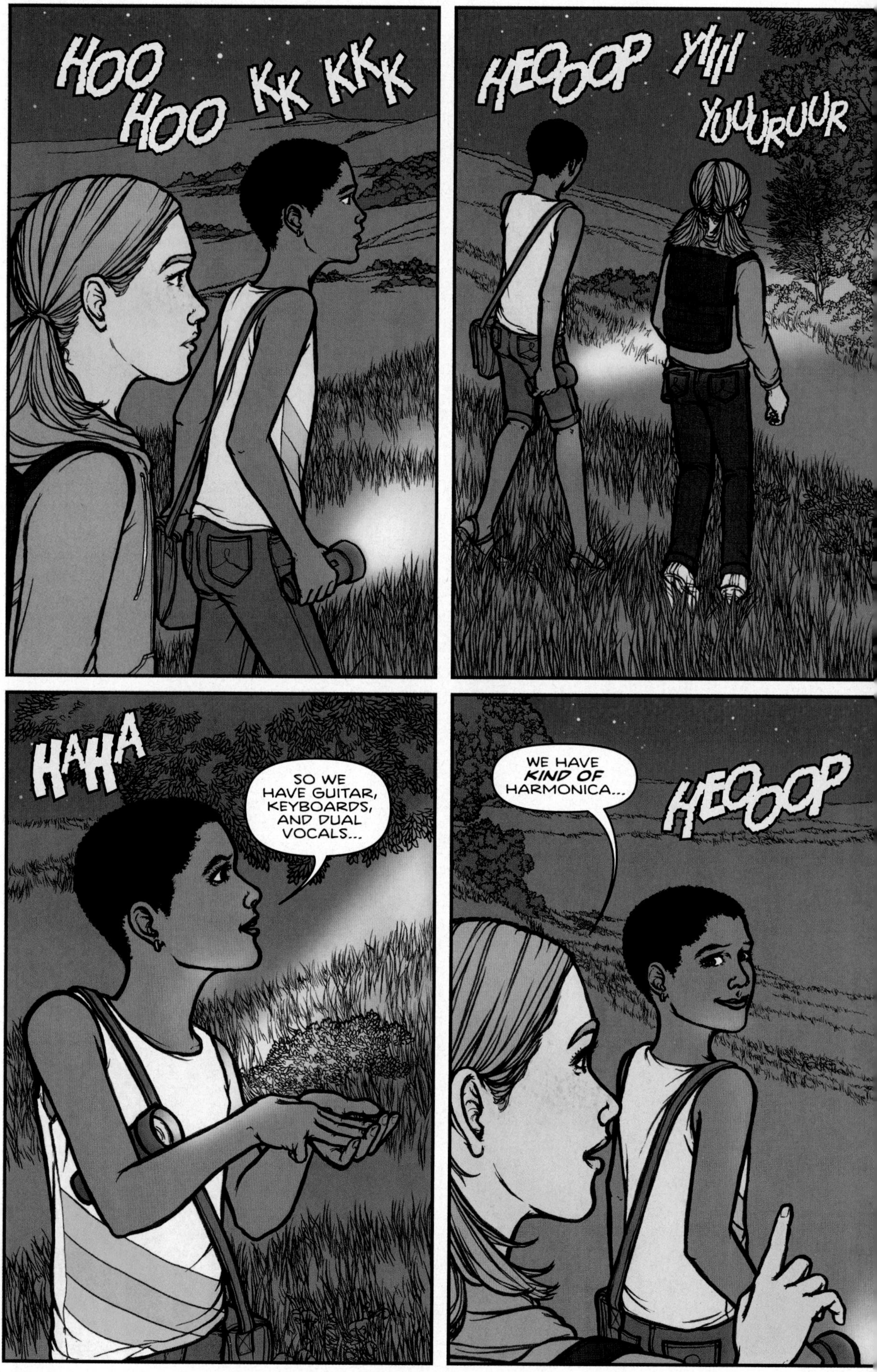
HOO HOO KK KKK
HEOOOP YIIII YUUURUUR
HAHA
SO WE HAVE GUITAR, KEYBOARDS, AND DUAL VOCALS...
WE HAVE *KIND OF* HARMONICA...
HEOOOP

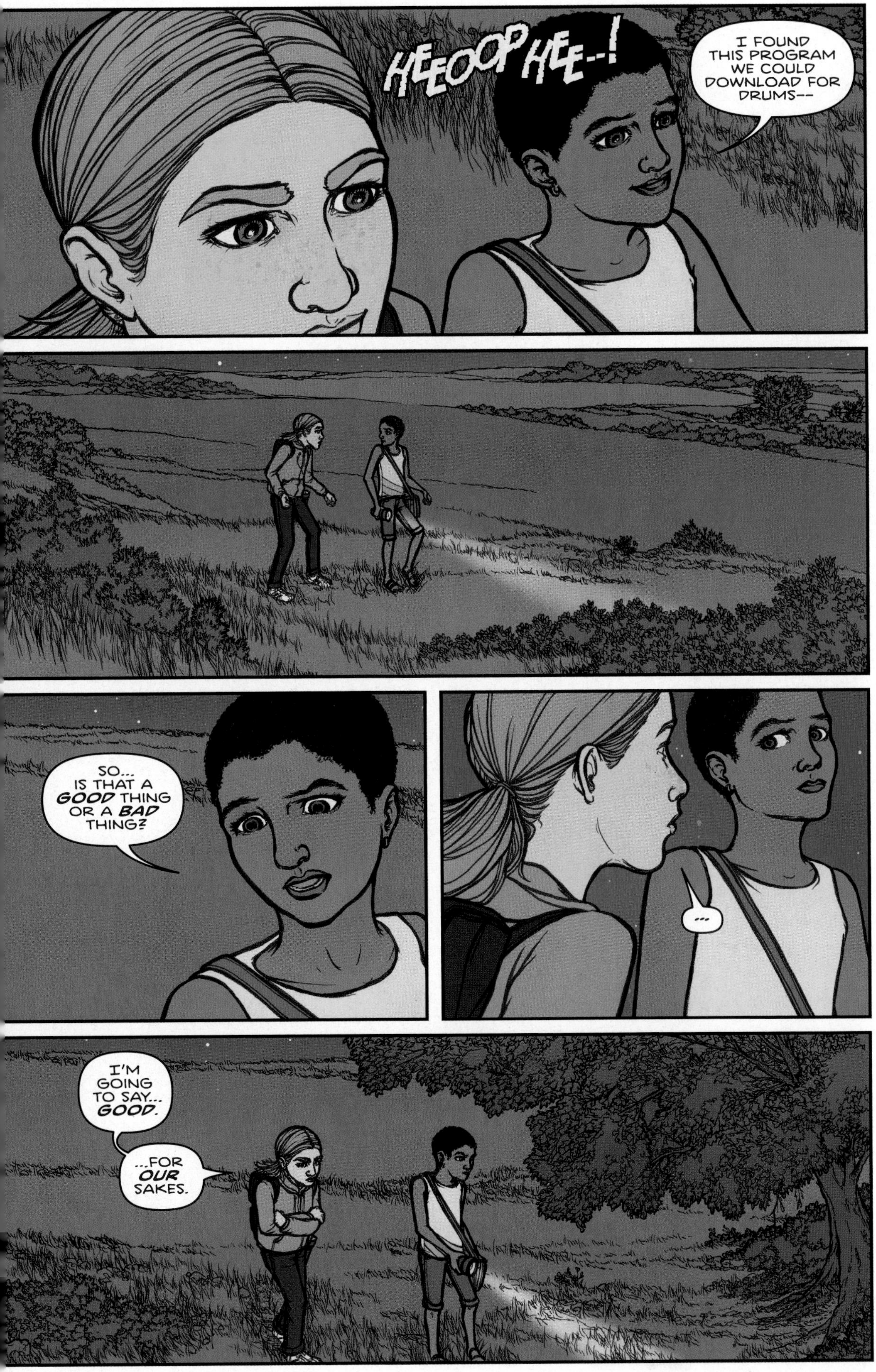
HEEOOP HEE--!
I FOUND THIS PROGRAM WE COULD DOWNLOAD FOR DRUMS--
SO... IS THAT A GOOD THING OR A BAD THING?
...
I'M GOING TO SAY... GOOD.
...FOR OUR SAKES.

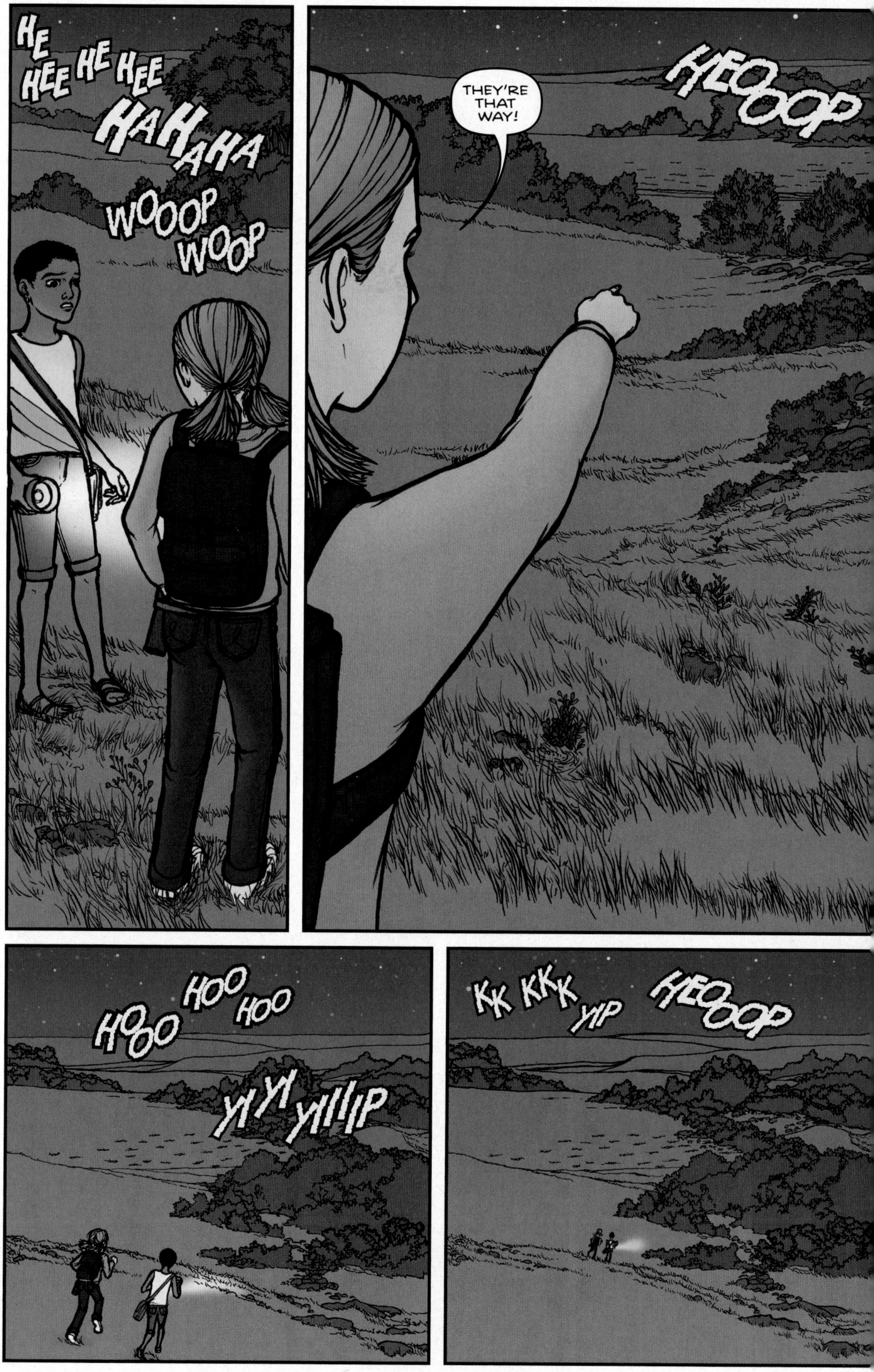
HE HEE HE HEE
HAHAHAHA
WOOOP WOOP
THEY'RE THAT WAY!
KEOOOOP
HOOO HOO HOO
YIYI YIIIIIP
KK KKK YIP
KEOOOP

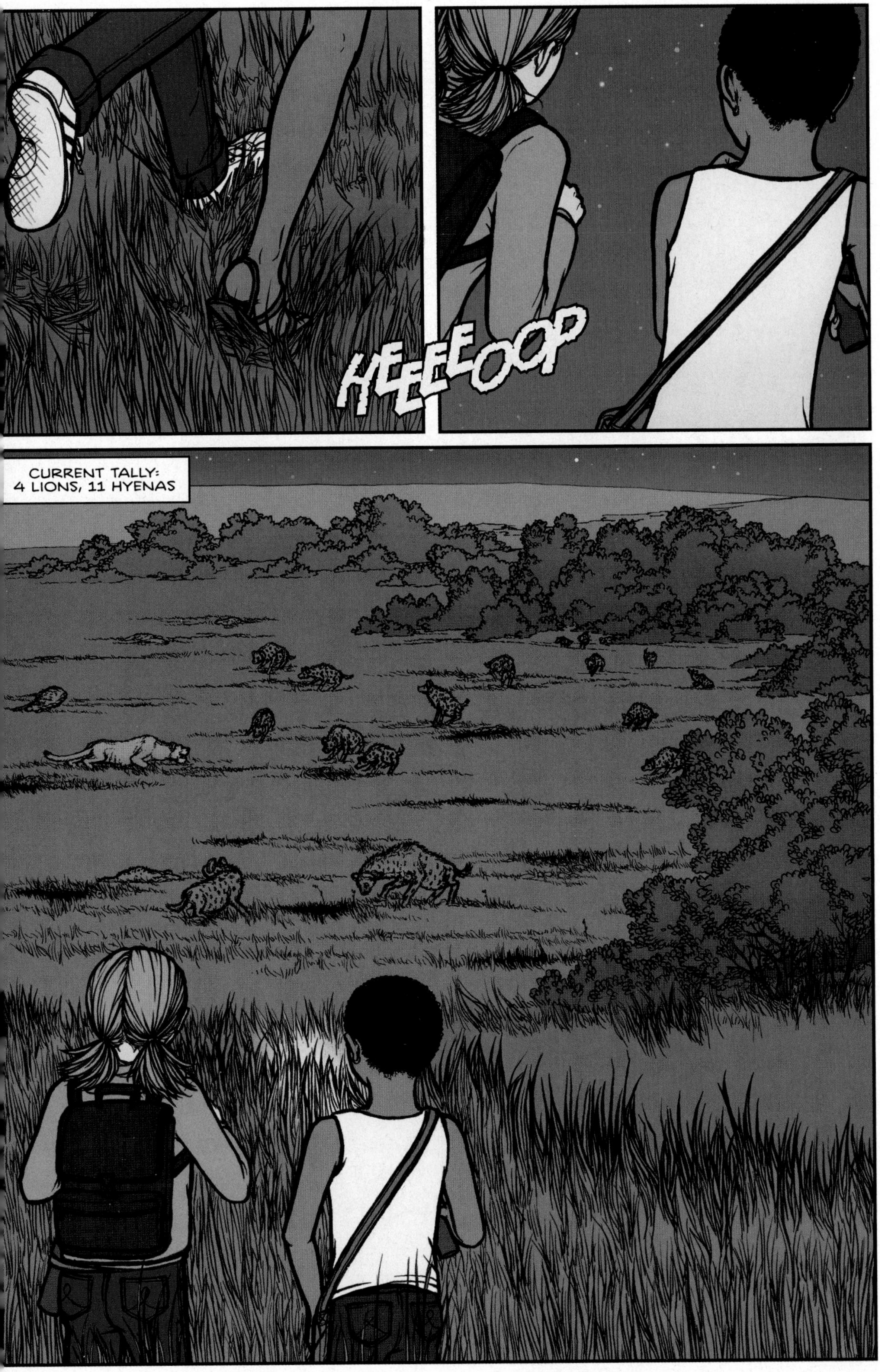
HEEEEOOP
CURRENT TALLY:
4 LIONS, 11 HYENAS

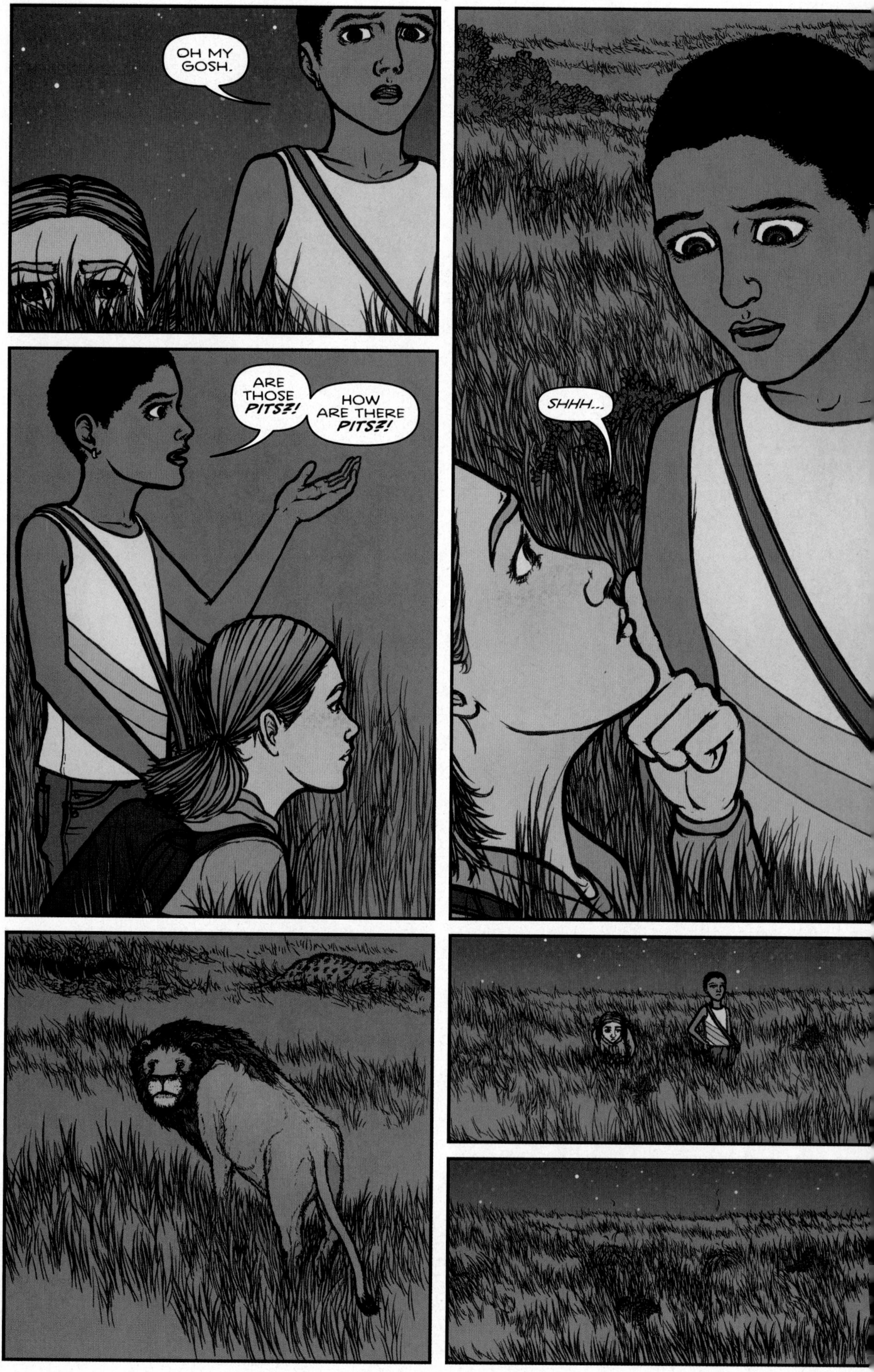
OH MY GOSH.
ARE THOSE PITS?!
HOW ARE THERE PITS?!
SHHH...

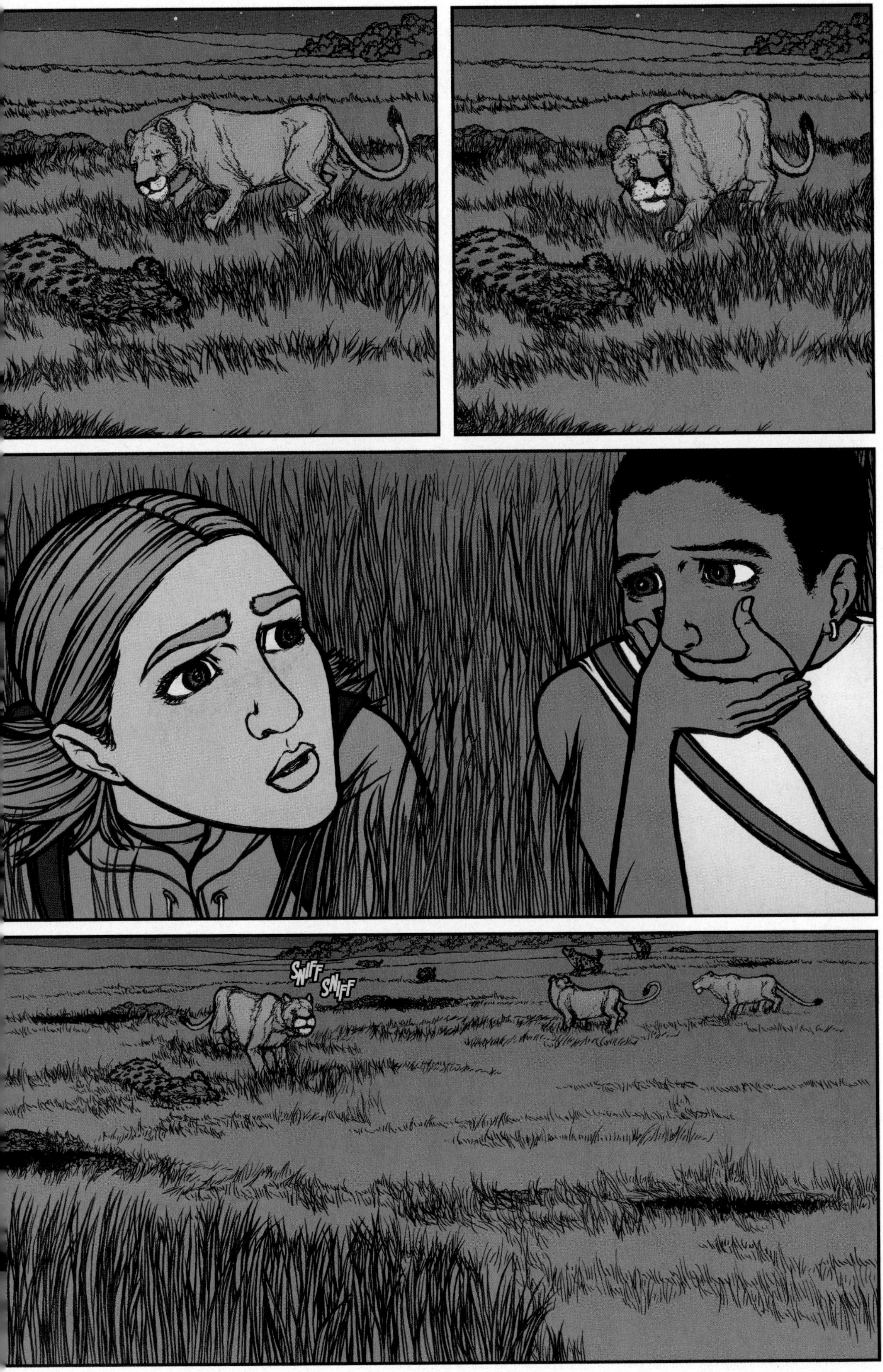
SNIFF
SNIFF

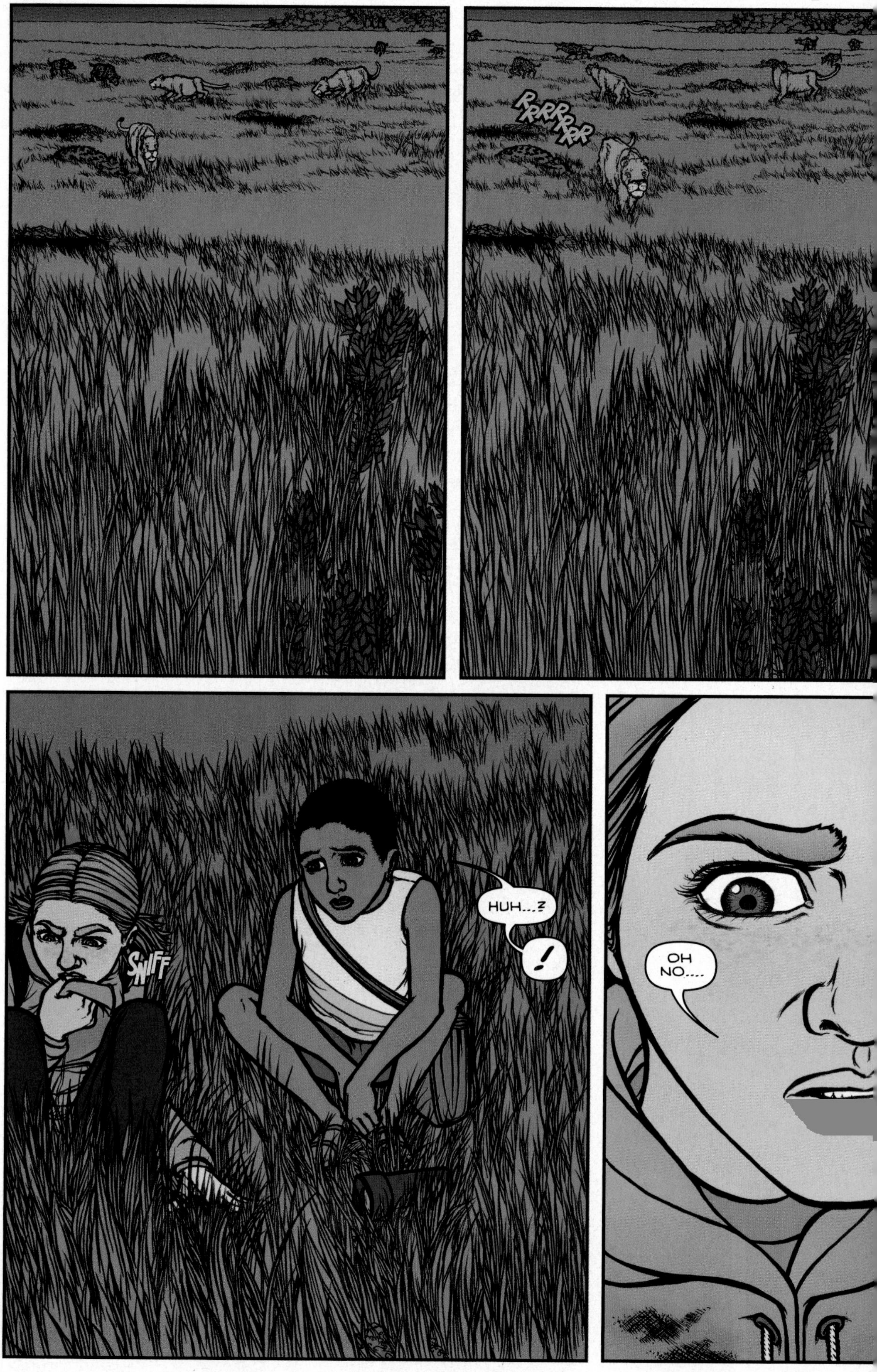
RRRRRR
SNIFF
HUH...?
!
OH NO....

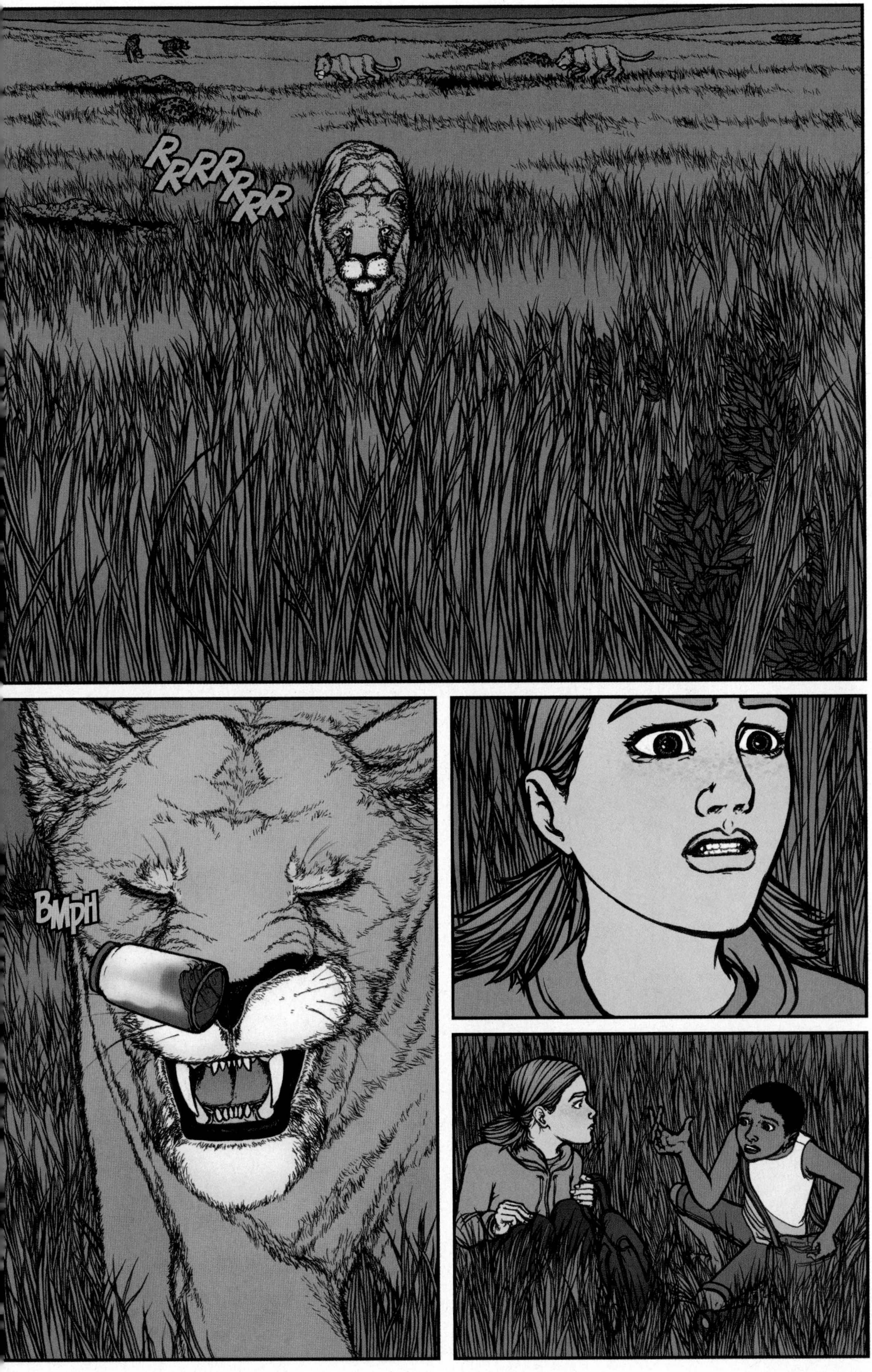
RRRRRRRR
BMPH

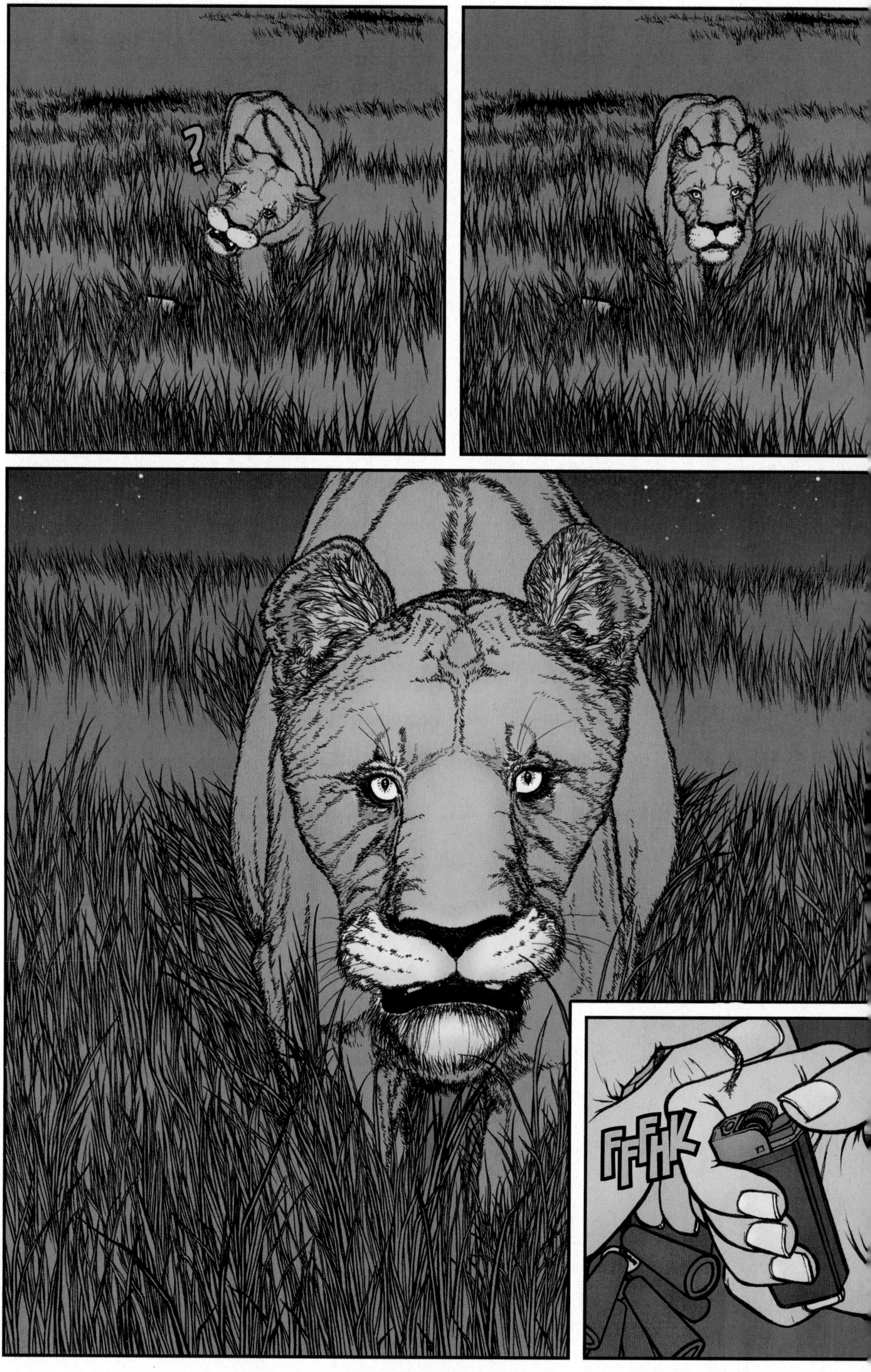
?
FFFHK

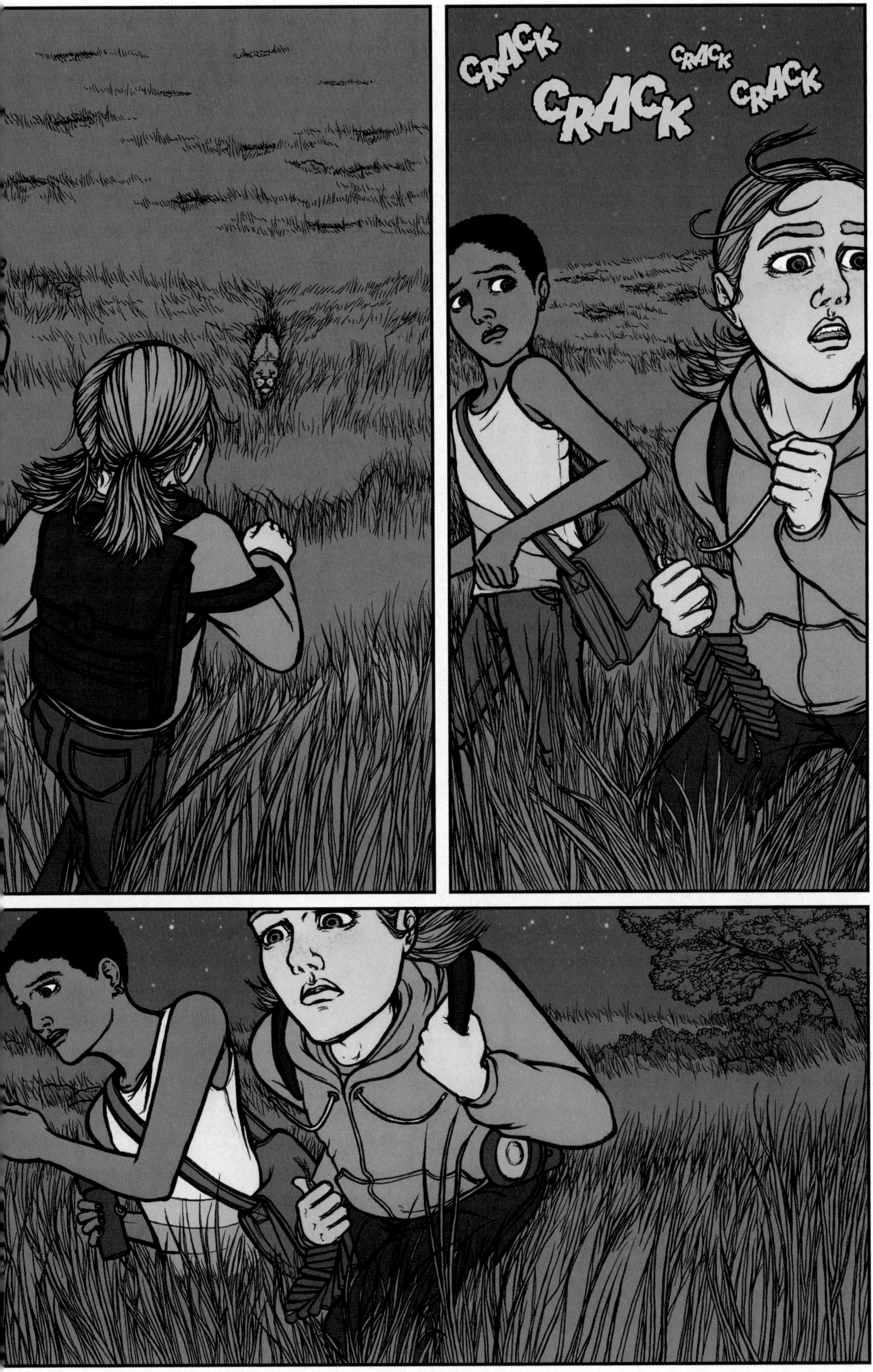
CRACK
CRACK
CRACK
CRACK

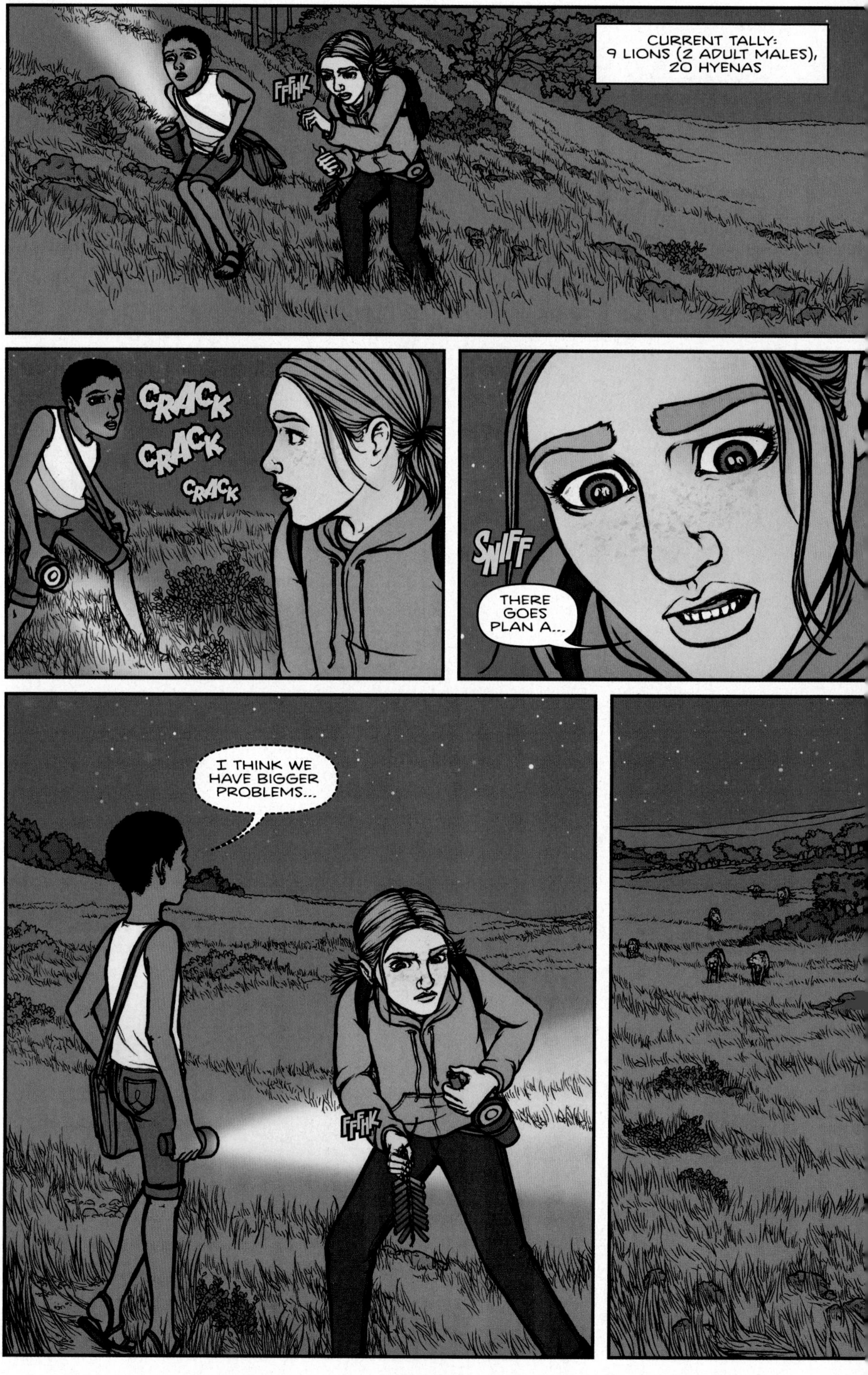
CURRENT TALLY:
9 LIONS (2 ADULT MALES),
20 HYENAS
FFFHK
CRACK
CRACK
CRACK
SNIFF
THERE GOES PLAN A...
I THINK WE HAVE BIGGER PROBLEMS...
FFFHK

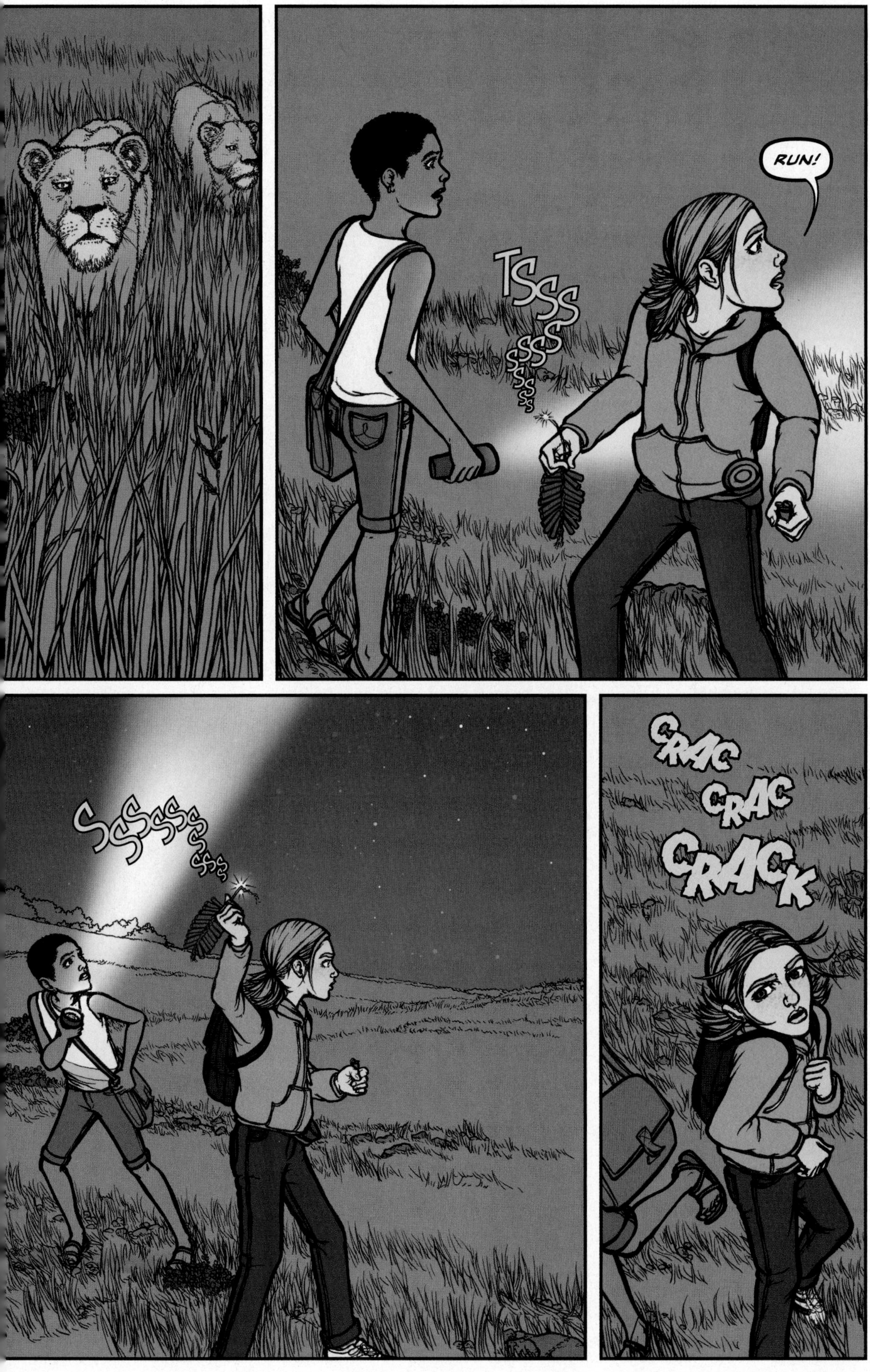
RUN!
TSSSSSSSSS
SSSSSSSSS
CRAC
CRAC
CRACK

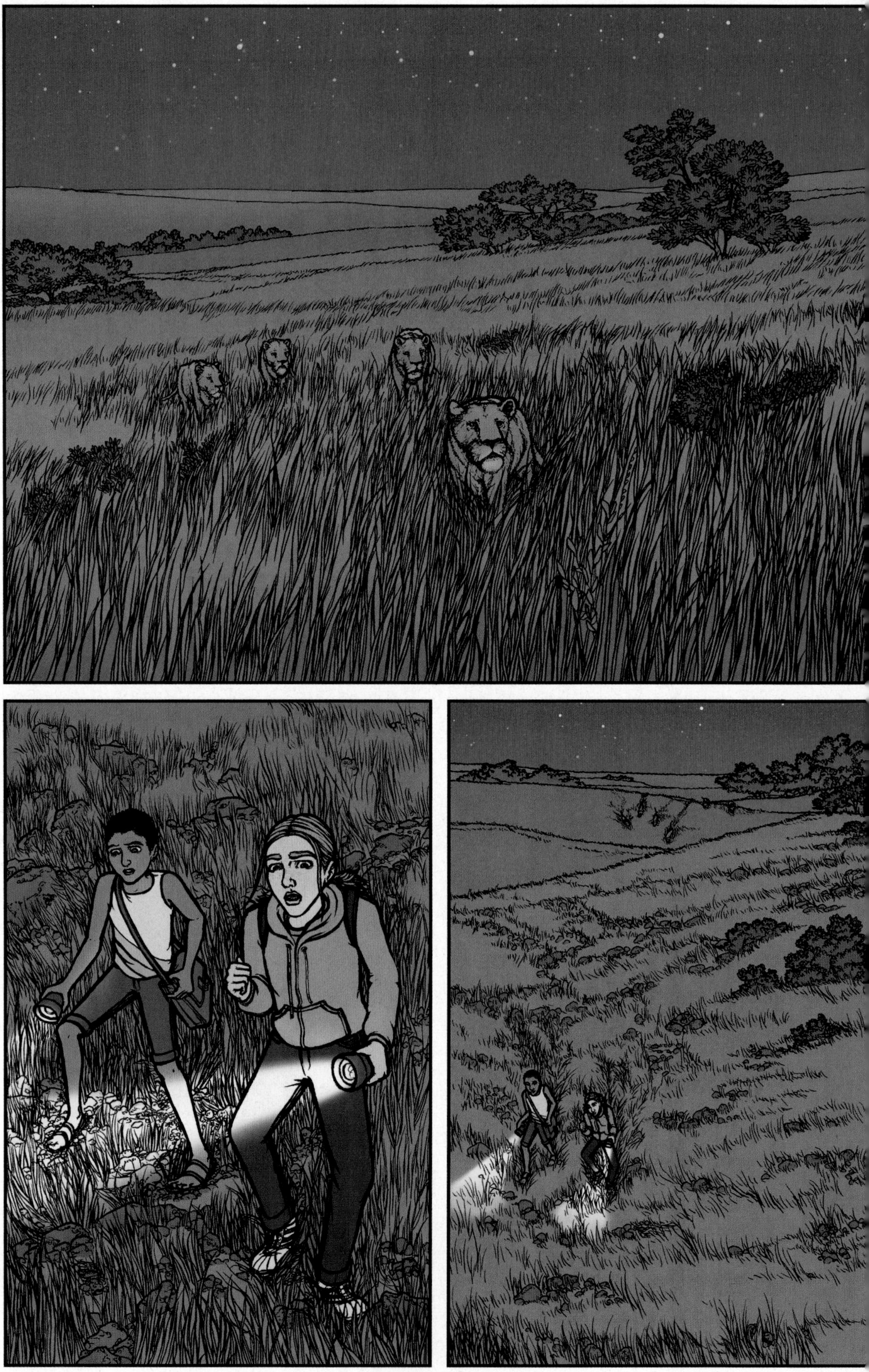

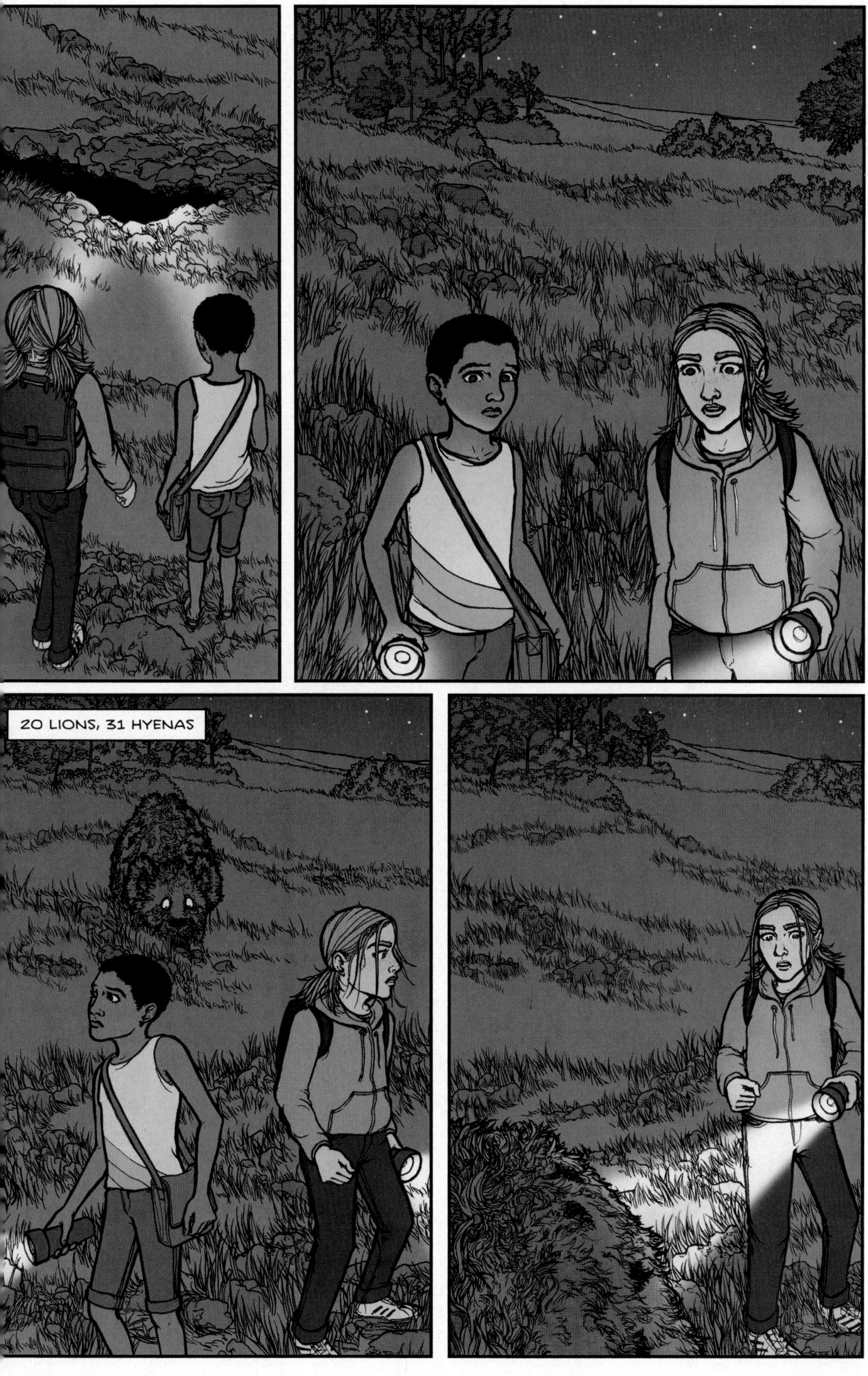
20 LIONS, 31 HYENAS

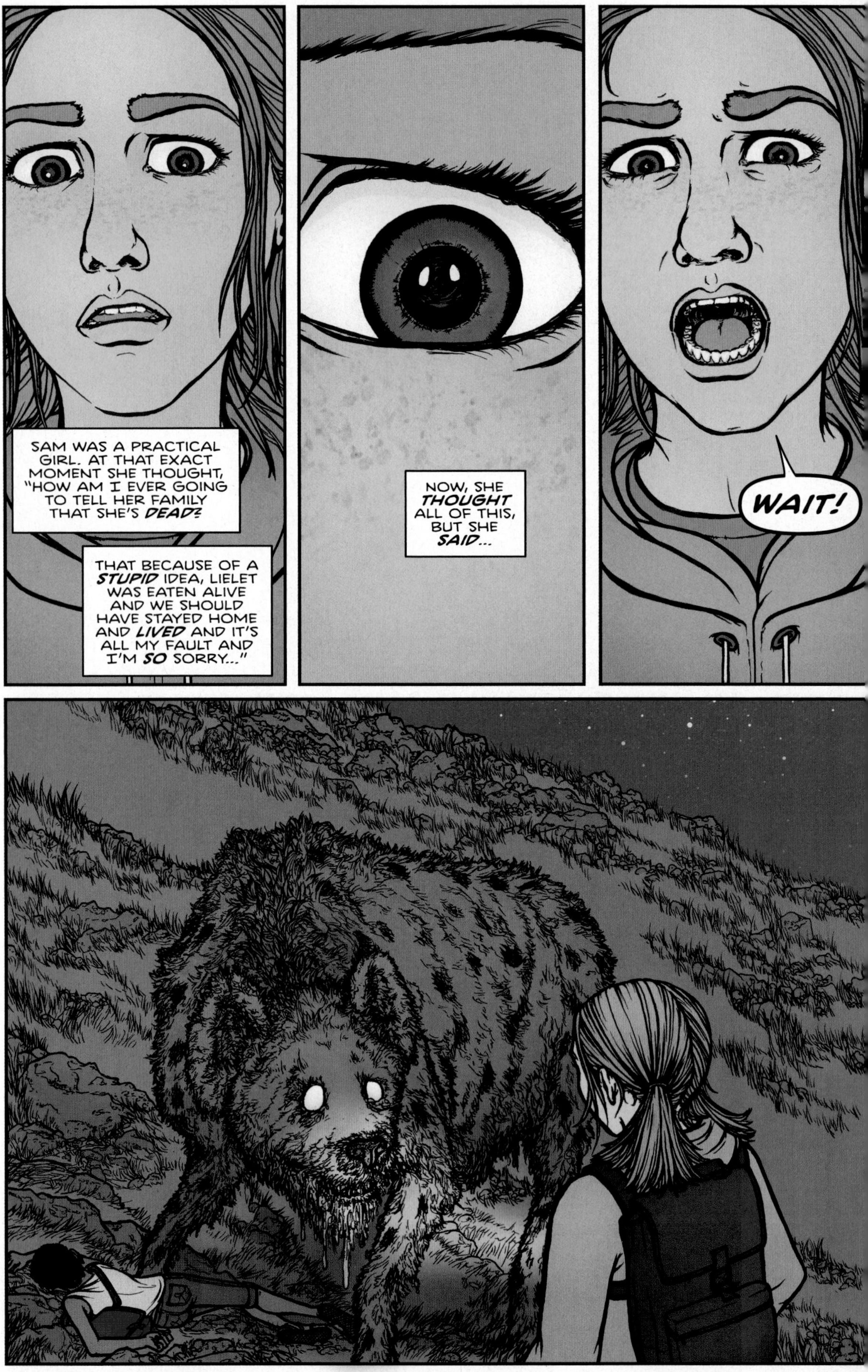
SAM WAS A PRACTICAL GIRL. AT THAT EXACT MOMENT SHE THOUGHT, "HOW AM I EVER GOING TO TELL HER FAMILY THAT SHE'S DEAD?
THAT BECAUSE OF A STUPID IDEA, LIELET WAS EATEN ALIVE AND WE SHOULD HAVE STAYED HOME AND LIVED AND IT'S ALL MY FAULT AND I'M SO SORRY..."
NOW, SHE THOUGHT ALL OF THIS, BUT SHE SAID...
WAIT!

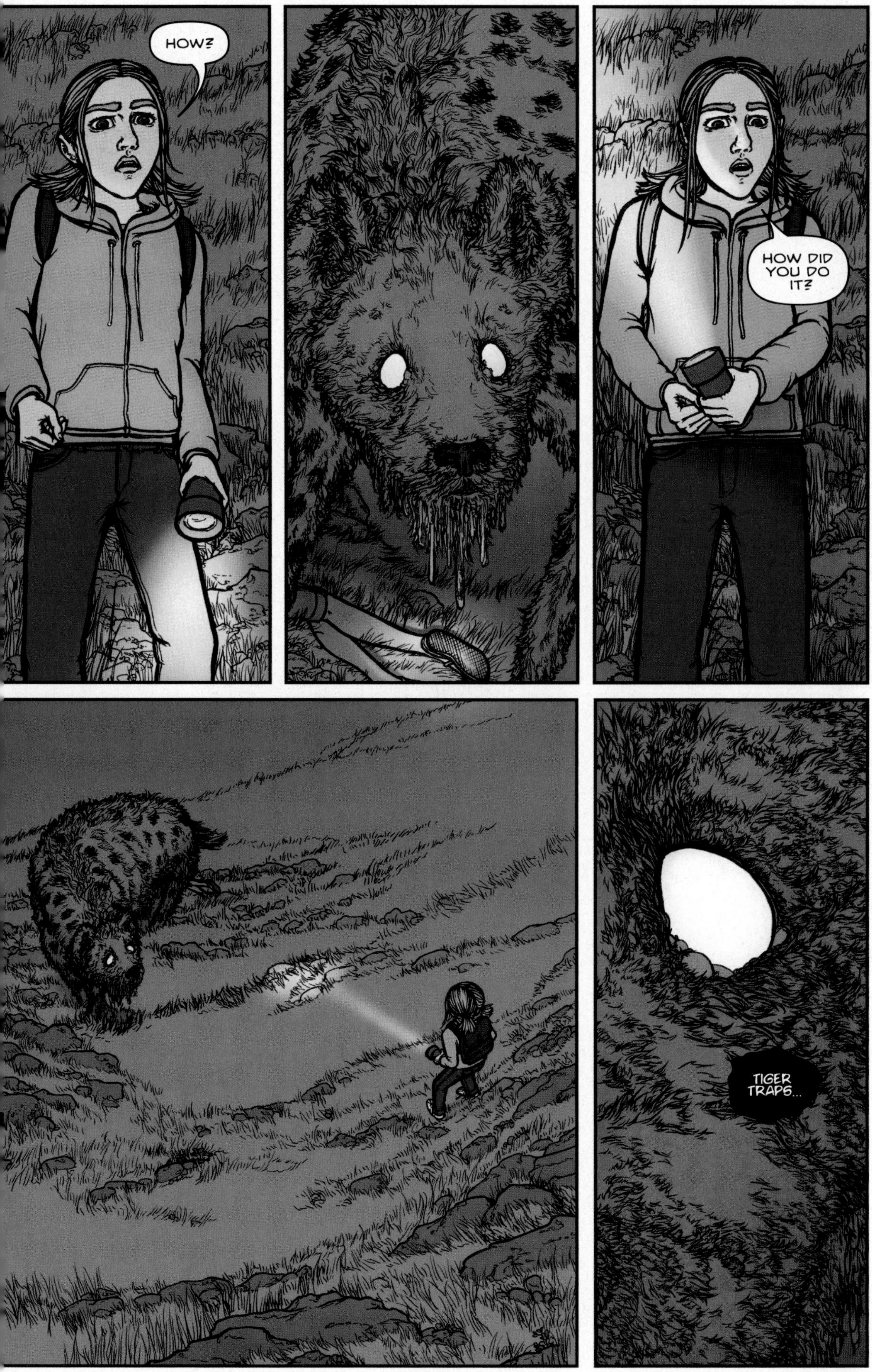
HOW?
HOW DID YOU DO IT?
TIGER TRAPS...

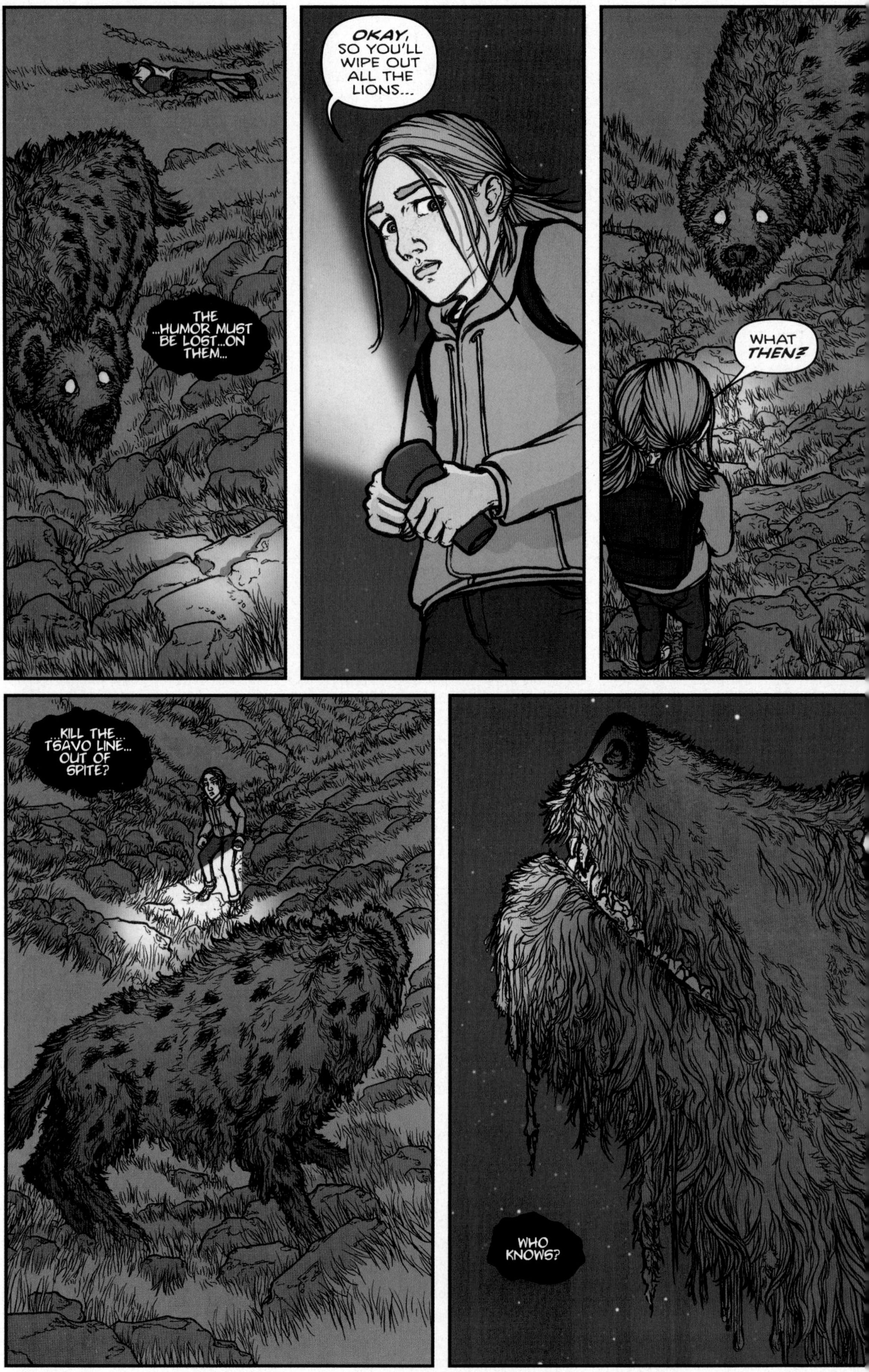
THE ...HUMOR MUST BE LOST...ON THEM...
OKAY, SO YOU'LL WIPE OUT ALL THE LIONS...
WHAT THEN?
...KILL THE TSAVO LINE... OUT OF SPITE?
WHO KNOWS?

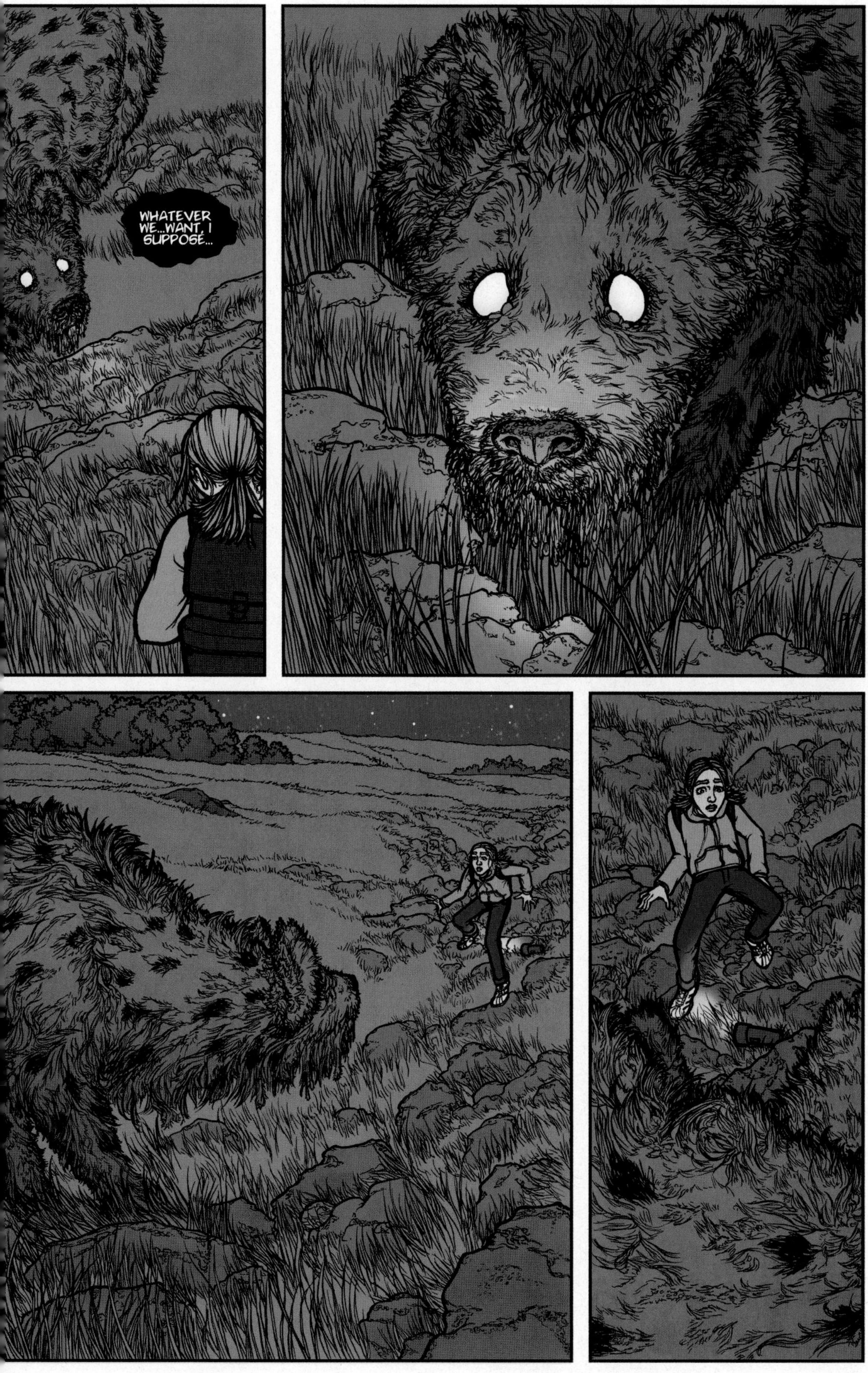
WHATEVER WE...WANT, I SUPPOSE...

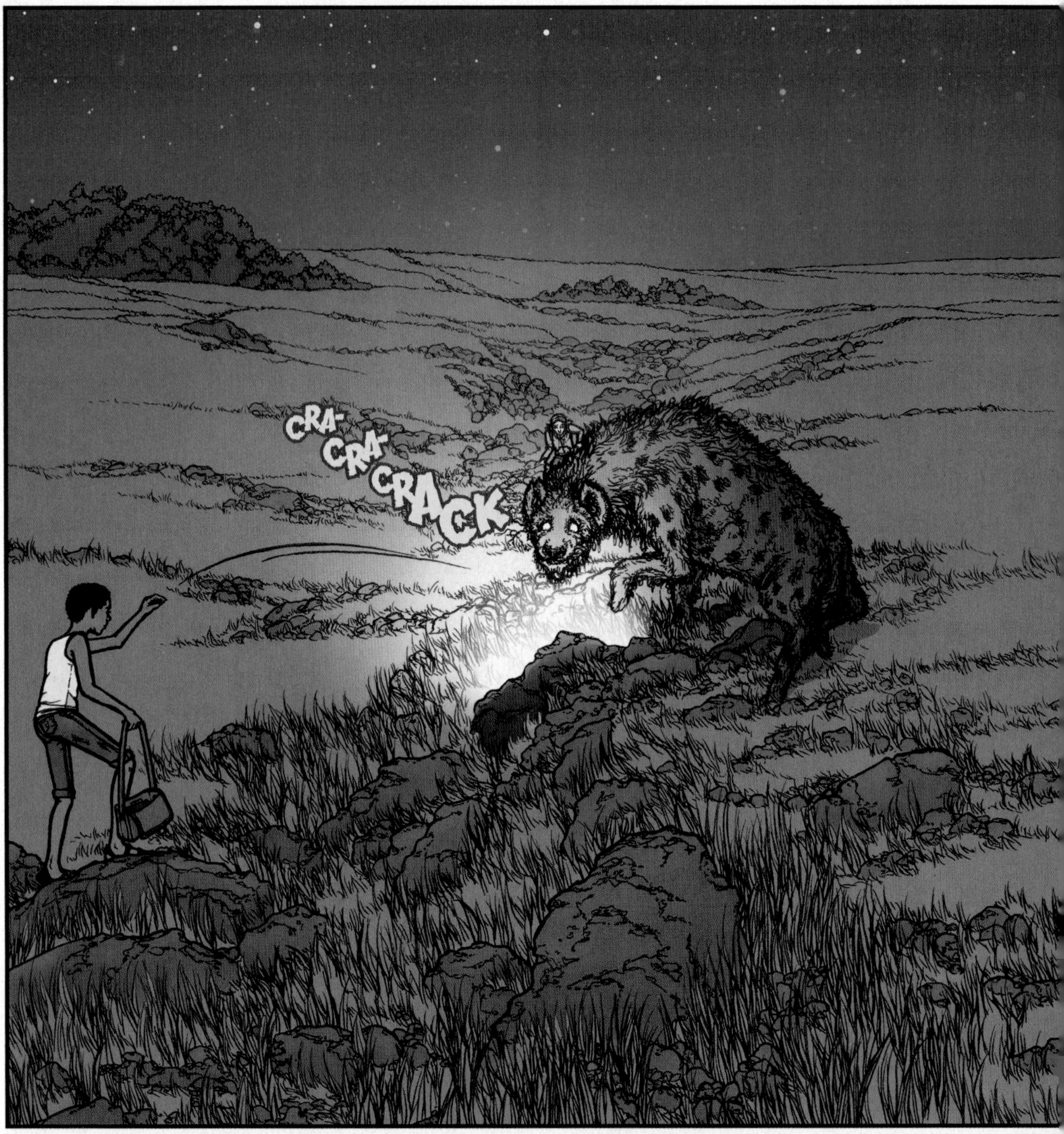
CRA-
CRA-
CRACK

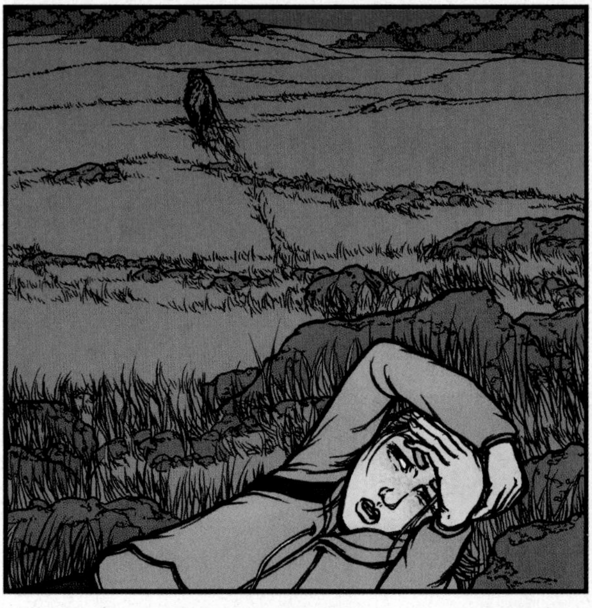

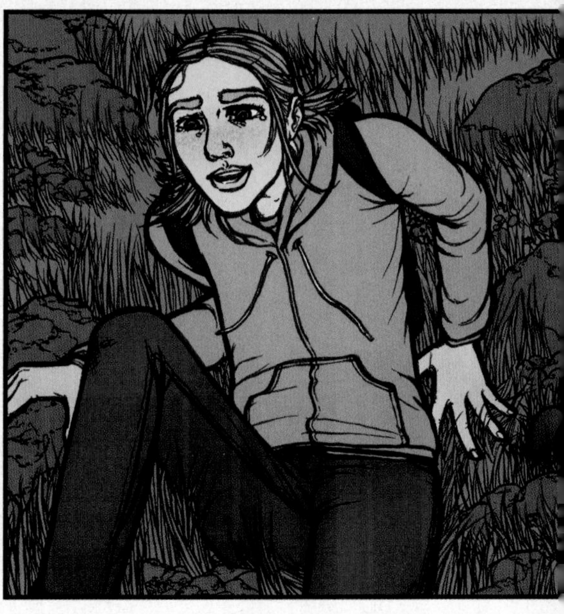

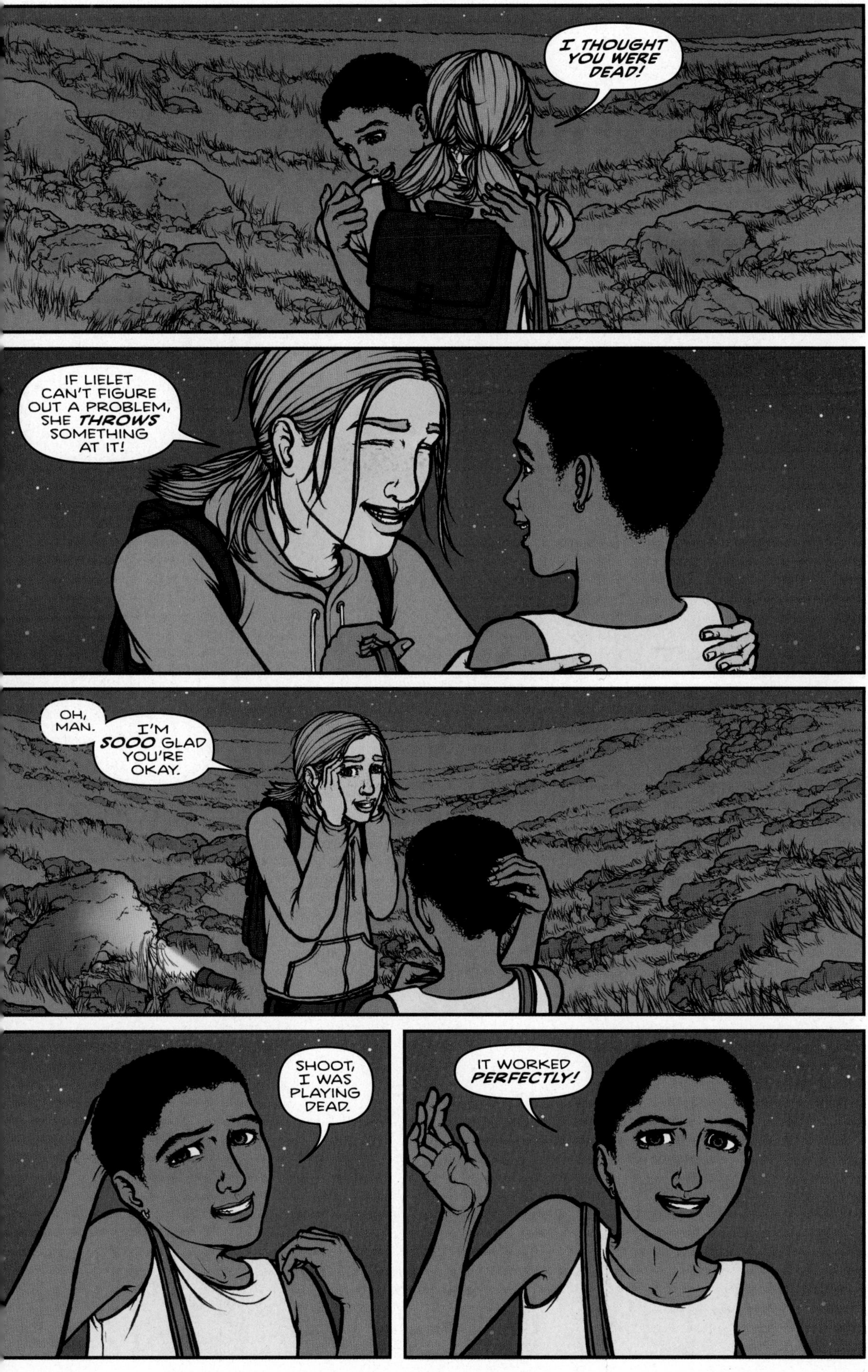
I THOUGHT YOU WERE DEAD!
IF LIELET CAN'T FIGURE OUT A PROBLEM, SHE THROWS SOMETHING AT IT!
OH, MAN.
I'M SOOO GLAD YOU'RE OKAY.
SHOOT, I WAS PLAYING DEAD.
IT WORKED PERFECTLY!

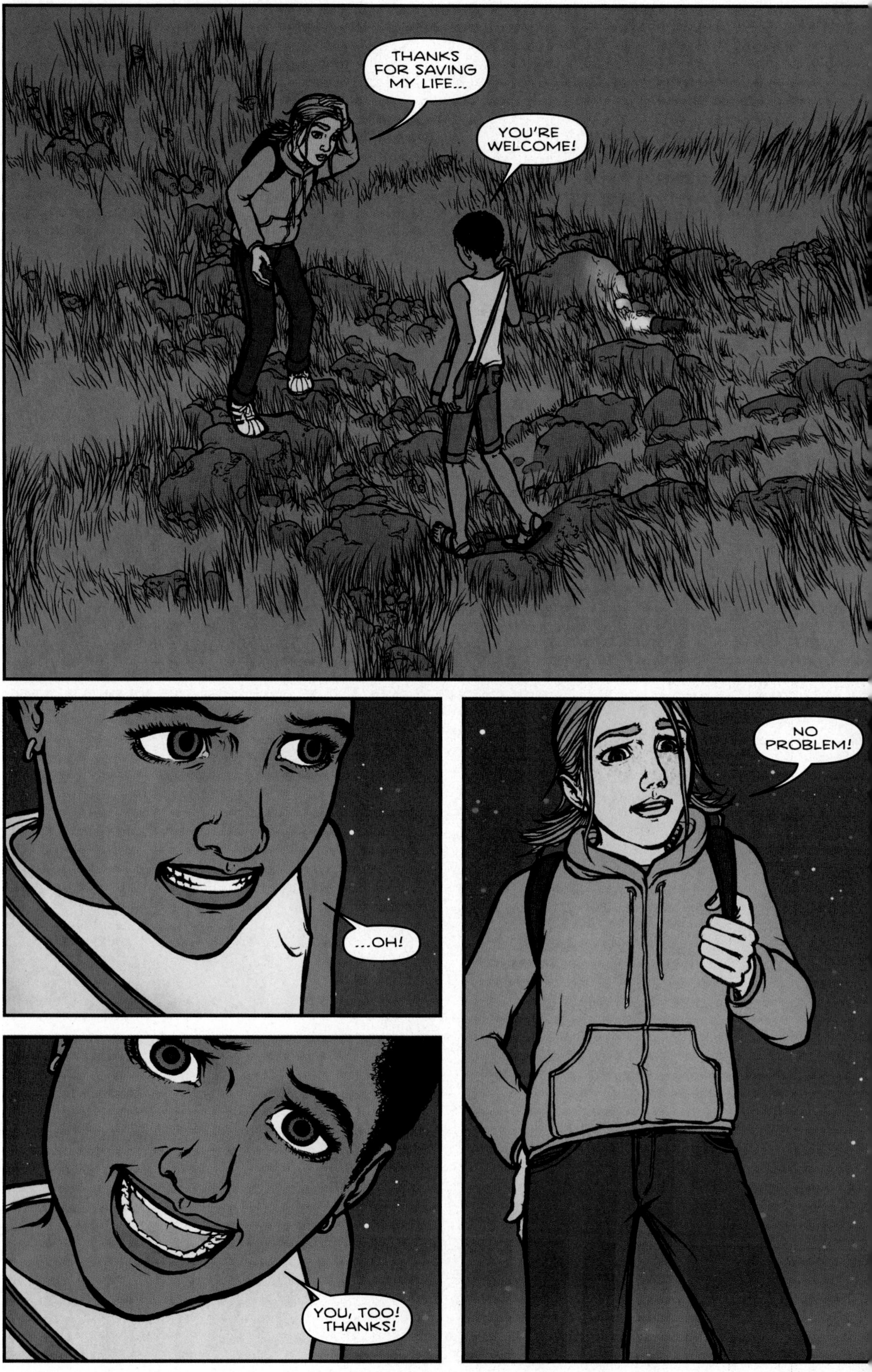
THANKS FOR SAVING MY LIFE...
YOU'RE WELCOME!
...OH!
YOU, TOO! THANKS!
NO PROBLEM!

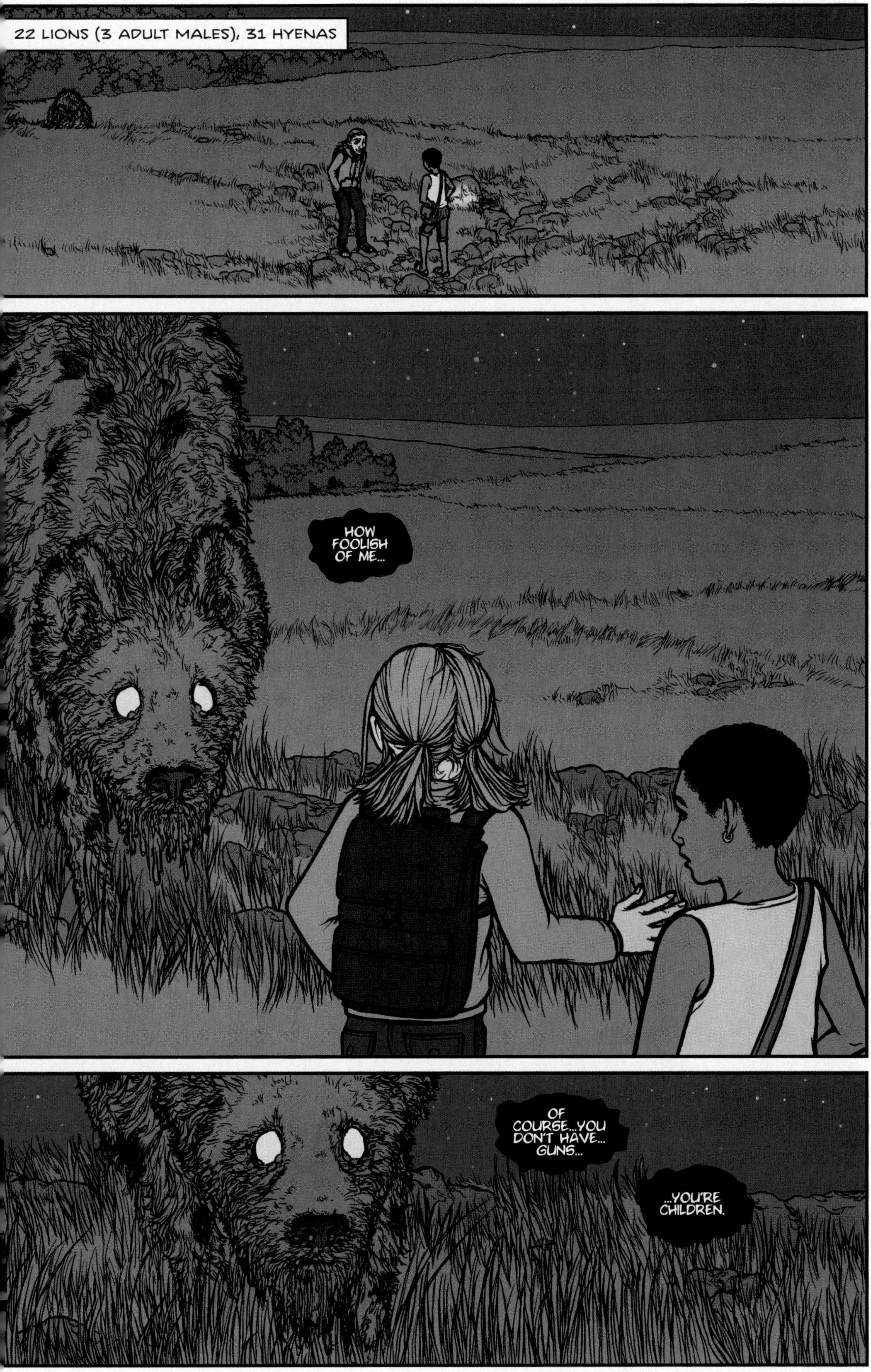
22 LIONS (3 ADULT MALES), 31 HYENAS
HOW FOOLISH OF ME...
OF COURSE...YOU DON'T HAVE... GUNS...
...YOU'RE CHILDREN.

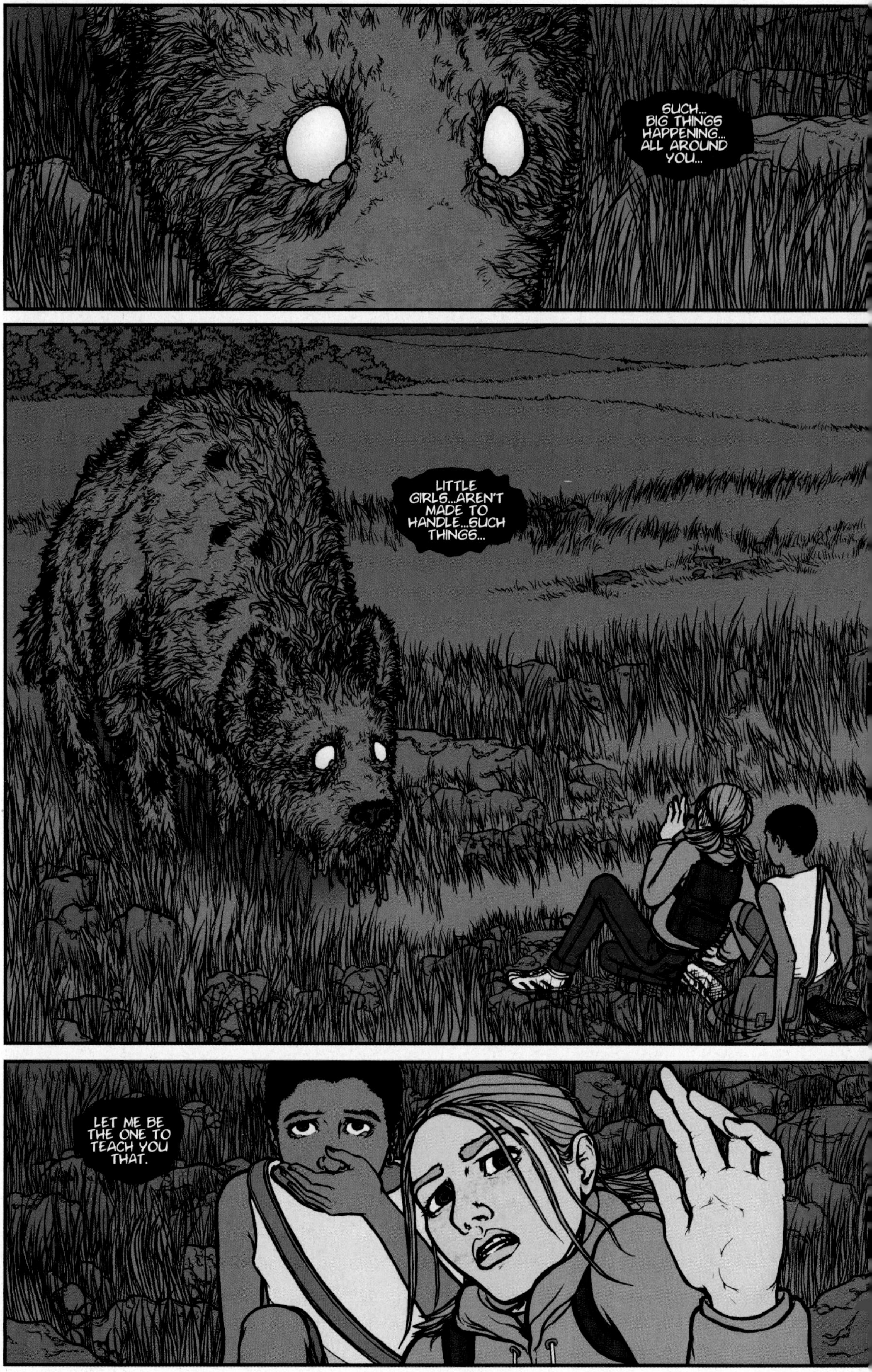
SUCH... BIG THINGS HAPPENING... ALL AROUND YOU...
LITTLE GIRLS...AREN'T MADE TO HANDLE...SUCH THINGS...
LET ME BE THE ONE TO TEACH YOU THAT.

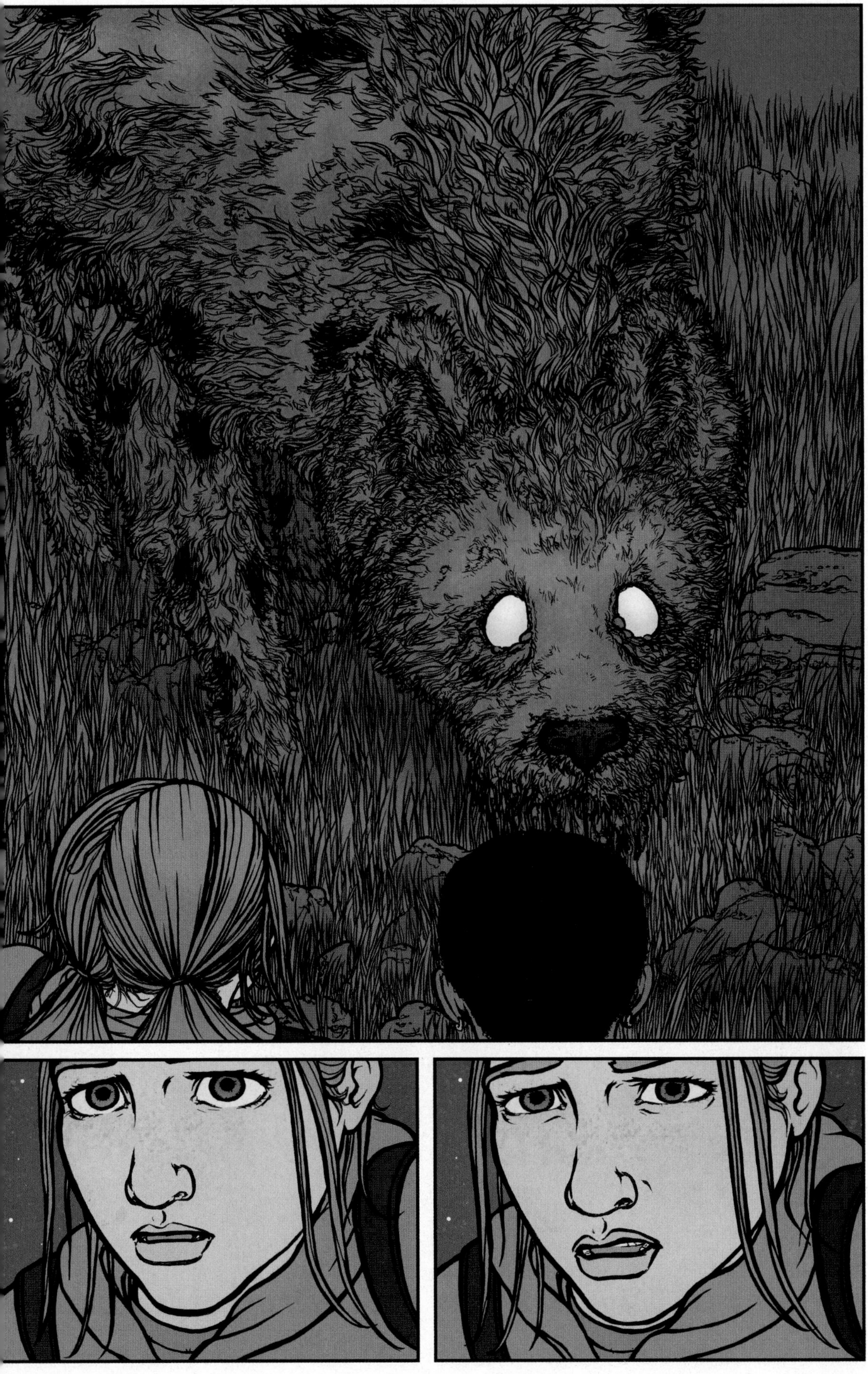

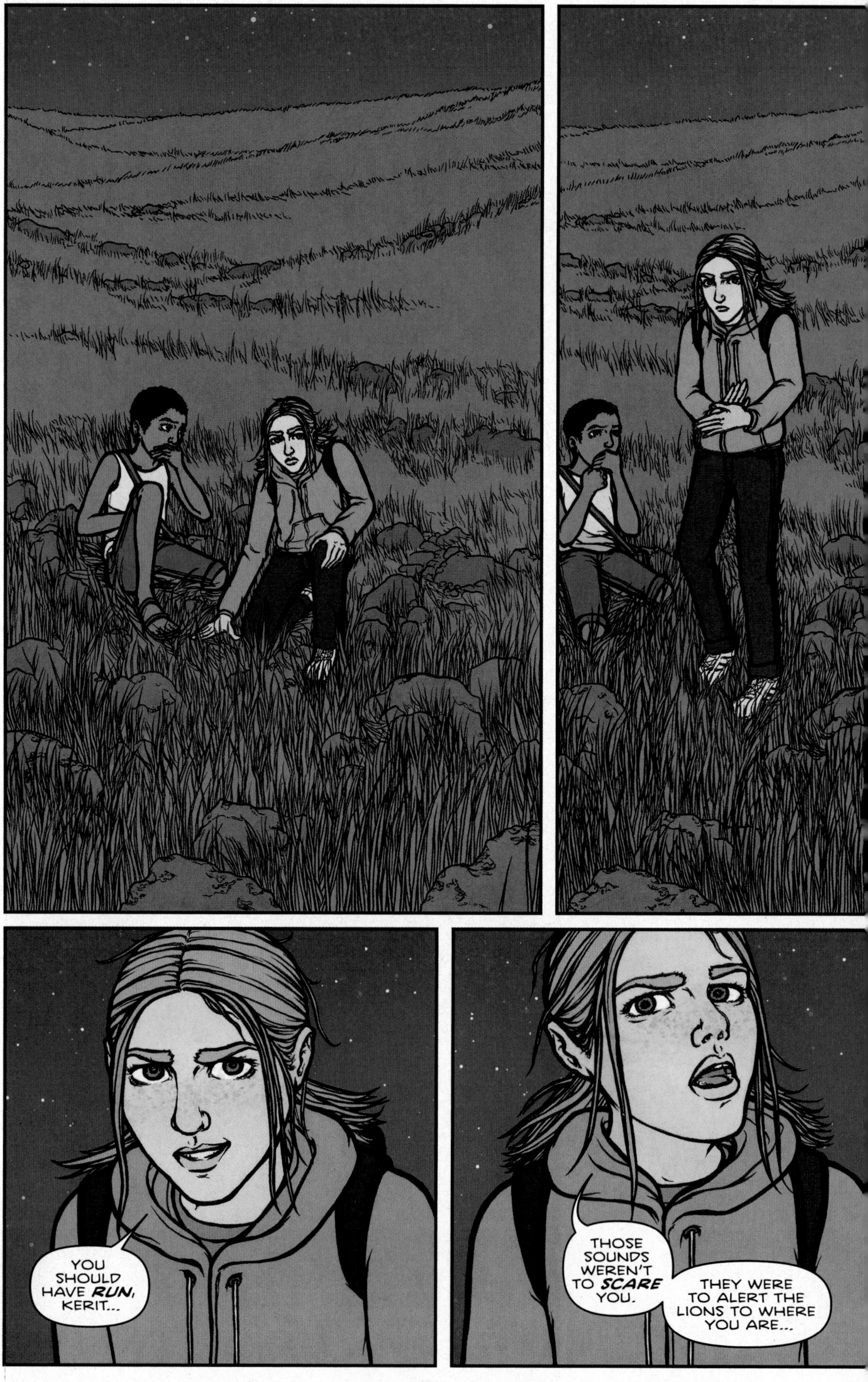
YOU SHOULD HAVE RUN, KERIT...
THOSE SOUNDS WEREN'T TO SCARE YOU.
THEY WERE TO ALERT THE LIONS TO WHERE YOU ARE...

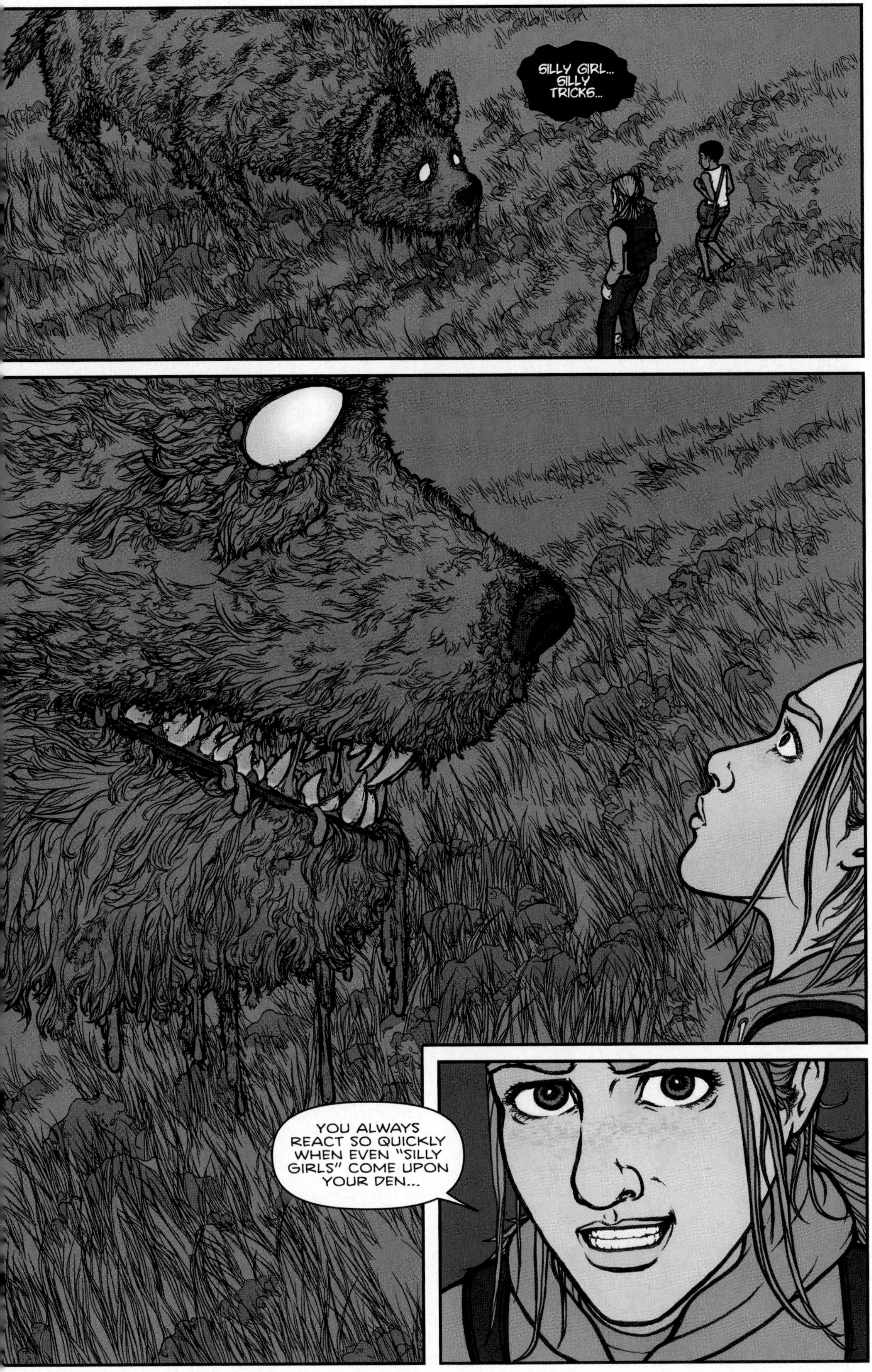
SILLY GIRL... SILLY TRICKS...
YOU ALWAYS REACT SO QUICKLY WHEN EVEN "SILLY GIRLS" COME UPON YOUR DEN...

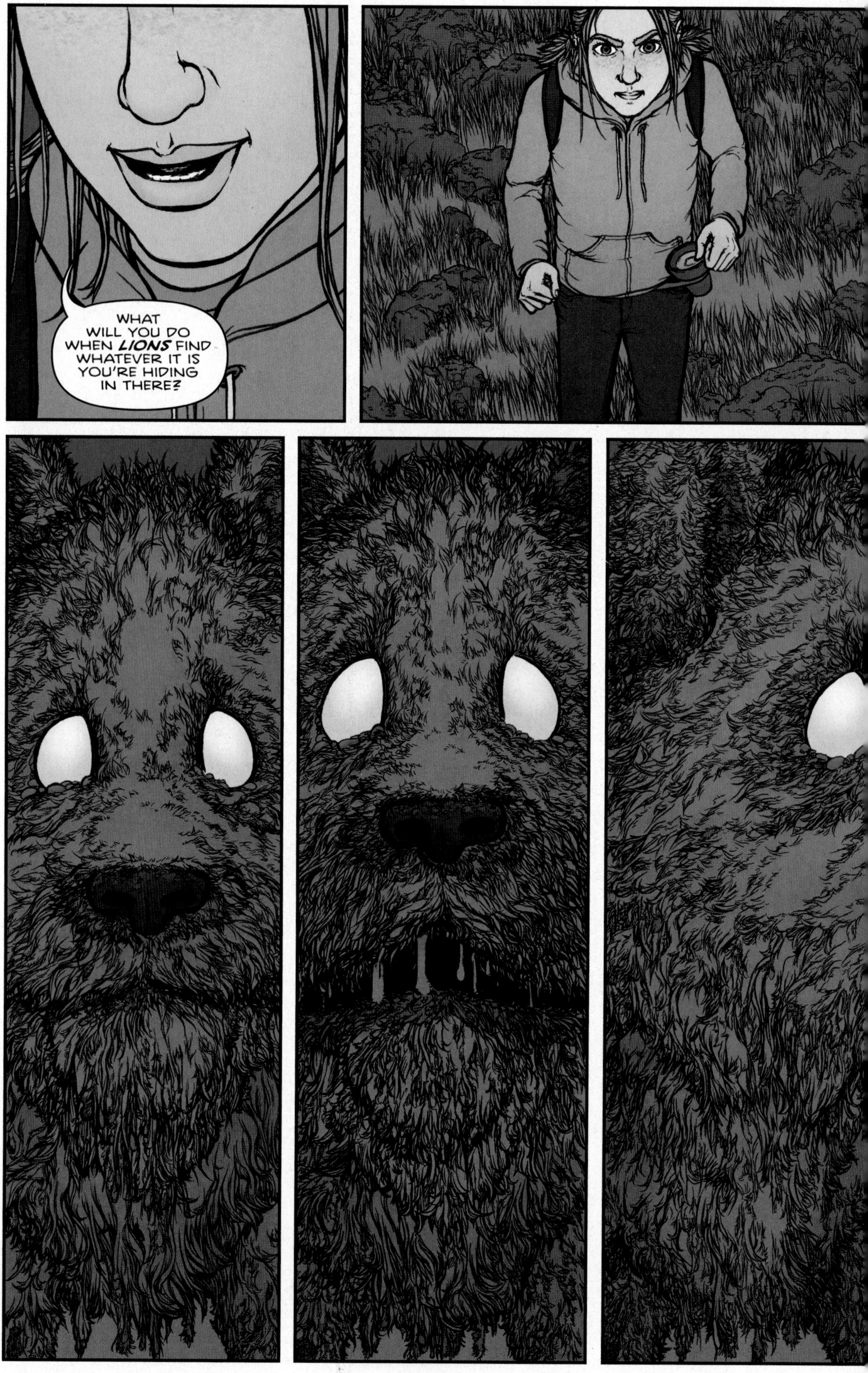
WHAT WILL YOU DO WHEN *LIONS* FIND WHATEVER IT IS YOU'RE HIDING IN THERE?

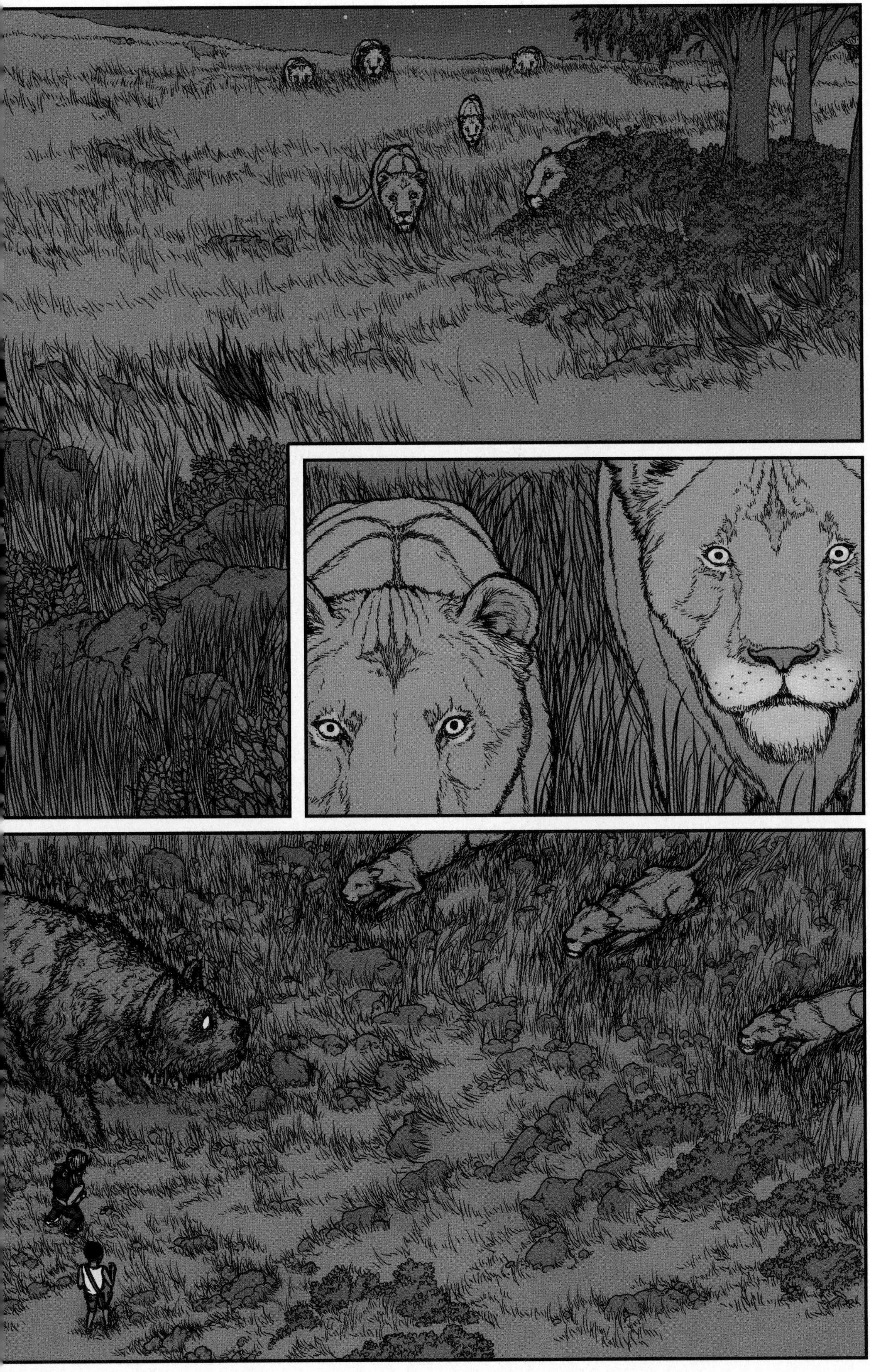

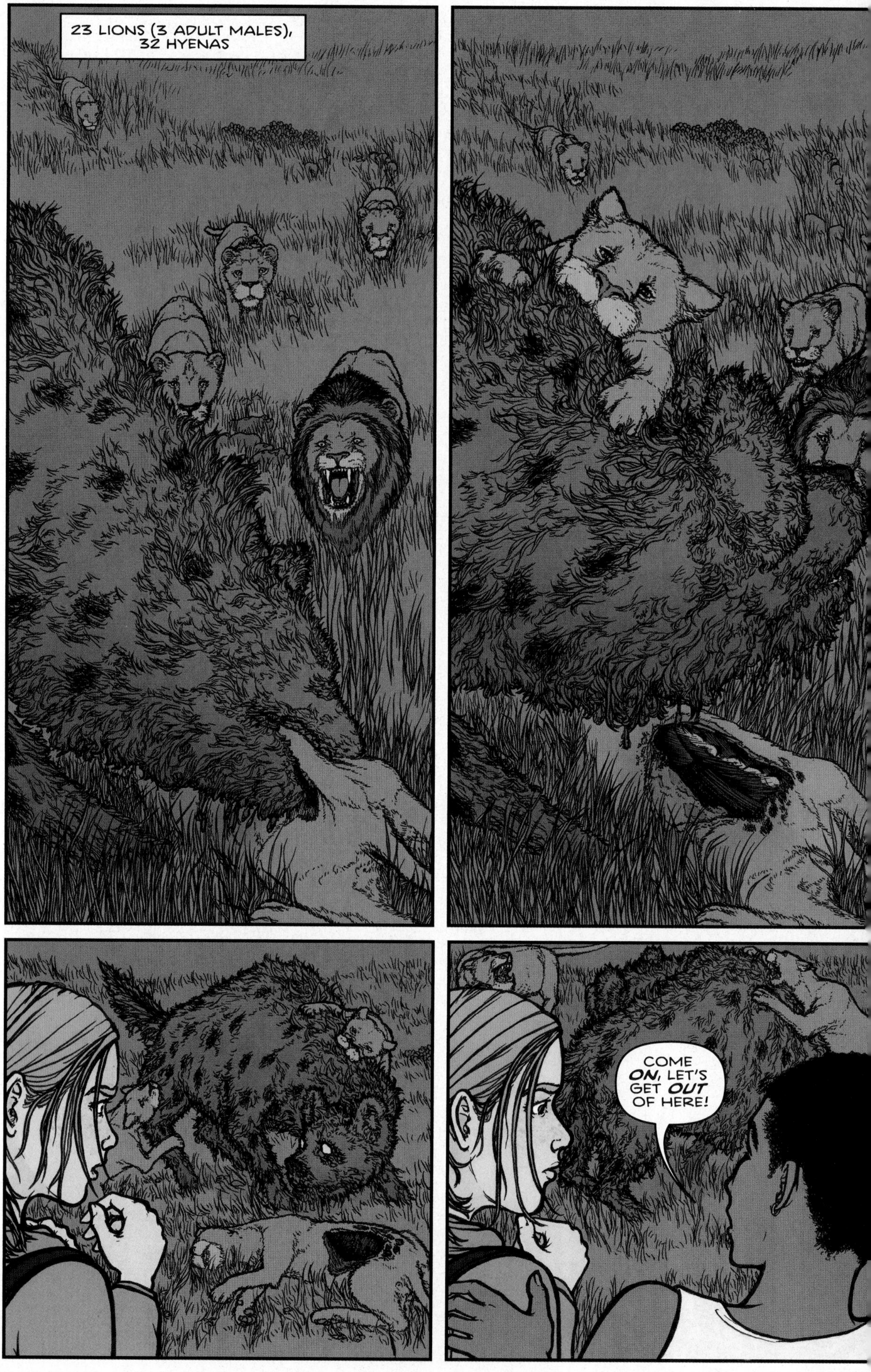
23 LIONS (3 ADULT MALES), 32 HYENAS
COME ON, LET'S GET OUT OF HERE!

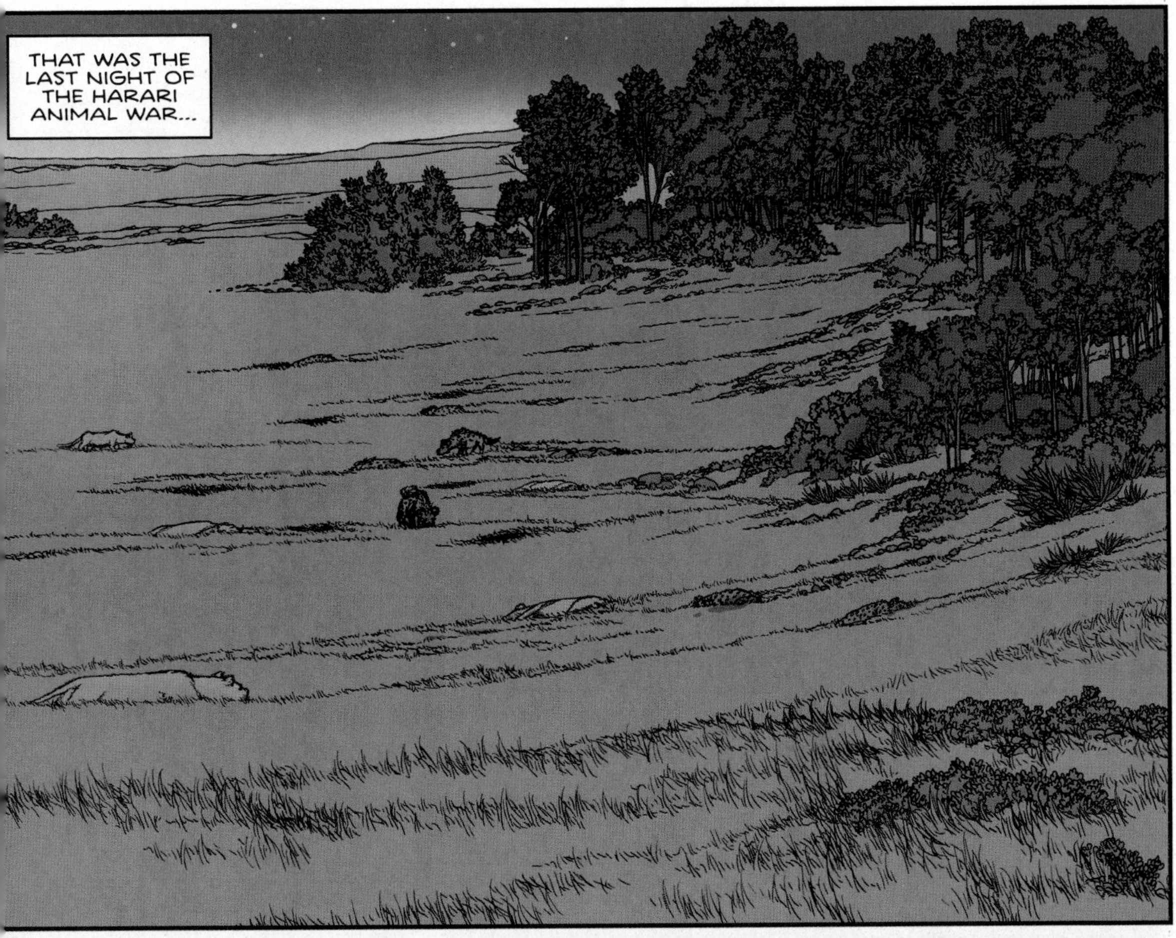
THAT WAS THE LAST NIGHT OF THE HARARI ANIMAL WAR...

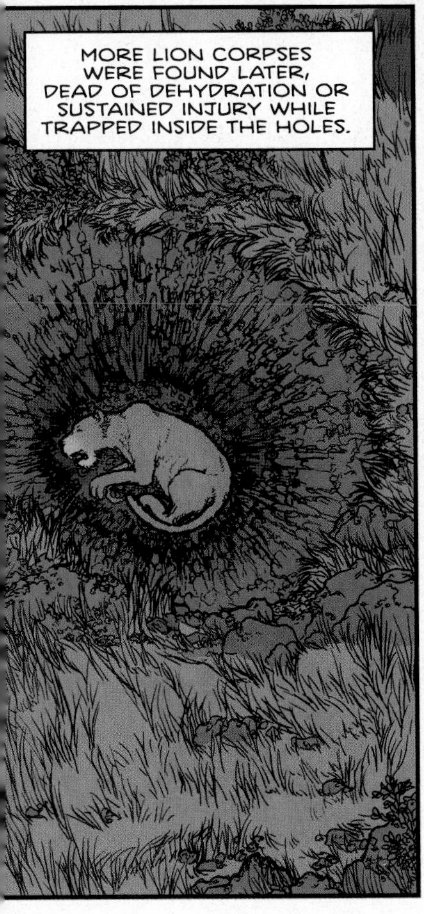
MORE LION CORPSES WERE FOUND LATER, DEAD OF DEHYDRATION OR SUSTAINED INJURY WHILE TRAPPED INSIDE THE HOLES.

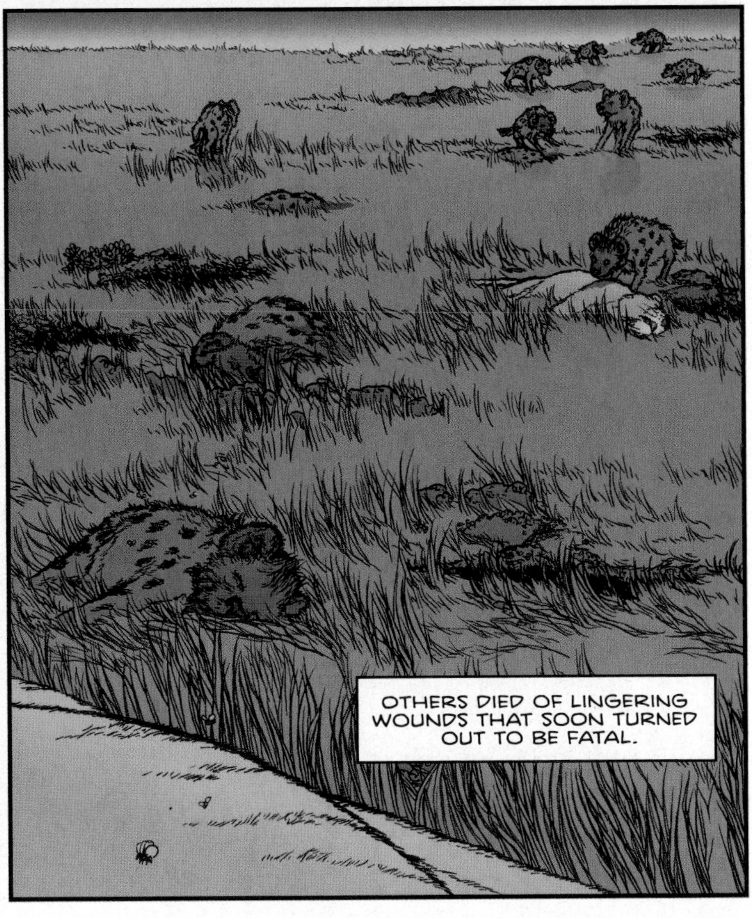
OTHERS DIED OF LINGERING WOUNDS THAT SOON TURNED OUT TO BE FATAL.

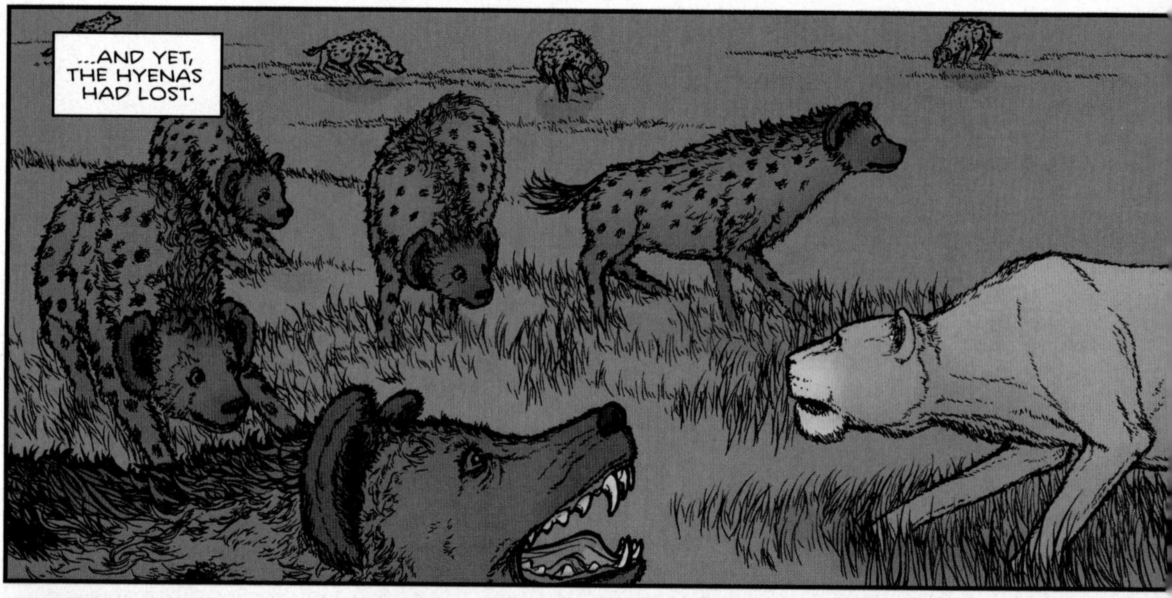
...AND YET, THE HYENAS HAD LOST.

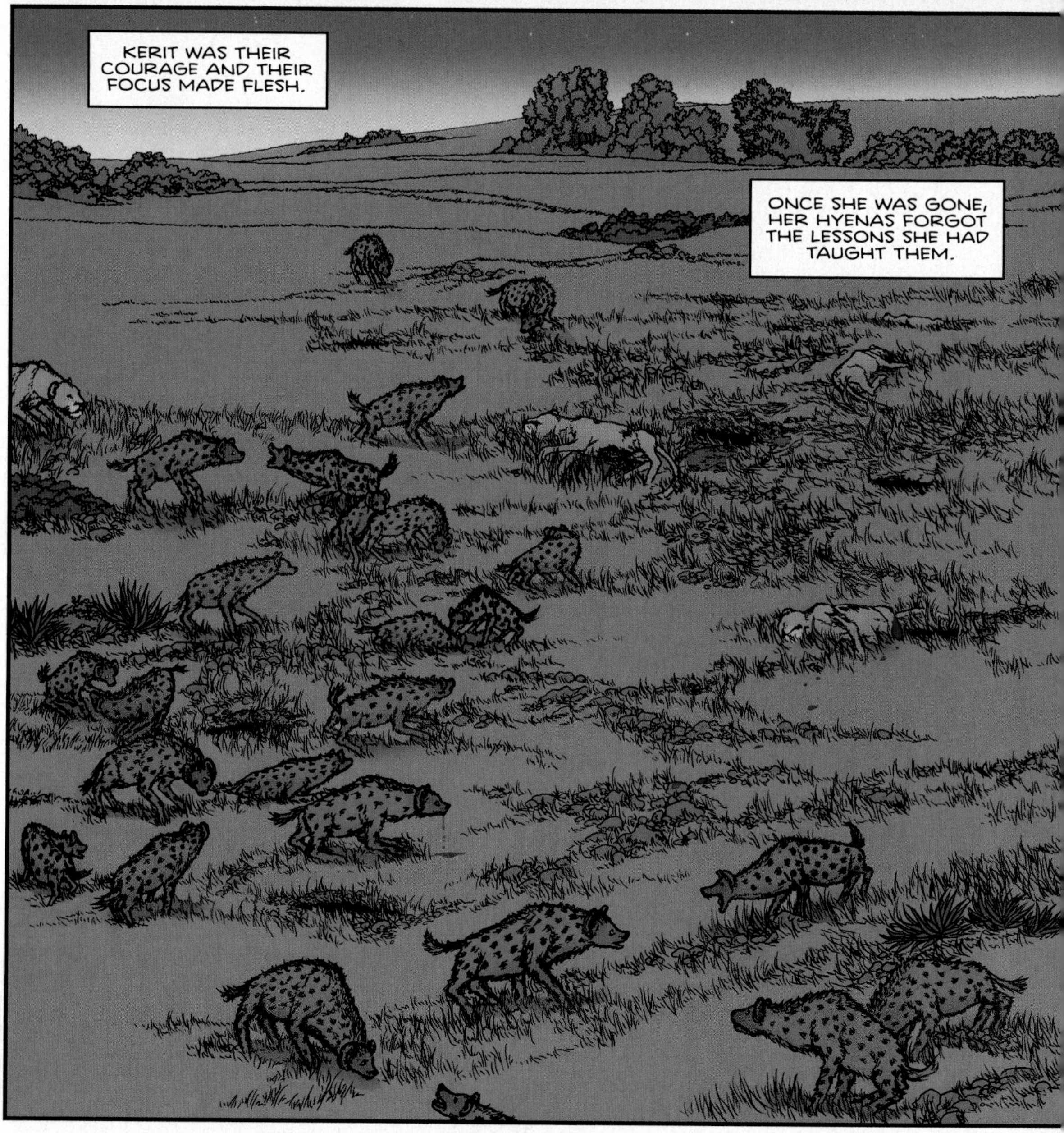
KERIT WAS THEIR COURAGE AND THEIR FOCUS MADE FLESH.
ONCE SHE WAS GONE, HER HYENAS FORGOT THE LESSONS SHE HAD TAUGHT THEM.

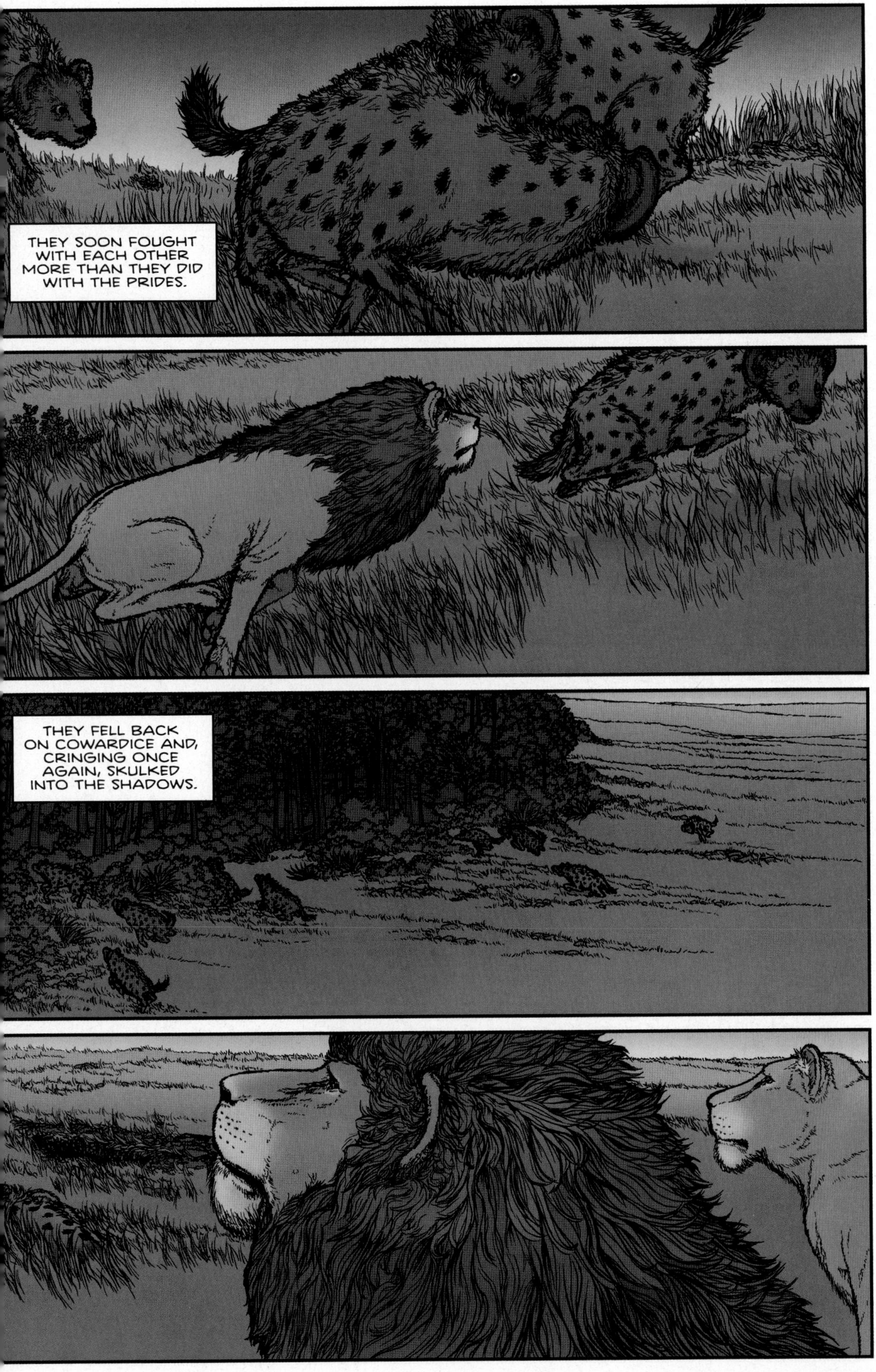
THEY SOON FOUGHT WITH EACH OTHER MORE THAN THEY DID WITH THE PRIDES.
THEY FELL BACK ON COWARDICE AND, CRINGING ONCE AGAIN, SKULKED INTO THE SHADOWS.

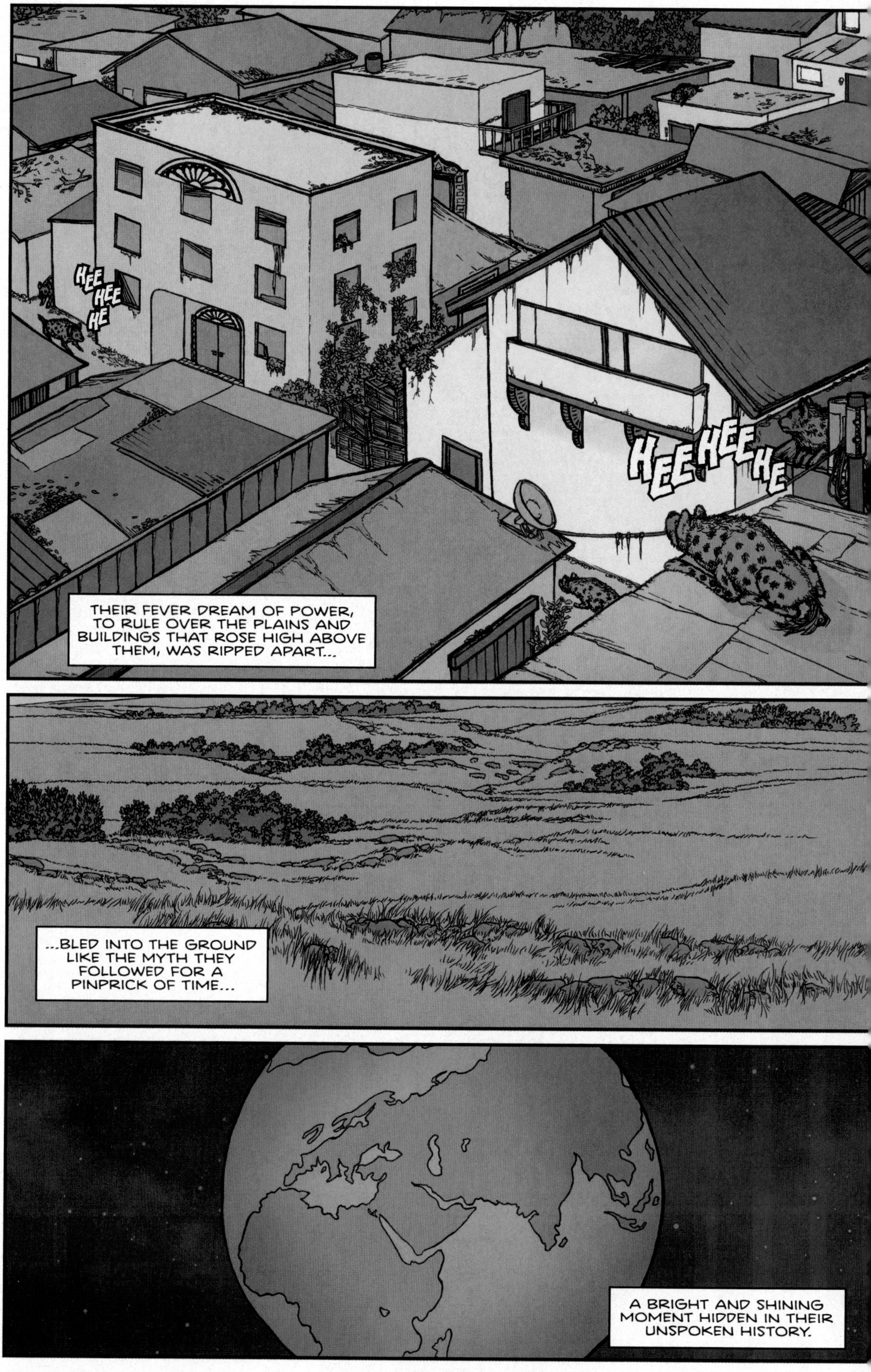
HEE HEE HE
HEE HEE HE
THEIR FEVER DREAM OF POWER, TO RULE OVER THE PLAINS AND BUILDINGS THAT ROSE HIGH ABOVE THEM, WAS RIPPED APART...
...BLED INTO THE GROUND LIKE THE MYTH THEY FOLLOWED FOR A PINPRICK OF TIME...
A BRIGHT AND SHINING MOMENT HIDDEN IN THEIR UNSPOKEN HISTORY.

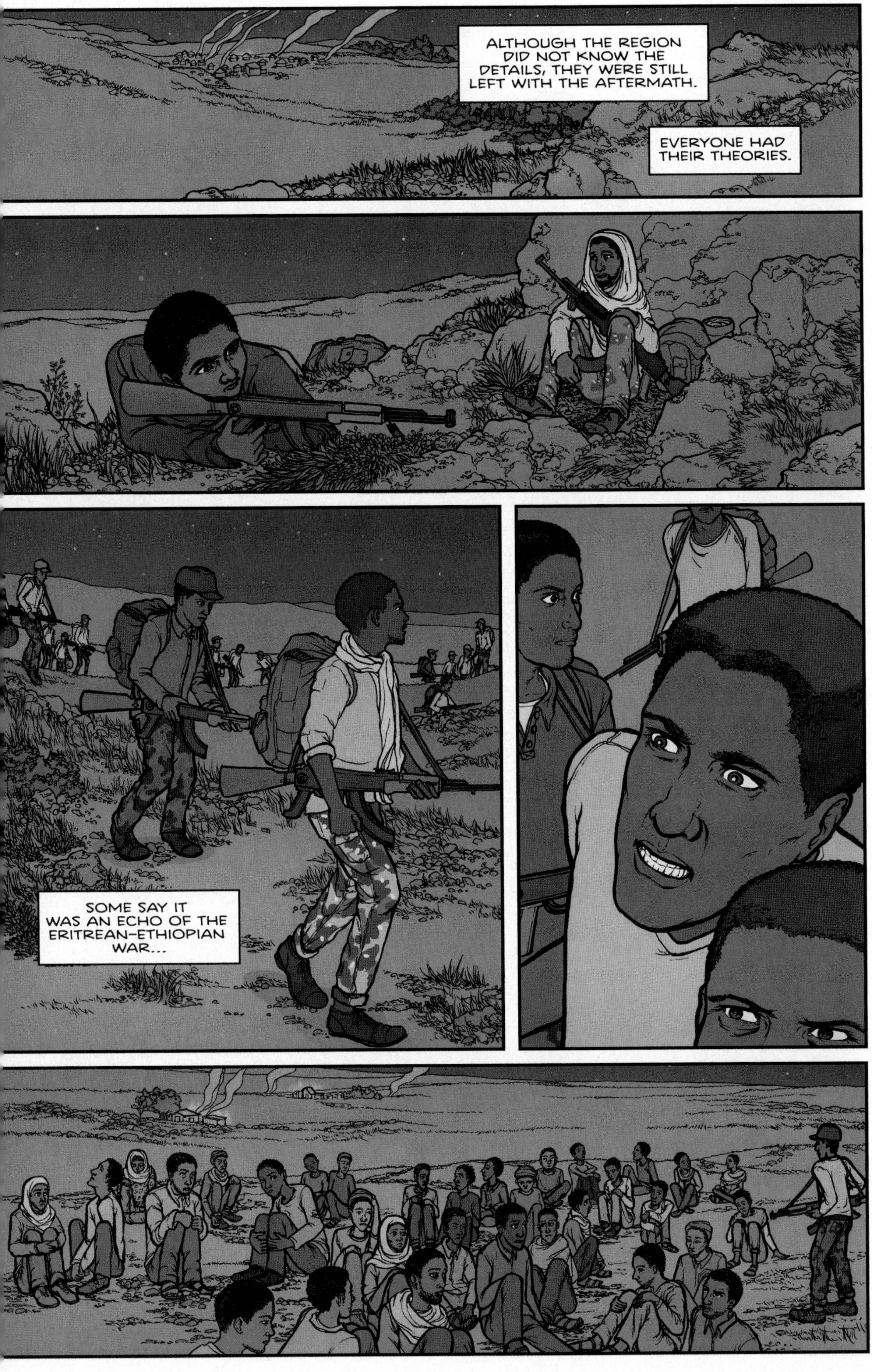
ALTHOUGH THE REGION DID NOT KNOW THE DETAILS, THEY WERE STILL LEFT WITH THE AFTERMATH.
EVERYONE HAD THEIR THEORIES.
SOME SAY IT WAS AN ECHO OF THE ERITREAN-ETHIOPIAN WAR...

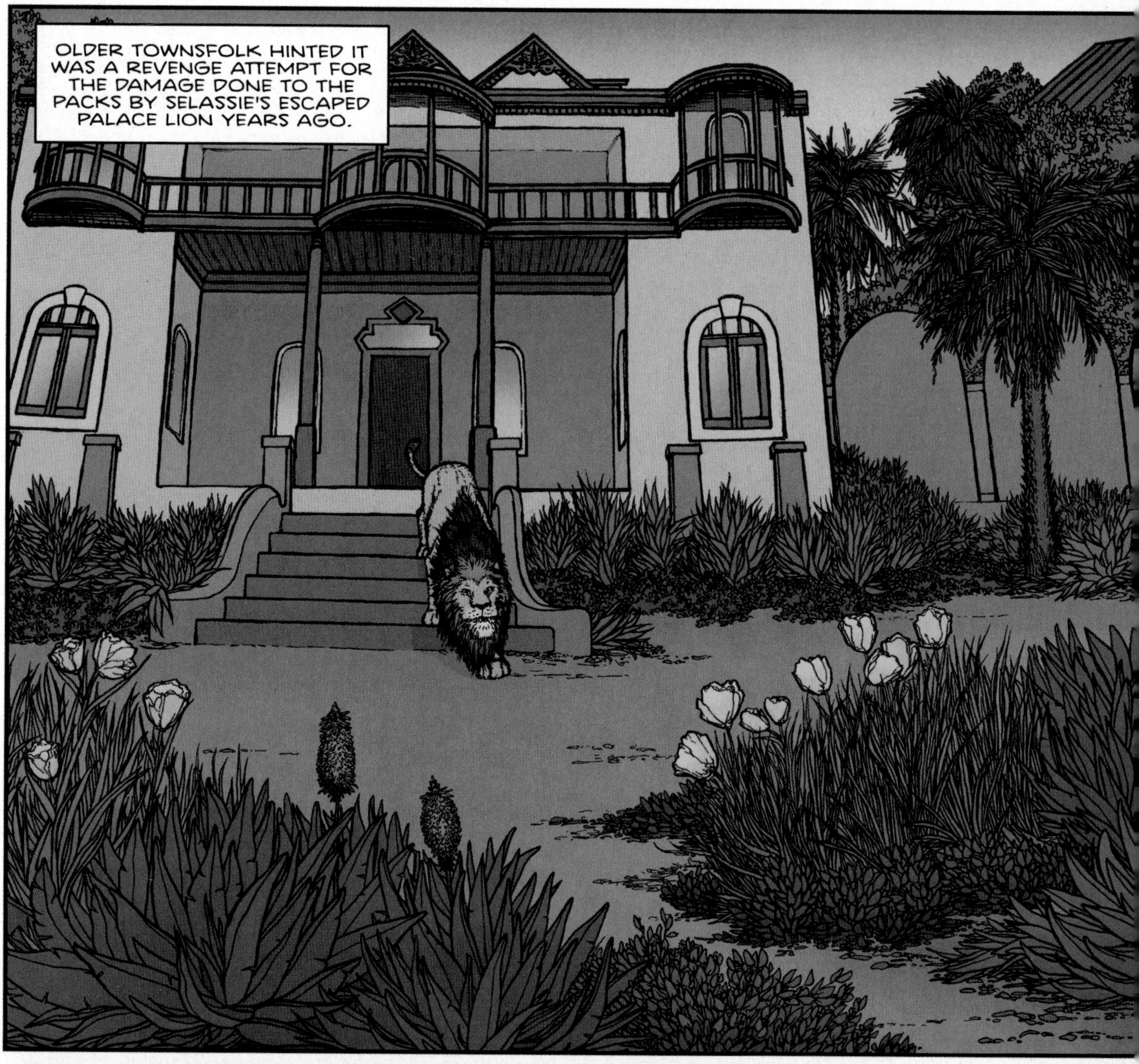
OLDER TOWNSFOLK HINTED IT WAS A REVENGE ATTEMPT FOR THE DAMAGE DONE TO THE PACKS BY SELASSIE'S ESCAPED PALACE LION YEARS AGO.

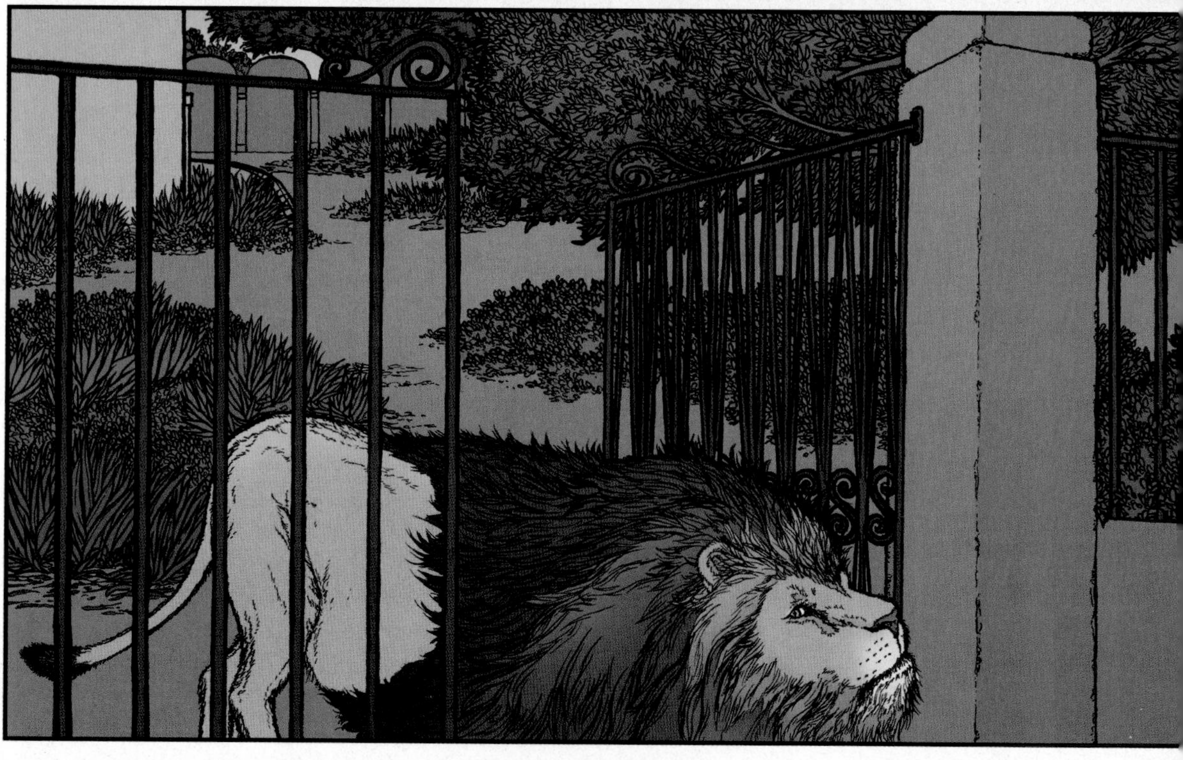

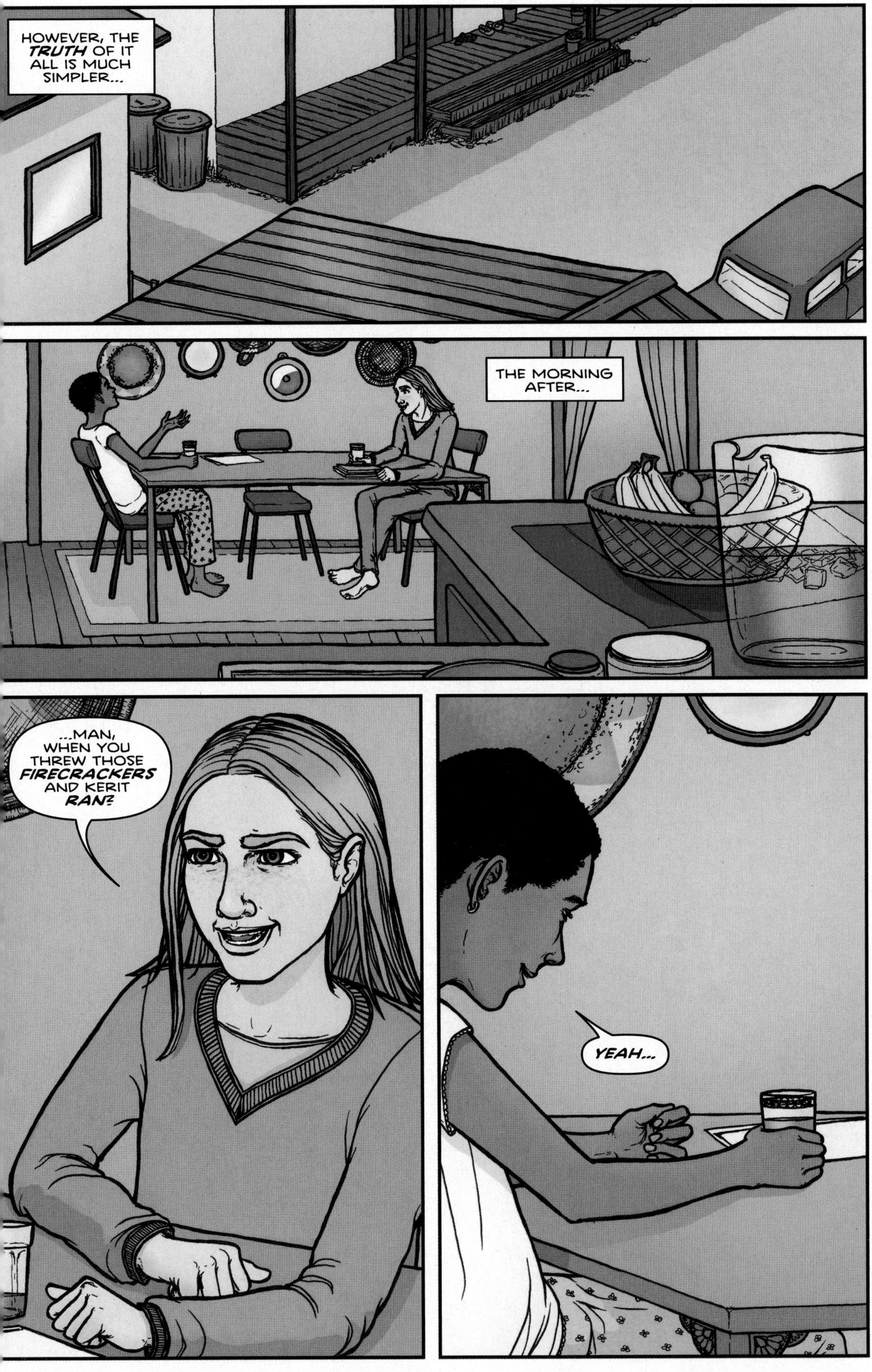
HOWEVER, THE TRUTH OF IT ALL IS MUCH SIMPLER...
THE MORNING AFTER...
...MAN, WHEN YOU THREW THOSE FIRECRACKERS AND KERIT RAN?
YEAH...

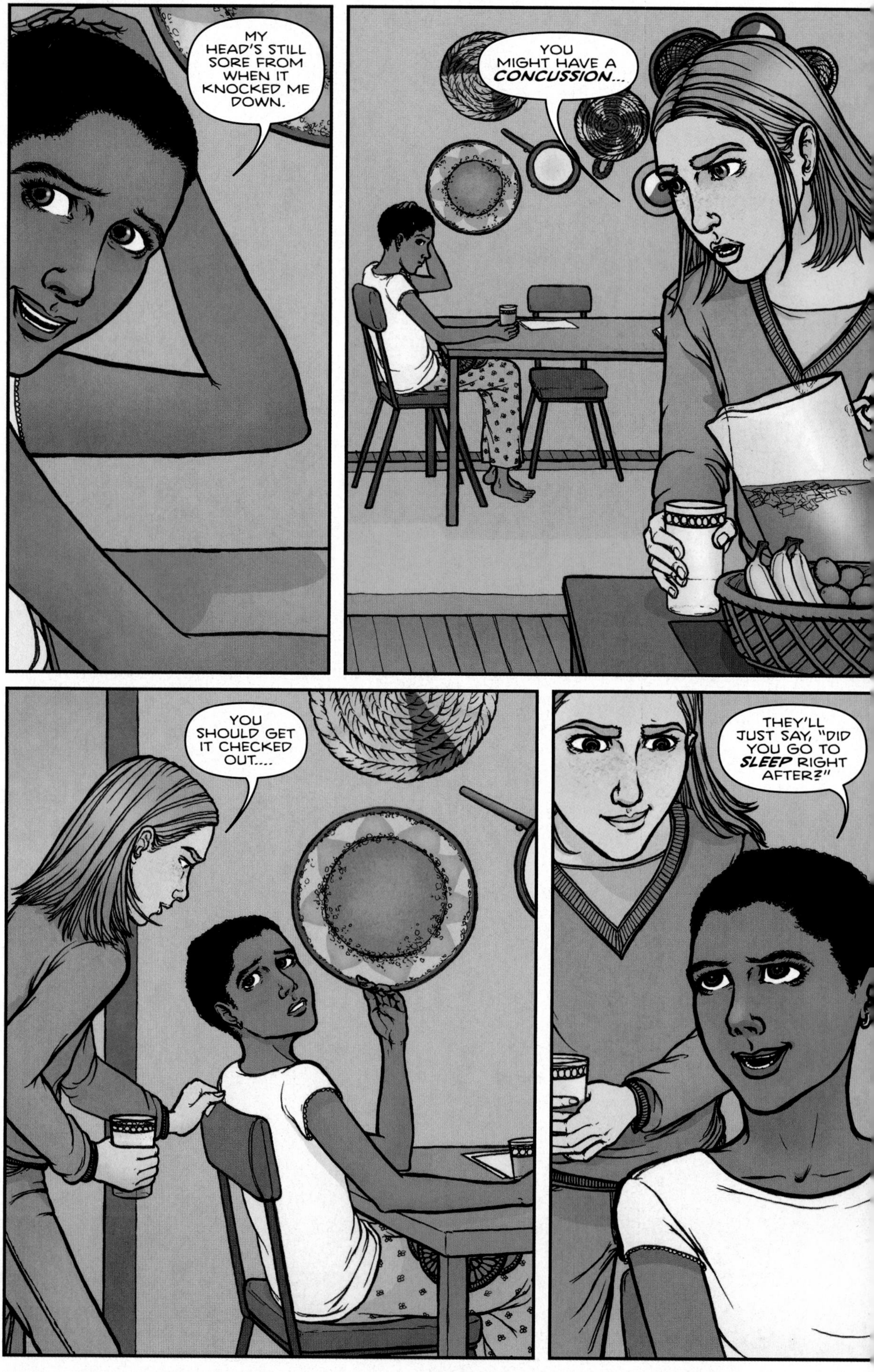
MY HEAD'S STILL SORE FROM WHEN IT KNOCKED ME DOWN.
YOU MIGHT HAVE A *CONCUSSION*...
YOU SHOULD GET IT CHECKED OUT....
THEY'LL JUST SAY, "DID YOU GO TO *SLEEP* RIGHT AFTER?"

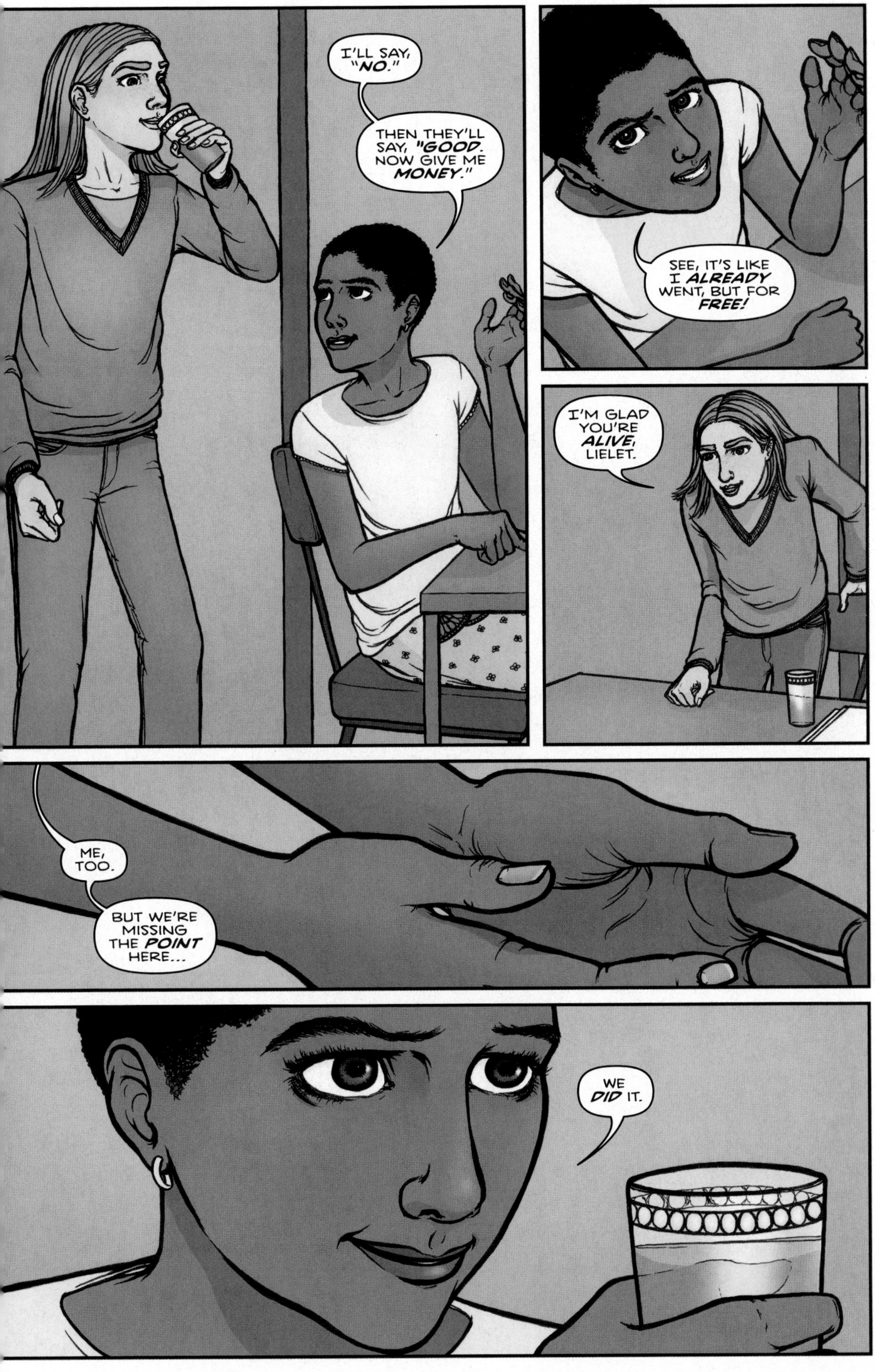
I'LL SAY, "NO."
THEN THEY'LL SAY, "GOOD. NOW GIVE ME MONEY."
SEE, IT'S LIKE I ALREADY WENT, BUT FOR FREE!
I'M GLAD YOU'RE ALIVE, LIELET.
ME, TOO.
BUT WE'RE MISSING THE POINT HERE...
WE DID IT.

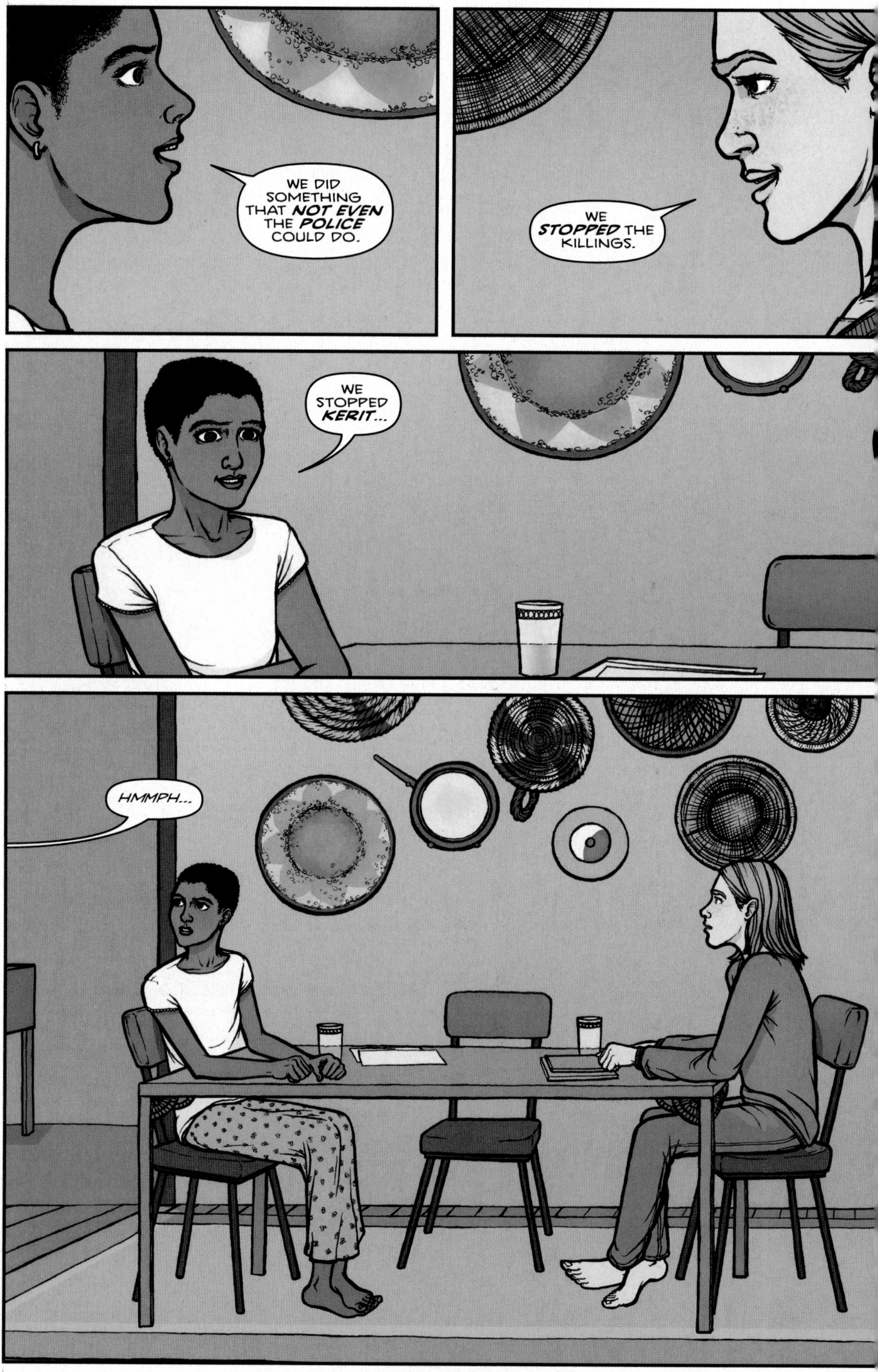
WE DID SOMETHING THAT NOT EVEN THE POLICE COULD DO.
WE STOPPED THE KILLINGS.
WE STOPPED KERIT...
HMMPH...

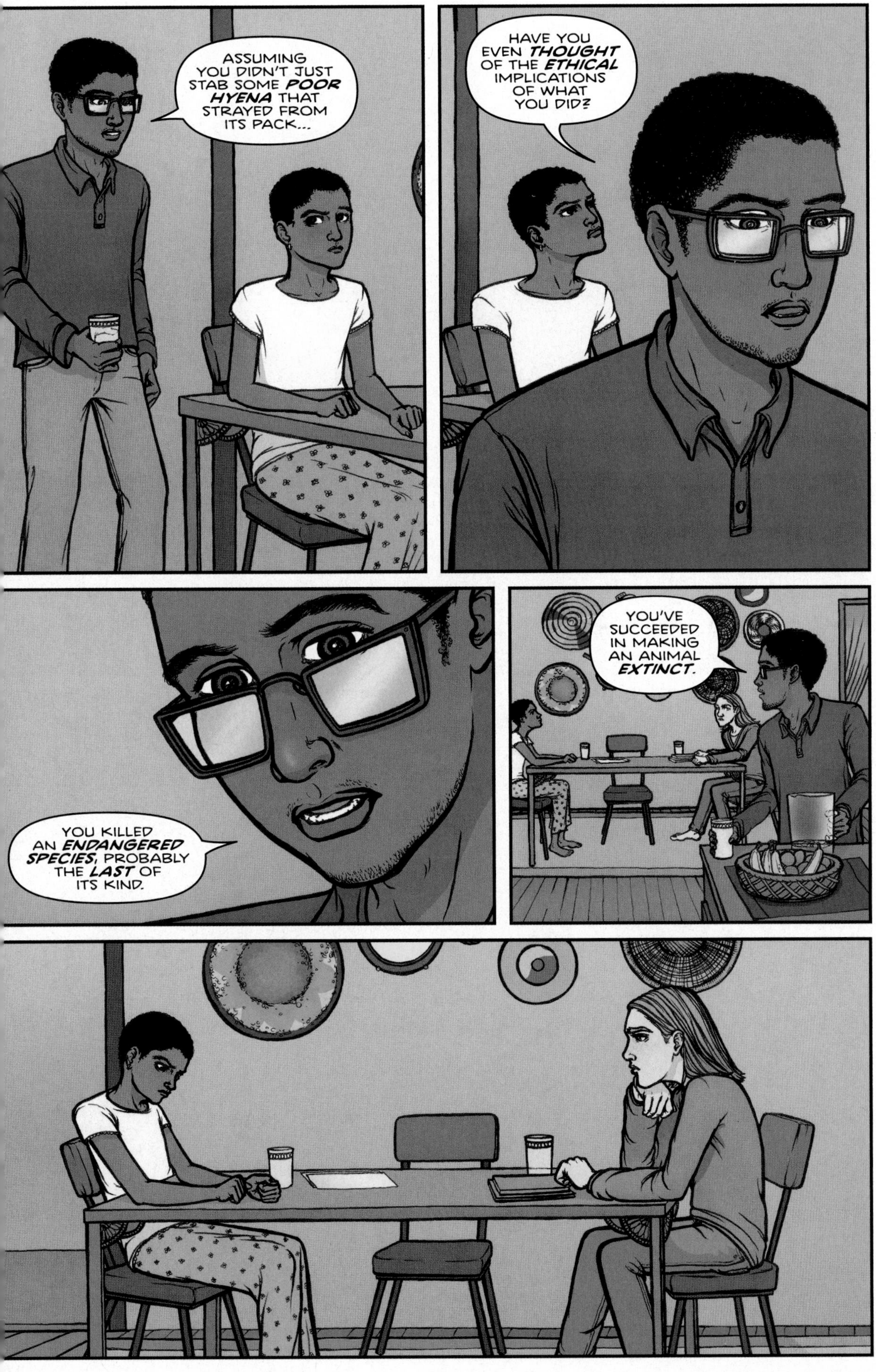
ASSUMING YOU DIDN'T JUST STAB SOME *POOR HYENA* THAT STRAYED FROM ITS PACK...
HAVE YOU EVEN *THOUGHT* OF THE *ETHICAL* IMPLICATIONS OF WHAT YOU DID?
YOU KILLED AN *ENDANGERED SPECIES*, PROBABLY THE *LAST* OF ITS KIND.
YOU'VE SUCCEEDED IN MAKING AN ANIMAL *EXTINCT*.

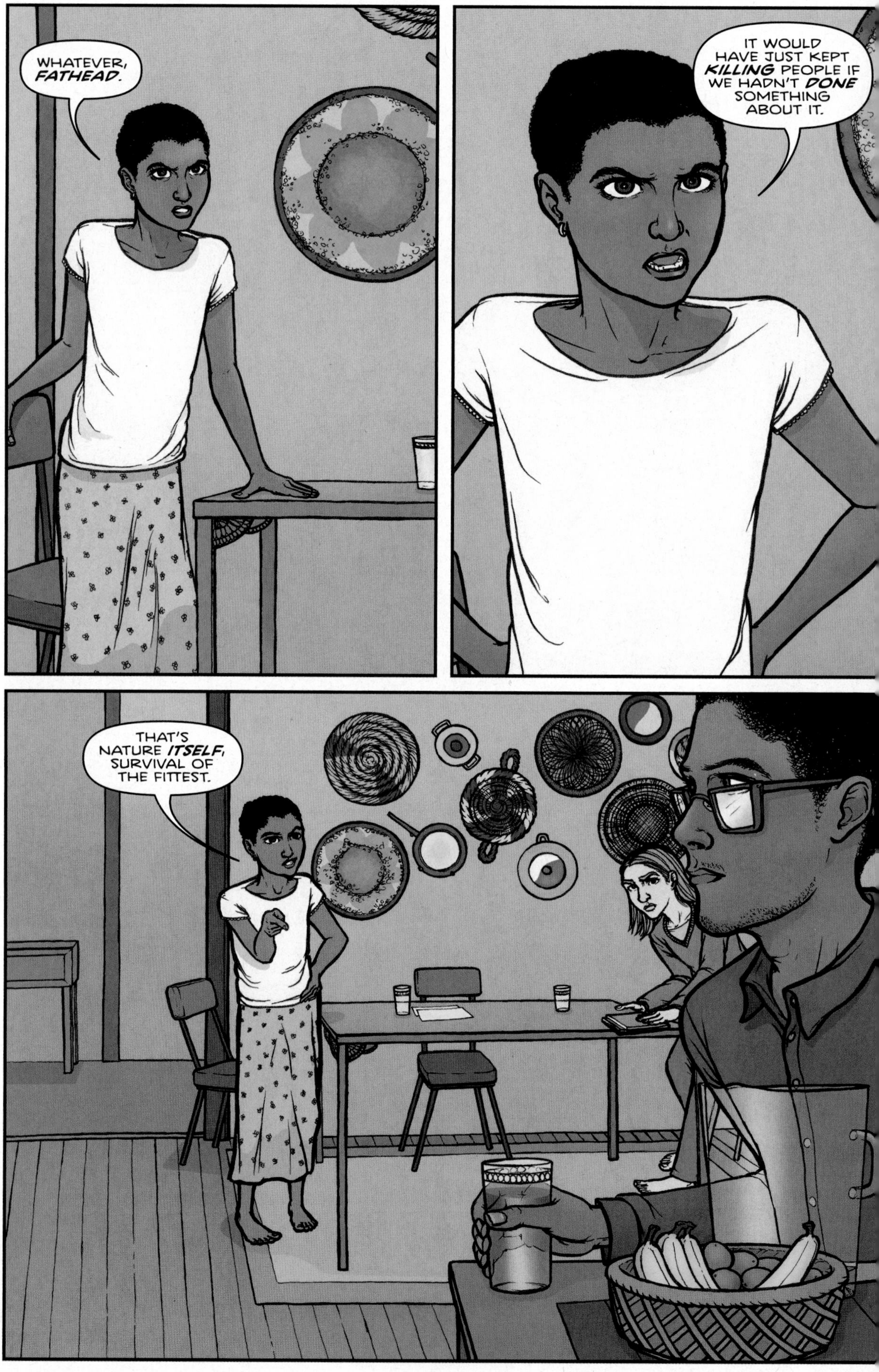
WHATEVER, FATHEAD.
IT WOULD HAVE JUST KEPT KILLING PEOPLE IF WE HADN'T DONE SOMETHING ABOUT IT.
THAT'S NATURE ITSELF, SURVIVAL OF THE FITTEST.

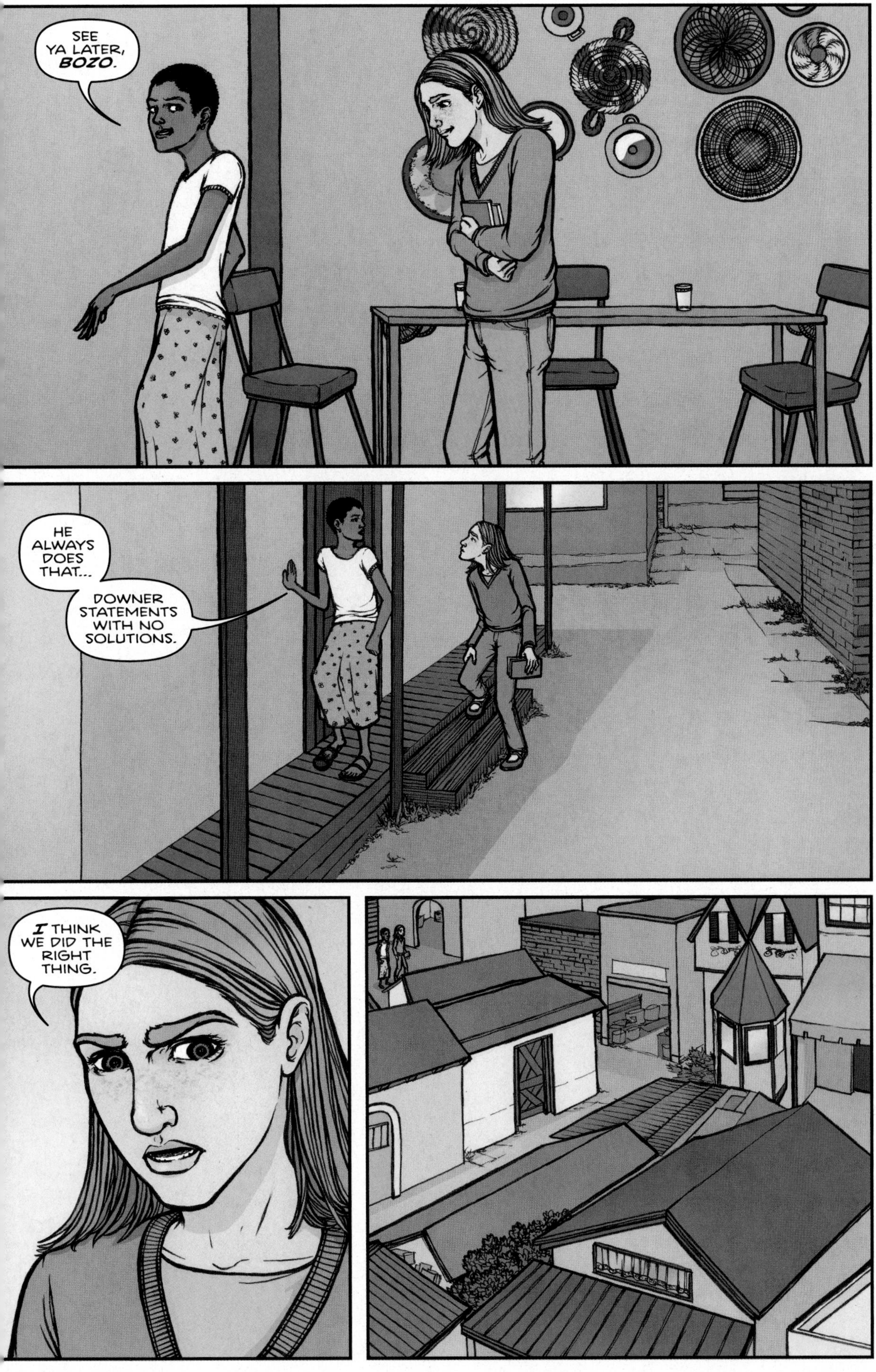
SEE YA LATER, BOZO.
HE ALWAYS DOES THAT...
DOWNER STATEMENTS WITH NO SOLUTIONS.
I THINK WE DID THE RIGHT THING.

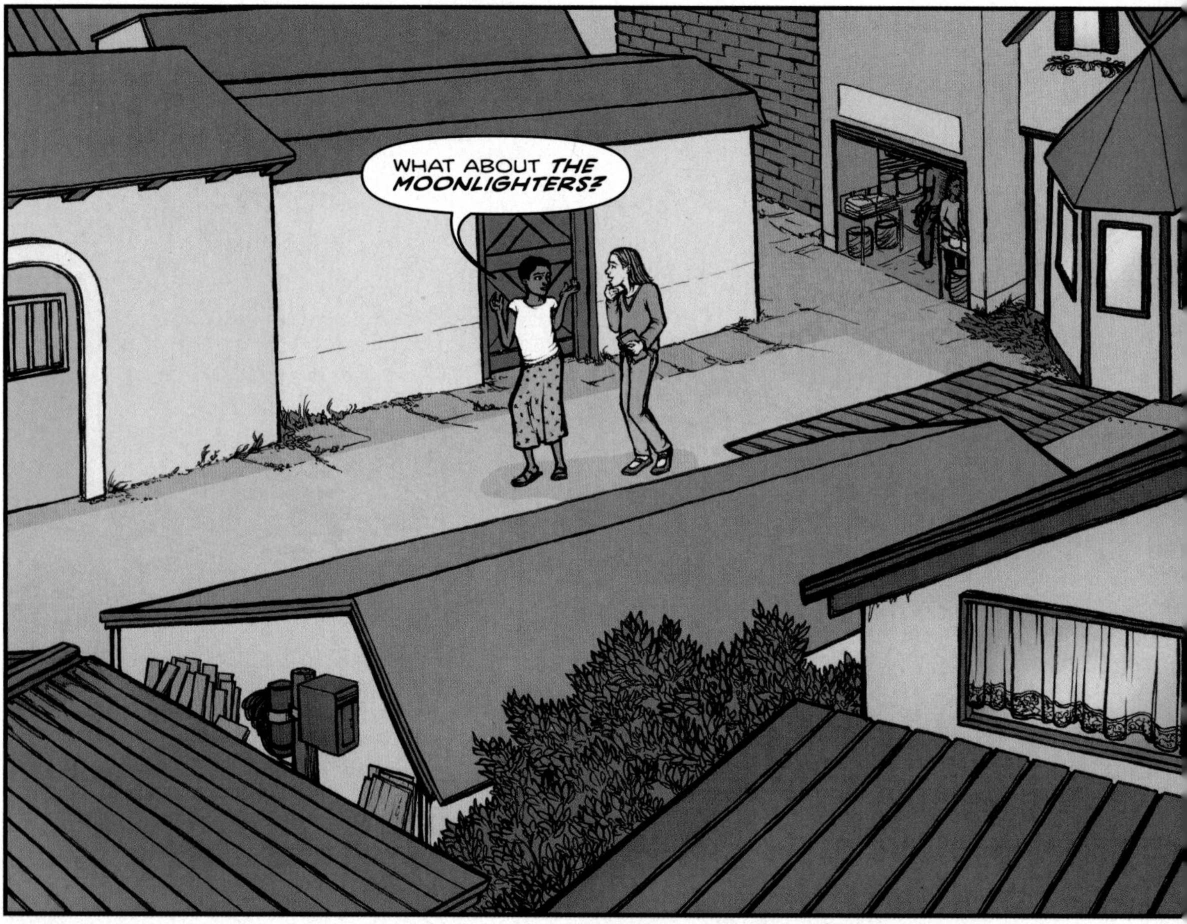
WHAT ABOUT THE MOONLIGHTERS?

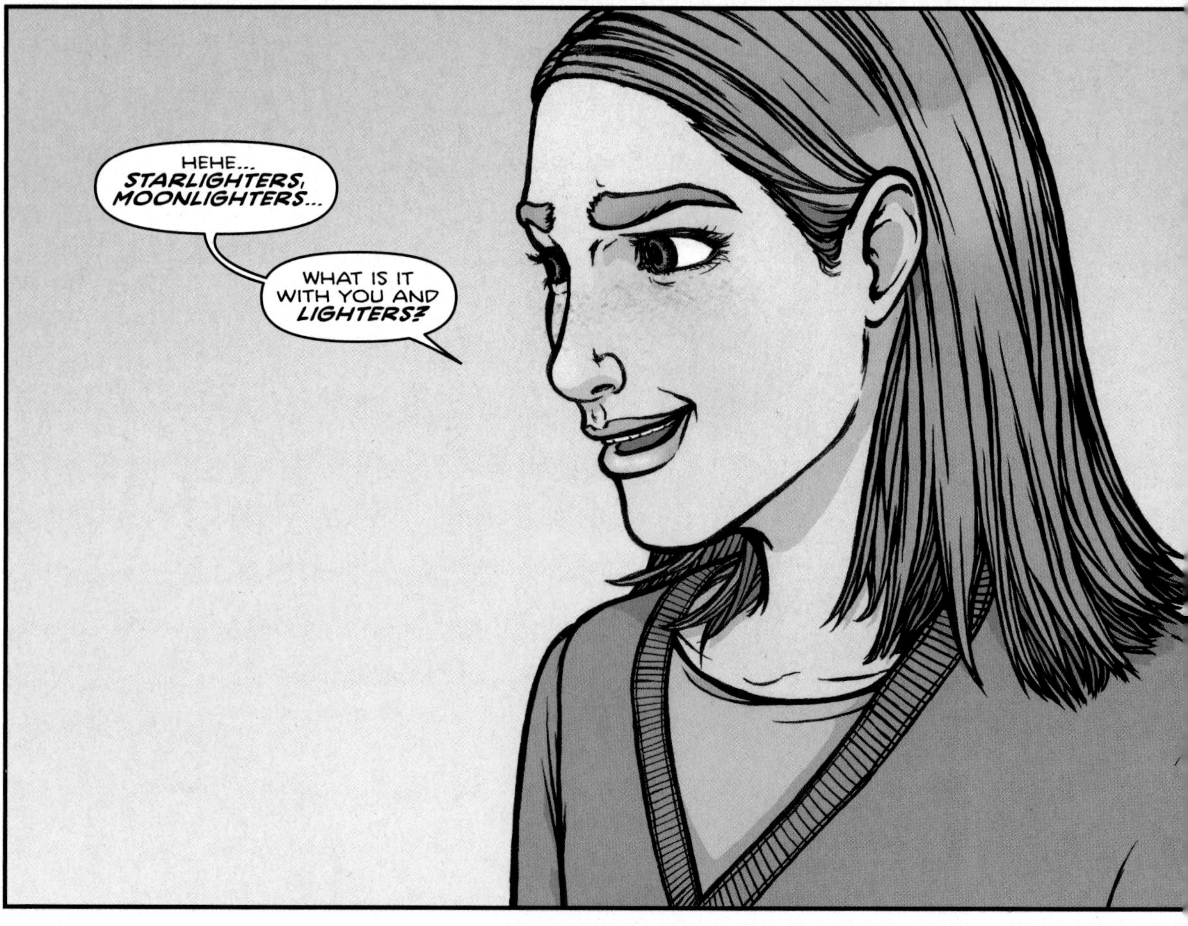
HEHE... STARLIGHTERS, MOONLIGHTERS...
WHAT IS IT WITH YOU AND LIGHTERS?

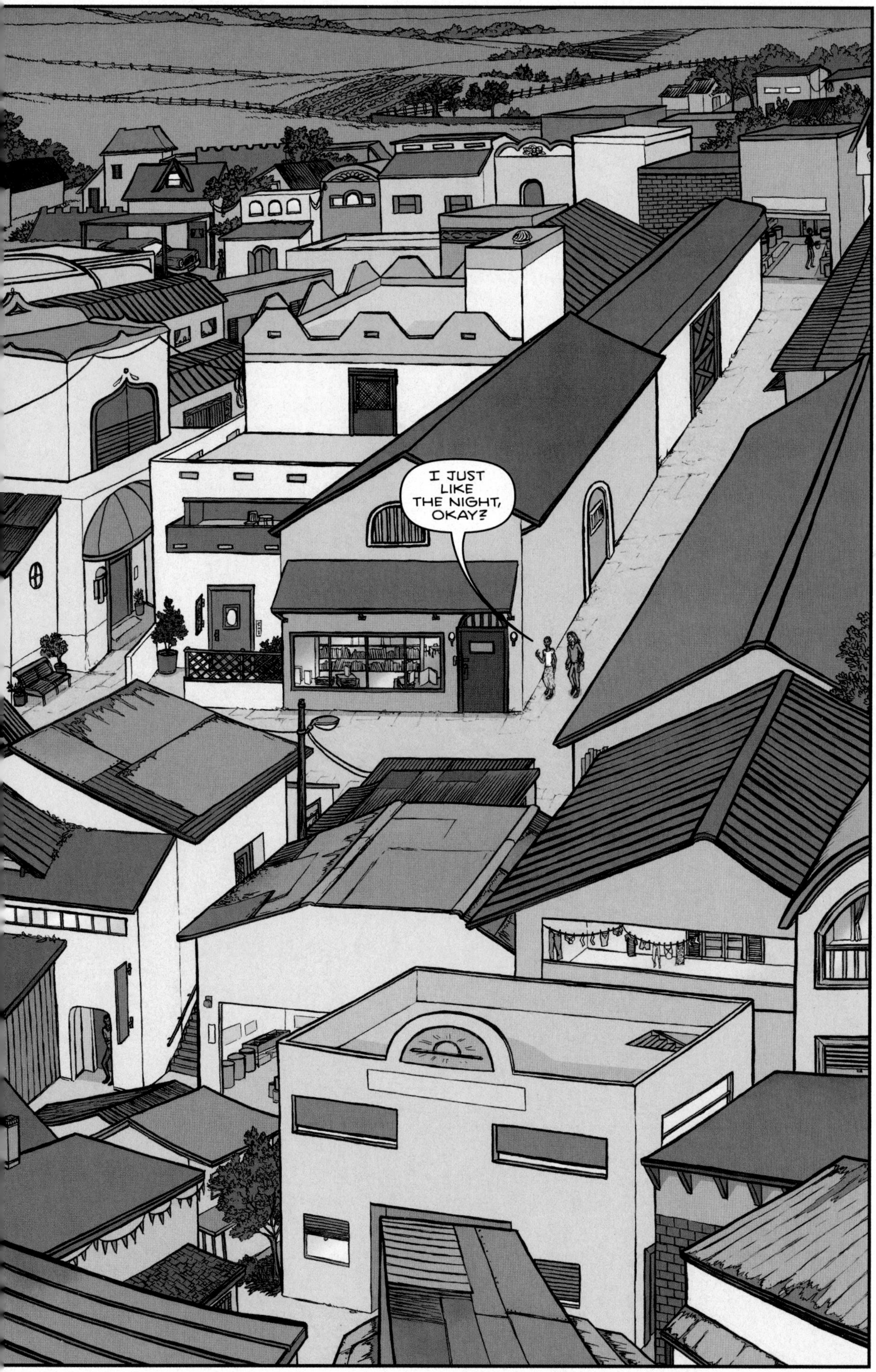
I JUST LIKE THE NIGHT, OKAY?

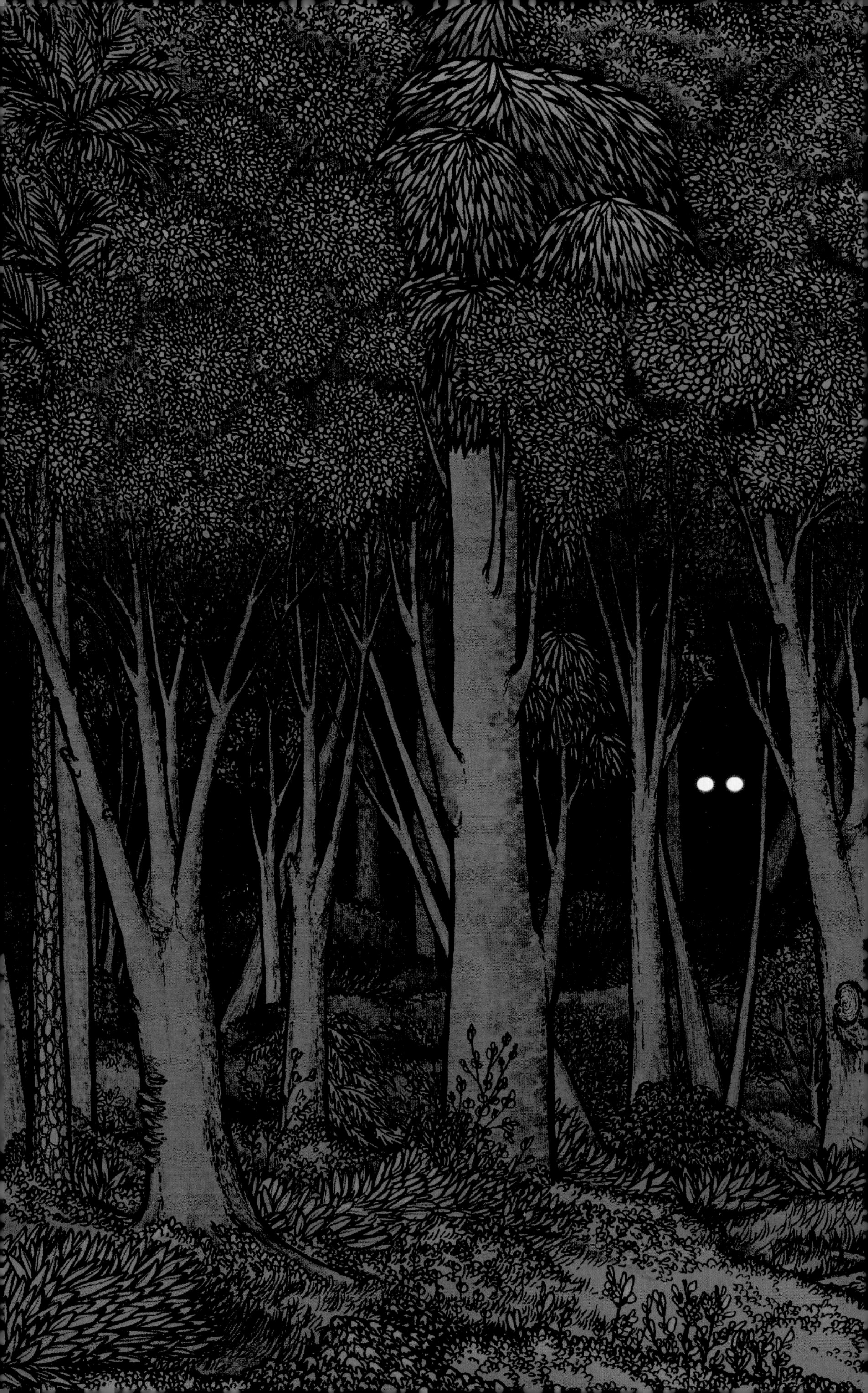

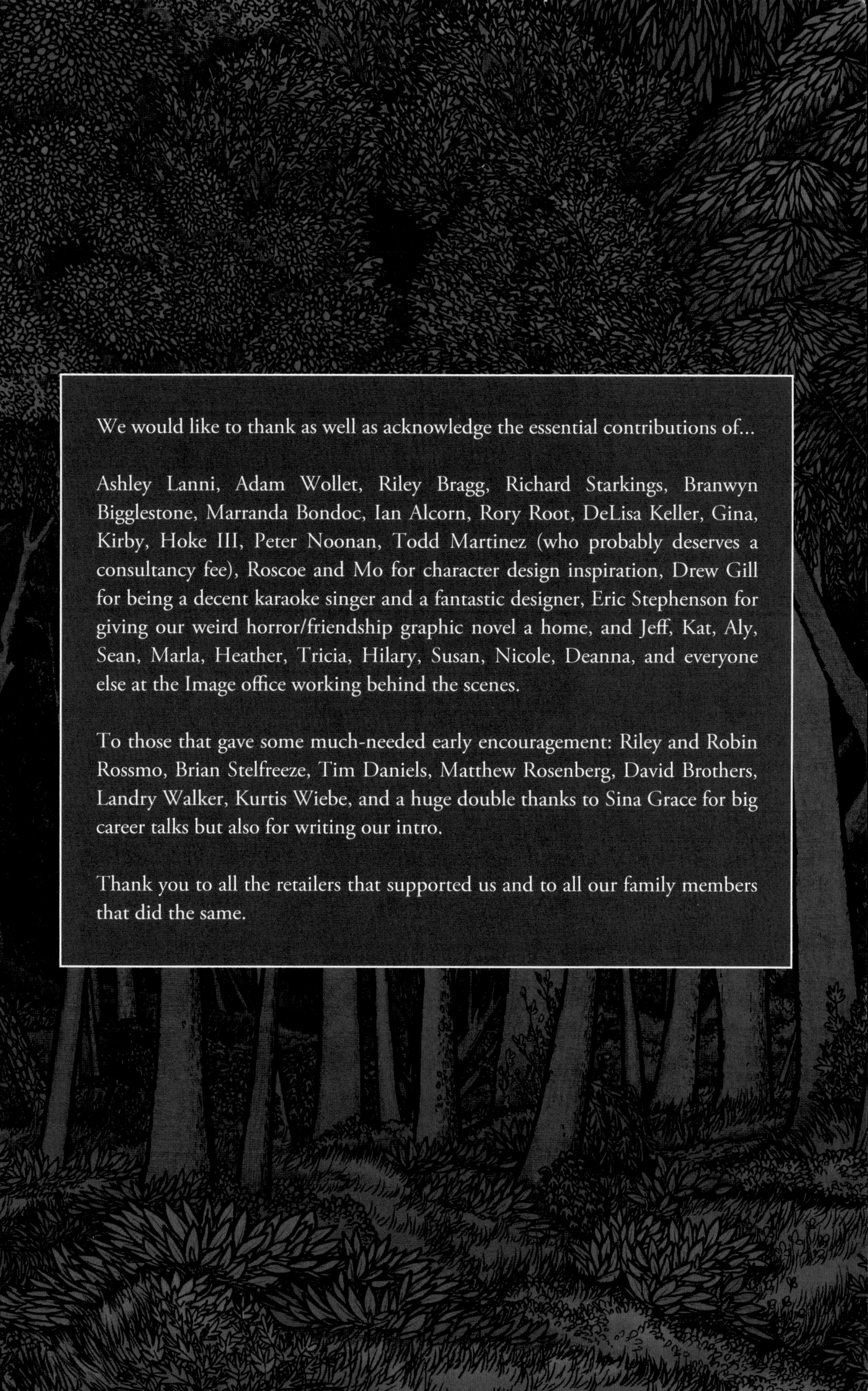

We would like to thank as well as acknowledge the essential contributions of...

Ashley Lanni, Adam Wollet, Riley Bragg, Richard Starkings, Branwyn Bigglestone, Marranda Bondoc, Ian Alcorn, Rory Root, DeLisa Keller, Gina, Kirby, Hoke III, Peter Noonan, Todd Martinez (who probably deserves a consultancy fee), Roscoe and Mo for character design inspiration, Drew Gill for being a decent karaoke singer and a fantastic designer, Eric Stephenson for giving our weird horror/friendship graphic novel a home, and Jeff, Kat, Aly, Sean, Marla, Heather, Tricia, Hilary, Susan, Nicole, Deanna, and everyone else at the Image office working behind the scenes.

To those that gave some much-needed early encouragement: Riley and Robin Rossmo, Brian Stelfreeze, Tim Daniels, Matthew Rosenberg, David Brothers, Landry Walker, Kurtis Wiebe, and a huge double thanks to Sina Grace for big career talks but also for writing our intro.

Thank you to all the retailers that supported us and to all our family members that did the same.

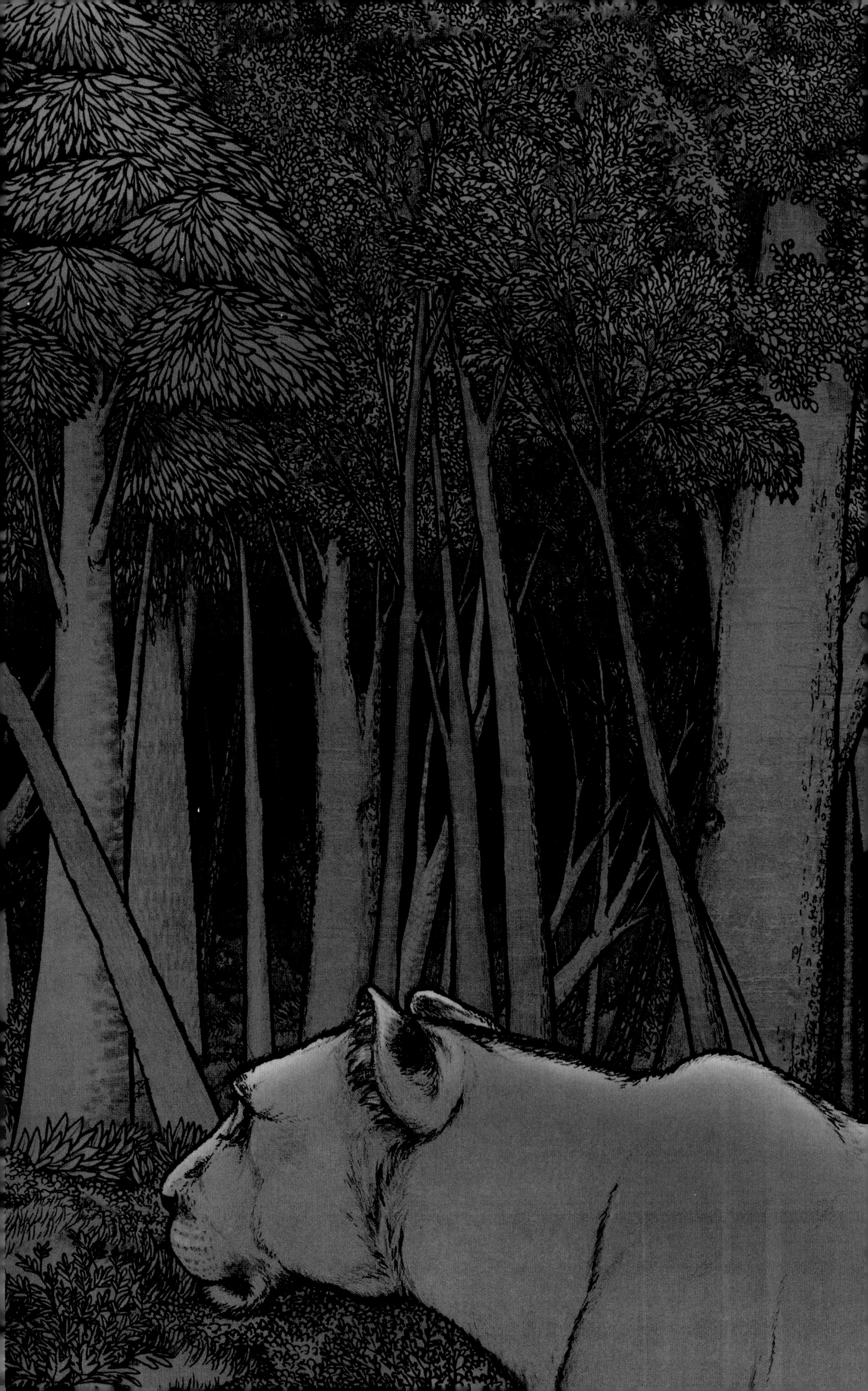

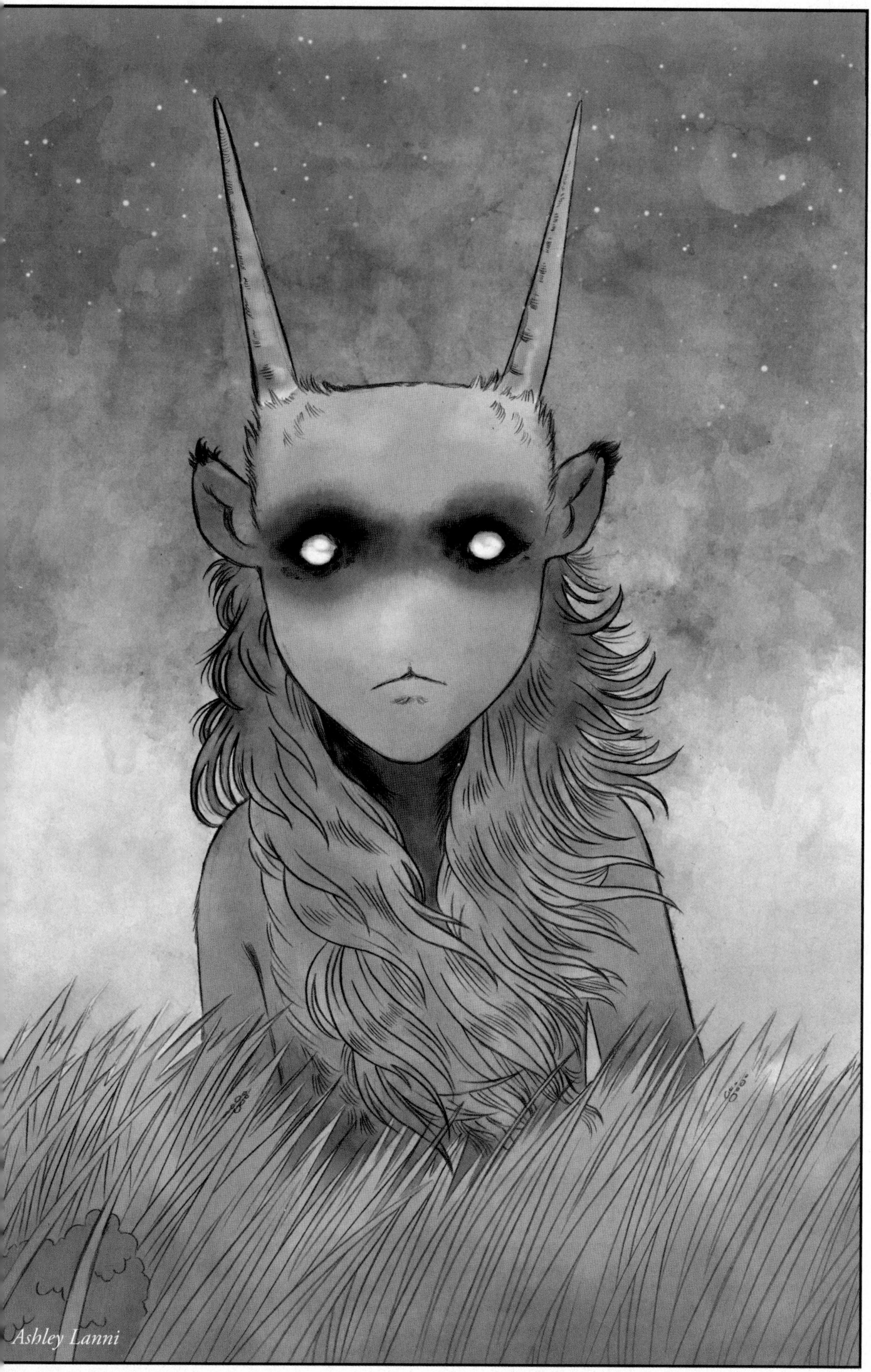
Ashley Lanni

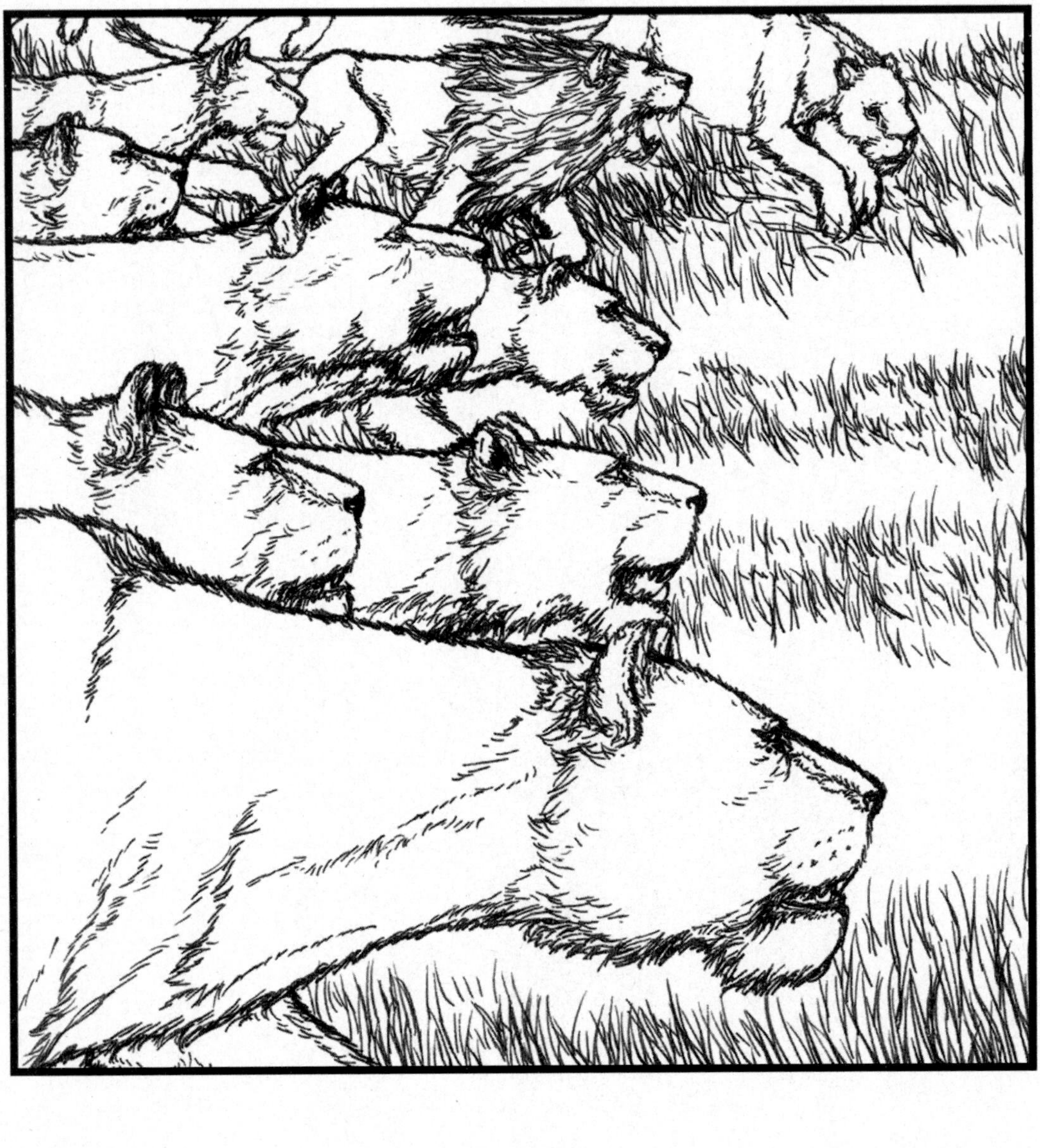

For additional ambiance with subsequent readings, visit

littlegirlsognmusic.bandcamp.com

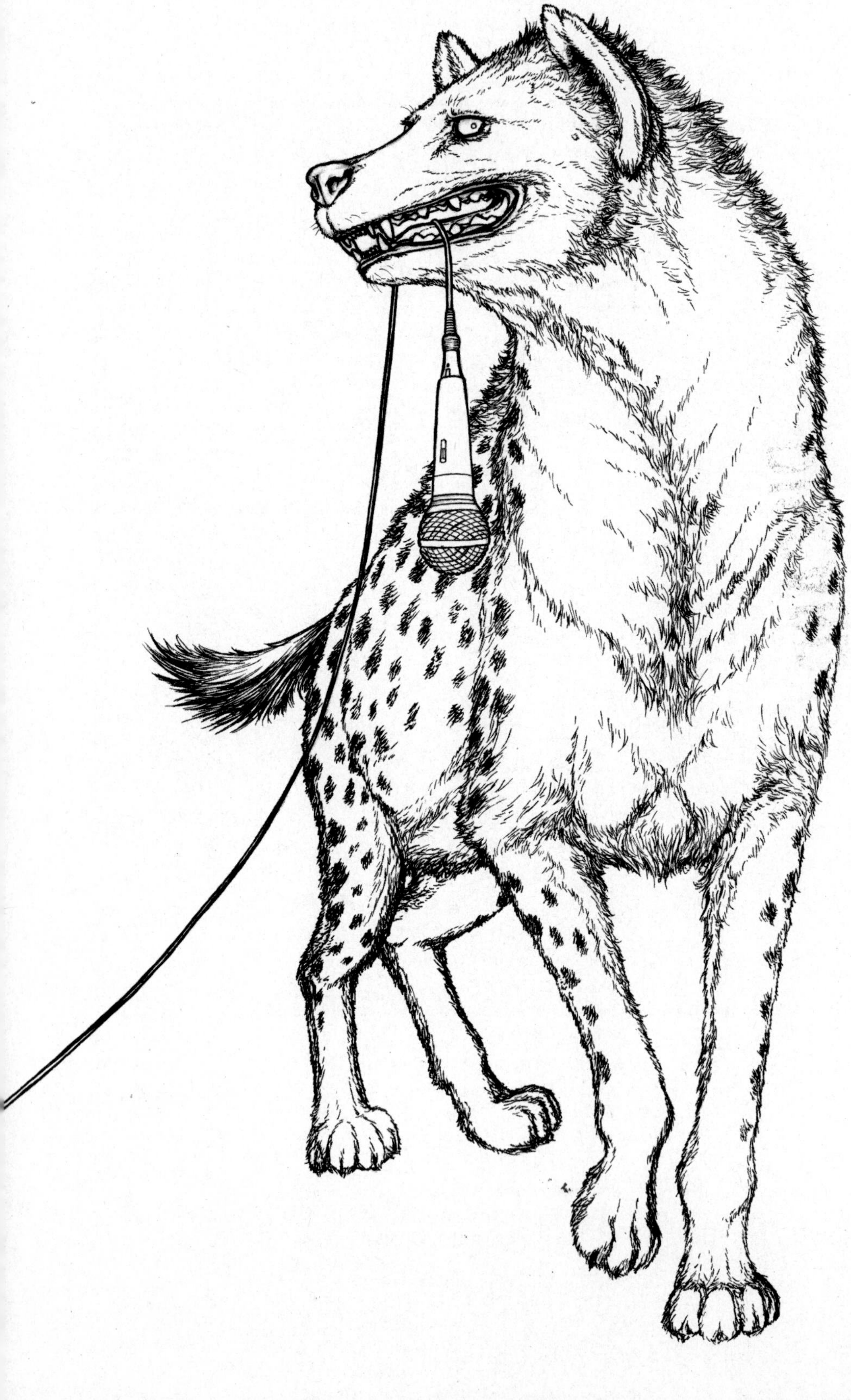